Arizona Territory

DUSTY RICHARDS

ARIZONA TERRITORY

PINNACLE BOOKS
Kensington Publishing Corp.
www.kensingtonbooks.com

PINNACLE BOOKS are published by

Kensington Publishing Corp.
119 West 40th Street
New York, NY 10018

ISBN-13: 978-0-7860-3663-9
ISBN-10: 0-7860-3663-X

First printing: August 2015

10 9 8 7 6 5 4 3 2 1

Printed in the United States of America

First electronic edition: August 2015

ISBN-13: 978-0-7860-364-6
ISBN-10: 0-7860-3664-8

Prologue

The redbrick Methodist church's steeple stood out against the darkening buttermilk skies. Hat in hand, Chet Byrnes knelt before the gleaming marble monument and gazed at the letters chiseled in the polished stone.

MARGARET BYRNES

MOTHER—WIFE—EQUESTRIAN—PARTNER

In God's hands.
May she rest in peace.

A cold wind swept across his wet eyes as he softly spoke to her spirit. "Marge, I've been bad troubled since you left me. The last few months without you have been tough, and we all miss you. Everyone says, though, it's time for me to get on with my life. So I've come here this time to tell you I won't pester you with visiting so often. I promised you I'd raise our son, Adam, and I surely will. He's a fine boy, one you brought into this world with a lot of sacrifice. I also want to tell you all the things that I probably missed telling you in our short marriage. You were the perfect woman for me. Your eagerness to pay all my bills when I first came here rose from your generosity toward one you thought was a down-at-the-heels Texas cowboy. When stage robbers murdered my nephew, Heck, you came and helped me through that tragic loss. With Reg's wife, Lucy, as our guide, we camped out on our honeymoon, and we found the high ranch. You've been a big part of my life, helping me build an empire in the Arizona Territory with my ranching and law enforcement efforts. I'll always have a place in my heart for you. May your soul rest in peace. Amen."

When he finished, he rose and gazed up again at her church and prepared to leave her gravesite. He closed the walk-through gate, mounted his roan horse, and headed back to Preskitt Valley and the big house. It began to rain. He shook out his slicker and looked at the sky. God must be crying, too.

Chapter 1

Two months later, Chet held a meeting with his various ranch foremen and, afterward, they left him in the living room to prop up his handmade Hyer boots and get ready for a new page in his life. Everyone came to talk about their plans for each of their operations. He took notes on all the things that mattered, ranch by ranch. He sure needed to hire an accountant. His late wife, Marge, and the Verde River Ranch foreman's wife, Millie, had kept the books, paid the bills, and handled all those chores. While he knew Millie was sincere, she had three children to raise, and it had been Marge's leadership that ran that end of the business.

Maybe his banker, Andrew Tanner, might know someone he could get. Millie said when Chet had to be away and until he found someone, with Tom's aid she'd keep the books up to date and pay the bills. Tom ran the widespread Camp Verde Ranch over the mountain in the Verde River Valley. Lucy took care of the books on the North Rim Ranch out by

Hackberry. His sister, Susie, cared for a newborn son, Erwin, and with her husband, Sarge, ran the Windmill over northeast—where each month they gathered the cattle to deliver to the various Navajo agencies over around Gallup, New Mexico.

Up on the rim, Robert and his new bride, Betty, ran the ranch's log operation, hauling logs to the big steam-powered sawmill. Leroy and Betty Lou Sipes operated the fruit farm in Oak Creek Canyon. His late brother's wife, May, and her husband, Hampt Tate, ran the recently expanded outfit that he called East Verde Ranch. She had two near-teenage stepsons, her own daughter, Donna, plus they had a new baby boy, Miles. The home ranch in Preskitt Valley was run by Chet's very strong foreman, Raphael, and his *vaqueros.* His other nephew, JD, ran Rancho Diablo, in the southern desert. His wife, Bonnie, waited in Preskitt for them to complete her new house down there so she could join him.

When Chet first arrived, Bonnie's mother, Jenn, who ran a café in town, befriended him, and she'd found him much of his help to start with. Later on, he brought her daughter, Bonnie, back from white slavers in Mexico, trading some valuable horses from his golden Barbarossa stallion for her to an influential *hacienda* owner in Sonora. She'd proved well worth it. Cole Emerson, who rode with him, was married to Valerie, who the three men, JD, Cole, and Chet also rescued in Tombstone and sent to Preskitt to help Jenn and Bonnie run the café.

Going over it all in his mind, he chuckled at the

thought that he actually carried all their names in his logbook, so he didn't leave anyone out.

His son's teenage nanny, Rhea Obregon, interrupted his thoughts when she brought Adam in the living room for him to hold.

"Rhea, sit down. You were Marge's choice to care for our son. I want you to continue to stay here and do that. Monica will help you."

Her tan face beamed at his words. "*Gracias,* he is like my own son."

"I know that. He needs to learn English. But he also must learn Spanish. Please talk to him in both languages."

"Marge told me that, and I do it."

He gently bounced Adam on his leg. "The goat's milk works well?"

"Oh, he never cries. He is growing so fast."

"I know he is. You're a good mother. The next three years will be important. If a baby can live beyond that, he should make it to being an adult. As long as you want one, you will always have a job here. Don't worry about him growing up, 'cause you'll never be out of work. You'll be very important to him. But he must mind you. You savvy that?"

"Yes. Monica and I talk a lot. I appreciate your trust in me. It will be a very hard job, but I will learn to read so I can teach him. I am not so good at numbers, but when he needs numbers, I will know them well when he counts."

"We'll hire a tutor for you."

"Oh, that would be very good."

He spoke to his infant son lying on his legs.

"Adam, your mother, Rhea, is going to educate you to run an empire." He kissed the good baby and handed him back. "I don't care if he goes to your church with you, but I want him to learn Marge's religion, too."

"I can do that. I have been in your wife's church. Can I have him christened in my church?"

"Certainly."

"Good, I have worried much about that."

"He will grow and become a good person under your guidance."

She crossed herself. "Oh, I am so relieved to have this talk with you."

"Rhea, you can always talk to me. I'm just Chet."

She nodded. "When you are away, I will have Monica write to you about him until I learn how."

"Good."

"Time for his nap."

"Good-bye, Adam. *Via con Dios.*"

"I have some lunch for both of you," Monica announced.

"Put mine in the oven. I am going to lay him down," Rhea said.

Monica nodded and when Rhea was upstairs she said, "What did you tell her? She sounded like she was in charge."

"I told her so. We need a tutor for Rhea. Can you hire her one?"

"Of course—"

"When she learns how to read and do sums, she'll teach Adam."

"Very good; your wife would have done that for her."

"You two are my wives here—now."

"Oh?"

He shook his head at her. "You must run this ranch, answer Raphael's needs, and decide things when I am gone."

"Alright. She and I can do that."

"I trust you two."

"You must feel like you should go to the south again?"

"The Force and Rancho Diablo need me to look them over."

"Did JD take Bonnie down there last week when they went home?"

"Yes, her house is nearly finished. I think they wanted to be together. I know if I was a newlywed, I'd want my wife down there."

"I didn't know if that marriage would work," Monica said, using a towel for a potholder to bring his plate from the oven.

He looked over his beef-cheese *enchiladas* and nodded his approval. "Best I can tell, seeing them together, they're very close."

"I think he grew up and she did, too."

"I hope so. Two lost souls before that."

"Will that be a great ranch someday?" Monica asked.

"I think so."

"But like the rest, they cost a lot to get them productive."

"Well, we're large. Markets like the one with the

Navajos had to be developed. In ten years, we should have rails here in the north. But economic conditions in the U.S. keep bouncing in and out of good and bad. To survive until then will be hard."

"Oh, you will figure it out. Your wife always told me that a hundred times."

He nodded and went to eating his lunch. "I plan to go down south. Jesus and Cole will meet me for the stage tomorrow. Remember, Tom or Hampt can be here in a few hours. If you or Raphael need them, they'll come on the run."

"Yes, I know that. I am so glad you take Jesus and Cole wherever you go. They have really grown up, riding with you."

"I'm glad to have them at my back."

"Will you keep doing the Force down there?"

"It's funded by the federal courts. Who knows what they will do and for how long?"

"Be careful. You are the one who holds us all together."

"Thank you, Monica."

The next day, under cold stars, the three men drove two buckboards to the Black Canyon stage office on the east side of Preskitt, where they loaded their saddles and war bags into the back of the stage. They were well dressed against the cold and had wool blankets to wrap in. The taller of his two men, Cole Emerson, was in his mid-twenties, and, Jesus, the young Mexican who held up his part of the team, was twenty. They covered Chet's back, and he trusted and listened to their thoughts and judgment.

The coach left at midnight and rocked its way off

the mountains to Hayden's Mill and Ferry on the Rio Salado to arrive on schedule about mid-day. Then they took the next stage south to Papago Wells and then to Tucson. The Tucson–Nogales Stage driver would let them off at the Morales Ranch gate below the village of Tubac. Chet would be glad to get there and join his Force, who'd been busy trying to end the banditry in southern Arizona.

He'd had many things on his mind since Marge's funeral. Had he been home that day when she took her spill from the horse, he couldn't have saved her. Jumping horses was her passion in life. She stopped riding them to carry their son, because she had never before carried a child full term. While the coach swept from the mountains to the desert, and owls flew the starry sky in search of prey, her death weighed on his mind. He sure missed her. At times, the sadness about overwhelmed him, but he had responsibilities to handle and he couldn't let go.

Inside the coach, the wool blanket turned away a lot of the chill, and he managed to go in and out of sleep. At the Bumble Bee Station, where they changed horses, he stepped off the coach to stretch his stiffness away. Deep in the canyons under the Bradshaw Mountains, he knew they'd soon be down on the much warmer greasewood flats that reeked of creosote and where the giant saguaros towered in the valley of the Salt River.

Finally, the next night under the stars, he and his men reached the Morales Brothers Ranch below Tubac, and the driver set off their saddles and war bags, then lashed the cover back down.

Chet tipped him a silver dollar and the man saluted him. "Good to have you back. I always feel safe when you're down here, Señor Byrnes."

The dogs heard them and barked and a light went on at the first small adobe house. Maria, Ortega Morales's wife, came on the run and hugged him.

"So good to have you back, señor. We all cried because we could not attend your wife's funeral."

"I understood. She would have, too. Is everyone alright?"

"Oh, *si*, no problems. They have finished JD's house and are working on mine." She beamed in the light of the candle lamp.

"Did you know JD's wife joined him? Have you met her?"

"No, but I will when I move over there. Are you hungry?"

"No, don't worry about us. We'll see you at breakfast." He kissed Maria's forehead and sent her back to the house. He considered her an angel. She cared so much for his outfit, fed them well, made sure they were all healthy, plus knew as much as any man about the land there and the people.

He turned to his men. "I don't know about you two, but I'm ready for bed."

"I feel beat up and beat down," Cole said.

"Me, too," Jesus agreed.

They went to sleep in hammocks and Chet woke in the predawn to the sounds of Maria cooking. Dressed, he joined her in the kitchen.

"Roamer coming back soon?" he asked.

"Three of them are just checking on things. It has really been quiet down here."

"That's good."

She poured him a cup of coffee. "How is your son, Adam?"

"Growing and fine. Rhea, the young girl raising him when I'm gone, wanted him christened in the Catholic Church. I told her to do that, but he had to be raised to know Marge's religion, too. She understood."

"Good. If you are Catholic, christening is an important event. You must have much faith in her."

"Yes, I do. She was Marge's choice, too."

"What will you do today?"

"Fill out the expense report for the federal court. It has to be turned in shortly. So I'll be busy."

"I can help you. I have been learning all about it."

"Good."

She topped off his coffee. "This law business has changed our life. We use to fret over a small store bill for food. Now we fret over buying more cows."

"Will you be happy over there?"

"Oh, yes. I like the house he showed me in the sketch. But I will miss the river and the birds here on the Santa Cruz. Near here has been my home all my life. Across the mountains, they are planting citrus trees and lots of palms. Someday, it will be a very nice *hacienda*."

"I would never have left Texas. Those were my people and my land, but now this is my land, from Reg's ranch on the high country to this place here."

"I hope you someday find someone to fill your life again."

"I'm not looking for anyone today."

Maria nodded that she understood, then said hello to Jesus and Cole joining them. "You are too good a man not to have a woman to share your life. Isn't he, guys?"

"Yes, ma'am," they both chimed in.

After breakfast, he went over the ranch books. As he closed the ledgers, the dogs began to bark. Through the window, he saw a fancy coach and several horses and riders coming into the ranch.

Maria put down her dishtowel, and Cole and Jesus came on the run. The two frowned at this fancy entourage with two teams of horses. Four outriders on Barb horses, in red vests and well armed, rode as the guard. A coachman in tails dismounted the fancy outfit and opened the door.

"Holy shit—" Cole managed at sight of the woman coming through the opened door. "Who in the hell is she?"

The coachman ran over and handed Chet a card. Elizabeth Delarosa Carmel.

Recent widow of Fernando Carmel, Los Indios Springs, Sonora, Mexico.

Chet removed his hat and went to meet her. The woman dressed in black satin was sure not some old woman, she was probably early twenties. Her dark hair hung in long curls to her shoulders. Great silver loops swung from her ears, and a large gold cross on a chain hung around her neck above the rise of her breasts.

"Señora, I am Chet Brynes. To what do I owe the honor of your visit?"

"May we go to your table under the shade? I have some wine I could serve you and your men. Sir, I wish to talk to you, if you have time for me?"

"That will be fine. This is Cole Emerson and Jesus Morales who ride with me. And this lady is Maria Morales. No relation to Jesus, but she is my hostess here."

She gave each her hand and then turned back. "I was headed home for Mexico when I learned you had returned here." She very carefully took his arm and holding her skirt in the other hand they headed for the shaded area.

"I understand you recently lost your wife?"

"Six months ago. Marge was a fine woman, and I miss her."

"I have been a widow myself for three years now. I understand missing someone. Life must go on, but that space they left is still there. They say it can be filled, but I don't think that way. All one can do is keep their faith and strive on."

There was no perfume in the air when they sat, but a scent. She smelled like cinnamon. The coachman set a half dozen wineglasses on the table and two bottles of wine.

She looked at each of them. "This is wine from my *hacienda*. I want to share it with you three. The señor, I have all day to talk to him, or until he runs me away."

The two men thanked her and Maria joined

them. A bottle was uncorked and her man brought Chet a sample to swirl around and taste.

Dry, sweet, but not too sweet. "Very good," he said, and handed his glass back. Thank God for Marge. She'd taught him how to do wine tasting.

The glasses were soon filled. Her man served her and Maria, and then the two men, and Chet last.

They raised their glasses in a toast to her, then sipped the wine.

She looked around. "This ranch is hardly a *federale*-style headquarters."

"We aren't fancy. We simply enforce the law."

"Oh, I know that. Bandits in Mexico respect you and your men. But I expected a military base like the fort south of here."

"We are only a strike force and my men are all cowboys. No *generalissimo* is here. We are low key, because we can't upset the county law enforcement. The judges in the territory are federal judges. We work for them."

"To your health." She clinked her glass to his and crossed her legs, making herself comfortable on the bench. Behind her façade of regal appearance, there was a little vixen in this handsome woman. Her words betrayed very little accent.

"They tell me you have a large ranch west of here?"

"Very large. You want to ride over it?"

She stopped. "You catch me off guard, señor."

"No, señora, call me Chet. And it was just an offer to show you the place."

Her composure returned. "Yes, Chet. I would love

to see all of it—with you. But you are a busy man to do that."

"Those two would handle the packhorses and cooking. You'd have a tent to hide in and we'd see every inch of the Diablo Ranch in a week."

She chewed on her lower lip and smiled. "Now I am the one that is scared. You are really serious. How many more ranches do you have?"

"Five more, maybe six."

"You don't know how many you have?"

"I can find them."

She laughed, then put her hand over her mouth. "How long do I have to answer you?"

"However long you need. I know you didn't come here to go on a long ranch inspection with a man who has a week's beard on his face."

She shook her head. "I have not said no to you."

"Nor yes."

"No, not yet, anyway. I understand you have a great Barbarossa stallion. What do I have to pay for a golden son of his out of a great mare?"

He just looked at her, poker faced. When he did not answer, she spoke again. "I think you are a horse trader of the toughest kind. I am talking about money. In dollars or *pesos*." She leaned in close and with a shake of her head, whispered, "Not me."

"I have no price on them."

She quick-like scowled at him. "You sold some to a Don Baca, who I know well, in Sonora."

"I didn't sell them to him. I swapped them for the return of the daughter of a good friend being held in Mexico."

"I am sorry. Baca said he bought them."

"He may have. Those two were with me." He motioned to his men. "She got herself into the wrong place and was kidnapped. We couldn't raise a force big enough to safely get her away, so I offered him the horses for her safe return."

Her dark eyes looked hard at him. "They were very high-priced horses then."

"What are horses worth when someone holds another human being against their will? Nothing."

"Yes, you are right." She tilted her head to one side. "I expected a bigger, louder man, but I think you don't need to be." A flick of her red tongue swept her brown lips. "If I take that excursion, can I see those horses?"

"No. I'm sorry. Not this trip with me. The horses are at Camp Verde. But you can see them anytime. My foreman can show them to you, if I'm not up there."

"I know the Barbarossa family does not sell any stallions. How did you ever get such an animal?"

"A young boy had a fast mare in Texas. He took her to Mexico and challenged the family to a race against their best horses. If he won, they bred his mare. If he lost, he lost the mare. He won the race and the mare had a horse colt. But they weren't rich ranchers, so they sold him to me."

"Did the family ever offer to buy him back from you?"

"He's not for sale."

She poured him more wine. "I would like to sponsor a *fiesta* here for tonight, to celebrate our acquaintance. Does that suit you?"

"Fine. What can I do?" he asked.

"Be yourself." Then she spoke to Maria. "Could we have a celebration here tonight?"

"It could be arranged. Someone will have to go to town for what I will need."

"One of the men can get what you need. Just make a list."

Maria nodded and drew a paper and pencil from her apron pocket.

"Good. Where can I change?" the young widow asked, looking around, and then spoke to him. "You would show me the river and this country on horseback?"

"I'm willing."

"Bring your things to my *casa*. I can help you change," Maria said.

"That is so nice of you. But you have to get ready."

Maria dismissed that, then took her and a valise to the house.

"Tell my men they can split cooking wood," she called back over her shoulder.

Jesus went to saddle both of them a horse. Cole tossed down his wine. "That is some lady."

Chet's stare followed her until Maria's *casa* swallowed her. "I have to say she is different."

The two of them rode over the countryside for a while in quiet companionship. The ruffled blouse she wore, with a divided riding skirt and handmade boots, showed off her figure. She was a handsome woman. When her head turned, silver hoop earrings danced, and the sunlight coming in spears through the tall cottonwoods glinted off them. Nearby, the Santa Cruz River ran over round rocks worn smooth by centuries of passing current. When she spotted the water, she asked him to stop.

They dismounted and she sat on a large flat rock. "Would you pull off my boots so I can wade in the water?"

"Sure, we all need to be free once in a while and do something like that." He gently removed them and her socks. When he pulled her to her feet, she kissed him softly on the cheek with a "*gracias.*"

That spot her lips touched burned through the week's beard stubble. She splashed about in the shallow water, holding her skirt up and looking pleased. Her laughter carried over the rustle of a million rattling cottonwood leaves in the warm wind. Free and clear, with the expensive brown cowboy hat cocked back on her head, he saw a very beautiful, proud, young woman. Everything else faded away and there was only the two of them in this world of streaming shafts of golden light.

"Where are you going?" she called out when he stood up.

"To get a towel to dry your feet."

"Ah—fine. I thought you were through with me acting like a schoolgirl."

He shook his head and smiled at her words. Actually, he could have watched her all day. Towel in hand, he returned to where she sat on a large flat rock. He carefully dried her small feet, replaced the socks, then the boots. She sat with her hands behind her, bracing for each boot to go back on.

"You are so good. Most men would have said, 'Come on, foolish girl, I have things to do.'"

He shook his head. "I think you're like a butterfly, flitting from one flower to the next one."

"Really?" They walked toward the horses, loosely holding hands. She stopped him. "That was very romantic to say to me. Thank you."

They set out again to walk to their grazing mounts, and when they reached the rise, she removed her hat, pulled him to her with her back to the rough bark of the giant tree. His guts roiled. If she stood there one more moment longer, whiskers or not, he was going to kiss her.

His arms gathered her up, and then she put her finger on her lips. "I will kiss you and make love to you, for you are such a real *hombre,* but never just for a horse. Do you savvy me?"

"Yes, I do." Then he kissed her, and all the grief and pain of the previous months faded away, leaving only pleasant memories.

CHAPTER 2

When the two rode back, Cole took their horses.

"Ma'am, that sidewall tent is yours to dress and sleep in," he said. "Your people put your things in there this afternoon, and one of the boys' wives, Consuela, said if you need help, she'd sure help you change."

She laughed. "My, your service is so good here, Señor Byrnes."

Amused by her words, he shook his head and spoke to his man. "Thanks, Cole. You all did lots of work for tonight." He indicated all the *fandango* preparation.

"That Maria can whip up a party in no time."

Cole left them to put up the horses.

"May I have some water and a bath?"

"I'm sure we can do that."

"That can be a lot of trouble in a camp like this."

He dismissed the idea with a wave of his hand and told her to wait. He soon found Jesus who agreed to attend to it. Then he led her over to his bench.

Soon, a good-sized washtub arrived and disappeared into her tent. Jesus gave Chet a sign the water was heating. He waved his thanks.

"Would it be too much to ask you to help me undress?"

Startled, he hesitated before finding his voice. "No, but you might get ravished."

"I don't think so. If you think I am too bold, let me say that I have never been with but one man in my life. That was my husband. You are not him, nothing like him. But today, I kept saying to myself that you will think I am too bold. But I know our time together here is short, and I have measured it carefully. I want you to see who I am. I know it is too soon since you lost your wife, but I want to be a candidate for her place."

"We only met this morning."

"Has it not really been hours and days longer than that?"

Chet looked down at her. "We have crammed a lot in during that time."

"Crammed?"

"It means overloaded the suitcase and sat on it to close it."

She broke out laughing and bent over. "Ah, yes. We have done that."

"They're taking the hot water to your tent."

"Will you come with me?"

"Yes. I need to get my razor and shaving cup. I'll join you."

He pulled her to her feet, wanting to kiss her, but didn't. "I won't be long."

Cole met him halfway there with his shaving gear. "You looking for this?"

"Thanks."

"Looks like your day, boss. She damn sure is a great Spanish treasure."

"I think so, too."

He ducked under the tent flap, set his things down, and tied it shut. Then he removed his hat and set it on a case. The smell of heated water drifted to his nose. She stood before him, dressed.

Hell's bells. She expected him to undress her. He began with shaky hands, and the entire time it was like unwrapping a surprise package. Damn, she said she wanted to be a candidate to be his wife. What would they do? Her ranch was in Mexico, and his own places sat miles away in Arizona. But this was too good to pass up. At last, he had his gift unwrapped. Oh, my God. She looked like an angel. He dropped his butt onto the cot, hypnotized by her beauty in the translucent light coming through the tent's skin.

She stepped into the tub. "And you didn't even kiss me."

"Hell, girl, I have all my life to do that."

Busy soaping a cloth, she never answered.

He went on, "Hell, I came down here to straighten out things, not fall in love."

"I stopped here to buy a stallion this morning. I had no notion who you were. Even what you looked like. I'd met your wife. But that was years ago in Mexico, before you married her. Do you think God brought me here?"

He stood up, then knelt down beside the tub.

With his hands on both sides of the tub, not daring to touch her skin, he kissed her. "I don't know if God helps fornicators, but he surely sent you to me."

"You are not disappointed?" She stood up and he grabbed a bucket of warm water to rinse her off. With the water pouring over her, she looked like a drowning urchin.

She reached for a towel to dry herself off. "Your turn."

He was soon in the tub, and she used a washcloth on his back. "Now that I can see you, you are a very big man."

"Does my size scare you?"

"No."

He shook his head. "Tell me why I'm not embarrassed to death with you here, and me naked, taking a bath?"

"The Mexican people have a saying, 'What is to be, is to be.'"

When he finished, she wore a robe and sat on the cot.

"Our day is fading fast. Maybe I am a silly girl you have found. Would you find a blanket after the dance is over tonight and take me to a haystack?"

"Nothing is ever silly in a serious relationship."

"I don't want you to remember taking me on a fainting couch. You are such an outdoors man, I want you to remember me when you are feeding your horses, being under the stars, going to bed on the ground."

"Tell me how bad you were offended when you asked me about the horse offer?"

"If I thought for an instant that you wanted me only for my body, I would never do this. It would have broken my heart. But you didn't know me then. I didn't know you. I also know now what your wife knew. You are a helluva bighearted man who, if you choose me, I will have to share with the world, but in the pages between, our lives will be rich. I must tell you in the four years of my married life I never bore him a son or daughter—"

"I entered my last marriage like that. Yet we were blessed with Adam."

"His name is Adam, you said?"

He nodded, then adjusted the small mirror on the tent pole and went to shaving. "You have your address on the card? I wrote my wife tons of letters."

"Yes, mail will find me. I will feel very important, getting letters from you."

"Don't expect poetry."

She laughed. "I am still thinking about the butterfly comment you said to me."

He squinted in the mirror and shaved his upper lip. "Just suited the occasion."

"What will you do tomorrow?"

"Ride over to Rancho Diablo and see my nephew, JD, and his wife, Bonnie."

"How long will you be gone?"

"A day to go, a couple days to look everything over, and a day to come back. You're welcome to come along."

She shook her head. "If I spent another day with you, you would never be able to get rid of me. I need to go home and be sure everything is working. It does well, but I am still the one who must run it. You understand? You have all those ranches."

"Yes, I do."

"I am wearing a simple blue dress tonight—for you to unwrap later."

"Fine, I am highly honored."

"No. If you find a better woman I can always say, I had him one wonderful, sunny, warm day, down on the Santa Cruz River." She drew a deep breath. "I feel like a dust devil who has been swept across the desert floor all day, whirling and dancing in a mad trip. May I burn candles in the chapel for your safety?"

"Sure, keep me in your prayers. You'll be in mine."

After they finished dressing, she stood beside him, ready to go out to the festivities, and she patted his shoulder. "This has been one of the greatest days in my life, *hombre*."

"Mine, too. I'm going to call you Liz."

"Fine. I will know who is calling me. No one ever called me that in my life." He kissed her. Strange, how wonderful things in life simply happened when least expected.

CHAPTER 3

When he and Cole and Jesus arrived at the Diablo Ranch the next evening, he was still looking back once in a while and thinking hard about her. When they dismounted at the corrals, the smell of hay brought the memory of her back to him.

That evening at supper, Bonnie sat at his side. She gently elbowed him. "Tell me about the Mexican widow you entertained yesterday?"

"Cole has been talking to you." He laughed at her curiosity.

"Since you all got me out of down there in Mexico, he and I are old friends. So, how about her?"

"She's a widow, and has a big *hacienda* down there. She's been a widow for a few years. And she and I just hit it off."

"Why did she stop there?"

"She wanted a Barbarossa stallion. She said she'd heard that I sold them to a friend of hers in Mexico. I told her I never sold any, except the ones I sold in

Texas for the train ride. That, instead, I had swapped them for a person's life."

"Yes, and, thank God, you did that for me."

"I'm still not sure she's not a *bruja.* No, she is not. She's very real. The two of us went off on a lark yesterday, and she waded in the river. We had a nice afternoon, and please keep this part to yourself, I started to kiss her. She stopped me and told me she would not kiss me for a horse, but she would kiss me for her love."

Bonnie stopped eating and put down her fork. "She told you that?"

Chet nodded his head. "Powerful, huh?"

"You'd only just met her, and all that happened yesterday?"

"Yesterday was over a month long."

"What will you do now?"

"Do my job here and up there. And think about her."

"Is she as beautiful as Cole said?"

"Maybe more than that."

"No one in our family will care. It's time you had a life. Marge would want that for you. Why don't you ride down there and grab her?"

"I better let it mellow. She has things to attend to down there. And I have things to do up here."

"Oh, Chet, it sounds like a romance made in heaven."

"Time will tell. But I had no intention of even looking for someone."

She rose and whispered in his ear. "Marge would never complain, knowing you were happy again."

"I hear you. Thanks."

The rest went easy. They had drilled two artesian wells on the ranch. The plan was to float some land cleared of greasewood and cactus, then plant alfalfa. Lemon and orange trees came next, then vineyards. Bonnie's house was well designed for the hot desert, an airy structure that caught the prevailing winds. Maria's house would soon be roofed and she'd move over there while her husband was on the south end, catching mustangs and shipping them to Mexico. JD promised him that the operation broke even, and it would eventually increase the range for cattle.

On his final day, before he left, they brought out a sixteen-hand, high-headed blue roan. "This's the horse we've been breaking for you," JD said. "I wouldn't ride him over the pass, but on the ground he should do alright. He's just green broke."

"How old is he?"

"Maybe four. He's a handful, but you won't wear him out."

"Great horse. Thanks, all of you," he said to the gathered crew. "They will be adding onto your *casas* soon, and you'll have gardens and even grapes. I'm very proud of all of you."

They applauded him as they left.

Jesus had his lead rope and JD walked beside Chet. "You going to Sonora and find her? Bonnie told me all about her. She sounds good."

"I have lots of things to do first."

"Hell, man, don't lose her. Bonnie told me you're afraid the family will think it's too soon to consider anyone. No one will think that. You do great things for all of us, but you have your own life to live. Do something for yourself."

"I think it's deeper than that. Hey, you're a great organized ranch manager down here."

"Thanks. It's a lot easier now that Bonnie is here. She makes me get real a lot of the time. And I probably need it. I'm thinking as much like you as I can."

"You're doing a good job and I'm proud."

"If I could get five hundred head of stocker cattle out of Mexico worth the money, what would you think about that?" JD asked.

"Buy them and let's try it."

"Thanks. Who do I contact for the money?"

"I'm going to get a man to do that. Wire Andrew Tanner at the bank in Preskitt. I'll let him know what you need."

"Good. I'll do it."

"Take care of Bonnie; she's a treasure."

"Oh, I'll do that."

As they rode back, Cole led the spirited roan, and they arrived back at sundown.

Maria had a wire waiting for them. Bandits had robbed a bank in Lordsburg in New Mexico, and they headed down that east side of Arizona for the border. They called them the Gimble Gang, a father, three sons, and two cousins. Wanted posters were available. Could he and his outfit head them off before they reached the border?

"What is it?" Cole asked.

"Some gang robbed the Lordsburg Bank. Where is Roamer? At the fort?"

"Down that way."

"I'll wire him and we can start that way in the morning, but I think by the time any of us get over there they'll already be in Mexico. Even if Roamer has a day on us. I doubt anyone can head them off."

"Give one of us the wire and we'll take it to Tubac and send him one anyhow," Cole said.

"Good idea. I'll do that. Jesus, you prepare a couple of packs. We'll ride out at dawn."

He quickly wrote both messages. Cole took off and he was alone at the table with Maria. She reached over and took his hand. "My husband was alright?"

"I never got to speak to him. He's down on the border, catching and selling mustangs in Mexico. I guess he don't write?"

"No, but I am fine. We all have so much going on in our lives. Tell me, did the young lady steal your heart?"

"I would say so. I met her so fast. In just one day, so much happened, and my head is still swimming. But, yes, she's an angel."

"You have any plans?"

"Yes, I'm sure we can reach an agreement—someday. She politely told me she only stopped by to see if I was here and to try to buy a horse."

"You turned her head that fast?"

"She turned mine. She said she knew about my loss and she wanted to be a candidate for my next wife."

"I knew she had turned your head. You two looked good, riding together. She is very rich and her *hacienda* is huge."

"Why she'd want me, I'll never know."

"*Hombre*, there are lots of women, married and not married, who would take you in a minute."

"Maria, you're a mess."

"I am telling you the truth. There are many I have heard say—that Marge has him, but if I ever caught his eye—I'd steal him."

He stood up and kissed her forehead. "I love you, too."

The Force left before dawn. The new blue roan bucked under Chet going out the front gate, but once on the road, he finally got him quieted down. But he did pace sideways down the dirt wheel tracks for several miles.

Jesus was trailing with three packhorses, and Cole rode with him and offered to swap horses with Chet.

"Hell, no. I'm fine. I'm going to wear him down today."

They both laughed at his words. Damn, he was one big tough horse. He must have come from the line of Barb horses the rich Spaniards brought to Mexico. But the stout gelding proved a handful until he got him rode down enough. He knew some horses never slacked in that power stage. JD and Ortega had chosen him well. He might save his life someday, and he could sure appreciate his big heart.

They made good time, and by late evening were over the Mule Shoe Mountains and in the border town of Noco. They put their horses up and Cole noticed Roamer's strawberry roan in the stables.

Shawn McElroy, Bronc Morales, and Roamer soon

found them. They went to a Mexican café across the wide border strip and ate supper.

"What's new?" Roamer asked.

"You should have seen this beautiful lady who came to see our boss at the Tubac Ranch yesterday," Cole said.

Chet held up his hand at their questions. "She wanted to buy a Barbarossa colt."

"Who is she?"

"Her name is Elizabeth Delarosa Carmel. Her husband's been dead three years."

"Whoa," Bronc said. "She is really rich, too. I know I have heard all about her."

"Maria said the same thing."

"Oh, she has a *hacienda grande* in Sonora."

"What are you going to do about her?" Roamer asked, then lifted his glass of beer to his lips and took a drink.

"If I knew that, I'd have already done it."

Laughing, Roamer blew part of his beer out and clapped him on the shoulder. "I ain't never heard you say that before. What did she think?"

"If things would have worked out—she'd probably say yes."

"Holy cow, you can find more rich women than a dozen men. And they are all pretty." Roamer held up his beer stein. "Let's toast the boss. Number one lady killer in the Southwest."

"Yeah!" they all cheered.

"Did the bank robbers get over here?" he asked, to put off their digging him anymore about Liz.

"Best we could tell, they beat us by twelve hours," Shawn said.

"They around close? Maybe we can herd them back across the border like we did that one gang."

Head shakes told him no.

Later, at the stables, forking hay for their horses, the memory of her came back to him. Why had he let her slip away? She was a real witch, a *bruja.* So much for that. But he couldn't rest until he'd written to her.

Dear Liz

We are in southeast Arizona. Chasing bank robbers, who beat us to the border, and we all went to supper in ole Mexico. Tomorrow brings another day. I hope you are home safe.

Chet

Wasn't much else to tell her, or his boss, besides reporting the border bandits were way down in Mexico. The feds might want to close the Force. His bunch had tried hard and brought most of the outlaws to the courts or left the others to feed the buzzards.

He mailed the letter to her, sent a wire to the Tucson marshal's office about the gang's escape, and went to his room in the hotel. His head on a pillow, he thought about her some more. She was damn sure hard to forget.

CHAPTER 4

When they got back to Tubac, he sent Roamer home. Shawn had no pressing reason to go home. While Roamer was gone, the five remaining tracked down three horse thieves and sent them to Tucson for trial. Cole and Shawn rode guard on a gold shipment from several of the Tubac mines to Tucson without incident.

Things were simply quiet on the border. When Roamer returned, Chet planned to go back home. Elizabeth sent him two letters, a few days apart.

Chet

I miss you so much. I know you have spoiled me. I know you are also busy. But even busy, you would have some time for me. I have never pined this much in my life for anyone. I will try to get busy and forget you, hombre.

Liz

The second letter read:

Chet

Read the last letter. And I am the same as I was then, the very same.

I miss you so much, hombre.

Liz

"How far south of the border is Liz?" he asked Maria.

"A hundred and twenty kilometers."

"A hundred miles, huh?"

"I think so." She frowned at him. "But you shouldn't go down there without an army."

"Maybe I will have her come to my house at Preskitt."

"That would sure impress her."

"But what if she's busy? And it's cold up there."

Maria laughed and pointed at her gold cross. "If I was her, and you invited me to your house, I would be there in the morning."

He shook his head. "I don't expect that."

"All she can say is 'no.'" Maria looked up at him. "I say she won't do that."

"Roamer is coming back. All we have are some horse thefts. It will take my answer a week to get to her and a week to get back." He shook his head. He still wasn't clear enough in his thinking about her and what to do. Was he just lonely without Marge?

One way to find out. "I'll send a letter and ask her to wire me if she can come. Jesus can meet her."

Maria dropped her shoulders and scowled in disapproval at his words. "No. You should meet her."

"My advisor." He looked to the sky for help.

"How sincere will she think you are, sending someone else, and not meeting her yourself?"

He laughed. "Damn sincere."

So he wrote her a letter.

Dear Liz

I want to invite you to come to my ranch at Preskitt. If you can come, wire me at Tubac and I will meet you at Nogales and escort you by stage to my home. Perhaps we can sort our lives out and resolve some things. We can get you warm clothes. It will be snowy up there.

Love, Chet

The three of them went to Tubac, where he mailed the letter, then they rode on up to Tucson to see about some horse thieves. They checked with several liveries and found that a man who called himself Fred Cousins had sold the stolen horses. No one knew where he lived, and the town marshal wasn't certain that was his real name.

Chet tried to straighten out the situation, but he found no way. Six horses with ranch brands were sold, and they'd been listed as stolen on the sheriff and brand inspector pages. He informed the livery owners they must keep a current list of reported stolen horses and check it before making any sales. He and his two men went to supper and discussed the situation. The Chief U.S. Marshal was out of town, and they slept in their bedrolls.

Jesus asked him. "Do you think she will come?"

"I don't really know how busy she is. It depends how much help she has to manage the place. I'm not in the know about her business."

The next day, they rode east to see about a ranch robbery they'd heard about. But the tracks were too old and faded to follow. Three border bandits did the holdup, and Chet had no doubt that they were already back across the border. He told the rancher that he needed to get them word quicker. The man agreed, but Chet knew no one would rob the same person twice, no richer than that man had been.

Roamer came back. His wife was fine, had plenty of firewood, and the kids all had colds. He laughed, telling Chet how Sheriff Simms had a burglar loose up there. The thief waited for folks to go to town and then stole what he could. Someone's ranch hands caught him and solved the crimes themselves.

No telegram. The next day, he got one from her.

CHET
I AM HONORED YOU HAVE ASKED ME TO YOUR HOME. I WILL BE IN NOGALES IN FOUR DAYS. I CAN HARDLY WAIT TO BE WITH YOU, HOMBRE. LIZ

"That was sent on Tuesday, and this is Wednesday. She'll be down there on Friday," Chet figured out loud, standing near Roamer. "We can go down there Thursday and wait for her. You don't need Cole and Jesus. They can go with me."

"Sure. Good luck," Roamer said.

"We'll check back. Be careful."

On Thursday, they rode down to Nogales. With the horses in the livery, he took two hotel rooms on the U.S. side. Across the border, they ate in a café with fine food, then went back to the hotel to sleep.

They got up early for breakfast. After the meal, they did some shopping in Mexico, and about noon the stage arrived. The three stood on the stage office porch and waited for his passenger to arrive. A nice-looking Hispanic girl came down the step first, but he relaxed when his smiling lady stuck her head out the window and waved at him. She wasn't wearing her silver earrings, but if she had they might have cost her those dainty earlobes, in case bandits had attacked and ripped them away.

She came through the crowd to him, and he hugged and kissed her. Whew, it was heart-warming good to have her in his arms.

"Anita, show Jesus what are our bags. Hello, Cole. You two do good work. He is not skinned up any at all."

She had Chet laughing.

Next, she fake-punched him. "You look good enough to eat, *hombre*."

"Nothing like you do to me. How long can you stay?"

"Until you throw me out, like old bathwater. Is that long enough?"

"Yes but . . ." He stopped. "The *hacienda*?"

"I have it being handled by my brother-in-law. He is very serious."

"That is sobering."

"I can go back." She held her arm out toward Mexico.

"Like hell."

She stood on the boardwalk, laughing. "Did I shock you?"

"Some. Time to get my sticks in a row. Do you and Anita need a room tonight? The next stage doesn't leave until early in the morning."

"She does. I don't." She looked over for his reaction.

One thing about Liz. She didn't mince words. "A room she will have."

"Am I being too pushy?" she asked him in a soft voice.

"No, you're not." He squeezed her hand. "The stage leaves at four in the morning for Tucson. It'll take two days to get to Preskitt. Cole is coming with us. He has a wife he'd like to see. Jesus will take our horses back to Tubac, then follow us home the next day on the stage line."

"Anita, I am so glad to meet you." He took the girl's hands in his. "We will have plenty of blankets. There may be snow up there. But the house is snug and warm."

"*Gracias, señor,* I have never seen snow. But I am excited."

He got Anita a room and their luggage was sent up. "We'll meet down here at five this afternoon and go to supper."

"I will knock on your door when we go down," Liz said to Anita.

She thanked her and went into her room.

Chet let Liz into his, then followed her inside and rested his back against the door.

She took off her cape. "Are you mad? I couldn't tell you my details in a wire."

"Mad. No. Shocked. Happy. I never figured how I could get it all done."

She buried herself in his arms and they whirled around. "Squeeze me hard. I have been trembling the last hundred kilometers and asking myself, 'Does he really want me?'"

"Oh, Liz, I've wanted you since you entered the race."

"Race?"

"You said you wanted to be a candidate."

She busted out laughing. "What else did I promise you?"

"Oh, I have a long list. Sit down. I want a few things settled. Can we be married in your church?"

"I am not certain. Why would you want to be married in my church?"

He put his finger on her lips. "I've thought hard about this. We'll talk to a priest. Your religion is precious to you. You could be denied communion."

"No, Chet Byrnes. You are the most important

thing in my life." She shrugged. "I would simply be your common-law wife."

"No."

"Yes."

"We'll see what we can do about that." He held her tight and kissed her. "We don't need to argue about it. I see a great road ahead for the two of us."

"I am so happy." She mopped at her tears with his handkerchief.

"You don't have to worry, we'll make it work."

They went to supper and enjoyed the meal with his men and Anita.

Once back in their room, under the threat that they must be awake and ready early, he unwrapped his present and the honeymoon began.

CHAPTER 5

On their coach ride to Tucson through the darkness, Anita asked Cole about Jesus. Obviously, the girl had been impressed by him.

"He's the greatest guy on earth. He had a girl in his village in Sonora and planned to marry her. But she died and he's been pretty quiet since then," Cole told her.

"Anita, she was kidnapped by white slavers, and fearing her plight, she hung herself," Chet said. "Cole was telling you the truth, Jesus did come back very sad."

"Thank you. He is a very polite man."

"My darling, all these cowboys are very nice men. They do many good things," said Liz.

"I am learning, señora."

"They are nice men." Liz lay back against his arm on the rear-facing seat. "How many times have you ridden in this coach?"

"Many times. But it beats riding horses this far. We've done that, too."

She laughed. "I feel like a little girl who is ready for her birthday cake."

"I hope you will be pleased."

"Don't worry about me. I will be."

She slept in his arms and felt such a part of him. This was his wife. Not wife-to-be, but his wife. He shook his head in wonder at the turns his life had taken. Not all that long ago, on a cold Texas winter afternoon, he'd lay under some cedars with three ambushers shooting at him. Two hour later, he rode away from there, and they weren't breathing anymore. Now, here he was under some blankets against the cold, holding this lovely butterfly and taking her home. Man, he'd been damn lucky.

Monica sent two buckboards for them. The two *vaqueros* driving them were excited, politely meeting the two females in the dark night. Their things were loaded and they headed for the ranch. The snow on the road had melted but covered the rest of the countryside and sparkled under the stars. Riding in the second seat, she held his arm tight.

"There is snow," she said.

"Lots of it has melted."

"Will it snow more?"

"We can hope so. It's valuable winter moisture. When you meet my housekeeper, Monica, speak to her in Spanish."

"Why? I have worked so hard to speak good English while here."

"I can't believe how good you are at it. I just love Monica. But you speaking Spanish will spin her around."

"You aren't ever mean, are you?"

"No, only with people I love."

When they drove up, he saw all the rigs parked in the yard and asked the driver, "Is everyone here?"

"Oh, *si*, *Señor* Chet, they are all here."

He sat back and shook his head. He hadn't expected this. "Forget my idea. Monica did this, bless her heart."

"I will get to meet everyone?"

He nodded. "Welcome to your new family."

"What did you tell her?" Liz was amused.

"I was bringing home a very important person and for her to be nice to you."

"She did what you said."

"That lady does not miss much."

The driver brought them to the front steps to drop them off, so they must all be in the living room.

"Wait," she said. She quickly put on her great silver earrings. "Are they alright?"

"Oh, yes. That's you."

"You hardly knew me without them in Nogales?"

"Yes, but I knew why you didn't wear them on the stage."

"So robbers would not steal them?" Amused, she laughed.

"Right, but your earrings are safe here. Come, this is my family."

Valerie broke ranks, ran off the porch, and tackled him.

"That's Cole's wife, Valerie," Chet explained. "Go ahead, Anita. No one will hurt you." He stopped and announced, "Her name is Anita. And this lady is Liz. In Mexico, they call her Elizabeth. Welcome her home to our ranch tonight."

The roar went up! Millie got her on the left side, and his sister, Susie, got her on the right. When he stopped on the porch to hug Hampt and Reg, they swept her away.

"Where is Lucy?"

"She's here."

Lucy soon rushed in and hugged him. He kissed her on the forehead. Then he did the same to May, who was close to tears. "Oh, Chet, she is so pretty. I see why you found her."

"I think she found me."

May nodded her head real fast. "I saw the smile on her face. She's very happy with you."

"So am I, with her."

Susie was at his side. "She's gorgeous. Where did you find her?"

"Southern Arizona. She stopped to talk to me about the Barbarossa horses."

"Really?"

He bent over and whispered in her ear. "She is much prettier inside than she is outside."

"I want that story."

"She owns a large *hacienda* in Mexico, and has been a widow over three years. She came to buy a horse and stole my heart. I never thought she would cross the border and leave her place for me. She said she would even be my common-law wife."

"Why is that?"

"They may not marry us in her church."

"You're certain? Reg was married in one."

He shook his head. "We will be here, regardless."

Susie hugged him and sounded impressed. "To me, she is the prettiest woman in the world."

He went and found a cup of coffee. His first thought was that he really wanted some whiskey, but he rarely drank it anymore. He needed to greet the rest of the family.

They finally all sat down in every chair and couch in the house.

"I'm so glad you all came to welcome us home. This lady's name is Elizabeth Delarosa Carmel. She has a great ranch in Mexico, and lost her husband three years ago. She can't wait to see the Barbarossa stallion. Two days ago, she got off the stage in Nogales and didn't have her earrings on and I blinked twice. I'd never seen her without them. I am honored she came up here to meet all of you."

He smiled when Rhea came in the room. She brought over the baby wrapped in a blanket and handed him to Chet.

"Thanks." His son in his arms, he walked over to Liz. "Here is the hell raiser."

"This is Adam?" Liz scooped him up. "He is so precious."

When she held him high, he yawned at her and everyone laughed. She found a chair and had her own conversation with the little one. Then she looked at Rhea. "I am so glad to meet you. I can see how much attention and care you have given him. I hope we can share him. I have never had a child of my own, and he is very precious. But I bet sleep is better for him than all these people who want to hold him."

Rhea nodded. She took him back and slipped away through the crowded room.

Liz caught Chet's look and nodded at him. "Those two are special."

"Come, you haven't met the one who runs this house." He pulled her out of the chair and led her into the kitchen. "Monica, this is Liz."

"I am so glad at last to meet you. I have not come to invade your house, but want to share my life with you. I will count on you to show me how to live in this far north and their ways."

Monica nodded, still looking steel-eyed at Chet. "When he sent me that letter, saying he was bringing another woman home, I packed my bags. Then I thought, he is bringing home a poor woman who does not know, and needs to know, what she is getting herself in for." Monica hugged Liz. "Welcome to our house."

"Uncle Chet." His ten-year-old nephew, Ray, took him aside and asked, "Does she like to fish?"

"I bet she'd fish with you."

"Tell her we really catch fish."

"I'll do that. Where is your brother?"

"He's treeing coons with a hound tonight."

"He treeing very many?"

"No. But he sells their fur for a quarter when he gets one."

"I'll find out if she fishes."

"Thanks. I like her."

When he caught up with Liz, Susie had her cornered.

"You know this is my sister, Liz?"

"Oh, we met earlier."

"Where's your husband?"

"Gallup, New Mexico, with a herd. In snowy weather, he and Victor team up to make the monthly cattle drive."

"We sell cattle each month to the Navajos. Susie and Sarge have the ranch about sixty miles northeast of here," he explained.

"You didn't drive over here?" Chet asked Susie.

She shook her head. "No, a cowboy brought me and the baby over in a buckboard. The boy is asleep. I'll show him off in the morning."

Liz shook her head. "You all are so busy up here. I met Robert and Betty who do the logging up on the mountain. And there is Reg and Lucy who have another ranch up higher than here. They have a baby girl?"

"Yes, Carla. And you met May and Hampt."

"Oh, Chet, you have such a large family. My poor head is swimming."

He hugged her. "You see why I had to bring you back here?"

She quickly nodded. "Your man, Jesus, is coming in on the stage tomorrow night. Anita asked if she could go meet him. She is a very nice young lady. He obviously impressed her quite a bit in Nogales."

"If she wants to stay up that late tomorrow night, I can arrange it."

She hugged his arm tight. "Your people are so nice to me, and I feared the very worst." She wagged her head from side to side. "They might think, what is this brassy girl from Mexico doing here? I know Marge has not been gone very long, and they might not like me."

"I know. I wondered, too. But she would have wanted this for me. She was such a bighearted woman. This would please her, that I don't have to raise our son alone. And that I won't be alone. But you don't have to compete with her. Be the butterfly that I met on the river. The woman I sealed this deal with in the hay. Damn, oh, damn, that had to be witchcraft. I haven't passed a haystack since that you don't come into mind."

She squeezed her eyes shut hard. "That is so funny. I wanted to impress you and I did. Good. I recall thinking once—If he thinks I will love him for the price of a damn horse, I will go home and let him break my heart."

"Yes, you shocked me with those words. I knew at once what you meant. Someday, you'll meet JD's wife, Bonnie. She's the one I rescued with those horses. I told her what you said and she said you were a special person, and she hasn't even met you."

"You've lived in my mind the last four weeks. Oh, I have rehearsed that day over and over. I saw you take your hat off when I stepped out of that coach and I . . ." She cupped her hands to his ear. "This is terrible to say. I about peed in my underwear."

He smiled. "Really?"

She laughed. "Oh, yes. Have you ever seen a horse for the first time and that minute you had to buy him?"

"Regardless of the price?"

"Regardless."

Susie came up to them. "Excuse me, Liz. He's our leader and, at such gatherings, we ask him to bless us all. He isn't real long winded, but we count on him to find the words. Chet, would you pray for all of us, and for your future wife, here tonight?"

The room quieted.

"Lord, we wish to thank you for once again bringing us together to meet and greet Elizabeth and Anita into our fold. Since Texas, we have expanded with several newborns and new members. Lord, we appreciate your grace you have on all of us. We are grateful for your forgiveness of our sins. Keep us strong in our hearts. Bless those on the trail and in the south. Make us all better people and help others. Amen."

He hugged Liz. Tears ran down her cheeks like large raindrops, and she was trying to help poor Anita who cried as well.

Susie, wet eyed, punched him. "You did it again. When you think life has evaporated, Liz, he'll bring you home. Thanks, brother."

Big Hampt was there, his arms over both of them. "Liz, he ain't a boss, he ain't ever forgot how he got here. But, by damn girl, he's the only man on this earth can say a prayer and get me wet eyed. God bless you two in any way you do it."

"Thank you so much." She dabbed at her eyes with a white hanky.

"It's been a real long stage ride. Let's put the rest off till tomorrow. Anita, do you have a room?" Chet asked.

"*Si,* I am sharing one with your sister."

"She may bite your head off. She's done that to me."

Everyone laughed. He showed Liz the staircase and they went to his room.

"You need anything to wear to bed?" he asked her in a whisper.

"With you? No."

"Good." He was opening a new book in his life with a neat partner. This time, in his own bed at home.

Chapter 6

The next day, after a big breakfast, almost everyone headed home. Chet promised them they'd have plenty of time to make plans for the wedding. And until they got it worked out, she'd be with him, unless he had law work to do.

When the company departed for their ranches, he spread out on the dining table maps of all of them.

"My, you have built an empire in the past three years."

"And the thing I like the most is, it pays for itself."

He stood with his butt against the table edge and held her by her narrow waist. "You looked shocked at me that first day, getting off the coach at the head-quarters."

Her brown eyes went to the ceiling. "I told you my reaction. Then I was off balance talking to you. Was this big-shouldered man real? Was he mean? Did he think I was some dumb little girl?"

"You amazed me, too. Here came this beautiful

Mexican woman and she had so little accent and she sparkled in the sunlight."

"I was very careful with my words that day. I didn't want you to think of me as some *puta* who came in a coach. But I realized and regretted I had so little experience with getting a man—one who I knew instantly that I wanted. Since my husband courted me, I had simply never desired another man. After his death, several men came to win me—you know what I mean?"

Chet nodded.

"I didn't want them. But here I was. I had seen your golden horses in Mexico. Don Baca showed them to me. He said a rancher in Arizona sold them to him. Do you think he owned Bonnie?"

She peered hard at him for his answer.

"I never was sure. If he didn't, I felt he could get her away from the men who held her. I had no army down there, nor a fortune to pay for her. But I had those horses that had no price."

"Well, anyway, I heard that this big man, Byrnes, stayed sometimes at that ranch by Tubac. So I stopped there to see this *gringo* horseman." She put her forehead on his chest. "And he was there."

She rose up, shook her head and her earrings gave off sparkles. "Lightning struck me. At first, I panicked. Then my mind began to think of things. I wanted you. You only made me more convinced by the hour, the minute, that hope grew inside my heart. But I also knew our paths might never ever cross again. So I had to take risks. Would he consider me a fool, or a—how you say—loose woman?"

He shook his head. "I love your story. Continue."

"I am baring my heart to you."

"I know that. I'm not laughing. Your honesty eats at my guts. You wore cinnamon. I could smell it."

"That is for good luck." She shrugged it away. He didn't.

"I was delighted when you took me for the tour. The river fascinated me. You have more patience than any man I ever knew. While I was wading, I was so busy thinking that you would say, 'Come on, let's go.'"

"Hell, I was spellbound, watching you. There was shafts of light reflecting off you and your silver. My brain kept saying God has sent her—do something."

"You were very patient. You dried my feet. Didn't Jesus dry his apostles' feet at the Last Supper?"

He nodded. "I never for a moment thought about it that way. I just thought that your feet would be wet when you got out of there. I'd get a towel and dry them. That way, I would get to touch you, too. No angelical thought in my mind. Maybe more lust than anything else."

"Well, see, I thought the other way. No matter what, it struck me about you doing that. What man dries a woman's feet after her wading in a river to avoid him?"

"You didn't think I would do that? I really got to dry your feet and put your boots and socks on."

"Then you said I was a butterfly. That was so nice, but I thought with concern in me, 'Who in the hell could catch a butterfly?'" Her brown eyes twinkled and she sparkled all over.

"Excuse me?" Monica said. "Anita and I are eating lunch. Rhea will be down soon with the boy. What are your wishes?"

"Thank you. We're near the end of the story. We'll join you."

"The *enchiladas* won't spoil. Since you are the boss *gringo*, you can come anytime."

He chuckled. "We'll join you soon."

"Sounds good." Monica went back in the kitchen.

"The party idea you brought up down there was very nice."

"Oh, that is no more than Hispanic tradition. I was through with my concerns over what I planned to do. I had decided I would go all the way. But how? I knew I needed to wear a minimum of clothing that evening. And I needed you—but not on some cot, not in some bed, but outdoors, in a place that only a boy would do such a thing to a girl."

He closed his eyes and hugged her. "And every time I'm around hay since then I think about you. I will all my life. That was brave of you to do that."

"Had you been courting me at my *hacienda*, I would never have been that impulsive. But I wanted you, paid the price, and won."

"It was the longest, best day of my life."

"Mine, also. Now, I will talk to Monica. I have help at my *hacienda*. Not as all-knowing as she is, and we will make a pact. I will speak more to Rhea. She is so dedicated to that boy, but I will be a part of him, too. Now, what else can I do?"

"Marge handled the books. She and Millie from

the ranch did it. Millie would rather someone took that lead, but will help you."

"Good, now I have a real job. You can show me how. All these foremen are so nice. You need to share your job with me. I love ranching."

"I will, of course. My story is long. But we are moving forward. I never could have done this much expansion in Texas. We got here early enough to beat the land speculators. In the next ten years, Arizona will get railroads, and then nothing will stop it."

"You are a leading edge now. One more thing about our arrangement. I know I told you right out that first day. I have never had a child. Doctors could not tell me why. You have an heir, Adam. He is a wonderful boy. But someday will you think it is my fault you have no more children?"

"Another nice woman told me that. I am not marrying you for your child bearing. I'm going to marry you for you. To me, you're the perfect wife. No holds barred."

"What does that barred mean?" She chuckled.

"In a prizefight, that means you can kick, bite, or gouge out his eyes."

"After that, we better go eat." Her arm around him, they went for the kitchen, laughing.

"Raphael is coming to the house with a man. Raphael is the foreman for this ranch," Monica said to Liz, looking out the back window.

Then she directed her words at Chet. "If that man needs to eat, we have plenty of food."

Monica turned to Liz. "People come all the time and need him. I bet this one does, too."

"Ah, good morning," his foreman said. "Mr. Talburt has a problem and needs some help from Chet."

"Raphael, step inside and meet my future wife. You missed the party last night."

"Oh, I go to bed early."

"Go on in and meet her."

"*Si*."

"Sir, what can I do for you?" Chet asked the man.

"Someone shot my brother in the back, and the law don't seem to want to do anything about it."

"Where is he?"

"Over by Four Peaks. It's in Gila County. Here's his wife's letter. I know you've been over there."

Dear Orville,

I don't know who to call on. Your brother Argus was shot in the back over three weeks ago by some men who live nearby. Despite my letters to the sheriff begging for help and asking others no one has came. He is laid up in bed. The neighbor took the bullet out right after he was shot. I don't think he could live through a wagon ride to Globe or Mesa. Who can I turn to?

Easter Talburt

"You know that country?" Orville asked.

Chet nodded. "Kinda strange that no one has investigated it. It's a dang long ride over there. My man, Jesus, will be here tonight. He'll need a day's rest. Then Cole, Jesus, and I will go over there and see what we can learn. Come inside. We're having lunch. Hang your hat and coat over there. I'll need a map on how to find her.

"Folks, this is Orville. His brother was shot over in Gila County. And no one will see about it."

Monica pointed her finger at Liz. "I told you so. Sir, do you drink coffee?"

"I do."

"Good, I will fix you a plate and cup. Sit down there. These two just started eating. Don't worry about a thing. We feed everyone at this ranch house."

Chet could see Liz was amused by Monica's take-charge style.

"Men come here all the time and act like they never eat away from home, and my cooking has not killed one of them yet."

Chet knew he was home. He shook his foreman's hand and winked at him. "Thanks, good to be back for a day anyway."

Raphael waved his *sombrero* at Liz, ready to leave. "We will talk another time, señora. So nice to have you here."

"Yes, we will."

"Things are back to normal here. The Byrnes detective agency is open for business again," Monica announced.

"Anita, you can tell Jesus when he gets here

tonight that he has one day to rest, and for him to show you Preskitt. The next day we'll ride for Four Peaks."

The poor girl looked around, lost.

"Don't worry, he's a real gentleman, and you need to see the town and the church. Tomorrow, your boss and I are going to go look at the horses that she came for the first time I met her."

Liz laughed and reassured Anita the situation would be fine. "And I really do want to see his horses."

They talked afterward. "I'm sorry people depend on me to straighten out these kinds of things for them. You'll have to share me."

Liz frowned. "Where is the law over there? It sounds like Mexico."

"We're building on that. Don't worry. We'll try to quickly settle it."

"I can see I will have to share you. I don't mind, so long as I'm part of you. We will squeeze in our time, too. Wading in shallow rivers?" she asked. "Well, it was the only foot washing I could think about."

He hugged her and swung her around. "It was nice."

They could work on the marriage business when he came back. She wasn't in any hurry and he wanted their union well done. They had no one to please but themselves.

CHAPTER 7

When Chet, Cole, and Jesus rode out the gate for Rye, Jesus was taking lots of ribbing about his showing Anita the town the day before. The weather wasn't exactly warm that morning, frosty but clear. Chet's other roan, the strawberry one, walked on his toes a lot, but never bucked. They led two packhorses. Chet counted on a three-day hard ride to get to the Talburt ranch.

"Now that we've teased you about Anita, what do you think about her?" Chet asked Jesus.

"I was shocked that she asked to meet me. Oh, she is a very nice young lady. But we only talked a few times in Nogales. When I got to the stage office, she came out of the night and hugged me and said she was glad I got there safe. I have never been on that stage line when it was being held up. Whew, I didn't know what to think."

"Did you have fun in town with her yesterday?"

"Oh, I did. We had ice cream at the drugstore.

Cole told me it was a better place for the two of us to go than the big saloon."

Chet and Cole shared a nod over that item.

"We went to the church, too. She prayed there and thanked me. She asked if I went there often. I told her at Christmas, sometimes."

They both laughed at his answer.

"She may be good for you," Cole said. "Valerie and I go to Marge's church. It sure won't hurt."

"Did she say anything about Liz's parents? That was one thing we never got around to," Chet asked.

"No, but Anita told me Liz really did run the *hacienda.* There are many people that live and work there."

"Her brother-in-law is going to run it. I never heard what killed her husband."

Jesus shook his head. "She never said. Anita is a very nice quiet lady."

"Had she ever ate ice cream before?" Cole asked.

He chuckled. "No, she never had. It was a big treat, she told me."

"Twenty cents' worth?"

"Yes."

"Them expensive dates are going to break you, buddy."

Jesus shook his head. "I can afford some more."

"If you can't, Cole can finance the rest," Chet said.

The warm sun shone on them as they trotted their horses northeast from Hayden's Ferry. Four Peaks, the highest mountain, loomed far to the east. The saguaro desert spread out, bristling with cholla, and the pungent creosote smell of the greasewood brush attacked his nose. They'd reach the Rye area by late the third day. According to his map, the turnoff was on the right-hand side of the road. And a half mile up that lane was where she lived.

"We've been up in this country before," Chet said, looking around.

"Jesus tracked some horses up here."

"I recall that."

The sign read TALBURT and an arrow mark showed the way.

"Lots of these folks don't have real houses, as I recall," Chet said, looking around as they rode uphill.

"Squaw shades, they call them."

Chet nodded.

"It is a poor land, much like Mexico. It isn't farm-land," Jesus said.

"Yes, I don't know how anyone can live off cattle sales alone up here."

Cole shook his head. "All farming is hard stuff. We grew cotton at home in Texas. Bumble bee kind. Land was so poor the bumble bees had to bend over to pollenate the flowers on them."

"You're saying you'd rather be a cowboy than pick cotton?" Chet teased.

Cole shook his head. "That isn't even a good question."

"I agree," Jesus said.

"I bet that shade on that hillside up to the left is hers." Chet pointed to some brush pole corrals and palm fronds stacked high on the peaked roof of the *remada.*

A hard-faced woman in her thirties came out, carrying a rifle. "What do you three want?"

"We're U.S. Marshals. Are you Mrs. Easter Talburt?"

"Yes, I am."

"Your brother-in-law, Orville, asked us to come see you."

"You came too late. My husband died yesterday."

"I'm sorry, but we couldn't have saved his life. This is Cole and Jesus. They're my deputies. My name is Chet Byrnes. We want to set down and talk to you about this matter, and we've ridden a long ways. Do you drink coffee?"

"Yes, but I have none."

"No problem. Jesus can make us some."

"I only have benches to sit on." She looked troubled about their encounter with her and held the rifle in one hand by the barrel.

"I know you've had some tough times, ma'am. Benches are fine. We can sit on the ground. We're simply cowboys who have come to help you." He moved uphill, took the rifle, and patted her shoulder to reassure her. "I'm so sorry we didn't come earlier."

She sobbed into his vest. "You didn't know. I buried him myself yesterday, but I didn't have the courage left to finish covering him up."

"Let's go inside and sit down. We can do that for you. We came on short notice. Your brother-in-law told us about your problem and then we had to get here. That took three days."

"I have no food to feed you. No coffee."

"Jesus can handle that matter. Sit in the rocker and I'll get a blanket. It's cold enough you're shaking." With her situated in the chair, he squatted down on the ground before her. "Cole, get a blanket for her."

He hurried away and returned quickly with a blanket to wrap around her.

"Start at the beginning of your story."

"Oh, I don't know what I can tell you. Argus worked in the mines at Globe. We thought we would move. We have, or had, some cattle. We planned to sell them and try to go somewhere else."

"Where was it you planned to move?"

"The mines at Crown King, maybe. This place was his dream. He wanted a ranch. We have a homestead patent on this section, but folks wouldn't let us alone. First, the Carpenters moved in and squatted on our land. He finally got them to leave. The Burris family came next. He caught the four of them butchering one of our calves and they shot him in the back. It was our calf."

"Is there any way you could prove they were butchering your calf?"

She dropped her face down. "No, that was just the start. They destroyed the hide, I'm sure. They told the deputy it was their calf, and the four of them swore he shot at them when they were butchering their own calf and they shot back."

"Where was your husband shot?"

"In the back. The deputy come around and said it

was self-defense. He attacked them and the calf they had killed was theirs—case dismissed."

"Who could testify they shot him in the back?"

"Stan Couples, who took the bullet out. I didn't figure Argus'd live to make it to Mesa or Globe riding in a wagon. We knew he was bad off. But they shot him and left him for dead. I think they thought he was dead when they rode off."

"You have run out of food and caring. I don't mean caring about him. I mean caring about your own life."

She nodded, and the rocker runners creaked some. "Reason I didn't bury him—I was going to shoot myself and lie in the same grave when they found me."

Disappointed at her answer, Chet shook his head hard at her. "Easter, suicide is not an answer."

"If you'd been through the hell I've been in . . . They ran my horses off. I kept one in the lot and they come back for him. I had the gate tied. One morning I found the rope cut and he was gone."

"Describe your horses." He held his herd book in hand to jot down the information with a pencil.

"The team was two bays, about five years old. Mustangs he caught and broke. They had two T's on their right shoulder. A paint, brown and white, some black in her mane, she was my horse and about seven. His gray gelding was, I think, seven, too. He wore a Hat brand. I have those papers."

"Did they steal them?"

"Maybe ran them off. I don't know. Those horses wouldn't leave the ranch unless driven away."

"Tell me about the Burris bunch."

"They live north of here. They've made other people leave. One day those folks were here, the next they had left. I know they scared them away."

"Easter, I need proof."

"How can I get proof? They ride in wearing masks, shoot up things, and who sees them?"

"I guess we'll have to look for witnesses." He dropped his gaze to the ground.

Jesus brought her a steaming cup of coffee, and one for him, too. "We need some firewood to cook supper," he said to Chet.

She shook her head like that, too, was impossible. "I've used all there is close around here."

"Jesus and I will ride out and find some," Cole said.

They had a few hours of light left before sundown, so Chet agreed.

A short while after they left, Chet heard a rifle shot.

"What was that?" she asked, her face turning pale.

"A rifle shot. One should be no problem. They may have shot a deer to eat."

"I'm just jumpy, I guess."

Cole soon came in with a slain deer over his saddle.

"We can hang him on the crossbar," she said. "I'll get my knives and tubs. You guys are sure some outfit."

Jesus came back dragging a bunch of mesquite brush on his lariat to make a fire.

She brought the two men some rope to hang the

carcass. With the deer swung on the crossbar, Chet told Cole to work on the firewood supply with Jesus. Cole went for his hitched horse and Chet began sharpening a knife to skin out the deer.

"I'm amazed. You are lawmen, aren't you?" asked Mrs. Talburt.

"Yes, but we are simple people and used to working outside when needed. Tell me all you know about these people who shot your husband."

"They're bullies. They came in here a few years ago. Started acting like they owned the whole country. Those boys of his raped a few young girls. But they never raped the daughter of any rancher who they knew better than to cross. At least, I never heard of them doing that."

"Most people keep or sell the hides of beef they butcher?" He was splitting open the deer's hind legs to peel the hide back.

"I don't know. Why?"

"If they have one wrong-branded hide, it can point to rustling."

"How do you find out?"

"Make a surprise search."

He started cutting up the middle of the carcass to divide the hide, careful not to split hair and get it on the carcass. That was where one got the raw deer flavor on the meat. This animal was fat and would make Mrs. Talburt lots of meat to jerk. The hide removal was advancing when Cole brought him two buckets of water.

"You're making good progress," Cole said. "I'm going to try to get some more firewood."

"The two of us will get this done."

She worked on one side to remove the hide, Chet on the other. He noticed right away that she was a hardworking lady, using a knife to peel back the hide. Maybe in her mid-thirties, but he had no doubt she could fight a bear if challenged. But she was too thin; no doubt she hadn't eaten much since her husband was shot. He couldn't blame her, since she had no one to help her.

With the hide finally off, she said she would tan it. Nothing would go to waste. He washed his hands and began to eviscerate the deer. When he dumped the guts in a tub, she took the liver and the heart out. She also cut out the kidneys and put them in a pan with the other parts.

Cole had come back twice with fuel on the end of his lariat, while Jesus was busy chopping it up.

Chet rinsed off the carcass. Mrs. Talburt took the parts to the cooking area, and came back with an ax.

"How do you want him cut up?" he asked her.

"Chop his ribs out, and I'll slow-cook them all night. They'll be good in the morning."

"I can do that."

"We can use the quarters for jerky, and eat the back strap. Do you have a wife?" she asked.

"I lost my wife a short time ago. She had a horse wreck."

"I wasn't prying." She had the big pan ready to go up the hill.

"Have I acted like I wasn't married?"

"Oh, no."

"There is a special lady at my ranch now, waiting

for us to close our business here so we can make plans for the future."

"I'll write a letter and thank her for letting you come. Oh, and call me Easter. We've dressed a deer together today, so we can call one another by our first names."

Chet, amused by her comments, concealed a smile and agreed he would.

Jesus had some onions to fry with the liver. The *frijoles,* he complained, were slow to get cooked, so he fried some German potatoes. They sat around the table, sipping his fresh coffee.

"How do we stand?" Cole asked.

"We still need to close the grave this evening. I want us to take a look at the Burris place. They may have some hides that don't belong to them. If we can't hang a murder charge on them, a rustling one will do the job."

"They dumb enough to keep a hide with another brand on it?" Cole asked.

"If they think they're tough enough, yes."

"How will we do that?"

"Ride up and search their buildings."

"You have a warrant?"

"We'll get their permission."

Cole laughed. "That should work huh, Jesus?"

"Sure. We have searched lots of folks. It should work. The food is done. Come fill your plates."

"I think a surprise visit, early in the morning, might be good."

The two men agreed with him.

"What if there are no hides?" she asked.

"I intend to put the fear of God in them."

"You three do this all the time?" Mrs. Talburt asked.

"When we aren't helping folks like you, we ranch," Chet said.

The men sat on the ground with their plates of food and she occupied the rocker. A bloody sunset showed off in the west and the temperature began to fall.

"Leave the grave until tomorrow. We didn't get it filled, but we'll be back and complete it for you."

"Thanks, you've been most kind."

"Do you have any relatives you can go live with when this is over?"

She shook her head.

"Your brother-in-law?"

"I don't get along with his wife, or she would not get along with me."

"Oh."

"You don't know her then."

"No, I never knew him until he came and asked for my help," Chet said.

"I'm amazed she let him do that."

"He came and asked me to help you."

"When the law would not budge, I had no one to ask anymore. So I wrote him."

"Well, I am trying to think where we could take you and you'd be safe. Obviously, this location is for some tough brush popper to run cattle. This bunch won't be the last bullies to come here."

"You're saying I shouldn't stay here alone."

"That sums it up."

"But I have no money to leave."

"I'll think of someone who needs you or needs a house kept."

"Thank you. And thank you for the deer and the firewood."

"We aren't done yet."

She smiled for the first time ever. "I know, but you have helped me so much."

"Set your alarm clock, Jesus. We're going to try our hand at routing them out of bed in the morning. Better get us up at four."

Cole pulled out his pocket watch. "It's six o'clock now."

Later that evening, Chet had a hard time going to sleep. Leaving Liz behind was on his mind. He'd asked her to come up to Preskitt and then rode off on her. Well, maybe she would understand and not leave him. Hispanic women could have a mad side—especially a rich one like her.

Strange, in all the foot-washing business and talks they had, she never mentioned her family. Her brother-in-law became the ranch manager and Liz sounded definite about that. There was too much he didn't know to make real good sense out of things. She came there to be with him, and to be his wife. And here he laid in a thick bedroll, two hundred miles away from her, listening to coyotes whine. It was not fair.

They woke in the starlight. Easter made coffee and oatmeal with bugs from Jesus's panniers. The deer ribs and *frijoles* were still cooking. In the lamplight, the three men saddled their horses and hitched them, then climbed back uphill to eat breakfast. She had hot water for them to wash their hands and a towel.

"I plan to be back here tonight and have this business settled."

She nodded. He noted that she'd brushed her hair and tied it back with a ribbon. Even wore a much nicer dress. Good, her esteem had risen. They finished their meal, thanked her, downed the last of their coffee, and rode out.

The second road north from hers led to the Burris place. It was several miles northeast, and there was an old broken-down wagon at their turnoff. With Easter's directions, it was easy to find under the stars. They rode up on the flat, hobbled their horses, and set out on foot. Each man carried a Winchester and plenty of brass 44/40 cartridges. They came up on a squaw shade beyond the corrals.

Cole took the assignment to sneak around behind and cover the back side, in case they decided to run for it. Chet and Jesus planned to sit and watch things from the corral. It afforded some protection and there was a slit in the fence where they could belly down and shoot through. The sun began to creep over Four Peaks. No one had stirred. The number of horses in the corral told him most of them would be there. Daylight began to creep up.

He fired two rounds in the air and yelled, "I have a posse surrounding the house. Hands high, or die. Any woman with a gun in her hand can expect to be shot. Now, get out here now or die."

The cussing and grumbling went on.

A woman screamed. "I have a baby. No gun!"

"Get out here and move to the left in plain sight."

"Who in the hell're you?"

"U.S. Marshal Chet Byrnes and my posse. Get out here."

"We're coming. You got the wrong place. Who you looking fur?"

"The Burris Gang."

Women in nightshirts led the way, herding crying kids. Then, bearded men in long-handles followed, hands high.

A rifle shot came from the back.

"I told you I had a posse. Any more in there want to die?" Chet shouted, angry at their disobeying him.

"No!"

"Cole?" Chet called out.

"Yah, Chet. I got one of them. He came out with a pistol in his hand."

"Get him around here."

"Can't, Chet. He's stopped breathing."

One of the younger women fell to the ground in a faint. As he came out of the corral, Chet saw her fall.

"That's his wife," the gray-headed man said.

Chet shook his head. "We warned you. Now who shot Argus Talburt?"

"He attacked us, butchering our own calf. The law in Rye will tell you so."

"I have a dying man's different version. He said you killed him. Besides, why would you butcher your own calf on the open range? Give me one good reason."

"We ain't talking."

"I can call for a cattlemen's trial today in Rye. If I read his letter in the middle of town, the three of you won't stand a chance of being acquitted. Or you can sign a confession that you shot him and stole his calf. That might get you five years on a plea deal in court in Globe."

"I'm getting a lawyer."

"You won't need a lawyer in Rye."

Chet looked up and saw Cole coming out of the house. "They have four hides with other brands on them in there. One has his brand."

"Well, Burris? That will be the convicting evidence in the court at Rye."

The man didn't answer him.

"With four stolen cattle, one of them Mr. Talburt's, and his statement, your necks will be stretched under a cottonwood tree west of town."

"Five years?"

"I'll tell the judge that was my agreement. You don't protest and if you admit doing it in open court, that will be the sentence. You, however, don't want to go to open court, for the prosecutor will demand you three be hung. Hides and his deathbed confession will get you hung in Globe."

He looked at the others. "He's got us by the balls, guys. I don't want no trial in Rye or Globe. I say sign it."

They nodded and the huddle of women began to cry. The kids cried, too. Jesus went for paper from his saddlebags, and ink and pen.

"Cole, get them dressed."

"After that, take the youngest, and have him saddle three horses. You women, feed those children and don't try anything. One is already dead. We'll kill the rest of you."

He wrote out the charges they confessed to and that he was a U.S. Marshal, and they had agreed to a five-year prison sentence with no pardon or parole privileges for the crime. Harold Burris signed his name first, with James Burris signing second. Then Robert Lee Burris signed under them. Chet signed and dated it.

The youngest of the boys might have been sixteen. The dead one was nineteen years old, the women told him, and agreed to bury him. He let the wives feed the prisoners, then they set out for Easter's place.

He dismounted below her squaw shade and she came down the hill. "You arrested them?" she asked, out of breath and looking warily at the ones seated on their horses in irons. She hugged him.

"They confessed to manslaughter and rustling. They're going to prison for five years."

She nodded.

"Best I could do. The fourth one is dead."

"You did miracles, after that deputy said there was no case."

"They say they know nothing about your horses. I'll send a bill of sale back up here for their three horses, along with someone to bring them back for you to use. Their horses go to the arresting officers. Don't wait till you're flat busted. Come to Preskitt, and we'll find something for you to do."

"My neighbor came by this morning. The man who tried to save my husband's life. He asked me to stay and marry him."

"Good, Easter. Keep your head up. You looked very nice this morning."

She blushed. "What is your wife-to-be's name?"

"Elizabeth. Call her Liz Byrnes."

"I am writing her a letter and thanking her for letting you and those two nice men come do this. God bless both of you."

The trip to Globe took the rest of the day and a half day more to get there. Court proceedings took up another. The sheriff grumbled about Chet interfering in his job. The judge and prosecutor, however, agreed to his plan, plus thanked him and his crew.

Chet and his posse left for Mesa on horseback, and a day later they rode onto Hayden's Ferry for the stage. From there, he telegraphed Liz that they would be there at midnight and that Jesus was bringing the horses and would be home two days later. They sent Cole's wife, Valerie, a wire, too, that he would be there.

The night air was cool after the coach left the ferry and, huddled underneath the blanket in the seat, he knew it would be a lot colder up in the mountains.

"I thought all the time up there he'd want to see that deathbed confession, didn't you?" Cole asked.

"Well, that was my bluff. He figured I had one and they hold up good. I could have read one to the cattlemen's jury up at Rye, but I didn't have to."

"Would you have had to do that?"

"No. I hoped not. My reputation in Rye isn't the best anyway. You knew that story?"

"Those two that killed your last wife's foreman, another ranch hand, raped a rancher's wife, and you caught them?"

He nodded.

"The person that wrote that letter to the Globe paper about you hanging those two made you famous."

"That story never had my name in it."

"Word spread fast. I told a buddy that I wanted to get on with your Verde Ranch crew. He said I'd better watch that guy that owns it, that he hung two outlaws by himself at Rye."

Cole went on, "Boy, I have never regretted getting this job. That first cattle drive trip we made to New Mexico and those damn Apaches attacked us. I thought I was in for worlds of hell. That buck you caught and left me with drew a knife, and I had to shoot him. Things were tough in those early days. The Force ain't been a picnic, but with those rewards we've split, Valerie and I have a start. I can recall back when you put her on the stage to come up here and help Jenn. Hell, I shook my head that night that there was no way I'd ever catch her. And now she's my wife—and we rode clear down here, killed a deer, stocked up that woman's larder, and the next day you had the rustlers confess to a crime the local law let them off on. Damn, Chet Byrnes. I love riding with you."

Chet nodded his head. "That Easter was who I was proud of—she blossomed."

"Yeah, she sure did."

"I have a good team in you two, as well."

"This has been one of your nicer operations. Hell, I am proud of all the folks we help and save. She did clean up like a new penny. You must be happy we're going home again. Oh, man, you have a real great wife, like I do. Them get-back-home reunions are damn sure great."

"Cole Emerson, I'd say you're a real happy man. You've talked more today than you have in a year."

"Well, I told Valerie how lucky we are. She's kind of upset the others are having babies and she isn't. I said one would come for us and it will. If God wants us to have kids, he'll send us some. You know Bonnie told Valerie she thought she might be with a baby."

"Hey, I have a son. Marge and I never thought that would happen."

"Liz never had a child with her last man?" Cole asked.

"No, and she warned me. But Marge did, too, before we got married."

Cole laughed. "Here came that fancy coach and out came this silver earring–flashing lovely woman, and before supper she was yours."

"You missed the greatest day. The day that Jesus took Anita to town, we went to the Verde Ranch to see the big horse and played with six of his sons and daughters. Liz really got excited. That was why she stopped at Tubac in the first place. She had seen those horses we sent to Mexico for Bonnie, and she wanted to buy some."

"They are great colts, but you found another

princess in her. What is the story about washing her feet? I only heard part of that."

"We were riding around like a pair of lost geese in a tall hay meadow. She wanted to stop and wade in the river. Hell, anything was fine with me. So she sat down and I took off her boots and socks. Then she went wading in the golden sunlight, with beams coming through the cottonwoods and dancing on the water. I could have watched her all day. She came out and I went after a towel. That move worried her. She thought I was going to leave her. Then, when I dried her feet, she recalled Jesus doing that to his apostles at the Last Supper."

"Oh, I see."

"Hell, I simply wanted to touch her."

They both laughed.

On their arrival at Preskitt, Liz had driven the buckboard to meet him. One of the ranch boys brought Valerie in another one. Valerie and Cole were hugging and kissing. Valerie pulled loose, ran over, and pulled Chet away from Liz. "Let me kiss him for sending Cole home early for me."

Valerie hugged him and kissed his cheek. "Liz, you're so damn lucky. He is such a good man to all of us."

"Oh, I know. I know."

Chet was back with his bride-to-be, all bundled up in a winter coat, but she wore her earrings under a red woolen shawl tied over her head.

"You can tell me how it went on the way home. You can drive," she said.

They shouted good-bye to the others and left for the ranch.

He explained how they arrested the rustlers and got them to sign a confession. He also told her how Easter had given up after her husband died.

"I did that, too. Such a bad thing to happen to anyone. But you know that. Oh yes, this week they brought me two of his colts from the Verde. Jimenez and I are working them."

"So you have your horses that you stopped by for, at last?"

"Oh, they belong to everyone in the family."

"I am teasing you."

She hugged him. "Ah, yes, now this Mexican tramp is stealing his horses."

"Does not being married worry you?"

"No, I just say that to be silly. *Hombre*, I am very proud to share your life with you."

"Let's meet the priest and ask him if he can marry us."

"He better. I am not moving out of the ranch house to please him."

"I'm glad. Everywhere I go I smell hay. I can't believe how you did that to me."

"I admit I did it. That was where a boy would have taken me that night. See, I knew you were still a boy at heart."

"I am curious about your childhood. Somewhere, such things must have filtered through."

"Oh, my parents were very rich. I was raised in a strict Catholic girls' school. I learned about boys from myclassmates. I never had a chance to stray.

Chaperones were always on hand. I learned to dance at arm's length. At such an event, I might have two dances in an evening.

"When my husband discovered me, I had never even kissed anyone. He swept into my life, kissed me, and we went off and danced in a *cantina* all night. My parents searched for me, and they even put a price on his head. A priest married us the next day, and by a fast private coach he took us from Mexico City to his Sonora *hacienda.* They disowned me. I have not contacted them since. That was their choice. My husband was an empire builder like you. There is a big *hacienda* in Sonora. His brother is not him, but he is capable enough to run it.

"I never wanted another husband. After his death they came from silly boys to gray-headed old men, even one with a cane. They came like peacocks, and they thought I was some weak sister who needed their skills on how to run a *hacienda* and to spend my money."

"You have no contact with your parents?"

She shook her head. "My father is a dictator. I won't put up with that."

"What does he do?"

"He is a big lawyer. He has been a *federale* judge."

"Your mother?"

"She does what he says."

"No brothers or sisters?"

"None."

"Your husband treated you well?"

"Oh, we had fun. So much, I never thought it would end. I don't think he spoiled me. Much like you did, taking me to the Verde Ranch to see the horses. I knew you wanted to be ready to go help that woman, but first you took me to see the stallion and his offspring, and before I could ask you if I could have one of them to train, you told Tom to bring me two."

Chet nodded grim-like. "I felt bad, fixing to leave you when you gave up so much to join me."

"You told me something I have thought much about. What is a person's life worth, compared to anything financial? I could be a rich woman, entertaining myself, or else I could share another person's life, and it be as exciting as being a wife to him had been. It was not hard, after that long day we shared, for me to see being alone was not how I wanted to live the rest of my life."

"All those suitors missed the point?"

"Oh, they were embarrassing."

He shook his head. "You didn't know me, climbing out of that coach in a black dress and your earrings flashing."

"I immediately knew that man with his hat in his hand was no clown. You have a real aura about you. You know what I mean? You could hold people off without using your hands. It encircles you. What did your wife do to meet you?"

"We rode together from Tucson on that same stage to Preskitt. At the time, I was obligated to a woman in Texas. I guess Marge thought I was a stranded cowboy and she started paying my bills. I had to gather them and repay her. She simply wanted to be sure I could survive. Headed home south of

Preskitt, road agents killed my nephew, Heck. She came to my aid. The lady in Texas had to stay there and care for her family, so I returned and Marge fell in my tracks. I owed her for helping me so much when Heck's murder shattered me. My entire family was moved here, and I was to go look at the rim country for a ranch—but Susie, my sister, said Marge wouldn't go on a camping trip with me—she has been to finishing school. But when I asked her, Marge said she'd love to go. I told her no, that I'd marry her first."

"That is what I expected, if you wanted me. But I am doing fine, fitting into your life. Are you still suited with me?"

"Yes. Perfectly." He reined up in the yard. "We must always keep talking, not simply as lovers, but partners."

"Oh, we will."

Monica had waited up and spoke up, "Are all his fingers and feet still on him?"

"Oh, yes. I think he is fine."

"What was the result?"

"One of the troublemakers is dead, the other three will serve five years for murder and rustling. The lady has a suitor who I think will see to her."

"Was she pretty?"

He shook his head. "Just a woman."

Monica nodded and served them cake.

"This is wonderful, thank you. Monica has been telling me about things in the past." Liz cut a bite off with a fork.

"She could fill a book."

"Not me. You would be the one," Monica said to him.

They both laughed. "We love you."

"I am going to bed. He will be up early, I have warned you."

"Good night."

He was home. Time to straighten out things.

"Tomorrow, we can find the priest, and you can meet my associates in town."

"Sounds great. I hope I am fitting in."

"You can't please everyone. You do me."

They went hand in hand upstairs.

"When you set our wedding date, I want time to invite your people to come here, so I can meet them," he told her.

"They won't come."

"If they don't, then they will lose."

"You have thought about that, haven't you? You are such a family leader and I have forgotten them. I was raised so strict, I have always resented that."

"I bet you did."

She laughed. "We will have fun."

They met Bo Evans, the land man, who had bought three more homesteads near the Windmill Ranch. Chet introduced her to Tanner at the bank. At the mercantile, she met Kathrin, the lady he brought back from Utah, and her husband, Ben Ivor. They had lunch at Jenn's Café, and she met Jenn, along with Valerie and another girl who took Bonnie's place. Then they went to the Catholic church. She put a shawl on her head, touched the holy water at the entrance, and crossed herself with a curtsy. She went to pray at the altar while he took a seat in the back.

"You are Chet Byrnes?" the priest asked quietly.

He started to stand and the man waved his effort aside.

"I am here with Elizabeth." He nodded toward her kneeling at the altar, praying.

"She is new here?"

"Yes, she comes from Sonora."

"One of your men brought her lady here. Morales?"

"Anita."

"Yes. And Jesus rides with you?"

"Yes, sir. But Elizabeth and I came to speak to you. We plan to marry."

"I am honored. You are not Catholic?"

"No, sir."

"I can marry you out in front of that rail."

"I heard that we could not be married in the church."

"Some strict members of my order might deny you. I won't."

"The lady who cares for my son wanted him christened."

"Oh, yes, Rhea told me. She has not set a time, since you were gone."

"I will have her set that date. The wedding date is what she says." He nodded to the returning Liz.

"I understand."

"Thank you."

They had an interesting exchange with Father O'Brian in his office.

When the marriage matters were about over, she spoke up to Chet. "I have thought about this. Would you let me hold Adam in my arms, when we get married?"

"That's fine with me, if you want that."

"I really want that. It is his infant son, Father."

"I have no problem with that," O'Brian said.

Chet shook his hand and they left his office. She held his arm on the way to the buckboard. "I think this has been another great day in my new life."

"I partner a saddle shop, so I want you to meet them, too." They went by and met Martin McCully and his daughter, Petal. Then he took her by the livery and they met Frey and his wife, Gloria.

Driving home later, he told her about Gloria's problems when her husband died and how Frey rescued her from the house of ill repute.

"She is a fine lady. He's a real man, isn't he?"

"Yes, and a friend who's helped my operation a lot."

"What next?"

"Get married."

"You are right. Let's plan it."

"You pick the date."

"Yes, that is my job. What will you do meanwhile?"

"On the open days, check on our ranches. You can go along."

"Would you be shocked if I wore britches when I ride with you to look at the ranches?"

"No."

"Good. I would not offend you or embarrass

you. Marrying a *Latina* may be a bad enough scar on you."

"Oh, don't worry about that. You are my choice. You have so little accent, who would say that?"

"Oh, some woman who wanted you."

"Too bad."

"I went back to my *hacienda,* scolding myself for acting so desperate for you not to forget me. I was very upset, then your lovely letters came. I about squeezed them to death. And I gritted my teeth so tight, they hurt."

"You're a mess. I thought I was just a page in your book of life and you would turn that over and go on."

She pounded his arm with her flat hand. "Did you not believe me when I said I never knew another man beside my husband?"

"I knew that. We were both shaking that night like teenagers."

"Yes."

"Don't worry. I knew I had a winner, but I feared I had no good hold until you answered me in those letters. Then it was a two-way road to me."

She quickly agreed. "You had lots of good memories behind you."

He nodded. "More are in front of us."

"I am glad we can talk, Chet. I am not insecure with you, but we have so much more to learn about each other. I want you to know I am here to be your—mate?"

"Mate is the right word."

"Do you feel alright to be married in the Church?"

"I have no problem with that. Father O'Brian is a kind man."

"Yes, very kind."

Things were moving forward. That pleased him.

CHAPTER 8

He planned to start his first evaluation of operations on the Verde River Ranch. Tom was a watchful manager and he did a good job, but this ranch was his largest investment and had the most acres in the north. However, the Quarter Circle Z Ranch was his lowest source of income and it had been expensive to build its operation. That was because the past foreman sold the calves at weaning time, along with other bad management practices. The market for cattle was the larger two- to three-year-old steer. They would only start to reach that goal this year. A tough cow culling had helped, but that only called for more replacements. The sale of three hundred head of steers this year would help. The next year looked even better when near all of them would be Hereford or Shorthorn crosses.

Replacement of the traditional longhorn cattle was the direction ranching was headed. The beef quality of the British breeding was a necessary move.

Liz set the first Monday in March as their wedding

day. He wrote a letter to her parents in Mexico City, inviting them to the event, but he didn't tell her.

"Will the snow be gone?"

"No," he teased her. "It might snow that day."

She turned up her hands and shook her head. "You are no help."

He hugged her. They were making plans to go to the big house at the Verde. It had been some time since Susie moved to the Windmill, so Monica sent two of the *vaqueros*' wives and one of their husbands to clean the empty house. Supplies were sent along for the kitchen and to stock the place.

He had no idea how long they'd be down there. Liz said as long as they were together, she and Anita didn't care. Monica said Lea would make them a good cook, and her husband, Polo, would help her.

Jesus drove Liz and Anita down there in a buckboard. Chet wanted two of his roan horses down there for them to ride. Cole and he left early. When the sun was up enough to warm them some, the others came along. Mid-morning, Tom met the two men at the big house.

Polo had the fireplaces going. Raphael had sent a lot of firewood, just in case Tom's bunch was too busy to cut any. Chet thanked the two wives for their hard work cleaning the house.

Most of the morning, the men sat at the table and talked about the blacksmith shop. John was making a lot of barbwire with a small crew. Their building of windmills had picked up, and they were buying the gears because the shop didn't have the milling facilities. Three were set at Reg's on homestead wells on places they'd acquired. Tom's operation set up two and Hampt got one for the East Verde Ranch.

"Can we buy them cheaper than building them?" Chet asked.

Tom sat back. "Give us another year on that?"

"Fine. We didn't come here to shut you down."

"Tom, you know of any artesian wells in the valley?" Cole asked.

Chet had been about to ask the same thing. "JD has a driller. He found two substantial ones. The water pours out from behind a shut-off valve, and in about two years, they'll irrigate several acres of alfalfa."

Tom agreed. "We could use a driller, if he didn't cost an arm and a leg."

Chet explained again, "Tom, we aren't here to tear up your plans. Things are going good. When I bought this ranch, we knew it would take three years to get a set of saleable steers."

Tom nodded. "We're building a great set of cows. By next year, we'll have over a thousand great cows. We'll also have over two hundred Hereford cows by then, too."

"We'll need some purebred bulls for that operation next," Chet said. "If the weather isn't too cold tomorrow, I want to show Liz the Perkins Hereford operation. She's never seen that many white-faced cattle in her life."

They laughed and agreed she needed to see them.

They discussed farming, and Tom spoke up. "We have a good hay program, and we're learning how to grow a seed corn I got from Mexico. Any corn we plant must tassel in June, before the real summer heat sets in and burns up the tassels. That'll ruin having a good ear corn crop in Arizona."

"Too much or not enough?" Chet sat back in his chair to listen.

"If we get much more to oversee, I would hire a farm foreman."

Chet shot a look at him. "Maybe we should look for one?"

Tom was not in favor. "I want us making money first."

"Cole, what do you think?"

"I think they're doing a real good job. The men tell me they'll have lots of hay to carry over. So, in case of a long drought, that will be a big gain for the future."

Tom agreed. "I think we're building a solid ranch operation."

"Will it take two thousand cows to have a real ranch?" Chet asked.

"Maybe fifteen hundred. That and the steer carry-over would be a helluva lot of cattle."

"Probably right. I see that Jesus has delivered the ladies. Let's break for lunch," Chet said.

He went to welcome them and kissed his bride-to-be on her cold cheek.

"What a wide world it is up here." She used her arms to show the expanse of the Verde Valley.

"You alright, Anita?"

"Oh, *si, señor.* This is a very different country." She shook her head as if she might be taken back by it all.

Arm on Liz's shoulder, he said, "Part of our world. Jesus, tie up the team, lunch is ready."

"I am coming."

"Ladies, this is the original house on the ranch. After we rooted out the crooked foreman, I lived here with my sister before I married my first wife. The big house has so many more conveniences than we have here, but it's warm inside."

"It is a very nice house," Liz said.

"Someone needs to live in it," he said.

Liz chuckled. "You have to choose between on top or down here."

"I guess. I fear an empty house will fall down with neglect."

"I have no answer. Was your house in Texas like this one?"

"No, the one in Texas was a walled fort against the Comanche. It even had big wooden gates. We hadn't closed them in years, but we could have. All we lacked was a damn cannon."

"The Comanche kidnapped two of your brothers and sisters?"

"No, three. A boy and twins, a boy and girl. We never found any trace of them."

"Oh, that was sad."

Liz left him to go speak to Lea. "Anita and I are here to help you. What can we do?"

She smiled at them. "We are fine. Millie was here and she offered to help me, too. I handled this meal. *Manana*, maybe I will need three to cook."

Liz thanked her and told her the house looked very nice.

"*Gracias, señora.* It's a very nice *casa.*"

Chet seated her and Anita at the table. They ate with the men, and the conversation covered their trip.

Anita commented, "It is a narrow mountain road. I am glad we did not meet anyone."

They laughed.

"Did you cross yourself?" Chet asked her.

"Yes, several times."

Jesus smiled and shook his head. "I told her I had never ran off that road in my life."

She frowned at him hard enough that Chet chuckled.

"Tomorrow, if it warms up, we can go look at the Herefords."

"We have a south wind. It should be warm enough," Tom said.

Liz squeezed his leg beside her. "I want to go."

"Sure. I think we can get back before dark."

Liz frowned. "If you can't, I can camp with you."

"We'll take our bedrolls."

The men all nodded they'd heard him.

"After lunch, we'll look at the ranch horses."

"May I go?" she asked.

He shook his head. "How could we go without you?"

"Get up at midnight," she teased him in a soft voice.

He shook his head at Liz while she complimented Lea on their good lunch. Monica had chosen Lea well. Her husband, Polo, liked his job and Tom told him when they got busy he could help work stock.

When they went to look over the ranch's working horses, Tom suggested they buy a few replacements for the *remuda* and break them before the spring roundup. Chet agreed and they checked out the Barbarossa colts, besides the two she had at the upper house.

"Will you eventually ride them as ranch horses, or sell some?" she asked him.

"Awful high priced to herd cattle on. We probably will geld most of them and sell them to folks who want high-priced horses to ride. I sold enough in Texas to take everyone and the wagons up to the panhandle by the new railroad going to Denver. But we're accumulating more now."

"Someday, I want a stallion for my *hacienda.*"

"You pick him. They're yours, too."

She hugged his arm and in a whisper said, "I suppose you will make me pay you for him."

He grinned and whispered back, "I hadn't even thought about that."

She laughed, shaking her head beside him. "Yes, you had. You had."

He found the ranch and corrals in good repair. Tom had forty-five weaned Hereford bull calves he was feeding corn and hay to grow them out.

She admired them. "You will use them this next year or the one after?"

"Tom likes to get them to a long two years, and that is only half as many as I need. We thought we'd be selling some bulls by now, but our own expansion keeps us buying more besides the ones we raise."

"A big place takes lots of things. Tell me about

that. I am anxious to see all those white-faced cows tomorrow."

"Fine. The place is being well kept, isn't it?" he asked her privately, surveying the curious young bulls over the rail fence.

She quickly agreed. "Tom does not miss details."

They were on horseback out in the river bottoms where the range herd of cows had been hayed earlier. She was amazed at all the haystacks, but being an observer, she commented how good the longhorns and half-Hereford cows looked.

"They are licking their sides and, to me, that says they are doing good."

"I think it's worthwhile, feeding them up here."

"Oh, with the snow cover you get up here, I think you would have to. Reg has to feed more?"

"He has lots more winter up there, and he also has to keep the elk out of his hay."

"I have never seen an elk."

"You will, in time."

"I know, but I wanted you to point some out for me. Oh, and I like this roan horse. I see why you ride them."

"Wait till you ride in the mountains on one. You'll really like them."

"I bet they are sure footed. What do they call them?"

"Bulldog mountain horses."

"I can see why. But you're a horseman. You knew that yellow horse would make money and bought him to fill your needs, like the train ride and getting Bonnie back."

"And he also got you to stop and have an affair with me."

"Oh, yes." Her eyes sparkled. "I had not counted on that, but I never would have stopped to meet a man who would treat me so badly if he had not owned a great yellow horse. I can't even believe that day really happened." She was laughing by the time she finished.

"I am truly grateful you did. But you said you ran off with your first husband to a dance and married him the next day."

She laughed. "I guess when I find a man I am—what you say in English—what is that word?"

"Impulsive."

She looked at him like that was a new thing.

"It means no holds barred."

She snickered. "Eye gouging and biting allowed, huh?"

They both laughed.

"I have tried to speak good English, since I learned it. But there are words I simply don't know."

"You do a great job. I won't get mad about you asking me anything."

"Wait till I am your wife, then I will be like a bulldog biting you."

"No, you won't. I know you better than that."

"Oh, we will see." She gave a toss of her head under the scarf and remounted.

They rode back to the big house with Tom, Cole, and Jesus.

"Tomorrow, we will see the Hereford cattle?" Liz asked.

He checked the sky for clouds. "Yes, if the weather stays open like this."

"Good, I appreciate seeing all the things that you do. Someday, I will transfer some of your ranching practices to my *hacienda*."

She had not mentioned much about her ranch down there, but she knew the ranching business. Running cows in a place where it never snowed would be a lot different from in the Verde Valley.

He looked forward to the night and holding her in his arms. At times, even as intimate as they had been, he learned new things about his mate. He hadn't thought much at first about Liz telling him she ran off and married her first husband. She ran off with his heart, too. Obviously, the *hacienda* had been her late husband's. For his part, he felt damn lucky she'd been available to become his wife.

A teenage boy came and knocked on the front door during supper. Polo went to see who it was and invited him into the dining room.

"Mr. Byrnes?"

"Yes, come join us. What can I do for you, young man?" He stood over his chair to talk to him.

"I hate to bother you, sir—my name is Brant Bates. Some outlaws hit our place yesterday. They stole several of our horses and shot my dad. My mom said you were the only man in this territory who could get them horses back for us. She said for me to start looking for you here, then go to Preskitt."

"I'm here. How is your father?"

"Shot up, sir. Else him and me'd be gone after them. I wanted to trail them down, but maw said they'd eat me for breakfast. I ain't much—well, I never shot another man and I don't know if I could before he shot me."

"You been to see the sheriff?" Chet asked.

"Maw said he was worthless as tits on a boar hawg."

There were snickers.

"That's pretty bad. Since we can't leave until daylight, sit down. Has your dad been to a doctor?"

"No, sir."

"Where do you live?"

"On the road they call Crook's Highway."

Chet nodded at him. "That's over east of Camp Verde."

"Yes." The boy thanked Lea for his plate of food and silverware. "I know you're busy, but we sure need them horses back."

"Oh, we understand. When did you leave home?"

"This morning, sir."

"Day's ride over there," Chet said, thinking out loud. "Well, I guess we'll be up before dawn and go see about his situation."

"I'm going," Liz said.

He looked at the ceiling for help. "It will be cold. Besides, I lost Susie's first husband chasing outlaws. I don't want to lose you."

"You won't, *hombre*. You won't."

"Jesus, find her some long winter underwear and

britches. If she wants to freeze to death, I won't deny her that."

"Where will those outlaws go?" she asked.

"Most of them go up to the Little Colorado Horse Head crossing. We chased some bank robbers up there last year."

"I hope they aren't headed for Utah," Jesus said. "We came close to freezing to death going up there."

"When was that?" Liz asked.

"Some outlaws kidnapped Leroy Sipes north of the Arizona strip country and held him for ransom in Utah. We went up there, found more wanted killers, brought him and that bunch back, plus the lady at the mercantile, Ben Ivor's wife, Kathrin, who you met. She was fleeing polygamy and had gotten swept up by this gang. She was a victim of circumstances, and we brought her back, too. Ben was a widower and they do fine together. They have a new baby. My land man, Bo, found that orchard property for sale in Oak Creek, so I bought it. The Sipes were having a tough time making a living on their place and I hired them to go run it. We've been eating produce—melons, apples, potatoes, peaches, and berries, ever since. We also have cabins up there. Good place to hide."

"Another ranch." She laughed.

"Hey, they brought us wagonloads of fruit to can last summer. Next year, Raphael, who you met at the Preskitt Valley place, is planting ten acres of beans—*frijoles*, pinto beans, to supply the ranches. We're figuring out many things to be more self-sufficient."

"You all don't do anything that isn't done well. But how did you assemble all these people?"

"Many of them had worked on the Verde River Ranch and that crooked foreman fired them. They all ate at Jenn's Café, and that's where they came from."

"Tell me about your sister-in-law, May. I love her."

"May was my brother's, Dale Allen's, second wife. His first wife died and she left him with three boys and a newborn baby daughter. Dale Allen married May, who was a banker's daughter, but I always thought he married her strictly to care for his young children. Her family was very mad that she married him, and disowned her."

"I understand that part."

"After Dale Allen was shot up in Kansas, his son, Heck, and May didn't get along. He was fifteen, so I brought him out here with me, looking for a ranch."

"He is the one the stage robbers killed below Preskitt, when you were going home?"

"Yes, and I told you Marge came to my rescue. Tough days."

"I bet they were."

"Hampt, the real big guy, married May. They have the baby, Miles, now, too. In Texas, May lived in the big house, and was the quiet one, raising kids. She married Hampt and he caught her singing and playing a piano. We never knew she could do that, and she was with us several years. Hampt has been really good for her."

"He is a gentle giant, isn't he? He cried at your family blessing."

"That's true, but if he ever gets mad, he's a grizzly bear."

"Your sister? Susie?"

"In Texas, she ran the house, fed the crew. Went with a sheriff at home, but they parted. She married a young man, Leif, who rode with me. He was riding with me when he had a horse wreck that killed him. Sarge, who handles the cattle drives to Gallup, is from the military. When she was widowed, he moved in and they got married and have the baby."

"She is so nice."

"In Texas, she always wanted me to marry a fat German farm girl who could farm and have lots of kids."

She laughed hard. "You never minded her."

"Nope. Now, tomorrow, wrap your hair up and we'll find you a larger hat. At first glance, I want you to pass for a teenage boy on this trip. Do you have a hand gun?"

"A new .30 caliber Colt. I can shoot it. The .44 was too big."

"I don't doubt that. Wear it, Deputy Marshal. Brant, is that horse you rode in on solid?"

"No, sir. He's a Welsh pony. They took all the big horses."

"Jesus will get you a good horse in the morning. Should I send a buckboard over to bring your father back to a doctor?"

The youth shook his head. "We have good neighbors. I am certain they would bring him."

"Then it's settled. Before dawn, we ride out. Bring a tent."

She shook her head. "Not for me."

Jesus returned Chet's nod, that he would handle it.

"See you all early in the morning. Brant, Jesus will find you a bunk. Get lots of sleep."

In bed later, she snuggled in his arms. "Thank you for taking me along. I won't slow you down."

"Not a matter of that. I may not want to get out of a warm bedroll with you."

"Oh, you silly guy. I am very excited. Thanks. You won't regret me being along."

"You may have to hold the horses for us."

"I can do that, too."

He kissed her. Despite some misgivings, he felt proud she wanted to go with him. That way he wouldn't miss her.

CHAPTER 9

Under the early morning stars, his men assembled the pack train. The breath of humans and horses came in clouds of vapor. Lea had fed them breakfast and they were on the way shortly. When they left, the sun still had not peaked over the mountains in the east. Liz wore a large-brimmed black hat Jesus found that fit her. She looked enough like a Mexican teenage boy to suit Chet.

Chet and Liz rode his strawberry roans and left in a trot. Cole had a spunky horse that bucked some, so he took the lead for Camp Verde Village. After passing through town, they began to climb the face of the north side. In a short while, they were in the pines, and Liz twisted in her saddle to look down at the great expanse of the river's route far beneath them.

Mid-morning, they took a short break. Jesus handed around some fried apple pies Lea made for the trip, and they washed them down with canteen water. Chet put Liz back on Baldy with a wink and they rode on. Mid-afternoon, with him pushing, they reached the Bates ranch. A woman in her thirties, wearing a black wool coat over a housedress, came out on the porch to greet them.

"You must be Chet Byrnes?"

"Yes, Mrs. Bates."

"You sure got back here fast."

"How is your husband?"

"He's making it."

"Does he need to go to a doctor?"

She turned up her hands.

"This is my wife, Liz."

"Nice to meet you, Mrs. Byrnes."

"Your name is?" Liz asked as they went on the porch.

"Oh, I'm sorry. I'm Doris."

She patted her arm. "Nice to meet you. May I see him, too?"

"Certainly. I sure hated to bother your husband, but I knew if he came there was a good chance he'd get those rustlers and our horses back."

"He's good at that," Liz said.

"I knew that. Andy, this is Byrnes's wife, Liz," Doris said to her husband.

The pale-faced man sitting up with pillows nodded. "Sure hated to call on you two, but I just couldn't ride far after them."

"I want your wife to take you to a doctor in Camp Verde. Who can we get to haul you there?"

Doris spoke up. "The Van Horns will take him."

"Send Brant to get them. I want all the information you have on these rustlers," Chet said to the pair.

"When they rode in here, I figured they were on hard luck. Three good old boys riding the chuck line, I thought." Pain caught him and he winced. "Anyway, Doris fed them and then they pulled a gun to rob us. Made me mad and I ran for my .44."

She made a face. "They gunned him down."

"You have any names?"

"Curly, Fan, and Pick." She shook her head. "Last name Smith."

Chet nodded. "Describe them for me."

"Long hair, whiskers. Curly had reddish hair, stood about five foot six inches. Fan had gray hair. I don't think he was that old. Five eight or so. Pick could have been Pike, I never heard it right. He's a bean pole, maybe six foot tall."

"The horses and brands they took?"

"They all wore our KT brand on their right shoulder, mostly bays, one sorrel. Seven head. They took all our horses but that pony the boy rode over to your place."

"The pony's at our Verde place. Brant's riding one of our horses. No problem. If need be, I'll trade for it. My nephews and nieces can ride the pony. Let's see when it's over."

"Your wife can stay here," Doris said.

Chet shook his head. "She expects to go with us. Thanks, anyway."

The woman frowned in disbelief at him. "Does she know how cold and bad it can get up there?"

"She won't stay unless I tie her up."

Liz stood there and nodded. "Thank you. I want to be with him."

Doris shook her head.

"We will stay here tonight. Maybe sleep on your floor."

"Oh, you are most welcome to stay here."

"My men are checking for tracks. If they get a good trail to follow, we'll leave before dawn."

"I'll send Brant to get a buckboard, then fix supper."

"I will help you," Liz said.

Doris started to say something, but instead nodded. "Thanks."

Chet and Andy talked about cattle. His neighbors were feeding his cattle hay.

Jesus and Cole came in.

"They went north. That many horses leave lots of prints. We can follow them," Cole said.

"Before sunup, we'll take up their tracks."

The men agreed. Andy was napping. The women worked on food preparation. In the warmth of the stove, Chet sat on the couch in the warm room and catnapped.

The wind in the morning came off the North Pole. They were on the move before the sun crept up. Clouds were rolling in and Chet was concerned that it would soon be snowing. If it reached any depth, that could sure halt their tracking them.

He checked on Liz several times to be sure she was warm enough. She scoffed at his worrying. "I'm fine. I have lots of clothes on and if I fall off this horse, you will need a rope and pulley to get me back in the saddle."

The men laughed. After a noon break, the snow started. Before dark on the short winter day in the rolling high country, they found an abandoned soddy with firewood and a fireplace.

"You own this?" Cole asked.

"I may. Bo buys these places all the time."

"How far is your ranch from here?" Liz asked.

"Maybe twenty-thirty miles west. I'm not real certain. At least we have shelter tonight."

She agreed and helped Jesus cook while he and Cole brought in the saddles and packs. The house had a particular odor he noticed as it warmed. It wasn't the horse gear, either. Smelled more like old socks to him.

"We may not be this lucky tomorrow night."

She hugged his arm. "Stop worrying about me. I am a big girl and proud to be riding with you. I know a woman along has you concerned. Don't be."

"Fine, you can just be one of the boys."

"Good. I want to be." They both laughed.

"How far are they ahead of us?"

"Not over two days, Jesus?"

"Two days. They aren't going as fast as we did today. Driving those horses slows them down."

"Did they ever say how much money they got?" Liz asked.

"All I heard was they robbed them."

Cole shook his head. "No, I never heard."

Jesus rose from his cooking. "I bet they didn't get much."

Chet agreed. "Not much cash in ranching cattle. We buy cattle from those folks, but aside from making a drive to some mining camp, cattle are not a large profit item."

"What do people do for money?"

"Most do without."

She nodded. "How many cattle do you buy in a year?"

"Over seven thousand head. Of course, some we ship are ours, but we've helped the small ranchers around the area by buying from them."

"That is a big business. I am impressed."

"Tell her about waiting for your money," Cole said.

"We get a paper from the U.S. Government at delivery. It takes up to six months to collect on that amount."

"Oh, so you have to wait?"

"Yes. That really worried me. Any time that much money is waiting and the U.S. Government is having so many financial problems, you can sure worry when they will pay you. But we're collecting on them now."

"But selling that many cattle is big business."

"I realize that, too, but we need to manage it well."

"Oh, yes, but I see why you can buy these homesteads, too."

"Deeded land belongs to you. Most are dry range homesteads and they have six hundred forty acres."

"People come here to scratch out a living, huh?"

Chet shook his head. "What can they sell to make a living?"

"I see. Thanks. I know you may not be having fun now, but all this ranch building pleases you."

"Damn near as much as having you along."

She shook her head at him. "He has supper ready, so let's eat. Is it still snowing outside?"

"Like a goose picking," Cole said.

"I figured so. Will we lose them?" she asked.

Chet shook his head. "No, we don't lose rustlers."

They set out again the next morning. The clouds still shed flakes and the cold wind threatened to burn the skin on their faces. Chet had found a kerchief for Liz to wear over her face and winked at his Mexican bandit. "It seldom gets worse than this."

"Don't worry. I am fine. I am with you."

He shook his head. "Helluva place to be."

By evening, they were on the Marcy Road and he made a decision to ride to the Windmill Ranch. "Let's go see Susie and warm up."

No one argued with him. Long past sundown, they arrived at the ranch and Sarge came out to see who it was.

"Sarge, meet Liz. Boys, put the horses up in a shed. We can unload them later."

"What are you all doing out here?" Sarge asked.

"Tell you in the house. We need to thaw her out."

The ranch crew quickly came and took over the horses.

Chet stomped his snowy boots off, with Susie saying, "Get in here."

"It won't take much pleading to get us to do that," Chet said.

"Whatever are you up here for?"

"Horse rustlers. They shot a rancher down on the rim, robbed him, and took all his horses."

"How long have you been out in this weather?" Sarge asked, taking their coats.

"A couple of days. We stayed in a soddy last night over east. Lucky it had firewood."

"That was the Colby place. It's yours. We had firewood there in case we ever got caught over there."

"We got caught. Liz, you thawing out alright?"

"I am fine. Thank you so much."

"She's damn sure a trooper. Said we couldn't leave without her."

"Well, you all are here and warm anyway. Did you lose their tracks?" Susie asked.

"We didn't think so. They were probably headed for Horse Head Crossing."

"The mail delivery for Preskitt will stop here tomorrow. If he's seen them on the road, he'll recall them."

"Good, we may stay a while till things thaw out."

"Fine with me," Cole said, and Jesus nodded in agreement.

"Whatever we have to do," Liz said, and they all laughed. "I wanted to go along and it was cold, but you were cold, too. It didn't kill me, and I got to see your fine house, Susie."

"Thank you. Me having female company is unusual. But it's good to have you here. We better fix some food."

"I am ready," Liz said. The bandanna around her neck, and still wearing the pants and wool shirt, she went with Susie into the kitchen.

Victor came in the house.

"Where is your new wife-to-be?" he asked. "We have the horses unpacked and your panniers in the bunkhouse."

Chet got up off the couch and took him in the kitchen. "Liz, this is Victor. He was our guide and helped us find Reg's ranch."

Victor spoke to her in Spanish and Chet understood enough to know she said her *hacienda* was at Indio Springs. He turned back to Chet, looking very impressed.

"She has a big *hacienda* down there."

"She came to see me at Tubac. She wanted to buy a Barbarossa horse."

"You sell her one?" Victor laughed.

"No. I got her instead."

She waved her hands at them. "No, Victor. I got him instead of a horse."

"I see. So glad you came to see us. Had you seen Susie's house before?"

"Not finished seeing it all."

"They did a nice job looks like," said Chet.

"Very nice," Liz said, and stood beside him. "It is good to meet more family. You all are so nice to me—the intruder."

"No, Liz, you are one of us." Susie shook her head from the doorway and went back in the kitchen.

Chet laughed. "Well, there you go, gal. The boss has accepted you."

"Welcome to the Windmill Ranch, anyway," Victor said.

"Thank you."

The cold sun was out the next day. They decided to let it warm up one more day. The mail driver stopped and changed horses. He hadn't seen the robbers on the Marcy Road. He drank some of Susie's coffee, ate a Danish, then thanked them and drove on.

Tom Dance, the mail driver, was a legend. A few years earlier, as it neared Christmas, the mail had been held up many times between Gallup and Preskitt. After robbers scattered the mail so often, looking for cash or valuable things in it, folks feared they wouldn't get their holiday mail.

Dance offered to get it through. No one knew how many dead, attempted robbers he left by the roadside. But there were several, and after that the mail ran flawless from Gallup to Preskitt. The broad-shouldered Texan had handled it.

"If he didn't see them, are those rustlers gone?" Susie asked.

"They just weren't on his road. Three men and seven stolen horses don't evaporate," Chet said. "Tomorrow, we'll look some more."

He'd spoken with Liz the night before about her staying there. But she was resolved to go on. He wouldn't argue with her.

"Tomorrow," Sarge said, "Victor and some of the boys want to help you find these rustlers. Cole and Victor can take two men. You, Jesus, and Liz, can take two more and meet them tomorrow night at Saint Johns. Spread out, you might better find them."

"Thanks," Chet said. "Leave it to an old military man to figure this puzzle out."

Susie hugged her man. "I'm surprised you aren't going along."

"I might."

"I'd damn sure be proud to have you, too," Chet said.

Sarge had several places he wanted checked the next day. They agreed his knowledge of the area was going to help, if the rustlers hadn't left the country. Armed with copies of the men's and the horses' descriptions, they rode out.

The sun came out, and with the three teams of riders they began checking out possible sites where Sarge thought the outlaws might hole up. Mid-day, Chet used his field glasses to scope a low-walled log cabin with smoke coming out the chimney. There were horses in the corral. One sorrel horse made him stop and try to see more of him, but the horse moved behind some others.

He turned to Liz, Jesus, and Monk, the Windmill crewmember. "There's a sorrel horse up there. It may or may not be one of them we're looking for, but Sarge told me he was suspicious about the people who live here."

"We keep an eye on that outfit. Hanson brothers," Monk said. "They aren't sterling citizens."

"Liz, stay behind us."

"Yes, sir."

He turned and winked at her. She nodded in approval and they spread out. No way to come up on that place without being seen. As they approached across the snow, he heard shouting and he nodded at his two deputies. "They're saddling horses. We've spooked them. Let's go."

They charged through the powdery snow and Chet fired two shots in the air. "U.S. Marshals, get your hands in the air."

One rider leaped in the saddle and fired at them.

"Take his horse," Chet said to Jesus.

His man slid to a halt, used his Winchester, and the horse rolled over.

"Sorry about that, but I didn't want to chase him down," he said to Liz.

"I understand."

"They're putting their hands up," Jesus said.

Four men with raised hands stood in the snow. Two of them were half-dressed, in shirts and long-handle underwear. A tough-looking woman stood in the doorway. Chet held his gun on them.

"Disarm them. Liz, check the horse brands in the corral."

"Is there anyone else in the cabin?" he asked the woman.

"Little kids."

"I'll go see," Liz said. "These are the stolen horses."

"Keep your gun ready."

"How is the one that had the wreck?" he asked Monk.

"Broke leg and he can't walk. I've got his gun."

"Let's see here. Who are you?" he asked the first man.

"Curly."

"You stole the horses."

He shook his head.

"Where's Fan?"

The outlaw pointed to the other man.

Chet nodded. "Pike?"

"That's the guy the horse fell on."

"What's your name?"

"Jim Hanson. I ain't no part of this business."

"You are now. That your brother?"

"That's Tad."

"Now we have five of you for horse rustling, and three for robbing those folks. Where can I hire a wagon, Monk?"

"I guess in town."

"Go rent one. These prisoners need to go to the Windmill. From there, we can haul them back to Preskitt ourselves."

"What about his leg?" Jesus asked.

"Better take him into town in the wagon and get it set."

They all agreed.

"We better not eat in there," Liz said with a frown and a head toss at the cabin. "We might die. It is too filthy."

"We can handcuff these rustlers and Monk's going after a wagon. Susie sent lunch along for us."

"Good."

With the outlaws all in chains, Chet walked with Liz behind the corral. "Well, did it go like you thought?"

"Very exciting. I wasn't afraid. Your men took charge of the situation. I know some people in Mexico live in squalor, but that cabin is terrible."

He hugged and kissed her. In a few hours, Monk returned with a wagon and team he'd rented and the outlaws were loaded. Cole and Monk were to take the prisoners to St. Johns and have the one's leg set. Then Chet told them to put the rustlers in the local jail overnight. The next day, they could bring them out to the Windmill.

The rest of the crew took the stolen horses to the Windmill. They left the woman one, and then rode west, driving the horses. The sun had melted a lot of the snow. Meadowlarks ran about looking for something to eat. A red wing hawk challenged them for being there.

"Future Mrs. Byrnes, what do you want to do next?"

"Maybe sleep for two days."

"We should get some rest tonight in a bed at Susie's."

"Maybe." Then she laughed. "You can see those snowcapped peaks from a long ways off. It is all new country to me. I am glad this is over, but I liked going with you."

"Cold and all?"

"Hey, I came to be with you. I meant it."

"I have no doubts. I simply didn't want to run you off."

"You will never do that. I must admit I liked the excitement. You are such a take-charge person, and that aura around you that I can slip into is wonderful."

She made him feel over-acclaimed. "Alright."

Then with a finger, she pointed at him. "Someday, when you work cattle, I will show you how good I can heel rope. Or in a pen, how I can rope four horses. You are not marrying a sissy."

"I never thought you were one. Aside from the cold and snow, this went easy."

"I will be ready the next time to go with you. I was never cold, but I bet I can dress warmer the next time."

"It was a hurry-up situation. I'll have some Windmill hands take Doris her horses and a letter explaining the arrests. Cole and Jesus can bring the prisoners to Preskitt."

"We can get up early and ride hard for Camp Verde."

"Maybe we should spend one more day with her and Sarge?"

"We can do that. No problem."

"You are too agreeable." She playfully poked him. "I like her and I know she does not get much company up here."

"Hell, there isn't anything going to die if we stay over."

"Oh, Chet Byrnes, I am so very lucky to have found you."

"Poor thing, drug through a blizzard and still glad to be here. I don't know about you. What were you thinking that day?"

"Monica said that you can always figure things out. I believed that, too."

That evening, Victor played his guitar and sang

with two other ranch hands in Susie's house with everyone there but his two men and the prisoners.

Susie remarked to Chet, "Times like this are like Texas, aren't they?"

"You homesick?"

"No. I love him, the baby, and this ranch, but I do get melancholy sometimes for the past."

"I know, but the things we've done here, we never could have done in Texas. This place and its operation are really making money. Tom's log hauling is amazing. Our ranches will soon all be profitable. When they forced us to move out here, it was a big favor."

Susie smiled. "Liz asked me about our place back there. She said you described it as an old fort. I told her it really was one."

"I can't get over her enjoying chasing down outlaws in the cold and snow."

"I can. She's very dedicated to you. She told me she ignored men until she met you and couldn't get over you. I told you several times about May wanting you. You loved her, but she wasn't to be your wife. Kathrin Ivor, she idolizes you. Every time you have had a crisis, she came to help. I bet she regretted marrying Ben when she learned Marge had been killed."

"All I did was save her."

"They can't help it. You did not encourage them. What does Liz call it? The aura."

"I love her."

"What's next?"

"Look at more of our operations and make them better."

"Well, you look much better in your earrings," Susie said when Liz joined them.

"I would have had icicles hanging from them on our chase."

They laughed. He hugged her, picturing long columns of ice on her ears.

His deputies and prisoners arrived. They put them in the bunkhouse, with plans to take them on toward Preskitt in the morning, with a stopover at the Camp Verde Ranch the next night. It would be a long drive, but his men were convinced they could make it.

Chet and Liz rode out about four o'clock the next day, planning to reach the lower ranch by dark. It was around freezing and threatened to warm up, so they rode the rested roans hard. They reached the ranch house about eight that evening. Lea was glad to see them and Anita hugged Liz. Chet figured Liz's lady had about given up on them ever returning.

The prisoners and his men got there after midnight. He heard them, but he was under warm covers with his wife and knew they could handle it.

The next day, they got back to the Preskitt Valley place, and ranch exams started, with Hampt's part next. His fenced hay meadows worked and his takeover of cattle on the Ralston place next door had worked. They sold off two hundred cull cows, which they hoped helped the range. Then they had driven another two hundred cows to Reg. There were lots of Shorthorn and Hereford cross cows in Hampt's original herd, but he had only begun the cross-breeding program on the Ralston operation.

"They sure look in good condition," Liz commented as they rode through them.

Hampt agreed. "Liz, I've been working hard to make this place work. It's been a challenge, but I can see us doing it."

"I can, too."

"Thanks. I'm just an old cowboy blessed with May and all these kids. You know after they fired me at the Quarter Circle Z, I was doing day work. Then Chet hired me and, boy, that was the great start for me."

Liz agreed. "I am so glad to be a part of this outfit. I understand your enthusiasm, for I have it, too."

Chet and Liz rode back together to the Preskitt Valley house.

"May is a queen," she said. "Those children all work for her."

"When we were in Texas, those boys were little and they treed her."

"What does that mean?"

"I had to make them promise not to make her cry."

"What happened?"

"May is so tender hearted. But now those boys have come to appreciate her and they even play piano with her. As I told you earlier, my brother married her to raise his kids. She does a good job now."

"Maybe Hampt helped her."

"He probably did."

"Susie told me about JD, too."

"He was a problem. We even had to go get him out of jail in New Mexico. But he married Bonnie, and I think they're doing good."

"Nothing is easy, is it?"

"Nothing."

"Next?"

"We'll postpone going to Reg's. I want it to warm up there first."

She laughed. "And I bought new underwear that fits me."

"Keep it. We may need it yet."

He reminded her. "In three weeks we'll be married."

"I know that. I'm fine. Monica and I have it all planned. I can't wait."

"I don't regret living with you for one minute. I have lived every day to the fullest and I will after we are wed. Can you see a difference coming?"

"No."

"Good. I enjoy every day."

"If you ever want to go off and have a man-to-man time, you tell me. I can accept that."

"Roundup is coming. I'd like to make as many of them as I can."

"I understand. Should we take a honeymoon?"

"That would be fine. Where should we go? There are cabins in Oak Creek."

"Maybe. Let me think on it. Alright?" she asked.

"No problem."

Time for the wedding came and they were to be married in the Catholic church with the reception at the upper ranch afterward. Chet found a circus tent in Tucson to rent just to be certain they had a dry reception. The carnival team brought it and set it up. She laughed about his concern, while she went running about to be sure things went just so.

Someone said to him, "You are sure spending a lot of money on this wedding."

"It won't hurt anyone."

"I guess not. I ain't paying for it."

Chet gave him a curt answer. "Right."

Two whole beefs were going to be cooked for the event. Cases of wine arrived from Liz's *hacienda.* Avocados from Mexico and lots of red chili peppers as well. Besides the array of Dutch ovens to make sourdough biscuits, three ranch wives were on hand to make *tortillas* as well.

Frijoles in big cast iron kettles were ready to cook. Rope hitch lines were set up, and many were invited. The *vaqueros* were in charge of parking and the weather looked favorable. They had white-washed every building. Extra outhouses were assembled.

Holding his son, while Rhea was getting everything ready to go, Chet played with him. Marge left him with a fine boy. He hoped he could make a rancher out of him. But no one knew what their kids would become or do.

Hours later, he stood outside the rail inside the chapel. Coming up the aisle on Hampt's arm, and carrying Adam, came Elizabeth Delarosa Carmel. The ceremony would soon be over and the *fiesta* would begin. Cole and Jesus stood by as his best men. The ring was new, but a simple gold band that she wanted.

The church was crowded. But before the ceremony

he noticed the ushers brought an older couple forward to be seated. They were well dressed and Hispanic. Were they her parents? He had no idea. They'd never replied to his invite.

He dismissed the moment and smiled as she joined him. Adam was well behaved while the priest went through the ceremony. She rocked him a little to keep him content.

The two of them answered the questions put to them by the kindly priest, and the ceremony was over before they knew it. Father O'Brian pronounced them man and wife, Chet kissed her, and they turned to go to the back of the church.

She caught her breath, but went on. "They came."

"I couldn't warn you. I thought it was them." From the quick look on her face, he saw how upset she was. He quickly said, "They can't ruin our day, Mrs. Byrnes."

"Right. I don't know what they want." She shook her head warily and said something to the baby.

Rhea took the baby so they could greet everyone in the line going out the doors. Liz stood with her shoulders squared, and he wanted to tell her to relax. But she wouldn't until something was settled. He had no idea what to do next. They shook hands and spoke to the many well-wishers. She kissed a few on the cheek. Her parents were coming. Some people went by with, "See you later."

Under his breath, he said, "Be peaceful."

She never flinched or acted like she'd heard him.

"Ah, you must be Señor Delarosa."

"You must be the famous border lawman, Chet Byrnes."

"I am, sir. This is my wife, Liz."

"Whose child is that you held?"

"Ours," they both said, and looked at each other.

"He is a handsome boy. You two are very lucky. My wife, Madelyn."

"Come to the reception out at the ranch today," Chet invited.

He shook his head. "We are only here for the wedding."

"One of my men will drive you out there. Cole, find a rig and take the Delarosas to the house."

"Got it done. There will be one here shortly, sir. Come this way, señor."

"My damn husband is a traitor," she said under her breath.

"They came a long ways. We can be polite. I see you in her face."

"He thinks that Adam is my child."

"He is now."

She looked to the ceiling for help.

"How are you, folks? See you at the reception," he said to the next couple.

When the line dwindled down, he thanked Father O'Brian. She did, too.

When at last they were alone, he asked, "Did I say how pretty you looked in that dress?"

"Chet Byrnes, the family peacemaker. No, but thank you."

"The photographer is waiting."

They stood for him, and Jesus came with Anita in a rig he must have rented to get them back to the ranch. Chet was about to laugh. Her parents had gone to the ranch in the one decorated for the bride and groom.

"They even took my buckboard," she said under her breath.

"Jesus and Anita, you two did wonderful."

Liz agreed. "Yes, very quick thinking. My husband planned for us to walk home."

He kissed her furiously. "Today is our day. Enjoy it. I won't ever marry you again. Today we are one; let's treasure our days."

"You don't know what I have suffered—"

"Today, we heal all that. I invited them and they came many miles. Our ranch is a place for healing, not wars. We have enough of that away from there."

"Chet, I will try."

"That is all I expect. How did Rhea get back with Adam?" Chet asked.

"The *vaquero* who brought her took her back. Those ranch hands would do anything for her or that boy," Jesus said.

"Thanks, I only wondered."

"They think he is their baby, too."

On the seat, Liz nodded, and more relaxed, snuggled against him. "You won, cowboy."

"Cowboys always win."

She laughed. "I am learning that."

At the ranch, she went upstairs and changed into a less formal dress. The sun came out and warmed things up for the vast crowd in the yard. Raphael's men acted as valets. After they unloaded their passengers, the men took the rigs up on the flat. Even the boys from the saddle shop were working at the parking.

Hampt and May cornered them. "Too damn much for us to get ready in time to be at the church," he said. "But we heard the ceremony went well."

"It did. Her mother and father even came."

"Wow, I want to meet them."

"You two are forgiven," Liz said, and hugged May and Hampt both. "I don't know how anyone is left in their right mind."

"No, missy, but we are so pleased you found us. This is just the foam on top."

She nodded at Hampt. "The real beer is coming, right?"

"Damn right."

She stood on her toes and kissed him. "May, how long is your bed?"

May held back a laugh. "Oh, a foot longer than yours."

They all four laughed.

JD and Bonnie congratulated them.

"The *vaqueros* told me you have two claybank colts?" JD asked her.

"Oh, the Barbarossa ones. Yes, Tom sent them to me."

"That was what they said you came for."

She shook her head with a big smile. "I should never have stopped. See what I am into?"

"I like what you told him the day of your meeting," Bonnie said.

"Oh?"

"The part about you wouldn't kiss him for the horses."

"He kissed me, anyway."

Bonnie nodded. "You are what he really needed. You make this place sparkle."

"Thank you. Someday I will come and see your ranch. He promised me that."

"Anytime. It's raw today, but I see a great ranch blossoming there in the future."

"He has a touch, doesn't he?" Liz asked.

"I would not be alive today, if not for him. He traded that man in Mexico those horses for my life."

They hugged and Chet noted that Liz sniffled. When they were away from them, she stopped and dabbed at her eyes. "Her story got to me. My face may be a mess."

"Anita won't be much help to you. Jesus has her and they have been dancing."

"I can go myself and fix it. I am not that spoiled."

"I won't be much help, anyway."

"Don't run off, and excuse me for a moment?"

"I can handle that. I'll be somewhere around here."

After they parted, he saw her parents talking to Raphael.

"Do they need anything?" he asked his foreman.

"No. We've been talking. They live in Mexico City," Raphael said.

"Yes, they came a long way."

"I told them how I met you and got my job."

"We had a rude introduction, but we made it work."

Liz's father looked at him and nodded. "I understand you are a U.S. Marshal?"

"Yes, there were a lot of border bandits, and I was asked to do something about it. I took some good men down there and we've put a stop to a lot of it."

"Oh, they talk about you in Mexico City. But how did you meet my daughter?"

"I was down by Tubac where we have our headquarters, and she came by to buy one of my Barbarossa horses."

His eyes widened in disbelief. "Oh, you have some of them?"

"Yes, I have a stallion. He's down on the Verde River Ranch."

He shook his head, firm like. "There are no such stallions from that ranch in this country."

"Come with me."

"Where?"

"The barn over there. Two of his sons are in stalls."

Raphael laughed. "He is not lying, señor."

"I will return," he said to his wife.

In the barn alleyway, Raphael took one out of the stall by the halter to show him.

Delarosa shook his head as the animal showed off some. "But, how?"

Chet told him the story.

"Did she buy one?"

"They aren't for sale."

"As spoiled as she is, I bet that made her mad."

Chet shook his head. "We spent a long day together. And, eventually, we became engaged to be married."

"This boy is yours, they tell me."

"He is ours now."

He nodded. "Why was he there in the wedding?"

"That was her wish."

"I see that you three are bonded."

"Exactly."

"Our family has been strained apart. There is no need in that. My wife has been very sad. I can tell she did not want us here, but I appreciate your willingness to invite us. Your boy will someday have all of her inheritance. Rumors told me she never was able to have children with her late husband."

"My first wife told me the same thing."

"Maybe so. He is still the firstborn."

"Thank you. I will ask Rhea to show him to your wife."

"She may cry."

"It's a good day to cry or laugh, right?"

"*Si,* I see why she took you. Something stands out in your character. I heard the border bandits call you, '*El Tigre* Byrnes.'"

Chet smiled at his words. "She calls it my aura. I don't know. I'm simply Chet Byrnes, rancher and lawman. Let me find Rhea."

"*Gracias.*"

"No. Thank you, for coming to our wedding."

He found Rhea and the baby and took them over to introduce Liz's mother. Their conversation turned to Spanish. Adam would not have any skin left on him after this day. Thank heavens, it was warm for the occasion.

His wife returned and asked him what he had done without her. He quickly explained how Adam was going to be her parents' heir.

"They really came to make up, didn't they?"

"We do things we wish we'd never done, wish we'd never said, but the real person has to eat crow and come to awareness; no one wins at any less."

She looked off toward the mountains. "My husband could settle wars. I will talk to them. They are our guests. I am not going to cry again, alright?"

"Fine, Mrs. Byrnes. I showed him the cause of all this in the barn."

"What did he say?"

"No one has a stallion from that ranch."

"Where is my mother?"

"Over there, holding our son."

"Someday, I will tell you how close I came today to killing you."

He stole a kiss. "I'm glad that is over and done."

She hugged him. "No tears."

He smirked at her. Her lashes held droplets that shone in the sunlight like small mirrors. "Good luck."

Susie came by with her own baby. "Great party. Who isn't here?"

"Damned if I know. Her parents even came from Mexico City."

Susie almost was aghast. "She told me they hadn't spoken in years. How did that go?"

"Peaceful."

"You tired?"

"How did you guess?"

"Brother, I know you. Have fun on your honeymoon. It won't be much different except her name."

After they parted, he found Monica. "You did wonderful. Thanks, my love."

"I would not say this to anyone but you. And I don't mean to dig up the past, but Marge would have been proud you did this. We both loved her, but we've mourned enough. Liz is fresh and generous. I can't believe she went on that snow chase with you. When I asked her why, she said as long as she was with you, she'd be fine."

"Thanks, Monica, we count on you."

CHAPTER 10

In mid-April, they branded cattle on Hampt's East Ranch with neighboring ranchers and Sam Holt the brand inspector. They had the Quarter Circle Z chuckwagon set up in a camp and a man called Hanson ran it with two of his boys. They were hired by the day, real good cooks and help.

There was a wild yearling maverick that the hands called "Spook." He lit out for high country and Chet set in to chase him. The first time, he missed with his head catch. Liz rode past him on a fleet buckskin horse and threw her loop and it settled around his stubby horns. Chet came in and caught the heels, and that dropped him between them.

Chet swung down and ran to tie his hind legs with a piggin string.

"He's one heckuva long ways from the branding fire," she said in disgust, coiling her riata.

Brand inspector Hanson rode down there. "No one else wants him. Stick your brand on him."

They were soon there with a hot iron and a sharp

knife to notch his ears and make him a steer. Chet and Liz rode back to the herd.

"You aren't bad at heading, either, sister."

"I warned you I could rope."

"I'm pleased. You do good." He rode in close, leaned across, and kissed her.

"But if I have to head from now on, I want a bigger, stouter horse."

He laughed. "Next time, I'll catch him."

"Maybe," she said flippantly and then smiled. "You don't miss very often. Dodging juniper brush makes it hard to rope around. I love to be with you doing this. This horse is very good and I will bite my tongue for sounding ungrateful, because I love you, *hombre.* I am the happiest woman in the whole world."

"Good, you are easy pleased. Your first man must have taught you how to rope?"

She shook her head. "One of his *vaqueros* had the patience. My husband didn't. You are much more patient with me than he ever was. Oh, he never was angry or mean talking, but I couldn't tell him things that I tease you about. I feel so free with you. I never feel confined. If I am—how you say—a tomboy, I am no threat. And you listen, so I never feel I said something to the wind."

"Good. I'm glad." The drum of hoofbeats caught his attention. "There's one of the *vaqueros'* sons coming from the ranch. I recognize the small horse."

"Something wrong?"

"Lord, you never know." He reined up to the youth who handed him the envelope.

"A wire came for the señor. Monica said you needed it."

"Tony, thank you."

He opened it and saw it was very long for a telegram, and from Samuel Severs of the First National Bank of San Antonio.

DEAR CHET BYRNES,
WE DID A LOT OF BUSINESS WITH YOU
DURING YOUR CATTLE DRIVE DAYS.
I NEED TO ASK A POWERFUL FAVOR OF
YOU. MY BANK IS HEAVILY INVESTED
IN A LARGE HERD OF CATTLE BEING
DRIVEN NORTH

—"It's from a Texas banker, and it's obvious he has a large problem with a herd of cattle."

She frowned at his words. "You know him?"

"I did. Let me read it through."

"Certainly," she said. Then she spoke to Cole who rode up to see what was going on. "It is a letter from a Texas banker. We'll let him read it."

"Sure."

BOB DECKER, AN EXPERIENCED BLACK
DROVER, TOOK THIRTY-FIVE HUNDRED
HEAD OF STEERS NORTH WITH THIRTY-
FIVE HANDS. THEY LEFT HERE IN LATE
FEBRUARY. THE NEW KANSAS LAW
PROHIBITS TAKING TEXAS CATTLE
ACROSS THE STATE, AND HE HAD TO GO
AROUND THROUGH COLORADO TO GET

TO OGALLALA. WE HAVE NOT HEARD A
WORD FROM HIM, NOR DOES ANYONE
WE HAVE CONTACTED KNOW HIS
WHEREABOUTS. I KNOW YOU ARE A
BUSY MAN, BUT I KNEW OF NO OTHER
MAN BESIDES YOU WHO MIGHT FIND
THIS OUTFIT AND RECOVER AT LEAST
PART OF THIS HERD.
I CAN OFFER YOU TWENTY PERCENT
OF THE PROCEEDS TO FIND THEM,
DELIVER, AND SELL THEM IN OGALLALA
FOR THE BANK AND THE RANCH OWNER.
PLEASE WIRE ME YOUR ANSWER.
SAMUEL SEVERS
FIRST NATIONAL BANK OF SAN ANTONIO
TEXAS

"What does he need you to do?" Cole asked.

"He's lost a large herd of steers headed for Colorado and on to Nebraska. He can't find them and offered me a twenty percent share to find them, then get them up there and sell them."

"In his low-cut shoes, he'd have a helluva time finding them out there in west Texas anyway." Cole went to laughing. "What'cha going to do about it?"

"Twenty percent is a lot of money, if they ain't been run off the end of the world, crashed, and burned."

Liz and Cole agreed.

"Where would they be by now?" Cole asked.

"West Texas. This man is black. I bet every hand he has is black. I'm not opposed to that. But it might be such a sorry outfit, they've left the cattle loose and went home. Hard to tell what happened. What do you two say?"

Cole yielded to Liz.

"Sounds like you could make a lot of money."

"We all could. If I ask men to go, I'll give them a share of it, too. This won't be heading and heeling at roundup. This could be a real tough job to straighten out."

"I'll go along," she said.

"Count me and Jesus in on the deal. Is there any way we could get Hampt to go, too?" Cole asked.

"I know what you mean. May might not let him go. But he's a tough guy, and it may get real tough where we end up with those steers."

"Them Comanche ain't real settled in that country, either."

"I know that. Let me think some."

Hampt came dusting across the sagebrush flat and slid his horse to a stop. "Something wrong? You got trouble in the south?"

"West Texas, a man lost a big herd of cattle, wants us to find them."

His blue eyes flashed at them in stern disbelief. "How in the hell do you lose a big herd?"

"If they knew that, they wouldn't ask us to find them. So far, I've got three volunteers. My wife, Cole, and he spoke for Jesus. Will May let you go?"

"Who'd take care of this ranch?"

"Tom surely has a man. We know you have obligations, but right off we said we'd ask you."

"How long will we be gone?"

"Three months, maybe longer."

"That's a spell. Let me go ask her. When will you leave?"

"Two days."

"What next?"

"I'm going to wire him I want twenty-five percent, and he pays expenses for the things we need. And if the herd isn't found, he owes us five thousand dollars for the search."

"Will he pay that?" Hampt asked.

"Listen, Hampt, this guy sits behind a big fat desk every day. How in the hell is he going to find that many steers?"

"I'll tell Vincent he'll be in charge for me, and then I'll go speak to May," Hampt said.

"Good. We're going to ride to Preskitt and send him a wire. We'll know his answer in twenty-four hours. If you don't want to leave your wife, I'll understand."

"She'll tell me what she thinks."

"I know you two get along good."

"Right." The big man swung his horses around to leave them.

Cole nodded. "I better get Jesus. Will Anita let him go, ma'am?"

"I imagine so." She laughed. "They are getting real close."

Chet watched him ride off for Jesus. "This will be a helluva trip. It was a long ways coming out here and it hasn't gotten any shorter."

"You think they are in that country where you left the train?"

"Unless the cattle stampeded off in a hundred

directions, then most of them are somewhere up there."

"What else?"

"There are lots of war-happy Indians there, too."

"You had trouble with them before, didn't you?"

He laughed. "One of our first drives to Gallup, Cole and I got attacked. I had an arrow stuck in my saddle fork. He shot one Indian and I roped the one that shot my saddle. I left Cole to bring the Indian in as a prisoner, but he drew a knife and Cole had to shoot him."

She was amused. "I never realized he was an Indian fighter."

"It really wasn't funny. Let's get home and get a telegram off to this banker. I think we're his best chance to find them, and we have some room to bargain."

"How far away are we from there?"

"Six hundred miles."

"Whew."

"Let's ride."

They headed out in a lope across the rolling upland of sage and juniper for the upper ranch. From the ranch, they drove a buckboard to town where he sent his answer to the banker, requesting twenty-five percent and expenses and a fee if they failed.

He came out of the telegraph office, took the reins, and they drove back home in the dark.

"What is a big cattle drive like?" Liz asked.

"Boring as hell. You drive cattle almost single file and they jog along for fifteen miles a day or so. They get road broke in a week, and then the herders wish one would break and run. At the back are the loafers, who you have to beat all the time to make them keep up and you eat tons of their dust."

"Sounds exciting."

"They stampede and run off any chance they can and, usually, in the dark during storms."

"That sounds awful."

"That's why I want us and the boys well paid."

"I can go along?"

"I would not recommend it. But I won't tell you no."

She rode in close and kissed him. "You spoil me."

"You won't be spoiled on a cattle drive, I guarantee you."

"I want to go."

"Pack light. Today is Tuesday. If he agrees, we'll leave Thursday."

"Are you two off on another lark?" Monica asked when they came into the house.

"We got a telegram from Texas today."

"I know. I sent the boy to find you this morning."

"A banker has lost a big herd of cattle in Texas. They want us to go find it."

Monica frowned in concern. "A needle in a haystack?"

"Maybe, but if we find the herd, we could make some real money."

"Or get scalped or shot by Indians," Monica said. She went off to do her kitchen duties, shaking her head. "You aren't going with them, are you, Liz?"

"I thought I would."

"I thought so, too. Both of you are crazy."

"We will know tomorrow if he wants us."

"Good, I will get some rest." With that, she hurried from the room.

"She mad at us?" Liz asked.

"She gets that way at times," he whispered.

The banker agreed to Chet's plan. May told Hampt to go along, that they'd probably need him. Cole and Jesus spent the next day making certain their horses were shod and sound. They put new girths on the packsaddles and new Navajo-made saddle blankets to save the horses' backs. Chet told them to plan for four packhorses, that would be enough. A sidewall tent was included for Liz. They might not have taken it along except for her. But he kept that a secret from her.

He planned for them to ride his roans. His first day's goal was to make Windmill Ranch in one day. That would show them they could make sixty miles in a day, and the trip in two weeks' time, when they'd start looking for the lost herd. There wasn't much he could do until they reached the Texas panhandle.

"Where could they water three thousand plus head of cattle up there?" Chet asked.

"I've never been up on the llano Estacada," Cole said.

"Me, either. I heard a lot about it, but there isn't much out there, is there?" Hampt asked.

Chet shook his head. "Lots of nothing. I believe he veered too far west to miss Kansas and to go up that eastern Colorado trail to Ogallala."

"Think we'll find him in New Mexico?"

"No telling, but when we get over there we'll start asking questions."

May, their baby boy, and her daughter were all at the main ranch house to see Hampt off in the morning. Valerie was staying over to see Cole leave. Several others came by that evening to send them off. Frey came by and told Chet if he needed anything he could do to contact him. Ben Ivor and his wife were there, too.

"How long will this take, Chet?" Ben asked.

"I hope not more than three months. But there's no telling where they went."

"You get paid, if you don't find them?"

"Yes. But we have to find them."

"Any idea?"

"You can't have over three thousand steers and all black cowboys somewhere between here and the Indian Territory, and not have someone who knows where they are."

"What else could have happened?"

"Things get trying, even in a smooth drive. Like ships at sea, they might have had a mutiny. I have no idea."

The men, who had formed a circle around him in the yard, all wished him luck. Chet was satisfied they thought he had a big lost cause, but no one got in his face and said that.

By wire, he put Roamer in charge of the force at Tubac, saying he would be out of pocket for several months searching for the herd. He sent over thirty enquiries on the wire about where that herd might be, to men who knew that country, giving locations where he could get their message if they learned anything. The first contact would be at Gallup in six days. Then at Bernalillo in twelve days, the next at Santa Rosa in eighteen days, and the last at Tascosa twenty-four days later. He assured them he would reimburse them for any expenses. And to send their costs to Quarter Circle Z Ranch, Prescott, Arizona Territory.

They left under the stars for the Windmill Ranch. He'd given Tom the places and locations to reach him by wire, as well as to Monica and May.

On the road, Liz privately asked him if he thought Susie would cut Liz's hair in a short bob that evening.

"I can see why you ask. You don't have Anita to help cut your hair, but I love it the way it is."

"It will grow back. Washing it will be hard. Let her cut it and I can easily care for it."

"You can ask her. I'm certain she'll oblige you."

"You won't be mad at me?"

He shook his head. "This is not a trip of conveniences. Do it, and I will only cry inside."

She rode in and slapped his leg. "No, you won't."

He had to pass on to the guys she was having her hair cut short at the Windmill. They agreed it was a good idea under the circumstances.

After that, day one was uneventful in the ride to the Windmill. Sarge told them all the places they could stop at safely between there and Gallup, and who was friendly and who was not. He marked them all on a map. From Gallup on, they were on their own. But Chet had no misgivings. He rode with three powerful men and a determined lady. Susie shook her head at Liz's short haircut as she sat on her horse, but wished them the best.

The days were long, hot, and breezy. Wind-driven sand pecked at their exposed skin and faces. Chilling rainstorms drifted around and on the third day hail battered them. They camped one night on the road, and the next one stayed with an Indian trader, and the last night a rancher. On day five, they rode into Gallup in the late afternoon. He checked the telegraph office with Liz, while the others put up the horses and made sure they were grained and rubbed down.

"I have five wires for you, Mr. Byrnes."

"If I get more wires, please send them to me at Bernalillo, New Mexico, and ask that they hold them. I'll be there in five days."

"No problem."

Chet and Liz took the wires to a standing desk. He read them, one after the other.

CHET
BOB DECKER CROSSED THE RED
RIVER IN MARCH. I THINK HE HAS
NO CHUCKWAGON, A GREASY SACK
OUTFIT ON A HALF DOZEN CRAZY
MULES.A DISASTER GOING TO HAPPEN.
WILEY HARPER

CHET
I HEARD THEY WERE GOING WEST
NORTH OF CHISHOLM'S TRADING
POST CROSSING ON THE CANADIAN.
THAT MEANS THEY'RE IN WEST TEXAS
BY NOW. MOST OF THEM COWBOYS ARE
BAREFOOTED AND THE SEATS OF THEIR
PANTS THREADBARE. THEY WERE WAY
SHORT ON A REMUDA, AND SOME WERE
ON FOOT WAVING BLANKETS. HELL
KNOWS WHERE THEY ARE NOW.
CLINT ROSS

CHET
WHEN THAT OUTFIT CROSSED THE
BRAZOS AT WACO BACK IN THE SPRING,
FOLKS LAUGHED. MOST SAID THEY
WON'T EVER GET THERE. ILL EQUIPPED,
PARD. YOU WON'T FIND NOTHING LEFT.
LEROY HAYES

CHET
I NEVER HEARD OF THEM IN WICHITA.
GOOD LUCK. HARVEY COLE

"What now?" she asked.

"Send a wire home and say we got here and have leads. When we get closer, we can buy a chuckwagon, supplies, and even britches, from the sound of things."

"I hope we simply find them," Liz said.

They both laughed.

They were in western New Mexico, as scheduled. If the herd went west at Jessie's trading post on the Canadian River, they may be following it west before they headed north. That could be real tough Injun country. From the sounds of things, this was not a well-supplied bunch to start with. Ten more days and he and his outfit would be in that region with no problems, but that would be a lot to ask.

Over supper in a Mexican *cantina*, everyone read the information on the telegrams.

"Sounds tough," Cole said.

Chet agreed. "I figured they had a low-cost outfit, but this sounds like they may be stranded with those cattle."

"What does greasy sack mean?" Liz asked.

"They've got all their cooking gear and food in some burlap sacks strapped on mules," Hampt said.

"Oh, I see now. You had a chuckwagon when you did this?" she asked Chet.

"Boy, yes. I don't even want to think about that mess." Chet shook his head.

"Be pretty sorry, but maybe them black cowboys don't expect much?" Hampt asked.

She made a face. "Hampt, even they deserve better conditions than that."

"I guess so. It's going to be interesting, but they ain't paying this much money 'cause this job is going to be easy."

"We'll search that country on the Canadian in west Texas?" Hampt asked.

Cole warily shook his head. "Big country, and they haven't got all those Indians out of there."

"That's on my mind, too." Chet worried about the Indians being squeezed off the plains and how desperate they must be.

"What will we do?"

"Get a chuckwagon at Tularosa. Plenty of supplies. Rifles and ammo. I don't know how well armed they are. Get as many horses as we can find and set out to find them."

"Sounds wild, boys," Hampt said. "But that's all we can do."

In bed that night, Chet asked Liz how saddle sore she was.

"I have muscles I never knew I had. But I'd never have seen this country if I had not come with you. I don't want to own it, but I am enjoying seeing it."

"Just so you don't get so damn bored, you'd quit me over this trip."

"I am not bored. I am surprised that you learned so much from those telegrams. That amazed me tonight."

"Those men I wired really know this cattle-driving business. Not much goes on they haven't observed or laughed at."

"But we are almost two weeks away from where you start to look for them and already you have many good leads."

"We'll need them all, I bet, to find them."

"I understand. You know, I guess I am more muscle

than fat now. Can you find me a pair of suspenders to hold my pants up?"

He laughed and hugged her. "Galluses coming up."

"They don't cost much, do they?"

"Heavens, no. I'll buy or find you some. We better use this bed and then get some sleep. Tomorrow, we ride on, my love."

Cole had an extra pair of galluses in his saddlebags. He chuckled when Chet asked for them.

"You need them?"

"No, Liz does. We've worn her to the bone, and she fears losing her pants."

Laughing, he handed them to Chet.

That evening, he presented them to her, offering to put them on her pants for her in the morning.

"Where did you find them?" she asked.

"Oh, on some dead outlaw."

"Where did you find a dead outlaw out here?"

He fastened the suspenders in the back and put the straps over her shoulders.

Busy snapping them on, he helped adjust them. "I shot him between them so you'd have a pair that was uncut."

"Oh, that is some joke. I couldn't believe you shot an outlaw for me to get suspenders."

He swept her up and kissed her. "Cole had them."

"I will thank him." She shook her head at him and ran her hands under the straps to flex them. "My pants won't fall down now."

He figured it would take ten days to cross New Mexico, west to east. It took them a lot longer than that to haul the wagons across there. But so far they'd been lucky. They had sound, grain-fed horses that were well shod. Plus, they'd taken good care of them as well.

Later, lost in their lovemaking, he thanked God for all the good things that happened to the two of them.

CHAPTER 11

When they arrived at Bernalillo, New Mexico Territory, Chet had more messages. He telegraphed Monica and May that they were well, and told the telegraph operator to forward any other wires to Santa Rosa, then tipped him well.

CHET
I GOT A REPORT THEY ARE ON THE CANADIAN RIVER WEST TEXAS. A TEXAS RANGER SAID THEY WERE CAMPED OUT THERE. DIDN'T KNOW WHAT THEY HAD FOR PLANS. THEY HAD SUPPLIES BUT WERE LOW ON HORSES.

"Why in the hell don't he wire San Antonio for help?" Cole asked.

"I bet he's illiterate," Chet said. "The telegraph wire is still a mystery to some folks and they don't trust it. Heck, it ain't even signed."

"How many folks would give a ragged black man,

all broke down, credit for more supplies?" Hampt asked with a headshake.

Jesus raised a brown finger. "That's the truth. Hampt knows."

"Boys, it's a big place out there. Wild Comanche, Kiowa, Cheyenne, are all out there. What's left of the buffalo herd is in that country. It's not a healthy place for white or black men to be."

"We're going to be close to there in a week, boss?"

"I hope so, Hampt. I really hope so." He looked at the towering mountains with the sunset shining on its walls across the Rio Grande. "We go uphill out of here tomorrow, but we cross around most of it."

They went to eat at a restaurant. His arm on Liz's shoulder, he asked her privately, "How are the calluses on your backside?"

She chuckled. "They're wonderful. Jesus and I don't have to cook."

"You're doing great."

"I am excited to be with you and these three great men. We have had little problems so far. I knew this trip would test all of us. But it is better than waiting for your telegrams at Preskitt."

"We worried about you coming," Cole said. "Now you're one of us, Liz."

"Good. I would never have seen this part of the country. The amazing thing is how big it is. I have not seen a place yet that I would trade for the Preskitt area and the pines. That has really grown on me."

The men held the door to the café open for her. They soon were seated and had food ordered. Afterward, they took baths, and the men shaved, and they slept in comfortable hotel beds that night. They ate breakfast in the predawn and crossed on the Rio Grande ferry to the east side. Saddle leather creaked, hooves clunked on the hard-packed road, horses snorted dust, and some danced a little before shifting into a rolling gait. They had miles to cover and Chet pressed them every day to make those miles. The third day from Bernalillo they arrived at Santa Rosa, the village of small lakes. He felt better after reading more wires he received there.

CHET
I AM SATISFIED HE IS SOMEWHERE ON THE CANADIAN RIVER. I TALKED TO SEVERAL DROVERS IN OGALLALA WHO SAW AND AVOIDED HIS SPREAD-OUT OUTFIT IN THAT REGION. NELSON DAY

CHET
PAUL NEWLAND SAW THAT BLACK OUTFIT IN THE CANADIAN RIVER COUNTRY. THEY WERE NOT MOVING. HE HAD NO ANSWER FOR THAT.
CHARLES HOLLAND

"Well, at least we know he exists," Hampt said.

"Tularosa is two days away or so. When we're there, and while we look for them, we'll start gathering wagons, supplies, and guns and ammo."

Everyone agreed.

"Do you feel better, now that you know they are

out there?" she asked him behind their hotel room door.

"They didn't take wings, anyway."

"You knew this would be tough."

"Oh, yes. Liz, I'm pleased we have some evidence they are somewhere up here. But getting things rolling won't be easy."

"You love challenges. Heavens, you chose me. You could have sent for a German farm girl."

Her humor had him laughing.

"I am blessed to have you." He hugged her tight. "Day in, day out, I look over and see that roan horse bob his head beside me and you riding on uncomplaining."

"I asked to come along. I love being with you. You are a tough leader, but those kinds of leaders win wars."

"We're going to win this one. Thanks."

"Tell me about Tularosa."

"It's a frontier town. Not much law, unless the rangers have straightened it out. Be careful, and stay with one of us all the time."

She yawned big and buried her face in his chest. "We will do this. Let's try to sleep."

They stayed the next night at a west Texas rancher's place. Herman Acres, a big man the size of Hampt, was delighted to introduce Liz to his Hispanic wife, Leona. His ranch crew were interested in their search and what they'd do when they found them.

Chet explained they had to find them first.

"We heard about them, but never exactly where they were."

"What's wrong?" one man asked.

"A Texas banker hired us to come from Arizona to go look for them."

"They figured they wandered that far?" another cowboy asked.

Chet shook his head with a smile. "I have no idea what they thought."

"Hey, guys, we're glad you stopped by, and come any time," Herman said.

When Chet rejoined his wife in the ranch house, Leona had found her a bath and Liz beamed. "I told them they needed to come stay in Oak Creek. I have never been there, but they can catch trout, and it is cool in summer?"

"Both. If you come, just let us know. It's a heavenly place. Those folks bring us produce all summer long."

Leona smiled. "We get brave, we might do that."

"How many horses could I buy off of area ranchers, if I need them?" Chet asked Acres.

"Oh, a hundred, I bet."

"I may need two hundred."

Acres narrowed his blue eyes at that number. "You figure that's his problem?"

"No idea, but it has been offered as one."

"That's going to be a real mess."

"A big one, I fear."

"Good luck. Send me word if you need horses. I'll gather them for you."

"Thanks, I may be sending for them."

They rode into Tularosa the next day—a town of adobe hovels, with skinny black Injun camp dogs that bared their teeth at them, and naked brown-skinned children who stood back and looked hard at them. Some fat, Mexican women ignored them and looked to be on a shopping quest. And two barely clad, skinny whores came out in the street to proposition them. They must have thought at first that Liz was a boy.

"Hampt, try the saloon. They may know something in there. I'm going to the telegraph office."

"Got'cha," the big man said, dismounted, and hitched his horse at the rack beside several other hipshot mounts.

When Chet walked into the office, the telegraph key operator nodded to him from behind the counter.

"Chet Byrnes. Any messages for me?"

The man nodded. "Only ten. You expecting more?"

"Glad to have any at all."

He and Liz took them to the stand-up table and she began unfolding them. Jesus and Cole stood back to listen.

CHET
THE PARTY YOU WANT IS CAMPED ON THE CANADIAN RIVER NORTH OF THE DEPOT ABOUT SIX MILES. I LEARNED THAT FROM A RANGER WHO TALKED TO THEM. GARDNER GREEN

"We're close, boys."

CHET
I CAN SHOW YOU RIGHT WHERE THEY ARE FOR FIVE HUNDRED DOLLARS. WIRE THE MONEY TO THIS ADDRESS.
MILLARD COLLINS

He shook his head, amused. "I don't think I'll do that, Millard."

They all laughed.

CHET
I CAN'T FIND OUT A THING. SORRY, I TRIED. NOLAN FILES

Chet picked up the next.

CHET
NO HELP. CLAUDE BARKER

The room was quiet.

THE SHERIFF IN KANSAS SAYS HE WILL RELEASE THEM FOR TEN THOUSAND DOLLARS. COTTON MULLINS

"Who the hell is that?" Cole asked.

"A smart aleck in Wichita." He read on.

SORRY, CHET. NO HELP. LEROY NEAL

"Here's another that knows nothing." He put it down.

TO LIZ AND CHET AND CREW
WE OUT IN ARIZONA HOPE YOU HAVE FOUND THEM AND ARE HEADED HOME.
WE ALL MISS YOU.
THE WHOLE BYRNES RANCH GANG

"That is probably May's," Jesus said. "She is big-hearted enough to do that."

BE CAREFUL.
MONICA RHEA AND ANITA

"The rest are nothing. They don't know a thing."

"Who are you looking for?" the clerk asked.

"Bob Decker, a black drover and a big herd."

"Oh, them niggers are up on the Canadian. I guess they're going to homestead up there. You want them?"

"Yes, you know what the problem is?"

"Water run out. They got here too late. All those moon lakes are dry. *Playas*, you know what I mean?"

"I know both words. You mean he stopped up there 'cause the water was gone?"

"That's what they say. You need anything else?"

"Yes, I want to send some wires home. Cole, write one to your wife. Liz, write one to Monica and the girls. I'll write one to May for Hampt."

Cole took off his hat and clapped it on his chaps. "Whew. We've made it."

"Can I send one to Anita?" Jesus asked.

"Sure."

"Thanks, boss man."

"No problem." He went to work on his message for May.

Hampt arrived and came in the door, fresh faced. "You all hear where they're at?"

Chet nodded and pointed north. "This man said they're stopped 'cause the water holes dried up. Here's the message I'm sending to May. You write the rest."

"We are writing them all," Liz said, amused.

"I want Cole, Jesus, and Liz to find us a house or rooms to rent and take care of the horses. Hampt and I are riding up there and see what the hell we need to do to get them rolling. We'll be back later tonight. Eat supper if we aren't back."

"We can handle it," Cole said.

Liz agreed. "Just be careful."

He kissed her on the forehead. "We will. You stay close to those two here."

They went outside, took their horses out of the string on the rack, mounted up, and rode northeast. In a while, they found the line of cottonwoods that marked the Canadian bottoms and headed east. It was obvious that the scattered, grazing cattle were a part of the large herd they sought.

"These cattle sure been rode hard and put away wet," Hampt said with a shake of his head about the cattle's thin condition.

Chet was upset about how they had found the

animals. "I agree. These cattle, big and small, are in tough shape."

"Is this grass no good up here?" Hampt asked.

"No, they didn't get like this overnight. I think he's pushed them too hard to get here."

Hampt looked deeply concerned. "What can we do?"

"Get organized."

A black cowboy rode off a nearby ranch to stop them.

He set the horse down roughly in front of them. "What you's wants?"

"Mister Bob Decker."

"He's a busy man. What's you need him fo'?"

"'Cause I'm his new boss. Now show us the way."

With narrowed eyes, the black cowboy glared at him. Then he snorted. "Hmm, he ain't taking no orders from the likes of you."

Chet put his hand out to stay Hampt. "Just lead the way to the camp."

"We may have us a thing here," Hampt said under his breath.

"We'll settle it. No problem."

Hampt looked skyward for help. "I hope so."

"We can work it out." The man began to lope his horse and they fell in behind him.

They came over a rise to see a scattered camp of tents and tarps set up with a lot of small fires and black faces raising up to see who was coming in. The guide jumped off his horse, went to the tent fly, and pointed back at them.

Way over six feet tall, the snowy-headed black man

who came out folded his arms on his chest. Some of his gold jewelry flashed in the afternoon sun.

"What can I's do for you?"

"My name's Chet Byrnes. Samuel Severs sent me here to ramrod this herd drive and get it to Ogallala. Would you like to see the paper he sent me to take it over?"

"He owes me—"

"I am authorized to pay you that agreed amount, if you assist me in getting them up here."

A larger black man with a bald head appeared to demand, "Who dis man?"

"Yeager Brown, meet Chet Byrnes."

Chet nodded to him.

"They sent him from San Antonio to take over."

"Who?"

"Sam Severs." Decker held out his hands. "He says we'll get paid, if we help him."

Yeager reflected on it a moment. "What you gonna do?" he asked Chet.

"Reorganize this train."

Decker held up his hands to stop them. "I's wants these boys paid. I asked dem to come with us. I will collect that money for dem."

Still not convinced, Yeager shook his head, squeezed his chin, and spoke. "How many slaves you own, growing up in Texas?"

"Me and my brother."

"Huh?"

By then Hampt and Decker were both laughing. Chet shook his head. "We never owned a slave. My people came from the hill country of Arkansas to

Texas. My grandfather and father fought for Texas freedom."

Yeager came right back with, "You a damn rainmaker? You don't look like one to me."

"No, that's God's job. But I want an inventory by tonight of your food, guns, ammo, and number of usable horses."

"What you going to do with dat?"

"Get this operation ready to move north."

"You must have damn deep pockets, mister."

"I have the authority to do whatever is necessary. Get me that information."

Chet dismounted. "This is Hampt Tate. I'll introduce the others tomorrow." Then he took a tablet from his saddlebags and two pencils. One of the hands came and held their horses, and they went into the larger tent. The tables were rough, weathered boards with benches set around them. Two open bottles of whiskey and some cups littered the one they sat down at.

"You want a drink?" Decker asked.

"No, thanks."

"We don't have any coffee left."

"I understand."

He wrote coffee on his list.

"Sugar?"

Decker shook his head.

"What do you have?" Chet asked bluntly.

"Two hundred pounds of rice. Three hundred pounds of *frijoles.* We'll open one sack of those tonight."

"No chuckwagon?"

"No."

"It was too damn hard to get dem from place to place out cheer," Yeager said. "We left it down in the Indian Territory."

"I'm going to buy one and we'll figure out how to get it moving. How many modern rifles do you have?"

Decker looked at his man. "Five?"

Yeager nodded in agreement.

"How many of your men have pistols?"

"Maybe a dozen. Why?"

"Every man here needs a working firearm. The damn Comanche, Cheyenne, and Kiowa all have working firearms. They haven't found you yet, but they could. Now, how many horses?"

"Maybe a hundred."

"How many can be ridden to herd cattle?"

"Sixty."

"How many horses did you start with?"

"A hundred and fifty."

Yeager shook his head. "Dat ain't right. Dey weren't all sound horses."

"That'll be the problem. It may take a few days or so, maybe more, to get them here. But I have a promise by a rancher to bring me some good ones."

Hampt spoke up. "Tomorrow, I want eight men to take rifle training. They'll each have a rifle and be shown how to use it, and keep it clean. They turn it in when we get to Nebraska, or pay for it."

"You think—"

"These Indians will kill black men as quick as they kill white. You just haven't faced them. You're an invader, and they won't treat you any better than a white cowboy." Chet dropped his head down and shook it. "My wife is with me. I expect her to be treated with respect. See that every man knows it. We can talk more tomorrow."

"Where you going to get the water for dem?"

"Yeager, I can't make water, but these cattle are in tough condition today. They'll die when winter comes unless we get them on some real feed and water."

"Where will you live?"

"My wife and men will be in your camp tomorrow, and we'll move with the herd until we deliver them. I'll be here, too."

"What about water ahead?" Yeager asked.

"We'll have to find sources. Maybe hire someone to help guide us northward."

He and Hampt shook their hands, then they mounted up and hurried for Tularosa in a long lope.

"What did they think they would do for food?" Hampt asked.

"I have no idea, but we have a big task ahead, and I can't see us pulling out of here in short of a week."

Hampt nodded in agreement.

They met the others in Tularosa and went to supper in a bar the hotel man said served good food. It was mid-week and there were few customers in the place, so they got a nice welcome from Johnny Reed, the man who owned the bar. When they told him their plan to move the big herd north, he nodded.

"We all wondered when someone would be in charge of that outfit. You'll need lots of luck to get that bunch to even get off their butts. Excuse me, ma'am."

"No problem."

They ordered supper and Chet explained his plans. He finished with, "We want to send a messenger out to Herman Acres's ranch, for him to send me a hundred and fifty using horses quick as he can."

"I can get a boy to do that. Write a note and he can deliver it."

Chet wrote the note and put two silver dollars down.

"One's enough. Two will spoil him." Reed left the other one laying there and went to take care of it.

"They have no horses?" Liz asked.

"Not very many. When you're driving cattle and not graining them, you need several changes to get anything out of them."

"Who cooks for them?"

"We haven't met that person yet. We only met Decker and his man Yeager. I was not impressed. They abandoned the chuckwagon—too hard for it to keep up. Maybe I can talk to the big storeowner tonight. I'll ask Reed about him."

When he spoke to the bar owner about the man, he sent a boy to find Phillip Rymore. Before they finished their meal, a big man arrived, took his hat off for Liz, and pulled up a chair.

Chet explained his plan to Rymore, and before he even listed his needs, the storekeeper told him he could get about anything they wanted. He might have to ship some of it up the trail to them after they'd gone.

Chet told him about the bank arrangement on receiving payment, and how they would honor his purchases. Rymore agreed that would work for him.

"Three dozen Winchesters?"

"I have a dozen. I can beg, borrow, and steal the rest. They sell for about seven fifty. I'll try to hold that price."

"Two barrels of flour?"

"No problem."

"Four hundred pounds of *frijoles*?"

Rymore nodded.

"Dried apples?"

"Got them—and raisins?"

"I'll need plenty of both."

"I've got some good dry sugar, too."

"I'll need it. Canned tomatoes and peaches?"

"I have them in stock."

"Lard, baking powder, bacon, Arbuckle coffee."

"That I have. I have some new potatoes, too."

"Good, add them in."

"Cinnamon, and red peppers," Liz put in.

Rymore nodded that he had them. "I have a chuckwagon in good shape. Someone brought it back and left it here and I can sell it to you for eighty bucks, which was what I gave for it."

"We can use it. Can you find us four solid mules and harness? They sure won't have any. I also want girths, and latigo leather, plus some bridle leather. And a couple of reels of grass rope."

"Those mules may take a day or so to find. But I'll get you some."

"I'm sending for horses from a man that promised he could find me some. I want some canvas sheeting, too. Some lamps, and coal oil, in the mix. Tomorrow, I want about forty cans of peaches for that bunch. Tobacco and paper. I'm going to meet with the whole outfit and tell them how this is going to work."

"Two sacks of old bottles for target practice," Hampt added.

"No problem. I have a big draft horse and a two-wheel cart, so I can send some of this up there in it for now."

"Sounds good. You have anything else for us?" Chet asked.

"I know an older man who's been up that trail several times. He really knows the water and the rest."

"Can I meet him here tomorrow night?"

"Sure, he could use the pay. His name is Lou James. Well, men, I appreciate the business. Thanks. I'll try to outfit you best that I can. Nice to meet you, Mrs. Byrnes."

"Liz will do."

Rymore smiled at her. "My wife is Hispanic. She would love to meet you."

"I don't know what I have to do for these guys, but maybe we can find the time to meet."

"Thanks again, and be careful. You know this hostile Indian thing is not over."

"We like our hair. We will," Chet promised him.

Later, in the hotel bed, he told her he thought

from his attitude and attention to details that Rymore was a good man.

"He certainly sounds like a real businessman. I know your head is swimming in all this business. Don't worry about me. I'm proud to be here with you. I will be fine, and I can help, if you tell me what to do."

"You keep track of what we order and what we get. I can work that bunch then, and not have to worry about this end of it."

"Good."

He drew in a deep breath. "I know it will be hell ahead, but we may make a good deal out of this lost herd business."

"Ooh, yes."

In the morning, Reed had their breakfast ready at five. After that, Hampt went by the store and it had the lights on. When he joined them, Rymore told them he had a boy to drive the two-wheel cart out to their camp and it was near loaded. Their horses were at the livery yard next, and they were loaded quickly.

Chet added a couple of glass jars each of peppermint and licorice sticks. He aimed to use all that as carrots to lead those men. No one had spoiled them lately, so he aimed to start. The peaches and tobacco were going to work for that day.

Mid-morning, they reached the cow camp and the men were assembled on a slope. Most sat cross-legged on the ground. Some of the crew stood, but Decker assured him they were all there.

"This be the new man," he said in a loud, deep

voice. "His name is Mister Byrnes. You listens good to him, 'cause we going to be on the move soon."

"Good morning."

No answer.

He said it louder, and they replied.

"My name is Chet. No mister about it. You work hard the next six to eight weeks and you'll get a bonus. If you don't, you can start to walk back to Texas. That big man is Hampt Tate, and that cowboy is Cole Emerson. That Mexican is my right arm, Jesus Morales. This lady is my wife, Miss Liz, to everyone. We came from Arizona to get you to Nebraska.

"These Injuns we may meet will want to kill you. Every man will have a rifle and ammo. If you are threatened, shoot first, ask them questions later. If you can't shoot an Indian, shoot his horse. We'll show you how to shoot it. If you shoot another cowboy, you'll hang before sundown. If you lose that gun, you will pay for it in Nebraska. Am I clear?"

"Yes!"

"My men will pass out tobacco and paper next. There are matches, too. Don't, whatever you do, set the prairie on fire."

As his men and the store clerk passed each man who wanted one a pouch of tobacco, paper, and some matches, the talk went on furious among the men. One bare-chested man stood up and waved.

"Thank God fur you's, Mr. Byrnes." A cheer went up.

Decker, sitting in his folding chair, shook his head. "They've been out for weeks. You impressed me a lot already this morning, sir."

"Dey going to lick you boots," Yeager said, and freely laughed for the first time.

"Listen up, men. We'll go to having good meals." He held up his hands to silence them. "But we're going to work hard, too. We may have to be in the saddle moving cattle for two days to reach the next water. So, sleep when you get a chance. Stay close to camp unless there's more than two of you. Indians will try to pick you off and get your rifle.

"I have more good horses coming this week. But be ready to pull out. I have, as a bonus, a can of peaches for each man this morning."

The cheers went up again. "File by and pick up one. Hoarders get none."

His men gave them out.

"Then get back to you job!" Decker ordered, then turned to Chet. "I want you to meet my cook next."

Three Orientals in silk clothing bowed to him.

"That's my cook, No Ling Ling." A short, angry-faced Chinaman carried a hatchet and wore a que.

The man bowed. "You got plenty food?"

"I'll have it here by tomorrow."

"Good thing. Damn near starve here."

"You won't with me."

"Good men no work good on empty belly." He pointed. "That my helper, Du Wang. That my number two helper, Nu Wa Tye."

"Glad to meet you all. Food and supplies are coming."

"The eight men you asked for are here. They've

all shot rifles. Maybe not good as yours, but they can shoot," Decker said.

"Hampt, you have gun class today. Show those men. Tomorrow, I want ten more new ones. Yeager, you go with him and help them."

"Yes, sah."

"Cole, you and Jesus look over the horses we have and figure out what we need to do."

"What else you need done?" Decker asked.

"A couple of nice men to put up Liz's tent and help her organize it."

"I can do that," Jesus offered.

"No, he has some men who aren't busy. We need to meet and get acquainted with them."

Decker smiled. "You will have them too spoiled to work again."

"Good. I treat people right. If they don't work, I don't need them."

Decker lowered his voice. "You don't smoke. Your men don't smoke. I think that tobacco was the best gift of all."

"I figured that. They get a pouch a day."

Decker shook his head. "I sees why dee boss man done sent you already. But you worried about Injuns, ain't you?"

"They have their backs to the wall. I've fought Comanche all my life. They kidnapped three of my family members. Today, they are even more desperate. If we don't have a fight somewhere on the trail, I will be so pleased I'll pay you a hundred dollars."

"You do be concerned. I'll be more watchful. I ain't seen none."

"Trust me, they've seen you and sized you up already."

"Aw, heavens, Mr. Chet, that don't be good news."

"You hear them rifles?" He indicated the shots from down range where Yeager and Hampt were holding a gun class.

"I sure do."

"If we get prepared to wage war back at the Indians, these will save us."

"Land, lands. Yesterday I wondered how to feed dem. Today, how to save dem."

"Lots of things are coming. Get ready."

Chet talked to Hampt at noontime. No Ling Ling fed the outfit a mid-day meal for the first time in six weeks. They had been stretching their supply that much, Decker admitted.

"Those eight were the best shots in camp and knew rifles. I'll use two of them each day to help me teach the others. It'll speed up my training. They told me that the men are pleased we're doing this."

"They'd seen Indians, hadn't they?"

Hampt nodded. "But I'd fight beside those we had here today anytime. We need more of them that are that efficient with a rifle."

"You telling them if they can't hit an Indian to shoot his horse?"

"Yeah. That shocked the first guys, but they agreed that an Injun on foot was better than having one on a good horse able to charge at you."

"We need them gun-ready in a week. When those horses I ordered get here, and when the chuck-wagon's road ready, we need to head north. I want Yeager to show Cole and Jesus the next water and to begin scouting. That old man they told us about might be a big help, too. If he's around, Johnny Reed will have him there for supper tonight."

Lou James was no young man. He chewed on a corncob pipe and had lots of white whiskers, his southern drawl was deep, and he flirted with Liz like a boy.

"By jeepers, ma'am, how did he ever get you all stirred up in this deal?"

"He owns a great stallion. You ever hear of the Barbarossa horses?"

"Yeah. They're all in Mexico. Big gold horses. Texans call them claybanks. But the word is Palomino, right?"

"Yes, that is so." She used her thumb to indicate her husband. "One is across the border in Arizona. He owns him."

"Whew. How in the world?"

"A long story for later," Chet said, amused at her storytelling. "Go on, Liz."

"He didn't tell you, but he is a U.S. Marshal. He runs the Force that puts down Mexican bandits in southern Arizona. So he headquarters on this ranch down there, and I was going back to Mexico, and my people learn that he is there. So I go there to buy a horse for my *hacienda.*"

Lou took his pipe and pointed at Chet. "I see. You came there to buy a horse colt from him."

"Yes, just to buy a horse. I get out and this *grande hombre* is standing there, hatless, waiting for me."

"My, my, you talk the best English of any woman from Mexico I ever met, but those English words weren't good enough for your description of him standing there, were they?" Lou went to laughing. The others did, too.

Liz about blushed. "Then you know the rest. I had been a widow for three years. I did not need another man in my life."

"He never sold you a horse?"

"No. I had to marry him to get one."

"Missy, I can see why he swept you away. You're a treasure that Mexico lost."

"I still have a large *hacienda* down there, but this man has an empire in Arizona."

Lou turned to Chet. "What do you need me for?"

"Water holes, and your knowledge about the trail to Ogallala."

He nodded with a pained face at Chet. "You're late in the year for finding much water. Been dry this spring, but we usually get some showers in the next two months. You willing to cross over the Kansas line in a place or two, to water them?"

"I want these cattle in Ogallala in six to eight weeks, in much better condition than they are now. How tough are those Kansas border watchers?"

"If they don't get the word you're coming, there

won't be many out there this time of year. Usually by now, the herds don't try to go up there. I've distracted the watchers before, but if they find me in Kansas you'll have to bail me out of jail."

"No problem. What will you cost?"

"Two hundred bucks."

Chet rose, leaned over, and shook his hand. "You start tomorrow. Welcome to the outfit."

"Obliged. This meal ain't half-bad, either."

Chet shook his head. "Your storytelling is worth half the price of hiring you."

The others agreed. He was not a rainmaker, but he did know the way and where water should be, if they could find any left.

"How far are we from Nebraska?" Cole asked.

"Oh, like the crow flies, three hundred miles."

"That's reachable." Chet was pleased they'd found the right man.

Rifle drill began again the next day. Hampt and Yeager worked with a new bunch. No Ling Ling listed things he still needed for Liz, who wrote them down to order.

Rymore found them the two teams of mules, but they'd never been worked together before. To get them started, Cole and Jesus were going to drive them to town for some needed things and back to camp. Cole drove them, and Jesus rode along on horseback to help him hold them down.

The store people assured him they could get there, but it took two hours longer than planned. When they did return, the black men came and secured the mules to a hitch rack and the two head-shaking cowboys joined them for lunch. "They're fresh, I take it?" Chet asked them.

Cole scowled at him. "They don't know getup from sic'em."

"First they balked," Jesus said. "The one team would go and the other one backed. Then the harness chains jiggling spooked them. A damn ground owl really spooked them and they ran off. We've been to New Mexico and back already."

"When Decker gets here, we'll get him to send us a mule skinner. Black folks know mules. You two are cowboys."

They agreed. All were sitting at one table, when Hampt and Decker came to join them. Chet mentioned they needed a mule skinner to drive them.

"Mott Halter," Decker said. He stood up and told a man in the food line to send Mott Halter up there.

In a short while, a big man, who looked like he'd had a fight with a wildcat, came. His clothes were in rags and he took off an old hat he must have found beside the road.

"What'cha need, Mister Decker?"

"See them mules?"

"Yes, sah."

"After you eats you meal, I want you to unhook dem and drive dem around."

"Oh." The big man smiled wide as Texas. "I sure nuff kin do dat."

"Mott, since you are going to have to drive the wagon back and forth to town," Liz said, "I have a new pair of overalls and shirt to fit you, so you can represent us better. Eddie, at Rymore's, will replace your hat, too."

"Ma'am, that be so nice of you. I pays you in Nebraska."

"No, you just drive them mules. These two cowboys will pay for that, so they don't have to drive them."

Everyone laughed.

Cole looked up at the hipshot mules and agreed. "Cheap price to sell that job."

Jesus agreed.

After lunch, they unhitched the two teams for Mott, who wore his new clothes. He took the first team in harness and with trace chains hooked up to drive them around.

To the waiting mules, he said real quiet, "Jack."

The mules were stomping around and he had them controlled, but they never heard him say, "Jack," again. Head shaking, they weren't listening when Mott said it the third time.

He drew back the long check line and snapped that right mule in the ribs and hair flew at the point he struck. The mule acted goosed. He held him down. "Jack."

The right-hand mule knew that word and he had felt the strike on his side. His head was up and his ears were up. Number two still had not heard him, but Mott overhanded, did the same thing to the second mule, cutting hair with a, "Whoa, Jack."

When he clucked to them, they scrambled hooves some, but soon both drove real smooth. In a short time, he had them backing and turning and backing more. The gathered men applauded.

"He's a real mule skinner," Liz said.

"I bet you could have them cultivating in no time," Chet said to Mott. "I want you to be the mule man. Pick a helper. Drive them to town tonight, and bring a bedroll. We'll feed you there. You'll bring back more supplies tomorrow."

Mott shook his head and smiled. "Miss Liz. I sure like dese clothes."

She dismissed his gratitude. "No problem. You are sure the mule man."

"That don't make you mad, does it, Jesus?" Cole asked.

"I told you. I only worked burros and not many of them."

"How was rifle training, Hampt?" Chet asked the big man.

"We taught the best ones yesterday. From here on, we've got our work cut out. Yeager is good talking to them, but they don't know a gun butt from a barrel. My trainers I chose are good, too. But these people we had today, I want back tomorrow."

"If we get a real attack, we need them all to be proficient."

"I know. Maybe we can do that. Oh, hell, Chet, the U.S. Army trains those dumb Germans to be cavalry troopers and they couldn't even understand English. I hope I have the time."

"Tomorrow, I want Lou and Yeager, along with you two, to ride north, say, sixty miles north, and figure out our first days on the road. Keep in mind there are Indians out here. I want you four back the next night in one piece."

Lou agreed that was how to start. Clouds clabbered up the western sky and thunder rolled from the distance. But they made it back to Tularosa, and he fed Mott and his man on the back steps of the saloon, plus had them served two beers apiece. They slept rolled up in blankets in the livery. Liz found Mott's new assistant, Horatio Knott, a new pair of overalls, and a shirt, and straw hats for both of them. They were thrilled.

"Acres sent word he was gathering horses and would have them here in a few days." Chet thought that would work. Ranchers on the frontier had miles to go to markets. Range horses were plentiful and the ranchers were cash short.

Cole nodded. "Your gunmen doing better today, Hampt?"

"They're learning, and ain't shot no one yet."

"Good thing," Jesus said. "It might have been you."

"I can't get over yesterday," Cole said. "I seen men like Mott in Texas do that. White man and colored alike, that could do that. Only a Mexican with a bullwhip could have done what he did with that long rein. That was impressive to me. I've seen men cuss and whip on mules, but he was a hand right off." Cole shook his head in disbelief, but Chet had seen other men do it as smooth.

"Jack," Jesus whispered. "They damn sure listened after that."

"I'd bet a dollar that man he has to help him is as good," Chet said.

They all agreed.

Later, Liz asked him if he thought she'd done right, clothing them.

"Better than their butts shining."

"Oh, I am being serious."

"It'll be alright. That can't cost over a dollar a man."

"Less than that."

"Dress them up. We're going to Ogallala."

"When are the water searchers going north?" she asked.

"Tomorrow. We're about caught up."

"Going north tomorrow, I sure am going to miss these good meals you been chocking down me," Lou said when they started to leave. "I see how you built an empire in Arizona."

"How is that?"

"You didn't tell Decker to get someone to drive them mules, you said get a mule skinner. He got one who knew what to do. These guys Hampt uses to train them know guns. It ain't, 'Hey, Joe, do this. Get me the man.'"

"You be the water man, Lou," Chet said.

"In the middle of a damn drought, too."

"If there's a way, I'm counting on you to find some."

"Does this sweet lady of yours have an older sister?"

"No, she's an only child."

"Hell, I wanted her older sister."

"What about Monica?" he asked Liz.

She shook her head. "No, she is too fussy for him."

"There I go again. Off with no woman."

"Johnny will have breakfast for us here at five thirty."

"Night."

CHAPTER 12

The four of them—Lou, Yeager, Jesus, and Cole—rode north the next morning. Chet hoped they brought him back a good plan. Only time would tell.

Hampt was teaching the shooters to assemble. One man was to hold their horses. In practice, he fired a shot in the air and the men who were scattered rode to assemble in groups, laid belly down, and fired their rifles at targets. Chet decided he had taught them a lot. They looked impressive to him.

When the four water scouts came back, they'd found water, but the first was the worst—thirty miles north. Yeager said he'd found it before, but wondered how they'd get there.

"We drive that first day to water. Take us all day and into the night. It will be tiring, but the next one is how far?" Chet asked.

"Twelve miles."

"Short day."

That evening at supper, Liz asked him when they'd leave.

"When Acres gets here with the horses and we get them straight. Decker has his bronc riders selected."

Lou shook his head. "Bronc riders now, huh?"

"We'll see."

"No, that old man knows how deep those boys go. That's why an illiterate man like him can run drives. Most men take cattle north with a handful of good cowboys. He's got forty hands, enough so they can do the job."

"I think you're right," Chet said. "Five thirty tomorrow morning."

They groaned.

"Better enjoy this bed," he told Liz later.

"Yes, we will share the old ground in a few nights. Saddle horses are all you lack?"

"Yes. He sent word today. Acres is coming. Hope he found enough."

"I love that old man, Lou. He's so sharp. He said, '*grande hombre.* I know what you found.'" She shook her head. "I don't have to be careful anymore talking to you, but I fear I will sound like those black cowboys next. You's got any?"

They both laughed.

Three days later, Acres and five teenage ranch boys arrived with a hundred and thirty horses. Everyone in Tularosa turned out to admire them driven through the main street. Corralled in the gathering pens for cattle, Chet had hay to feed them for the night. He took Acres and his hands to supper, and his wife, Leona, too, who drove the buckboard loaded with bedrolls and supplies for the crew.

"How is it going?" Acres asked him.

"Exhausting. We go north in a few days. I believe we'll be ready."

"It took me more time than I thought it would. Several outfits had turned their horses out and they had to gather them. But I knew you needed this many, or more, so I got every one I could get."

"You did great. I'll wire the San Antonio Bank and have them pay you what I owe for them."

"Have them send it here to my account in the North Texas Bank."

"We can arrange that."

"Are things going as you planned?" Acres asked.

"Too slow, but we are about to start."

"What was the holdup in the first place?"

"Dry year. First water north of the Canadian of any amount is thirty miles."

"Yeah, it is getting late," Acres agreed.

"Maybe a good thing he stopped. They're in tough shape. The rest here may have helped them. We needed those horses you brought. I've culled over a dozen out of what they had. This will really help us."

"I bet it does. I want to see them. The boys and I would like to see your outfit."

"Sure, and I'll tell Liz to ride out with Leona in the buckboard tomorrow. We can bring the horses out in the morning."

"You tired yet?" Acres asked.

"Ain't had time to be that."

Acres motioned to the two wives at the next table. "Looks like they got plenty to talk about. Your wife looks the same as she did at our house."

"My wife is a tough lady."

"I know. She is sure pretty."

"Big help, too. She knows every penny we've spent, both ours and the bank's."

"She's rich, isn't she? Leona told me she left a big *hacienda* in the hands of her ex-brother-in-law?"

"Yes, isn't that amazing? I was busy figuring how we might visit, and she came lock, stock, and barrel to meet me on the border."

"Is Arizona nice?"

"I like the north. Pine country. Southern Arizona is cactus country. I have a large ranch down on the border that my nephew runs. Water is the largest issue."

"Never snows down there?"

"Maybe once in several years, a little falls."

"I guess someday I'll get out there and see you."

"You're welcome anytime. If I'm home, or not."

"That might be hard, to catch you there. You have a son, too?"

"Adam is eight months old. His mother was my first wife. She had jumping horses, and they were her life. She'd been married before and was twice widowed. She had never carried a baby full term. She quit jumping to carry our son. After he was born, she went back to jumping. While I was away, she had a serious wreck on a jump. She was a wonderful woman. I had no ambition to find another woman, when along came Liz."

"You were lucky, my friend. My boys' mother died of a fever. I was alone for a long time and then Leona lost her husband. They had an epidemic that killed her children before they came up to Tularosa. He was killed in a wagon wreck. I talked her into marrying me."

"Hey, you were lucky, too. She's a great lady."

"Oh, yes. But I can't believe how yours rides with you all over hell."

"She told me I couldn't go without her. She's a tomboy, is all I can say. But she never complains about anything."

They both laughed.

The horses were well received at the cow camp. A rope corral was set up with lots of the cowboys on hand. Decker's chief wrangler was Apache Joe. Chet had no idea where his name came from. The short man could make a lariat fly over two horses and settle on number three's neck. He picked a sorrel horse from the new lot. His first rider was another wrangler, Dickey Joe, with his saddle in his right hand and more hands ready to bridle him.

The horse bridled and blindfolded, his saddle in place and cinched twice, Dickey flew onto the saddle, jerked off the blinds, and rode the gelding in a circle, reined him around and nodded. "Damn good horse."

He stepped off and the third man in the wranglers was Jerry Bird. His bay horse bucked pretty hard, but he straightened him out. The bay proved to be a reining fool. He could spin on his hind legs, and lots of eyes bugged out watching Jerry rein the horse around on his heels.

Apache Joe beamed. "That is a real good one, huh?"

"A dandy," Chet agreed.

They spent all day testing them, and Chet was a little amazed at the chief wrangler's referral to some horse earlier that a new one resembled. Chet was satisfied that by dark, he'd know them all.

"He can't read or write," Chet said. "But he knows every horse they rode."

"I saw that, too. They should make enough mounts. Acres did a good job finding that many," Cole said. "He tell you what they cost?"

"Thirty bucks a head. He didn't get rich."

"These men are impressed. They never had this many good horses. They may even believe they're real cowboys."

"I hope so. This drive will not be like going on a picnic."

"How much longer?" Cole asked.

"Two days and we go north. I told Decker that an hour ago and he agreed."

"Yes, let's get it behind us."

"This is hot country," Cole said, drying his neck.

"Yeah, it would be nice to be back at Preskitt, drinking lemonade with ice on that porch."

"I'd like to be at Camp Verde and dance on Saturday night with my wife."

"We'll get back there," Chet promised him.

"I know. Having these horses does make it look like we may become a real outfit moving steers, too."

"I think Liz has them dressed for the trip, anyway."

"Boy, she did good at that." They both laughed at Chet's wife's efforts to dress each man in a new shirt and overalls.

Things were going fine. They greased the loaded chuckwagon axles and hand-sewed and waxed the seams of the new cover stretched over the bows. The last night before they set out, to celebrate, No Ling Ling baked some big fruit turnover cakes, peach and apple ones, in his largest Dutch ovens. The cooks planned to ride some gentle horses and let the mule skinners drive the chuckwagon. That suited Chet, since he doubted the Orientals could handle those mules anyway. Ever since they ditched the first chuckwagon in the Indian Territory somewhere, they were used to riding horseback. He didn't know the entire story, but he imagined they wrecked it. Mott and Horatio knew that driving mules beat riding drag on the herd, and Decker threatened them with that job if they lost the rig.

Before they left, he settled his accounts, grateful for his wife's neat paperwork. He notified the bank in San Antonio to pay the suppliers, including

Acres's horse account. He mailed them a copy of her accounting as well.

"If we make fifteen miles a day, we will be there in three weeks," she said.

"If we make that mileage, but I want some weight gain."

"We are closer to leaving then?"

He hugged her. "Hell, yes, girl. We are finally that close."

"Speaking of hell, it wouldn't hurt for you to say a prayer for us tonight." She hugged him around the waist.

"You're right. He will have a big hand in getting us there."

"Do it tonight."

Yeager came in. "I saw some of dem Injuns 'bout an hour ago. They be setting on horses and taking our roundup in."

Chet nodded that he heard him. "They're good at that. Now what they will do next, is the big question. Thanks. Tell Hampt, too."

"What was he saying?" Liz asked.

"Indians were watching us."

She frowned. "Oh, you said they were out there."

"You stay close. Comanche are the meanest, toughest, Indians that I know."

"You've fought them before?"

"As a boy, yes. Several times. But the worst I can recall, we were going to San Antonio and they jumped us. We got holed up in some rocks. Dale

Allen shot two of them with a shotgun. Both times that shotgun put him on his butt. He was maybe twelve. Some folks heard our shooting and came to run them off, or they might have got the whole family. Dad bought Dale Allen a pistol after that."

"How many were there?" she asked.

"I was only about fourteen then. I thought there were a hundred of them, but I imagine now there were maybe eighteen. Some of those fighters were my age. But their shrill screaming chilled my blood."

"You were fighting Indians at fourteen?"

"Yes, and I can recall it like it was yesterday."

"I hope they forget us here."

"It would be nice. They won't. No matter what happens, don't let them separate you from the men and the herd."

"I hear you."

"We will be on the edge of the knife blade all the way to Nebraska."

She nodded. "I am ready to go there."

"You're amazing. We'll soon be on our way."

"Don't forget to give them one of your prayers tonight."

"I can do that."

After supper, he rose and in his best voice said, "Tomorrow we leave here. I am going to ask the good Lord to bless and protect us on this dangerous journey. You may kneel, stand, or sit. The good Lord knows that we're out here.

"Our most heavenly Father, before we begin our

trip north, we want to thank you for getting us this far, and for our many blessings. All of these hard-working men and I will travel north tomorrow and the days after. Lord, be in our hearts and give us the strength and encouragement to work hard and get these cattle to Ogallala so we can return safely to our homes and families in Texas. In his name, amen."

"Amen," echoed across the field of cowboys. Many of them waved and thanked him for the prayer.

His wife squeezed his arm as they headed for their wall tent. "Thanks. That even helped me."

"Thank you for reminding me."

"I had to. Your sister wasn't here."

"She's always been a big help to me. Susie supported me when I brought that Texas bunch to Arizona."

"But she never found your Hilda, did she?"

"I think she looked hard for her." They both laughed.

She removed his boots, and he shook his head in the shadowy light of the tent. "Here you were living a sheltered life on a nice *hacienda*, and you chose to run off with a guy crazy enough to try to make money out of a busted cattle drive."

"Oh, it might have been a sheltered life. But I didn't laugh this much. I didn't feel as warm and wanted as I do in your arms. I knew I missed something—but I ignored the fact that it was having a real man.

"You blame me for the smell of hay bothering you. That night, when we made love in the hay, a brickbat fell on top of my head. This is exactly what I had not had. The experience was so revealing to me, I even wondered if the novelty would go away—at your house, it was even better. I wasn't jittery that night in the hay. I was playing around with a man I did not know much about, and me trusting him with all my love."

"In the short times we have been together, you never say no, you never have a bad day, you never fail to smile when we make love. That I realize and appreciate."

"Should I?"

"Hell, no. Is there anything you regret about us?"

"Yes."

"What is that?"

"I didn't find you sooner."

"Maybe it was best you were a widow all that time. I never looked at another woman when I was married to Marge. You could have come and gone. I really was as faithful with her as I am to you today."

"Then I will stop telling myself how foolish I was not having a man in those times."

"Those two that ride with me will tell you I never let any woman bother me, except for my wife. The two were shocked, I think, when I met you, but they pushed me in your direction."

"I know Jesus found me a bath. Boy, I had to swallow a lot to get the nerve up to ask you to wash me. You were not shocked, were you?"

"No, and yes. That was an exciting event. I was shaking inside so bad, I couldn't dare touch you."

"What a horrible thing to do. Here I was like some *puta* showing you my body, trying to be intimate with you so you could never forget me—I hoped. No, I prayed for God to forgive me for my wild ways, but I had faith you would not forget me, either."

"The diffused sunlight coming through that old canvas shone on your tan skin. I can see it now—all over again."

"I washed your shoulders later and thought how powerful you must be."

Then they were in each other's arms, making love again. All his concerns dissolved about taking off for the time they spent making love. Cattle drive or no cattle drive, he had her for himself.

CHAPTER 13

To get things rolling the next morning, they sent Apache Joe and his two wranglers north first. That way, the horse herd didn't get scrambled up in the herding operations. Then Mott and his skinner took the chuckwagon, and the three stick-like figures of the cook's party on horseback followed it. Poor Orientals looked like the round bottom boys, bouncing on their mounts in a stiff fashion going north.

Decker was riding around blowing a trumpet, no music involved, just blasts like some bull bellowing, and the ear-shattering bawling of upset cattle accompanied him. The great bell on the lead steer clanged, plus, at the same time, all the horses with their riders that cussed a blue streak filled his ears, too. The lost herd began the long trail that crawled northward.

This day would challenge them. Cole's estimate was thirty miles. But it was the first adequate water source and, no doubt, why Decker stopped where he did on the Canadian where there was water. At last, under way, he wanted the cattle's body condition to improve, not get worse. They had obviously been out of water too often, and run too hard in a combination of events before, so they needed to heal. Decker was already balking at some of the ways Lou James said they must go on this trip. Lou's way was to zigzag on short daily trips northward to water sources, something Decker didn't like. No doubt, that was why he stopped where he did and threw his hands up. So Chet had to stubbornly deal with him to overcome his reluctance, but so far he'd heeded Chet's plans.

He could tell that part wasn't over. In the old Chisholm Trail days, there was usually adequate water sources back east to follow a straight trail, but in this arid country you had to crisscross to get to water. And if it took two weeks more, who cared, just so the cattle put back on some of their earlier weight loss.

Hampt had done a helluva job of making soldiers out of those black cowboys. That first morning, Chet rode beside his wife parallel to the herd and avoided the dust of thousands of cloven hooves. He could only hope Hampt's efforts were enough to hold off any attack they encountered from any renegade Indians.

The day was hot, and the distance long, and he hoped the *playa* had enough water to satisfy their thirst. Hour by hour crept by. Noontime came and went. Thank God, the summer days were long. He watched a distant wall cloud build in the west and then vanish.

Cole and Lou joined him. He knew they must be close to their first destination. He and Liz shared a nod of approval at their appearance.

"See any Injuns?" he asked.

Both men shook their head.

Cole looked over at the long line of cattle. "You made good time today."

"Perfect trail drive boredom. If there's enough water up here, I say we rest tomorrow."

"There is."

"What will Decker say?" Cole asked.

"He will grumble. He's either hurry up or totally stop. But I run this drive and he works for me."

The two men nodded.

"Do the point men know how to swing the herd into this place?"

"We told them," Lou said. "The rest are not bad hands on keeping them rolling. Today has been a damn long one."

"Yes, but they have been resting, too."

"Oh, yeah, day after day will take a toll."

"Have you seen any buffalo?" Liz asked. "I have never seen one. I hope to get to see them one time."

Cole shook his head. "None yet. But they have sure killed a lot up here 'cause bones are all over the place."

"If we find some, we can go look at them," Chet promised her.

"Good."

"I better go tell Decker we'll stay here for one day. You two ride with Liz."

"We will."

He found Decker and told him the point men really knew how to circle them in on the water. "It's been a good long day. We'll graze them here tomorrow and move on the next day. It's only ten miles."

"I suppose it's sideways, too," Decker grumbled.

"Listen, we need more beef on those steers. That will set the price. I know cattle, too, and we'll eventually get there, but they'll be in much better condition."

"Hmm. You can do dat up there."

"Listen, don't challenge my judgment. These cattle will be fatter this way."

"Bunch of foolish bullshit—alright, you be dee boss. But it be worthless doing it dis way."

"That's how it will be." Chet didn't intend to argue another minute. Decker knew that, too.

"Get it straight?" Liz asked, smiling when he returned.

"We had some words. We'll camp here a day."

Jesus returned.

"See any sign of them?"

He shook his head. "There are some scouts out there. I cut sign of them, but I never saw a camp or any smoke out there."

"Good job. I can't believe that with us being the last herd this spring that they won't try to at least steal our horses. To an Indian, to own more horses is wealth. Since we've got some better horses, I think they will try to steal them. You seen Hampt today?"

Chet looked around for him. He had not seen him since morning. Had he even seen him then? Where was the big man? Not unusual, he didn't check in sometimes. They had washed up, when a couple of horsemen driving some horses ahead of them came in their direction. One of them was Hampt, and the other a horse wrangler of Apache Joe's.

Hampt sent the boy on to the cavvy with his dozen head.

"Those our horses?" Chet asked.

Hampt took off his hat for Liz. "They are now. I came up here with Joe and the *remuda* this morning, and as we crossed a grassy ridge, I thought I saw someone driving some horses. I got Dickey Joe and we went after them. I soon seen they was only some teenage bucks, and they'd probably stolen somebody's ranch horses for a lark.

"I shot two of them. Dickey caught their horses and the bunch they stole. Well, since there ain't no ranches we can find, I said we'd take them back to ours. So we brought them back to use."

"You need to be careful and take more guns along doing that."

Hampt wrinkled his nose. "The rest were somewhere else."

"They could have come to their rescue. I don't aim to go home and tell May I let you kill yourself."

"Alright. I'll take more help next time, but we've got fourteen more horses. Two that you got to mount on the other side."

"That was the good part. Better eat."

"Hampt," Liz said, "you did wonderful."

"Thanks, ma'am."

"I just don't want him killed," Chet said.

"I know, but he's such a big, wonderful bear. I see why May is so happy to have him."

"He does better for May than my brother ever treated her. He's great."

When they were alone, she asked, "Why did he treat her so badly?"

"He never beat her, he just married her to raise his kids. He spent hours working by himself on farm machinery; we didn't have a buggy, wagon, or farm implement that wasn't in top shape. We never lacked a fixed thing."

"Why?"

"He did that like some people drink. He lost his first wife having a baby girl. That event scarred him. It was like he couldn't find himself. He argued all the damn time about my decisions. Then he met May and eloped with her. Her parents disowned her. She had a prettier sister they just idolized and who could do no wrong. Poor May had a lot to deal with especially how to handle Dale Allen's kids. Heck, his oldest son, was a rebel and who his father ignored. Even those two little boys treed her."

"They made her cry?"

"Oh, yes. I had to get them to promise not to do that.

"Heck went to Kansas with his dad on that last drive. They shot Dale Allen. How he ever did it, I will never know, but Heck rode clear back to Texas to get me."

"He's the boy—"

"Yes, the one. We'd bought the big ranch and were headed back to move the family out there.

Stage robbers killed him, and when Marge got word, she came down there and saved me."

"And then some silly widow came looking for a golden horse."

Chet closed his eyes. "Best deal I ever made in my life."

"You are easy pleased." She laughed and shook her head.

"Oh, darling, but there is no telling what will happen next."

"Yes, there is. You will be off on another adventure. I hope I can ride along."

"You were married how long?"

"Three long years. He had about built the *hacienda* when he took me for his wife. Oh, I just knew when I married him that I would have a hundred children for him."

"A hundred?"

"Well, lots. But none came.

"A doctor had us do many things. None worked. He did not know why, so we saw another. He didn't know, either. Then, one day, bandits shot my husband, in our own *casa.* That was a very bad day in my life. I was upstairs, dressing to go to an occasion in the village. There were shots. I knew they were happening down in the entranceway of the house.

"He shouted, 'Stay up there.' Then more shots in the house. I took my pistol and rushed out. I met one bandit on the stairs and shot him in the chest. Then another shot at me from the foyer. I steadied the pistol and shot him, too. He died also, but beside him, in a pool of his own blood, was my dearest husband—dead.

"I didn't know which one killed him. But I shot both of them again in the head until I ran out of bullets."

"Oh, my God, Liz, that was horrible."

"Do you know on that day in the Santa Cruz River with me wading in that water, that whole terrifying day of his death evaporated. Like a flash of lightning, it faded for the first time, and then you washed my feet and I thought about the Christ-like thing you were doing to me."

"I see why you did that. In reality, all I wanted to do was get my hands on you."

"And when you could have, you gripped the edge of that bathtub so hard your knuckles were white."

"Oh, girl—that was a great day."

"I felt sixteen again."

"Me, too. I better do some checking. We need to see if everything is ready for tomorrow. I won't be long."

"Take care. I will go to the tent."

He kissed her forehead and went to find Yeager. He found the man squatted on his heels by the chuck-wagon wheel. "Did he tell you about tomorrow?"

"He grumbled about it. But he done told me we'd stay over a day here for the cattle to gain weight."

"We need more meat on them. We will gain it going slow up north."

"I savvy what you plan. I'll check things tomorrow, too."

"Good. No Indians today."

"And the big man he bring in mo' horses. He be a big man alright. I never hear of any one steal an Injun's hoss before. Dey usual steals dee other folks' hosses."

"Hampt's alright. See you in the morning."

They turned in early. Sure was nice to have her along. He wouldn't ever forget the worst day in her life, either, and knew the reason why she'd never told him about it before. Whew, that much bloodshed had to have been a real sorry day in anyone's life.

And here they were, honeymooning again, and her laughter ringing out. Wasn't hard to tickle her, that was for sure.

CHAPTER 14

Three more grimy, dust-eating days north, and in the early pre-dawn hours, Jesus woke them. His words whispered in Chet's ear, jarred both him and Liz into instant awareness.

"Apache Joe brought the horse herd into camp. Said he heard too many daytime bird calls out there in the darkness."

"Smart."

"They are waking everyone up. Hampt is organizing things. We figure they want our horses."

"Yes." Chet had his pants on by then. "Liz, you get in the chuckwagon and stay low. Keep your head down."

"I'll be fine."

"Do as I say."

"Yes, boss man."

There was lots of activity going on. Hampt ordered his gunmen to spread out on the ground, either kneeling or flat. "Shoot horses if you can't shoot Indians."

Yeager doubled his herd guards to try to hold the cattle, when all hell broke loose.

"Don't blow that trumpet, it might spook the cattle. We don't need to run them down."

"What will they do when they come screaming in here?" Decker asked.

"We'll have to shoot them."

"I hope to hell it works."

Chet got in Decker's face. "So do I. They don't want the cattle; they want the horses."

"How many you figure?"

"Indians are strange. They may fight, they may not. The cavalry had been hounding them. I don't think there are any big camps out here like years before."

Dawn became a pink rim out east. A roar went up and the drum of many horse hooves came from the east. At first, he thought maybe he was wrong, but there were a lot of them coming. The first volley of shots laid down several attacking riders and horses. The screaming, shot horses thrashing on the ground made it more difficult for them to come back through. But they did charge again and had hell coming through the field. But the endless rifle shots blocked that charge and not an Indian came within seventy yards. By then, most of the warriors' horses were shot or the rider shot off of it.

In full daylight, the sun's great ball blasted his shooters' eyes, so Hampt led the charge on foot at the Indians. They shot wounded Indians and horses until they were on the eastern brink of the rise. Then more shots rattled the air.

Chet rode around the far side and found the herd riders had the cattle herd secure. A lot of cattle were on their feet, but they'd held them. He met Yeager on the west side and shook his hand. "Great job."

"No. Hampt and his shooting done did that."

He agreed. "But your men held the herd."

"I be pretty proud of us all."

"Me, too."

"We'd never done dis wit'out you. That bank man he must of heard what my old daddy say, 'Don't you's send me no gawdamn boy when I's needs a man.' Chet Byrnes, you be dee man."

"Thank the men every chance you get. They deserve it."

Yeager promised he would.

Chet rode back to the chuckwagon and dismounted.

Liz climbed down off the wagon. "Me and the cooks are unharmed."

He hugged her and swung her in a circle.

"We did this one, darling. We did it."

Someone had taken Hampt his horse. In the midst of it all, he was giving orders. The men were making certain all the Indians and shot-up horses were dead.

They also were taking guns, arms, knives, and trophies.

"There's several good saddles out there that these men can use," Hampt told him. "No doubt, stolen from white men."

"Have them gather them. We'll have a saddle lottery for the men, to see who gets to ride them."

Hampt agreed and sent more men to get horses to pull the saddles off the slain horses.

"We stay here today?" No Ling Ling asked.

"Yes, but after breakfast, we'll move your camp over there." Chet pointed north a ways. "I know the buzzards will be bad."

Mott came about then and the head cook yakked at him.

"What does that damn crazy chink need now?" he asked Chet.

"After breakfast, move him north a good quarter mile. There will be too many buzzards around here in a short while."

Mott wiped his face and neck with a rag. "Boy, that was a helluva fight. That Hampt be some Injun fighter."

Chet agreed.

Hampt rode back. He was holding a great eagle-feather headdress that about drug the ground. "Miss Liz, this trophy belongs at the Preskitt Ranch house. I don't know his name who wore it, but he won't need it where he is now."

"Why, Hampt Tate, I will be honored to have it. That is perfect."

Chet agreed. "We can hang it on the bows in the chuckwagon for now."

Some returning men set their rifles down and volunteered to put it up. Coffee was soon ready for everyone. They brought in twelve good to usable saddles. Liz set out to make raffle tickets while they drank coffee at the host table.

When Decker and Yeager joined them, Chet told

them about the raffle. They thought that was a good thing to do, and told Liz the headdress was great. Cole, Lou, and Jesus joined them.

"The rest of them are gone," said Cole. "My last count, eighteen Indians were left dead. We have nine good horses. We collected about twenty rifles. Ones don't work, we bent the barrels and busted off the stocks. Nine pistols and a big crate of knives, tomahawks, and hatchets. Lots of gunpowder and ammo. There's a like-new .52 caliber Sharps buffalo gun and a dozen cartridges. I figure they got that from a buffalo hunter they caught out here."

"That should be Hampt's trophy," Chet said.

"Yes." Liz applauded. The hangers-on agreed.

The first hungry, sky-drifting buzzard must have sent a signal up. Hundreds of them soon glided in, ignoring the nearby people. They began their clumsy stalking about, fighting, and trying to be the first to peck the eyeballs out of the dead. That was their delicacy and they sought them before anything else.

Only four of the men were scratched, and none seriously wounded. Decker told them when they finished eating to go relieve the herders and scatter them out for the day. They'd move ten miles the next day.

"You men did good today. I won't ever doubt you again. I thought we'd be slaughtered," Decker said. "You saved us. Why, I never saw such a bunch attack a train like they did."

"Decker, your men did that job, not me."

"These bucks be Comanche?"

Chet nodded. "Yes. Back in Texas, they took two of my brothers and a sister. I don't have much use for them."

Decker nodded. "You evened the score today."

"No, you can't ever take a life for one taken. Humans are too valuable for that."

"Move these dozen saddles to our camp," Liz said. "We will draw tonight for them."

Hampt said, "Don't fret none. Soon as we eat, I'll see they are taken up there."

They went northeast the next day. Decker grumbled, but Chet ignored him. The cattle had begun to fill out. Some of the range they stopped to graze had gotten rain earlier, and the green grass mixed in with the dry forage made a rich mix and their sides began to swell. Orderly watering of the stock, driving them short distances, and finding better graze, all meant improved conditions for putting weight on the mixed-age steers.

Lou took him aside. "You ready to duck into Kansas for a few *playas*?"

"How far in?"

"Not too far. But there's some good water over there. No one lives out here. We've been scouting and haven't seen a Kansas lawman."

"These cattle are doing great."

"The water is a short run."

"Let's do it and say we lost our compass."

They slowed the drive to a crawl, making five miles a day, watering, and resting. In a week, they only made forty miles, but the cattle were recovering. They stayed three days on the Arkansas River close to the western trail, then they went north. They were getting close to Nebraska.

One afternoon, when they were camped for the cattle to graze, three men wearing suits rode up. Decker came by and told Chet they looked like trouble.

He agreed, seated outside his tent. "Tell every man not to shoot them. I'll handle it."

A big man under a wide-brim Stetson Boss of the Plains hat rode up. "Whose camp is this?"

"What do you need to know?"

"You the ramrod?"

"I am. Who are you?" Chet rose from his chair to face him.

"My name's Trumbo Rodman. I'm a chief of the Kansas State Police."

"What are you looking for?" Chet asked.

"Trespassers."

"Oh, you've been tracking them?"

"I have been for days, and you have been trespassing."

"No, I'm in Colorado."

"You have violated the acts of the Kansas legislature driving Texas cattle through our state."

Chet noticed that many of the cowboys had quietly come to sit on the ground nearby with their Winchesters on their laps. Rodman started frowning. "I am a state policeman."

"In Kansas. You're not a lawman in Colorado."

"Why have all these blacks got rifles?"

"Comanche tried us. We turned them back."

"What the hell does that mean?" A cross look swept his face.

"Tell your men to sit real tight on their horses. These men of mine are all experienced Indian fighters. They don't take any prisoners."

"You threatening me?"

"Mister, you're a simple camp robber in Colorado at this time."

"I'm—"

"How far is Kansas from here? A couple miles?"

"I don't know."

"I guess there isn't a fence. I never saw a sign for the past fifty miles. Why don't you ride back to Kansas?"

"I'm going to arrest you and your men for trespassing."

Chet dropped his head and shook it. "No, you don't understand. You're not in Kansas. You try to arrest us where you have no authority and I will say you were camp robbers and we killed you in the act."

"You can't do that."

"Lower your voice. Those boys killed Comanche 'cause they tried to rob our camp. All I have to say is 'shoot them,' and you'll be dead. Now, get back across that line. Walk back to your horse and mount up and go back to Kansas."

Chet rose and held out his hands to stay his crew. "These good men are riding back to Kansas. No one has got hurt."

"You ain't seen the last of me."

He walked him to his horse and the lawman mounted.

"I better have."

When the three men turned their mounts to the east, Chet reached up over his head like he had a gun and pulled the trigger. His men mimicked his action with their rifles, and their shots made the riders' horses near bolt out from under them as they tore off for Kansas. The crew cheered and laughed.

"That was more dangerous than the Comanche," Liz said, holding his arm, standing beside him.

"Not when you have an army."

"I guess we better stay in Colorado till we get to Nebraska."

Chet agreed. "We better."

"Sorry I got you in that situation," his scout Lou said, riding up and dismounting.

Chet shook his head. "We're moving north in the morning. Things are fine."

Lou nodded.

Decker had his arms folded and nodded. "They really be that dumb?"

"They had no authority over here. But most folks listen to them and go in and pay a fine. I didn't have time for them today."

Decker snorted out his nose and slapped his pants legs. "You sure be dee man."

"I want Lou and Cole to head for Nebraska and find us some pasture, so we can sort these cattle into three classes. Yearlings, two-year-olds, and the big steers."

"You ain't going to just sell them?"

"No. Those big ones are a premium class. Midwest farmers want them to fatten. The twos can be wintered easy and sold next year. Those yearlings will require lots of feed and are two years from turning a profit."

"Why, we be weeks sorting them."

"I don't think that long. No matter, we need to sort them."

Decker left him, shaking his head. Yeager caught Chet later. "What be happening?"

"I told him when we get up there we'll have to sort the cattle into the three classes."

"That will be work."

"My share of this deal depends on the total sale. I want the most out of them."

"It pays everyone's wages, huh? When we be down dere, I never thought I'd get a penny fur dis job. Now it looks better, we can sort cattle."

"We'll get them sold."

Yeager agreed.

The next day, Lou and Cole went to find or rent sorting ground. That day, the cattle buyers rode out to meet them and frowned at the mixed herd.

"We'll sort them when we get there," Chet assured them.

The next day a man with three cowboys rode out and spoke to him.

"Rusty Harold. These are my boys. Not sons, my cowboys." He laughed.

"This is my wife, Liz. I'm Chet Byrnes. What can I do for you?"

Harold removed his hat. "Ma'am, *buenos dias.*"

"I speak English, Mister Harold. Nice to meet you."

"I was a little homesick for some *el español.*"

She rattled some Spanish greeting off and he laughed. "Thanks. Made me homesick already. How did you two get hooked up?"

"She stopped at a ranch where I stayed to buy a Barbarossa horse in southern Arizona."

"You from Arizona?"

"From Texas first."

The man narrowed his eyes in deep concentration. "You have some Barbarossa horses?"

"Yes."

"You have her and some of them, too. That makes you a real lucky man."

"I am. You looking for cattle?"

"They said you had yearlings?"

"I have."

"When you sort them off, I'd like to bid on them. We have a helluva lot of hay and grass."

"If my count they gave me is right, that could amount to a thousand head."

"You said the count?"

"A friend of mine in Texas asked me to find these cattle and get them up here."

Harold frowned some more.

"They were stranded down there in the panhandle."

"I came up here two years ago. Did Kansas catch you across their line?" Harold asked.

"They rode over in Colorado and accused me."

"You pay a fine?"

"No. They had no authority over there."

"You're right, but they buffalo a lot of guys." Harold pushed his hat up some and laughed. "I really can't believe your beautiful wife has ridden all this way and looks that pretty."

"She is a trooper. Join us for supper. We can feed your men."

"Thanks, we will. Where did you say you ranched?"

"All over Arizona," she said. "He has many ranches in the territory."

"Mrs. Byrnes, do you have a sister?"

"No. I was an only child."

"Damn, there go my chances."

She laughed and bumped her shoulder into Chet. "Hear that?"

"I am listening. But I have the Barbarossa horses, too."

She agreed. "He does have some good ones."

"He must have some good foremen, too?"

"Oh, yes. I have a *hacienda* myself in Sonora. But he has some grand ones."

"You two just met?"

"Six months ago. I heard this man who had sold some of those horses was at a ranch below Tubac, which is south of Tucson. I stopped with a coach and my entourage, and here was this big guy who ignored my pleas to sell me one."

They all laughed.

"He had lost his wife and I fit in." She shrugged her shoulders. "And he has this huge extended family."

They all laughed.

"Well, you ever need a roof, come see me. Are you from Texas?" he asked Chet.

"I went out there so I could find her," Chet teased. "No, my family was involved in a bitter Texas feud in the hill country. So I sold out and have been busy ever since."

"Those feuds were real bad."

"Yes, we thought the Comanche were bad, but feuds were much worse."

Harold agreed. They talked about cattle prices and conditions. Later when Chet and Liz were by themselves, Chet told her she had a place to go if she left him.

She laughed. "He is a big flirt like you are. I am not leaving you."

"I know that. I can't believe he does not have a woman."

"She hasn't come by yet."

He hugged her. "As long as you don't leave me, I don't care."

"Don't doubt about me, *hombre.* I never thought I'd see so much country. I like Nebraska. It has lots of wonderful grass, too."

"Cattle growers can see that at a glance."

"Yes, yes. But I fear it gets cold up here."

"I bet it does. I will take you to town in a few days, unless you want to go and the guys can take you."

"I am fine. I enjoy sorting cattle."

"I don't want you to be bored to death."

'That will never happen in my life with you."

Cole and Lou made a land rental of two sections

of grass on the Platte River for three hundred dollars a month. Chet hoped in a month they'd be finished and ready to return home.

"We could've rented it cheaper for a year," Cole teased him.

"No, thanks, you two did great. We'll move up there and start sorting in a day."

Hampt and Lou rode over to look it over and figure out how to use it.

Traffic from potential buyers picked up. Chet figured out there weren't many cattle sent up there that had not been sold. That could mean he had some advantages in marketing these cattle, but they were in mid-August. He wanted to be home before winter set in, and they were a long ways from home by horseback.

He wired Sam Severs at the First National Bank in San Antonio that they were at Ogallala. The cattle were in an improved condition, and they would sort and sell them in the next two weeks, if they could.

In reply, Severs said he was relieved and to keep him informed.

THANK GOD FOR YOU CHET BYRNES.

He also wired everyone in Arizona they had made it to Nebraska and were planning to sell the cattle in the next few weeks. Monica answered that she, Anita, and Rhea were all burning candles for their safe return. Tom said the ranches were doing fine. They even had some rain. May said she cried and prayed for all of them. She and the kids really missed Hampt.

Cattle sorting began. They had three teams to handle the divided herd. Several unemployed cowboys came by asking for work and Chet hired the best of them. So he had a dozen more real cattle sorters with them on the crew and things began to go faster.

Apache Joe knew the best cutting horses in his *remuda* and issued them to the best riders each morning. Hampt was in the center, with Cole and Yeager both taking on a herd. Things went fast and furious. Chet and Liz helped, too, plus met the cattle buyers and discussed how many cattle they expected to have for sale in the three herds.

"You think the split is about a thousand head in each bunch?" Wayne Bolt asked him, sitting a good using horse with them.

"They left south Texas with thirty-five hundred head. I took over control of the herd in the panhandle. Since then we've lost a few head."

"How come you took over this bunch?"

"No one could find them. They were out of horses, food, and water."

"They look pretty good today."

"Liz bought them all clothes. They were pretty shabby dressed."

Bolt laughed. "I can imagine that."

"You ready to bid on them?" Chet asked.

"Not serious. I planned to offer you twenty bucks a head."

Chet shook his head. "Those big steers are worth eighty dollars a head."

"Oh, no. More like forty."

"The twos are worth that."

"How high you got those yearlings?"

"Twenty-five a head."

"Oh, they're trash."

"Well, I am not taking that for them."

"I can see I can't buy your junk. I better go back to town."

"You have ten days to put a price on them. They'll be separated and ready by then."

Bolt shook his head. "Before this is over, you'll come and talk to me and take my prices. I bid forty, fifteen, and ten on them."

"Thanks, we'll see," Chet said.

His wife sounded mad when Bolt left. "Boy, he is conceited, isn't he?"

"Oh, just a cattle buyer, and they come in all forms. I have had my backside chewed off before because I didn't sell to a cheaper buyer."

"Really?"

"Oh, they will do anything."

"I'll be glad to get the sale over."

"I agree. We will and head home."

"Wonderful." She threw her hands in the air. Then she hugged his arm. "I still appreciate you having me along."

They lost a good horse that day. A wreck with a wild steer, and the horse and steer both had to be destroyed. The white cowboy was alright, but Chet figured he'd be sore in the morning. The weeks dragged by and the cattle were at last sorted.

Two days later, he met with the buyers in the Elkhorn Saloon at ten in the morning. His wife shopped for some things she wanted, while he held court in the near empty saloon.

"The top bid on the big steers is seventy-eight dollars. Anderson and Schmell have that bid. Any more bids?" He waited for any move—none. "I will sell those big steers to them."

Both men waved from where they sat.

"Two-year-old steers sell for sixty-eight dollars. Hiemer, Cook, and Donaldson get them. Rusty Harold bid twenty-five dollars on the yearlings. No more bids, he gets them." He paused. "Beers are on me. Thanks."

The cattle processing required four more days. The sales amounted to one hundred ninety-six thousand nine hundred and fifty dollars. Chet's share amounted to over forty-nine thousand. After payroll expenses and the costs were deducted from Severs's account, Chet sent him the bank's share to Texas via Wells Fargo.

He told his three men he would pay each of them three thousand apiece when they got back to Preskitt. He wouldn't listen to their protests that they didn't need it, and Liz backed him.

Severs wired him back.

I THANK GOD. THE BANK DID NOT LOSE A SINGLE DIME. THE MAN WHO WE MADE THE LOAN TO HAD BEEN SHOT IN

ROUND ROCK IN A CARD GAME BEFORE DECKER GOT OUT OF TEXAS. IT MADE FOR A LONG LONG SUMMER. THANK YOU AND ALL YOUR EFFORTS. SAM

"We don't need to talk about the money part around the others. They may think they earned a share," he told Cole, Jesus, and Hampt. They all agreed with him.

Later, Liz asked how much he had left.

"Forty thousand."

"Ten thousand a month, right?" she asked. "You were well paid."

"Hey, I haven't paid you yet."

She hugged him. "I loved it. You don't owe me anything. You know that. Well, let's ride home. That banker should be glad that you sorted them; they'd never have made that much money otherwise. I heard that Bolt's offer."

"It isn't always getting there with cattle, but how you sell them, that make things work."

He dreaded the long trail going home, but he left the horses and wagon for Decker to sell and split the amount they brought with his crew. They'd been paid the money promised them, besides his gift.

His outfit crossed west to Denver, and Chet took Liz to an opera and some other highlights that really made her days spent there. Down the road, they went to Santa Fe and enjoyed the festive spirit of *fandangos* for a few nights. Chet thought his wife would bust over their stay there. She attended church every morning and they danced till the last song each evening.

His wife was wading in the Santa Cruz again in his eyes. When she was high on things like the *fandangos*, he loved watching her. Then, back in the saddle again. They rode on, crossing arid western New Mexico, but the nights grew cooler and the days shortened. They stopped a day and reshod some of their horses in Continental on the Great Divide, then went on to Gallup. By the time they got there, his herders would already be back at the Windmill from their September delivery.

Five days later, they met an excited Susie who tore out of her house to hug Liz and him. They had a great reunion, telling her about the long ride. Susie also hugged Cole, Jesus, and Hampt.

Chet heard Susie ask Liz if she was pregnant.

His wife's answer was, "No, but we haven't given up."

He went off listening to them laughing.

That night in bed, she asked if they were going home or staying at the Verde.

"Oh, we better stop here for the next night. You and I, and Jesus, can talk to Sarge. Hampt and Cole will leave early for home, and I don't blame them. If you weren't here, I'd have rode all night to get back to you."

She hugged him tight. "And I'm so glad I got to see so many things and places. But after I first saw that tramp camp of those black cowboys and those gaunt cattle, I said to myself, 'What will my poor husband ever do with this mess?'"

"It wasn't a picture of paradise, was it?"

"That little man in San Antonio, who wears those low shoes that your two men talk about, owes you a lot more than you charged him. I thought you were robbing him when you first told me what you planned to charge him. But he would not have ten cents on his dollars you got him if you hadn't straightened it all out."

"Oh, everyone worked on it."

"Everyone worked, but Hampt made them soldiers. I know you have good men, but they are like keys that all unlock different things. Cole and Jesus knew he was the man you needed, but they think like you do. The whole thing awed me. And taking me along was such an adventure. I will never forget." She was shaking in his arms. "I, of course, had seen lots of Mexico, but seeing that vast land was what Coronado saw when he came up here exploring, centuries ago. I read those reports and knew where I was in them."

"You never told me anything about that."

"I did not want anything to distract you. I saw the set in your jaw, the determination in your eyes. You could have run Decker off, but you simply pushed your points on him. You have that aura, but you also have been the boss since you were a boy. I am so glad to be your mate."

"You knew what they were singing in that opera?"

"Oh, yes," she said in agreement. "Spanish and Italian are not that different. Oh, I loved it. My first husband would never have thought to take me there. He was never anything but nice to me, but the opera, that was so great for me to attend. Only you would have thought to take me there."

"The only person who didn't see it, who would have loved it, was May."

"Oh, yes. She is such a treasure and I never even thought about her and the opera."

"You will someday know these people like I do."

"I listen. Your sister asked me tonight if I was pregnant."

"I heard her."

She whispered, hardly able to keep from laughing, "Let's go to work on that."

"I love you, Elizabeth. I really do."

"Thank God."

Chapter 15

The two married men left to join their wives in the early dawn. Chet had them on fresh horses and told them not to kill them, and to change to fresh ones at the Verde Ranch. They thanked him and galloped off under the waning stars.

"I bet if it had been me, I'd have rode all night to rejoin my wife."

Jesus touched Liz's arm to get her attention. "He would have, too."

They laughed and went back to have the rest of their breakfast and talk with Susie and Sarge.

"Well, I know a young lady who will be glad to see you," Liz said to Jesus.

"I will be glad to see her, but we drew straws last night for who went home this morning."

"Aw, hell, this close, you could of gone," Chet said, shaking his head.

"You are also the good guy," Liz said.

"You can tell her that," Jesus said.

"I will. You two guys are rascals. You two aren't

going to leave him unprotected, despite all the women in the world."

"Oh, we are serious about our jobs."

"And about Anita?"

"We will see. She is an excellent lady, but I am not him." He pointed at Chet.

"Oh, Jesus, you are him. You have rode with him long enough that I see lots of Chet Byrnes in you."

"Maybe your eyes are full of sand."

"No, I have slept most of that out. You can't deny both you and Cole think and do things like he does. That is great. I will light a candle for your success with her."

"That is real sweet of you."

"I think you made him blush," Chet said.

She caught up with Jesus and pounded him on the back. "She would be lucky to have a man like you."

Jesus about melted.

"What is happening?" Susie asked, ready to refill their coffee cups.

"Liz is playing cupid with Jesus."

"With Anita?"

Chet nodded and winked at her.

"I thought she was a lovely girl the night I met her. We shared a bedroom."

"She is very nice," Jesus said.

"Well, it is interesting." Then being sure they were alone, Susie leaned across the table. "How much did you make?"

"Tell her," Chet said.

"He paid each of the three men three thousand

dollars apiece. And he is putting in the ranch account forty thousand dollars."

Susie put her hands to her face in shock. "That's my brother."

Liz agreed.

"We did well and like we always said, we'll need that money someday," Chet said.

Susie quickly agreed. "He has been doing this for years and that's why we are all so well set up here in Arizona."

"We better make more coffee. All the men are coming in and will want to hear the entire story," Liz said, seeing them through the window.

They relaxed at Susie's the rest of the day. That evening, they had a parley with the crew at the Windmill Ranch. Chet told the story to all of them.

"You didn't bring any black ones back to help us?" one hand asked.

"No, but I bet Robert could have used a black guy named Mott. They brought us two teams of big wild mules out from Tascosa to the camp, and they were all Cole and Jesus could handle. Tell them, Jesus, about Mott."

"He was a big *hombre.* Thick arms. Real quiet. He had those mules unhitched and trace chains up on one team. He said, 'Jack,' real quiet. Mules not hear him. He said it over. Mule still not hear him. When he said it again, he cut hair off the mule on the right side with the check line. That one heard him. Whoa. He held him down and did that same to the one on the left. Hair flew and Jack number two knew his name. Then he drove them around like they were Shetland ponies."

Jesus drew back his arm with an imaginary line in hand and said, "Whoa, Jack. Them mules had improved hearing."

Everyone laughed.

Chet spoke up, "No one asked me for a job before we left Nebraska. They were so tired of driving cattle, they probably never want to see one again."

Then they ate supper and harassed Jesus some more.

The next day at the big Verde Ranch, Lea and her outfit had things in hand at the big house. She made them a big supper and told Liz she really enjoyed the job and the house. Chet hugged her before they left and told her what a good job they did.

They had a big time repeating the cattle drive story with Tom and his crew.

The following morning, the three went to Preskitt. Monica had word they were coming, no doubt from Cole. When they arrived, she stood on the porch with her hand up to shade the sun from her eyes, watching for them. Beside her stood Rhea, holding Adam, and Anita.

Chet hitched his horse and Liz shooed him on. "I can dismount myself. Go hug that boy of yours. I am next."

Rhea handed Adam to him and he kissed him and rocked him. His son had become so stout in his absence, he couldn't believe it.

"He is so strong," he said to Rhea.

"He is all boy, huh?" She beamed.

"Sure is." He kissed her on the forehead. "You have done wonderful."

She blushed.

He hugged Monica next. "All is well here?"

"Yes, peaceful and quiet. Now all hell breaks loose, huh?"

"I hope not."

"It will. It always does. You are home."

When he looked back, Liz had Adam and was clucking to him. He smiled and laughed. "I brought her back with me."

"Well, I hoped you would," Monica said. "The poor girl is probably bushed from riding that far and long."

"No, but her old pants don't fit her. Any news from Roamer, JD, or Reg?"

"They seem to be making it fine. Oh, Bonnie is going to have a baby."

"I bet Jenn is excited."

"She is, indeed, very excited."

"You hear that, Liz?"

"Yes. This boy has really grown. I am excited. He will soon be walking, Rhea says." Liz swung the baby around and made him laugh.

"I expected that; he's a Byrnes."

"Oh, go on. He's quite a little man."

"Does he have an aura yet?"

"No, but I bet he has one by his teens."

"Oh, I have a letter for you from Mexico," Monica said to Liz.

"Thanks," she said, and handed Rhea the boy, then took it.

"Who sent it?" Chet asked.

"My superintendent, Manuel."

She opened the envelope and took the pages to the lamp. "He says hi to everyone in Arizona. He is writing to tell me about how things have gone since I came up here. The wine business is strong and doing well. They have a good harvest of grapes and he has little of the old stock of wines left in our warehouse, so things are fine.

"In the spring, he is marrying a young lady name of Rickola who is a member of a prominent Sonora family. He hopes I will bring you, Chet, to his wedding, and everyone misses me. Wine sales are very important for my *hacienda,* so he must be handling things quite well—"

Chet handed her his bandanna because she was about to cry. "See, my lovely wife, you aren't quite as tough as you thought you were."

Then he hugged her. "Write and tell him we will be there, and we'll bring a Barbarossa colt as their wedding gift."

"Really?"

"I said so, didn't I?"

"You people don't know," she said to those assembled in the kitchen. "This big *hombre* took me to an opera in Denver coming home. We went to two orchestra symphonies and a play. Then we stopped in Santa Fe and danced our boots off at some *fandangos.* This has not all been shooing cows to Ogallala."

Everyone laughed.

Chet rose up and stretched his near-stiff frame.

"Family, I want to sleep for forty-eight hours. Where is Raphael?"

"He went over with two of his men to help Vincent at Hampt's place this morning and has not returned. Something about squatters on that Ralston place you bought."

"If he's not back by morning, I better go check on him."

"Hampt should already be home?" Liz asked.

"Yes, and he can handle any squatters. But the matter must be serious for Raphael not to be back."

Monica agreed.

He'd figure it out early in the morning. "Come on, Liz, I want to sleep in my own bed one night."

She hugged his waist and looked smug-like up at him. "You crazy *hombre.* I am with you about that. But I want to go over there with you in the morning."

"Yes, alright." He surrendered. "I'm sorry we have so many tales to tell, and that we did that much riding. But it turned out very successful for the ranch."

They went off to bed.

"It is nice to be back," she said, undressing in the dim lamplight.

He stopped and hugged her around the waist. "I know it was tough, but when you have men like mine to help there isn't much they can't get done."

"But many people don't know how to teach people to lead others," she said.

He agreed and rocked her back and forth. "I don't know anything about these squatters, but we'll find out in the morning. Some of these people think they can take what they want."

"Why not?" She smiled smugly at him and slipped under the covers.

"What do you mean?"

She scooted over under the covers to kiss him. "I did that with you."

"Damned if you didn't." In each other's arms, they both laughed.

He would never win.

Chapter 16

They rose before the sun came up on a nice early fall morning. Everyone was eating breakfast with Monica, Anita, and Rhea, when Jesus joined them. Monica waved him over and fixed him a plate.

He thanked her.

"Cole is in town?"

"I didn't send him word. I figured we could handle it."

Chet agreed and went back to eating his eggs, ham, and biscuits. "He needs some time off with his wife. You hear anything about these squatters?"

"Some of the crew thinks they wouldn't leave when Vincent told them to. He sent for Raphael to come help him. They didn't know we were coming home last night."

Chet agreed. "Strange that he didn't come back last night."

"He is a home man," Jesus said. "Hampt is home, too. He should have gotten there yesterday. Him and Cole got fresh horses at Camp Verde. They split up on top of the mountain, and Hampt went south and Cole rode west to Preskitt."

Chet agreed. "In a few hours, we'll know how things went."

"I have a nice dun horse saddled for you," Jesus said to Liz.

"Thanks."

"And some cranky bucking horse for me," Chet said, buttering a new biscuit.

The table residents all laughed.

"Someone has to ride them," Jesus said, never looking up. "You get them rode."

"I'm just picking on him. We don't have to ride sixty miles today or drive cattle. All we need to see about are some squatters, and we should wind that up in a short while."

"Amen," Liz added. "It is so good to be back here. It was sure hot and dusty on that trail. I missed the mountains and here."

"On top of that, she never complained one time on that trip. Bad as it was."

"That's right. She was like a tiny flame that kept us all from griping," Jesus said.

"Well, we missed you three," Monica said.

"So did we, miss all of you," Chet said, downing his coffee. "We better ride out of here."

They left the yard in a long trot. Chet's horse never bucked and they made good time going across country to the east ranch.

There was a congregation in Hampt's yard when they arrived. At a distance, Chet spotted the familiar *sombrero* of his Valley Ranch foreman, and wading out of the crowd of men came Hampt.

"What's happening?" Chet asked, and swung down.

"They shot at Vincent and wounded another cowboy, but they ain't bad hurt. The squatters took over that old home place near the Verde River on the Ralston property. Vincent went down there with Buck Eaves and tried to be nice to them. He told them that was not an abandoned homestead, but deeded Byrnes property. I guess they scoffed at him. He came back and sent for Raphael to help him."

Raphael came out of the crowd and welcomed Chet home. "Glad you are here. Like Hampt said, he wasn't home yet when we went over there, and they started shooting at us. Vince and Buck both got small wounds. But they had women and children down there, and we didn't want them hurt, so we came back and saw to the wounded men. Hampt made it home, and we have been planning what to do."

"I guess we better go see about them. Who are they?"

"Yates is their name," Hampt said. "They drifted in here way before you bought it. They've kept to themselves pretty well. Must have been there for a while. They were settled in. Them Ralston cowboys probably never checked on them, so they think they've got some kinda squatters' rights."

Hampt whispered to Chet, "I think one or two of their women might have traded favors for the rent with that bunch we run off."

He nodded at the gathered men. "Is this the party going to move them today?"

"We aim to," Hampt said.

"Chet Byrnes, you better not ride out of here without hugging and giving me a kiss." May came hurrying through the riders and men. "Hi, Liz. You going, too?"

"I go everywhere he lets me."

"The cattle drive didn't hurt you. You look fresh this morning."

"May, I am happy anywhere he is."

"Nice you brought Hampt back. Thanks. We've been in a mess here without him." She hugged Chet and kissed his cheek. "You be careful. That bunch will shoot at you."

"I'm always careful."

"Not always, but close to that. Lord, we wouldn't know what to do next without you."

He kissed her forehead and shook his head at her. "I better get rid of these folks. We'll be back."

He shook hands with a few neighbors who had joined them and they set out. Liz rode beside him.

"Think they will fight?"

"They did yesterday, huh?"

"Two men shot. Things must have gotten tough. What will you do today?"

"Try to talk to them."

"Don't you become number three."

He reined the big bay in closer. "We'll just have to see what we can do. I should arrest them for shooting those two men, but if they leave, I won't have to support their families while they're in jail."

His wife shook her head. "Oh, my, I fear this will be some event."

"You have to think about those things sometimes."

"What if they won't listen and start shooting right away?"

"In that case, we shoot it out. We have more guns and ammo than they have. But I don't want women and children hurt if we can avoid it."

"How far away is it?"

"I expect two hours anyway."

Hampt reined up on his left. "I think I could have handled this. But I'm glad you're here. There were a few rumors about them that I should have checked. I planned to when we finished roundup, but we left for Texas so fast. I don't think other than a cowboy or two gathering cattle, we'd been that far over there. I didn't know where your line was, and if it was a homestead deal."

"No problem."

"While we were up there with the herd, May read the land description and decided it was our land. Vincent and another hand rode over there and told them they were trespassing. They didn't take him serious, I guess. Just before I returned, he went back and they went to shooting and hit him and Buck."

"What are they doing over there?"

Hampt shook his head. "Probably eating our beef."

"Probably," Chet agreed.

They rode, headed for the cottonwood tops in the distance that lined the Verde far below. The juniper country spread out on the east slopes of the mountain beneath them. His picture of that range was what he expected—eaten down. Maybe selling off all the culls and moving two hundred head of cows to Reg would let the range recover. It needed to.

When a single streak of distant smoke cut the azure sky, Chet knew they were closing in on the place. He told Liz he'd be back and swung out to talk to one of Hampt's men who'd been there before.

"Herb, did you ride over here with them?"

He reined his horse over to Chet's and they rode side-by-side down the dim tracks. The fortyish-year-old ranch hand nodded. "Yes, but we never figured they'd shoot at us like they did."

"How many had guns?"

"Three or four. I'm not sure. But Vincent was hit. I caught his horse and we got the hell out of there. Leaving there, Buck got another bullet that grazed him. It's a wonder they didn't blast us all away."

"Maybe we better split up and not ride straight in there?"

"Yes."

"What are you thinking?" Hampt asked as he joined him.

"We need to send Jesus around back with some men. The others rode straight in and got shot at, so we need to be careful."

Hampt agreed and Jesus joined them.

"Take about three men with you and circle that place. Herb, here, kind of knows the lay of the land, so take him and a couple of others. We don't need to ride in and get shot."

"Maybe we better eat first. May sent some fried pies," Hampt said.

"Pass them out. We'll take a break. Feed Herb and

his men first, and let them get around to the back side."

Hampt nodded and held up his hand to stop the posse. "Take a break. We're sending some men to get around back in case they want to fight."

Everyone went to dismounting. Many handed their reins to someone close and went behind the junipers to relieve themselves. The whole crew was polite to Liz, though it was strange to some of them to have a woman around. Chet saw how different it was having a woman along, but he didn't care. They could be courteous to her. This was her ranch, too.

The fried pies were a big treat and cheered everyone up. When Chet figured Jesus and his men had a good start, they rode on toward the squatters. When he saw the place in his field glasses, he saw some women in the yard, but no men.

"What is it?" Liz asked, seeing his frown.

He made a face. "I think the men left them."

"Why?"

"They figured the law would be coming."

She nodded. "How will we know if they really left?"

"Ride down and challenge them."

"Don't you get shot," Liz said, her brow furrowing into a frown.

"We better make a flag," Chet said, and rode over to Hampt who fished out a white feed sack. The news spread among the dozen men drawn up on the rise. They were sending in a man with a truce flag—Hampt.

"That will beat getting any children hurt," Chet said.

Hampt rode in and spoke to four women in front

of the house. Even at that distance, their dark eyes kept checking on the posse. Their men were gone. He had another mess on his hands, about like the one he had on the ranch down south.

"Come on," he said to the posse. "We need to make plans to move this bunch. Who has two wagons to haul them to Preskitt?"

"I can provide them," Raphael said.

"I'll put Jesus in charge. We'll set them up there and they can find work. Save them eating Hampt's cattle all winter."

"What about their men?"

"Hampt will file charges against them for wounding his men. We'll let the sheriff arrest them, if he can. No need in us spending our money and men on those worthless trash."

Cole, seeing there was no threat, rode in and joined them.

He came back with Hampt. "Their men are gone?"

"Obviously. I want a list of the women's names, and Raphael has the wagons to haul them. I want Cole to rent them a place for three months in Preskitt. We'll furnish them enough food for three months. Then they are on their own."

Cole, Hampt, and Liz all nodded in agreement with him.

"Who's the leader?" he asked Hampt.

"Mrs. Taylor."

"You gonna shoot us?" asked the tall woman with stringy gray hair.

"No. There'll be two wagons here to move all of you to town. I'll furnish three months' food and rent. Then you must find work and be on your own. The law will want your men for shooting my men. The sheriff will, no doubt, arrest them if they come around. You'll not be my wards, nor will I be concerned after the initial food runs out. They'll move you there in the next few days."

"You that Byrnes guy?" she asked.

"Yes, ma'am, I am, and this is my land. Be ready to move."

"Why can't we stay here?"

"If you don't accept my offer, you can start walking. I consider it generous." He checked the big horse.

She dropped her shoulders. "We'll be packed up when your wagons come for us."

"Each of you, give your name to my man. I also want the names of your men and children. Cole, get that for me."

"Yes, sir."

He turned to the posse. "Thanks to all you men who rode with us. If Quarter Circle Z can ever help you, call on us. We'll return the favor."

Then he rode among them and shook their hands. He told Liz to find Jesus and tell him that they were going home. When he had the names gathered, Cole could come on with Raphael.

"Hampt, this matter, I think, is settled. Tell May and those kids I love them."

"Good to be home, boss man. I'll tell them."

Jesus joined them. "I told Cole and Raphael to come on when they got the names."

"Let's ride." He smiled at his wife, and the three

left at a lope. It would be late getting home, but they'd sleep at the Preskitt Valley Ranch in their own bed.

When they reined down to walk the horses, Liz said, "You are generous with them."

"Only for the children's sake. Those women can do what they want. The kids were my concern. I helped Indians when we first got here. Those little ones worried me more than the grown-ups."

"It was still nice of you to do that."

"Owning all these ranches sure has its drawbacks."

"I was proud of you. They may not appreciate you, but you are a fixer. What next?"

"Get my business going better."

"What does that include?"

"I need to find some more British-bred bulls. You and I may go on a search for them."

"With Cole and Jesus."

"Yes, ma'am."

Jesus chuckled. "Good. We still have work."

She turned in the saddle, laughing. "Yes, you do. I agree with Monica, he needs you two to look after him."

"How in the hell did I make it this far?"

"You didn't always head an operation the size of these ranches."

"Mrs. Byrnes, I will take them along, and you, too."

"Good. I am happy to be a part of this whole operation."

"We are, too," Jesus said.

"Jesus, tell Cole when he gets back tonight, he can go see his wife, if he wants. We won't leave tomorrow."

"Good," Jesus said. "I can do that. He won't be long behind us."

Liz gave Chet a firm nod. "That was nice of you. He will appreciate some time with her."

They put their mounts into a gallop. When they reached the ranch, the sun was low. They dismounted and two boys came to get their horses.

"You can stay at the house," Chet offered Jesus. "We have plenty of beds."

"Thanks, I'll do that."

Monica met them. "Have you three eaten anything?"

Chet smiled. "No, we've hurried to be back in your company."

"I have some food in the oven I planned to throw out if you didn't get here."

They laughed. Liz came to their aid. "Sounds wonderful. Thanks."

"Did you get them?" Monica asked.

"The men had run off," Liz said as the men washed up. "Raphael and Jesus will move the women to town tomorrow. Chet will feed them for three months."

"More folks to feed, huh?"

"They had several small children," Chet said. "How are Rhea and Adam?"

"Fine. Gone to bed. Anita is, too."

"We rode as hard as we could."

The roast beef, potatoes, and carrots were delicious and Monica sliced freshly baked bread for them. Anita must have awoken, and came down dressed nice. After supper, she and Jesus sat in the living room to visit.

Sipping coffee at the table, Chet and Liz smiled over the couple.

Cole and Raphael rode in, and Jesus came into the kitchen. "I'll tell Cole about our switch."

"That's fine."

Jesus went out to tell Cole he could handle the women the next day with Raphael, and Cole could go home. He came back laughing. "That wasn't hard, to send Cole to his house. He'll check in, or we can send him word."

Chet agreed and told Jesus what room he could sleep in that night.

When they went upstairs, Chet and Liz left Jesus and Anita standing close to each other in the living room.

When they were secure in the bedroom, Chet kissed her. "Nice to be in our own bed."

She stretched out. "I want to include, nice to be with you all day. I had never seen that country and it was interesting. I love your understanding of the range like you do. I look a lot closer at grass and things."

"I ever tell you I simply love your body?"

She went limp. "I wanted to tell you all the good things you do."

"How about making love?"

She drew a deep breath. "That would take all night."

He hugged her tight. "I love you."

CHAPTER 17

Come dawn, he was dressed and went down to watch the ranch operations. Raphael was giving orders for the day. Four men were going back with Jesus and two wagons to bring the women and children to town the next day. Already up and with the men, Jesus was quietly overseeing things.

"You get much sleep?" Chet asked him.

"Enough."

"What will I tell Anita?"

Jesus shrugged his shoulders. "I was going to talk to her before I left, if she was up." He looked at the back porch, but saw nothing.

"You stop by and see her before you go. I'll find a place in town for the women today." He motioned Jesus toward the house. "Eat breakfast, too."

"I will. Funny, about yesterday. We went up there to make war and ended up feeding them."

"Either way, we did the right thing."

"You are right."

Chet went to thank Raphael.

"Hello, Patron."

"Morning, I'm just Chet, remember?"

"Oh, I remember, but where I was raised we always called our boss patron."

"Chet will do just fine. You've done so well, going to help Hampt, and moving those women and kids. We'll have a *fandango* for everyone tomorrow night. Tell the women to get the food for it today and put it on my bill."

"Good, we need to laugh some."

"Liz and I need to find the women a place to stay today. Have the boys hitch us up a buckboard to use in a little while."

"Sure, Chet."

"That's better. I'm not much of a patron."

"Oh, yes, you are a good one. I love my job, and if you need anything, I can get it done."

"Raphael, I appreciate you. And remember, *fandango*, tomorrow night."

"Ah, *si*, like I said, we need one."

"You had breakfast yet?" he asked Jesus, who still hadn't left.

"No, I was going to arrange the wagons."

"Raphael has men to do that. Come and eat breakfast. Anita may be down by now."

"Sure, *mi amigo*, we can hitch the wagons," his foreman said.

"Oh, alright. I am coming."

"There they are," Monica said as the men entered the kitchen and she delivered Chet's plate of food to his place at the table.

"Boy, we are up early today," Liz said, entering the room. "I asked her if you had left me."

"Just arranging things," Chet said, and hugged her, then kissed her on the forehead.

He noticed Anita coming from the living room and acting backward. "Better get in here and eat with him. He was fixing to leave without breakfast."

She smiled and thanked him.

With Anita and Liz seated, he took his head chair. "We need to find a place for those women today. And Raphael and I decided we need a *fandango* tomorrow night."

"Can I do anything?" Liz asked.

Monica shook her head. "The ranch women are great at doing this. They are so proud when he calls for one, they bust their buttons to get it done."

"Can I go on the house search?"

"You bet," Chet said. "I noticed one of the ranch men hung your Indian headdress in the living room where you wanted it."

"Oh, how nice." She started to get up.

"We'll go look at it after breakfast," Chet said.

"They did that last night," Jesus said.

"It is a real trophy," Liz said.

"Well, it's better to have his hat in here, than him," Monica said.

They all laughed.

With things rounded up, Chet and Liz drove to town. Bo had a few places for them to look at. They found a big enough house to shelter the women and children and close enough to walk to town. He rented it for three months for sixty dollars. They would buy their food the next day. He'd get Raphael to bring a wagonload of firewood to cook and heat with. Then the women would be on their own.

Jenn was pleased to see the two of them for lunch. She fussed over them and chattered to Liz about her daughter, Bonnie, being with child, and writing her letters about the ranch operation down south.

Chet went by and talked to Ben about ordering four more mowing machines and dump rakes to expand his farming operation for the next spring season. While the men talked, Liz and Ben's wife, Kathrin, looked at some household things the store had just received in stock.

Going home in the buckboard, Liz spoke to Chet about Kathrin. "She and I had time to talk today. I knew part of the story about you saving her in Utah. But she gave me a lot more information today. You know she never got over you doing that for her. She still feels she owes her life to you. She said I was lucky to have you. You were so dedicated to Margaret, she knew there was no way for her to ever have you, but she told me I am lucky to have you, and she understood why—but if we ever needed anything, she wanted to help to repay you."

"I was only doing what I thought was right. She needed a break from her situation."

"Well, woman to woman, I got the big confession and I thanked her."

"Susie said once, 'Oh, my God, haven't you even noticed her? She's been there to help whenever you had a crisis.'"

"She and Ben will have another child next spring."

"I'm glad they have each other and a family."

She hugged him. "I am so glad I have you, *hombre.* You still plan in November to go to the south?"

"Yes, the citrus will be ripe. We can bring home a wagonload for Christmas. You want to go home then, too."

"Yes, if I don't risk your life."

"I'm not afraid of Mexico. My men will ride along. They are about out of federal funds for the Force, and Roamer has been promised a job with Wells Fargo. Whenever we shut things down, Shawn McElroy wants to come back home. The two younger Morales brothers have enough cattle to start a working ranch of their own at Tubac. Ortega and JD are getting along well, and the Rancho Diablo is working."

"Will you miss the law work?"

"No. Things are going better in the territory, law wise. I wish they'd leave the capital up here at Preskitt, but in the end, the compromise is for a new capital that will be in the valley. It'll be in the Salt River Valley at the village of Phoenix."

"Not Hayden's Mill and Ferry?"

"More politics are involved. Phoenix will get the dome someday."

"We are still going elk hunting?"

"You bet."

She squeezed his driving arm. "You are so good to this poor Mexican girl you found wandering in the desert."

"Oh, no, the princess who came in the white and red coach from Mexico, and I stole her in a wild, crazy fairy tale."

"What wonderful memories I have of our life. It has been a fairy tale."

"You ever have an ounce of regret, leaving your land and coming to mine?"

"Oh, no. I didn't need—even want—a man when we arrived at what I thought was a goat ranch. Surely, they had made a mistake bringing me there to find the man who owned such a high-priced yellow horse. This lawman who struck fear in the hearts of Mexican bandits would not be there. Then he was standing there with his hat at his side—I knew then I was at the right place. My heart hurt. I was a young girl all over again. I must have blushed that day."

He smiled and nodded. "Before I left for Tubac, I spoke about our life to Marge's spirit at the grave, and closed the book softly like a final chapter. But I needed no woman. I promised to raise her son."

"Here I was. You offered to show me a ranch, no strings attached. My mind was like a dust devil churning up the land, whirling me around about what to do. Then you dried my feet like Jesus did his disciples at the Last Supper." She laughed. "Somehow, I had to have this *grande hombre.*

"Oh, I was bold and shameless after that. I thought I may not win you, but I will do my damnedest to do that."

"That's how your husband did you when you met him?"

"Yes, but I was a very innocent girl back then, not

the owner of such a large *hacienda* of so many *hectares.* I wanted to escape with him. He was very much another man, but you two are so different. If he came by after I became a widow, I doubt he could have turned my head like he did the girl in me back then. Oh, his death was a greater loss in my life than the Grand Canyon you showed me."

"Two things I recall the most was the cinnamon you wore for perfume and the haystack."

"Oh, I told myself not to make love to you in a bed or hammock. You are a man of the outdoors—I could tell that camp not being fancy did not bother you. You were a man who easily slept outdoors. Where would a boy seduce me and remember it?

"I worried so much about what I did that day. My chances to impress you were desperately short on time. Would he think I was some whore? That was my conscience needling me. I saw you were a big man in frame, but in that bathtub you were a giant."

"Did that scare you?"

"Some, but I was so brazen by then, I had to have you—at any cost."

"What if I'd made you pregnant?"

"I never considered it. My luck at that had been so slim, I had written it off."

"No worry."

"It really would not have mattered—I would have had a piece of you."

He drew the team down to a walk. "I knew that yellow horse was a good investment, but I never figured he'd get me you."

"Bonnie told me about her life. How she ran off

to find a more exciting life and then regretted it, but she was in too deep to get out. And you trading those colts for her life."

"Even if she went back to her old ways, which I'm glad she didn't, she was well worth two horses."

"And you paid for Cole's wife to come up here, too."

"Another lost girl. We met Valerie in Tombstone while looking for Bonnie. She really hated the trade, but was trapped. I gave her a few dollars for expenses and bought a one-way stagecoach ticket to Preskitt."

"I knew nothing about your past, except I met Margaret in Mexico before you married her. I knew she had died, but I don't think I put two and two together until the coach door opened."

"I'm glad you came."

"My only regret is I am not with your child today."

"That's up to God. Nothing we can do but try."

She laughed all the way down the lane to the house. "Thank God, you haven't given up on me."

"I won't. We may get some rain this afternoon. Clouds gathering and all."

"Good, we can hide out and be by ourselves."

"Amen."

CHAPTER 18

The next morning at breakfast, Chet was already at the table when Liz joined him.

"Are you going to get those women food today?"

"Yes, they stayed here last night. And we can get what they need today when we get them moved."

"Good idea."

He went out and spoke to Raphael and they squatted on their boot heels to talk. The land prep for the *frijoles* planting next spring was complete. They'd leveled it into borders, and Chet felt they were on the right track. The pipe project to water it came next. A young man from Preskitt had surveyed and staked it out for them.

"I think we can water it alright," Raphael said.

"That will be a big savings for us if it works."

Raphael laughed. "*Vaqueros* are like cowboys, they don't like to grub sagebrush."

Amused, Chet agreed. "How many bulls do you need for next year?"

"Twelve?"

"I'll have to find them and get them here."

"That would make all my bulls either Shorthorn or Hereford."

The cool wind that swept through, moving a few pieces of trash along, reminded him they would soon be having winter. The two men squatted around the corner of the white-washed barn, out of the breeze.

"Winter is coming."

Raphael nodded. "I am so grateful to have this job. Cold weather never bothers me anymore. We will have a good celebration tonight. *Gracias.*"

"You and your people are an important part of the ranches. Thank you, *mi amigo.*"

He went back to the house, kissed his wife seated at the table on the cheek, and stole his boy from Rhea so she could eat. Then he went in the living room with him in his arms, talking to him about Raphael needing more bulls. Finding good bulls for all the ranches was a constant demand on Tom. Even he wondered where they could get more of them—Arizona without rails was like an island. Besides, the Southern Pacific's effort to get across New Mexico to reach Arizona was weak. It would take a long time to get to the northern part of the state covered by a rail connection.

After breakfast, they loaded the women and children, a sullen outfit despite the fact that Raphael's cook had fed them supper the night before and breakfast that morning. They'd slept in a clean warehouse and no one had hustled them. He knew they, no doubt, figured their men couldn't easily contact them in town. But that was not his fault. Warrants had been sworn out with the sheriff for the ones that shot at his men.

Raphael had a wagonload of wood to go with them to town that morning. Jesus planned to take the lead woman to get the groceries and get back after noon. So it looked like that bunch was all set. And the ranch women, as he called them, the wives of the employees, were hustling around getting ready for the *fandango.*

Liz and Jimenez worked the golden colts on lunge lines. The young man had really worked them while they were gone, and when they got back, she was proud of his progress.

When she worked the colts, Chet could see how far they'd progressed. He could have watched her every move, working the two and so involved, but he left to check on the books. Millie had come up and worked on them. Everything looked current and well done—his operations were doing great. He needed to get Liz involved, but so far things looked good.

Jesus was back in mid-afternoon. The women had food and were settled, so that was over. Cole and Valerie came back with him, ready for the big *fandango.* Valerie kissed Chet on the cheek and thanked him for her husband being home for a few days.

Late in the afternoon, a wire came from the marshal's office in Tucson.

CHET
I HAD WORD YOU WERE BACK HOME.
A GANG HELD UP THE ARIZONA
NATIONAL BANK IN THATCHER TWO

DAYS AGO. THREE MEN. TWO DESCRIBED AS ARMY DESERTERS AND A BREED NAMED LOGAN BLUE WERE DESCRIBED AS THE GANG MEMBERS. THERE MAY BE TWO OTHERS INVOLVED, BUT WE HAVE NO NAMES OR FACES. THE TOWN MARSHAL TOBY HANKS THINKS TWO MEN CASED THE PLACE BEFORE THE ROBBERY WAS HELD. THEY STOLE OVER TEN THOUSAND DOLLARS. THE UNUSUAL LARGE SUM WAS THERE FOR SOME PAYROLLS. THE LAW THERE THINKS THEY HAD INSIDE HELP AS WELL. THE POSSE LOST TRACK OF THEM IN TWENTY-FOUR HOURS. BUT THEY SUSPECT THEY WENT NORTH. COULD YOU MOVE THAT WAY AND LEARN ANYTHING? I KNOW IT WILL BE A NEEDLE IN A HAYSTACK SITUATION, BUT YOU HAVE THE REP.

PAUL CONNORS THIRTY-TWO DESERTER U.S. ARMY. CONVICTED. ESCAPED WHILE BEING TRANSFERRED TO PRISON IN KANSAS. KENNETH SATTLER TWENTY-EIGHT DESERTER U.S. ARMY ESCAPED WITH CONNORS IN NEW MEXICO. LOGAN BLUE PART APACHE MEXICAN AROUND THIRTY YEARS OLD. KILLED TWO AGENCY POLICE. WAS WITH THOSE TWO WHEN THEY ESCAPED FROM THE GUARDS MOVING THEM TO PRISON. LET

ME KNOW YOUR PLANS. I UNDERSTAND
YOU ARE BUSY RANCHING. I HAVE
WARNED FEDERAL LAWMEN IN NEW
MEXICO AND COLORADO TO BE ON
THE LOOKOUT. THANKS.
ACTING US MARSHAL GREG ERSKINE

Liz had taken the boy from him to allow him to read it. "Bad news?"

"Any time the acting U.S. Marshal sends you a wire this long, there's trouble attached. A gang of three to five men held up the bank in Thatcher and got away, headed north. Two are Army deserters, and one is a breed who killed two Indian police. There may be two more. He doesn't know much more, except they eluded the posse sent after them. Probably Hanks included some businessmen on horseback for the search, and they're usually a poor excuse for a posse."

"What will you do?"

"See if we can find them over east. It may be a futile trip, but if they went north they either went to Horsehead Crossing on the Little Colorado and pushed on to Utah, or rode for New Mexico."

She smiled at the baby boy who she had laughing, and shook him gently. "We leave in the morning?"

"I won't tell you no, but these chases are never nice."

"Chet Byrnes, I will be with you and those two nice partners of yours. It will beat me rolling over at night in bed without you."

"I agree. It is just more tough camping out and riding hard after ghosts."

"Oh, now we are ghost chasers?"

"At times, it will seem like that. I better get hold of Cole and tell him. He and Valerie can stay here tonight. They can get her back to town tomorrow."

"Jesus is here?"

"I think so. When I don't have plans, he helps Raphael. I'll catch him. You need to go to town and get anything before we ride out?"

Liz nodded. "Yes. I can take your wire back to him. I will be back in time for the celebration tonight. Why do you look so grim?"

"I worry about you getting in on these tough cases."

"I understand, but I obey you and keep my head down."

"It isn't you. It's the worthless madmen we run down that worry me. Give me that boy back. Rhea needs him, and you need to make your plans. I'll write the wire for him and you can send it."

"He is fun to play with." She held Adam out for Chet to kiss.

"I'll take him back to Momma Rhea," Liz said, and took him to the kitchen.

He heard her tell Anita they'd go to town. He put the last newspaper back on the stack. His next move needed to be to get those girls a buckboard hitched and find Jesus.

The boys at the barn rushed off to hitch up a team. Liz and Anita promised to make a short trip. They left in a cloud of dust and he smiled. They wouldn't miss any part of the festivities.

After the women left, Chet found Jesus busy replacing a girth on a saddle.

After he spoke to him about the robbery, Jesus made a grim face. "Bank robbers. We need to try to head them off?"

"Yes. Can we leave tomorrow?" he asked.

"Yes. Liz is going along?"

Chet smiled. "She says so. She's going to town to deliver my answer and get some things. We need to tell Cole we're leaving, so he and Valerie can stay here tonight."

"I will find him. These men must be desperate criminals?"

"Bank robbers and Army deserters, plus a breed who killed two Indian policemen."

"Real nice citizens, huh?"

"Real nice ones."

Jesus asked, "Where were they going?"

"North from Thatcher. The posse lost their trail the first day."

Jesus shook his head. "I bet you said, 'businessmen ain't posse men.'"

Chet clapped him on the shoulder. "You're learning, partner."

"Where will they go from there?"

"What I know about that country is that it's damn near as tough as any. The gorge for the Salt River is up there, and they say it rivals the Grand Canyon in depth and high sides. Maybe west of that would bring them out at Young. That's Mormon country. We were up there chasing other outlaws above the Tonto Creek—Salt River Fork."

"Oh, yeah, the ferry deal, where they sunk one."

"That's the place. The ferry was cut loose and crashed in the rapids."

"Will they go to Horse Head Crossing?"

"There or New Mexico. I would suspect they'd go to New Mexico. Lee's Ferry is the only way to get out of Arizona on the north side."

"I know that well. Sounds like another wild goose chase."

"You and Cole have been in many cases we solved. We will do all we can on this one."

"And Liz will ride with us. I really love her. She never complains, she's funny, and she works hard as any man you could hire."

"She spoiled me bad on the cattle drive. I'd be ready to kick someone in the ass and she'd say, 'He don't know any better,' and I'd relent."

"She is a man's woman. But you knew that before Cole and I did. She has a way of supporting you, and she is not like most women. She doesn't need any big deals to be sympathetic, but is sincere."

"I'm glad I found her or she found me. I worry about her riding with us. But she came to be with me and I understand that."

Jesus nodded. "I will get the supplies packed and be ready to leave at dawn."

"Good." He thanked him and went over where all the ranch women were working on the *fandango.* They were singing and doing lots of food preparation.

"Señor, do you need something?" a middle-aged gray-headed wife asked.

"No, you girls have it under control."

They laughed at him calling them girls.

"Patron, we are so glad you have these events, we don't care about the work to get ready. You want a *fandango*, we are ready anytime."

A cheer went up to support her words.

"I know who you are," he said. "I applaud all of you."

He went back to the house and found Monica in the kitchen, baking pies and cookies.

"They are all mad; they didn't want a *fandango*."

"Oh, yes, they are so mad." She shook her head. "Crazy man, they love them. Did your wife get off?"

"She went to deliver my telegram, and must be shopping. Are you worried about her?"

"No."

"Should I send someone to check on her?"

"No. Just my motherly ways. Tell me, you are happy?"

"Yes. Is that wrong, in your opinion?"

"No. I have said before, Marge would be unhappy if you had not picked up your life."

"I know you were so close to her, closer than maybe I even was. And she and I had a great life. This woman is a different person. I love her and she fills my life, but in a different way, but it doesn't matter. I am really glad she came along."

"So am I. You would be a bear to live with." Then she laughed and turned away from him like she had things to stir. But not before shining tears filled her eyes. God bless that woman.

He went and read more of his papers until he

heard some shouting in the yard. It was five o'clock by the big grandfather clock. He hurried to greet them.

"Hey, you two stayed in town all day?" he shouted at them from the back door.

They were getting hatboxes and dresses in tissue paper from the buckboard.

"No, we were getting fixed up to represent you tonight."

"Good." He went down to help them and kissed her. "You two will be sparkling."

"We hope so, don't we, Anita?"

"This lady I work for is radiant in any clothes. She bought me a dress to wear tonight."

"Ha, will Jesus like it?"

She looked over at him. "I certainly hope so."

He hugged her. "Anita, he will be pleased."

"No big deals today?" his wife asked, loading his arms with dresses.

"Not a one."

"No more wires in town or much mail. We still are leaving in the morning?"

"Yes, and see what we can find."

"Good. I will be ready."

She glanced at the house. "I bought Monica a dress to wear, if she will come to the event tonight."

"That was sure sweet of you."

"If not, she can wear it to church on Sundays."

"They are really working hard to get ready."

"I suppose Anita and I can help them."

"They will be fine."

"I know you are pressed by our leaving." Anita held the back door open for him.

"Here, while you are not cooking, try this dress on." Liz filled Monica's arms with a tissue paper–covered outfit.

"You should not have—"

"Go try it on." She headed her toward her room.

Chet carried Liz's packages upstairs, and Anita took hers to her room.

Alone in the bedroom, she put down her things on the bed and then hugged his neck. "I count my blessings here every day. Not because you are so generous with me, but because I know I can count on you. I never have had any doubt but that you would support me as your wife."

"Good. I never doubt you, either. I really enjoy our life together. I never expected you to want to traipse along on these law trips, but I love having you there."

"Where are Rhea and the baby? I bought her a dress for tonight."

"She laid him down for a nap a while ago."

"Will Victor come tonight?"

"It depends where they're at in getting ready for the next cattle drive."

"Good." She squeezed him tight. "This wife business is busy, too. More fun than I expected."

"I hope you stay this happy."

"Why would I change?"

"I have no idea. When you get time, thank the women who are working so hard on the party. They like the attention."

"Yes, I'll go do that."

"We better see if Monica likes her new dress."

She kissed him. "For being my man."

They went downstairs, where their housekeeper looked great in the new dress.

"Does it fit?" Liz asked.

"Perfect, but kind of fancy for me."

"No. No. It looks wonderful."

Chet went to catch up on the latest newspaper she'd brought in. His mind wandered onto looking for the outlaws in a land as vast as the territory. Maybe a needle in a haystack might be easier to find. But outlaws were not the smartest individuals and usually they showed off enough to be found.

The party was a big success. Several came from the Camp Verde Ranch. Hampt and his crew attended, and Chet danced with his wife, May, and several others. He also danced a waltz with Kathrin Ivor who was showing her second pregnancy.

"I'm so glad you asked me to dance, Chet," she said. "I believe we never danced before. Now, you dance with both me and the baby."

"You and Ben are happy?"

"Oh, yes, he is a good man. He may run me off, for I keep getting with babies."

"I doubt that. I know it's a long ways from Utah, but you've done a great job of becoming a wife and mother."

"You know how beholden I am to you, for letting me have a new chance?"

"Kathrin, we both are lucky we didn't freeze to

death coming back. Jesus still thinks Utah is the Arctic. And no regrets. I'm proud of you."

"Good. I see your new wife and you have fun."

"She is a swell person. I wasn't looking to remarry and she wasn't, either."

"She was very smart; she chose the right man."

"It was that time."

They both laughed.

He wondered if their talk had settled her any. Susie had even noticed Kathrin's concern about him. He'd never made any pass at her or said anything. He knew he'd helped her out of a bad situation. But she didn't owe him anything.

"You having fun?" Liz asked, sweeping up in her new dress.

"I am. Are you?" he asked as they swept the wooden floor in the hallway of the barn. "That dress is beautiful. And the two girls' dresses look great. Did Monica come down?"

"No, but she says she will wear it to church Sunday."

"Good. I see Victor made it."

"He and Rhea are a fine couple."

"Monica must have the boy?"

"Yes, she does."

"I am going to talk to Hampt, Tom, and the others. We need to rise early, so we can't stay up all night."

"Yes, my love, but these *fandangos* raise my blood up."

He hugged her tight and kissed her. "I love you."

"Me, too. Tell them I said hi. Oh, I told Valerie that she gets the next dress. I really forgot her when

I got the others. She was almost embarrassed when I told her I would. When I get back, I am going to take May to town, too, and get her some dresses. Can I do that?"

"Yes, ma'am."

"You are so hard to please. How do you put up with me?"

"It is damn hard." He left her laughing and shook Hampt's hand.

"You three—four—be careful. because you won't have this big old man to back you," Hampt teased Chet.

"I know. We may need you, but stay here, you have a good operation going."

"I sure am busting my buttons on the whole deal. Will Ray need to go to some prep school to go to college somewhere?"

"Damned if I know, but I'll find out."

"You do that."

'Take care of yourself. You and May make a good team."

Hampt nodded his head. "Crazy outfit, the two of us. But we're getting along good right now."

Chet and Liz excused themselves, went to the bedroom, and honeymooned. He did have a good life, and he thanked God for her before he fell off to sleep.

CHAPTER 19

The last thing he thought about was to not trust the weather. They had some winter clothes in the packs because, despite the sunny days, fall was sneaking up on them. The foursome settled their horses on the road the next morning in the cooler air and headed for Susie's house in a long trot. The first day passed and they were at the Windmill by dark.

Susie, with Erwin in her arms, rushed out to welcome them. Cowboys took their horses and Jesus supervised them.

"Have a good party? We sent Victor." Then she laughed.

Liz hugged both her and the baby. "Oh, he made it and danced with Rhea. Good to see you, even under the circumstances."

"What are you after, another lost herd?" Susie asked.

"No, bank robbers."

"That could be dangerous."

Liz shook her head. "All we do is dangerous. We will be fine. The big man is in charge."

"You've sure been hoodwinked. I've known him all my life."

"Oh, Susie, he is the one to handle this, too."

"Besides," Chet said, "we haven't found them yet."

"Come inside. Sarge is gone to check on some cattle. He'll be back in a few hours."

"That boy is sure growing."

"Oh, Liz, he is growing so fast. How was the party?"

"Very nice. We went to bed early to get up here."

"How serious is Rhea about Victor?" Susie asked.

"Monica babysat Adam last night, so it looks pretty serious."

"I'm glad she's serious. Brother, how are things going?"

"Fine, if we can find these outlaws."

"Do you think they came this way?"

"No, I think they went to New Mexico. There's nothing north of Arizona but Utah. I'm sure they're looking for more fun than that holds."

"Be hard to buy a drink up there," Susie agreed.

When Sarge came in he looked over Chet's papers and the posters of the outlaws. "Pretty sorry pictures. I couldn't tell who they were."

Chet agreed. "I may have to ask them their names, huh?"

"Yeah, I couldn't tell them from those pictures."

"Most wanted posters are cheaply printed. But they're real people, and if they came north, someone saw them."

At daybreak, Sarge told Chet about the "good people" he'd met on the cattle drives there and who would help him on their route. He made a list of names and how to find them. They reached Joseph City, a sleepy Mormon village on the Marcy Road. Sarge recommended he talk to Alex Hamilton who ran the mercantile. The store was closed, but they put their horses in the livery, ate supper in a small café, and then slept in the livery hay section. His men did not think the so-called hotel there was worth anything.

The liveryman, Hogan, knew Sarge and had bragged on him earlier. Chet recalled Hogan saying, "Sarge don't keep no hell raisers in his outfit. And Victor, neither. Them boys that come here are polite, and after they leave, you can't tell they've even been here. Some of them Texas outfits come in here and all they've got is drunk, gun-happy hell raisers."

He discussed it with his wife that night in whispers. "Nice to know your crew is polite, anyway."

Snuggled against him, she agreed. "Those are both serious men. I really like Victor, and I know him better because he is a nice flirt to talk to."

"Do you miss people who speak your language?"

"No. I came to Arizona to be your wife. I could have stayed in Sonora and spoke Spanish."

"And slept in a nice bed with servants to wait on you."

"Boy, that would get boring, after all this get up and ride business, huh?"

He hugged her. Even after all that, he couldn't imagine any female not missing the luxury she left behind to become a saddle tramp with him and sleep in the hay. Well, he needed to count his lucky stars for finding her. That fancy lady that got off that coach was damn sure a prize, and his nose was full of sweet hay—wow, he was riding a cloud.

After breakfast in the café, he met Alexander in his store. No one there had seen the three wanted men in the area.

"So you're Sarge's boss?"

"He and Victor are my men. They've been a vital part of my ranching efforts."

"I'd say so. But that is a good bunch of men. They're like clockwork. You can tell the day of the month by their passage through here. And every head is in good condition. I get word from over there—those folks count on your men being there on time and right."

"Sarge said he quit the Army because all they fed him was beans, but he knew how to work men and get a job done right. When I bought the first ranch, he came to me for work as a simple cowboy. He proved himself and never failed. Victor has done the same. Cooked for the crew, learned the business, and now he's as good as his boss."

"I don't know if you know it, but you are a legend around here. Selling cattle ain't easy this far from anywhere, but you do it every month."

"We've been lucky. I wish we could talk more, but I need to find these robbers."

"Come by. You need anything, I'll try to get it for you. And, good luck finding them."

"Thanks. We'll need it. Nice meeting you."

When he walked outside, Cole asked him, "He know anything?"

"No, but he thinks the Quarter Circle Z is a helluva outfit."

Jesus nodded. "We hear that all over town, huh?"

Liz reined her horse around as Chet mounted. "They have a good boss."

"Oh, yes," Jesus said, and laughed.

They headed east. So far nothing, but they would be near the border of New Mexico soon, and he expected to learn something over there. Maybe they had seen them in Gallup. And there was a chance the threesome broke up. Not likely; with a successful robbery they'd probably stay together for more of the same.

"Don't you get upset, not hearing a word about them?" Liz asked mid-day when they stopped to water their horses at a trading post.

"It's like panning for gold. You have to swish lots of water around to find any color. Then one day, bang, you hit a mother lode. Are you discouraged?"

"I guess you're right. They leave tracks two feet wide coming across a land of eternity."

He smiled. "If they came this way, we'll find them. These kind pop up like prairie dogs, to find women, pleasure, whiskey, and hell raising. As you well know, we haven't passed through many islands of such paradise since we left Preskitt."

Laughing at his words, she rode in and slapped his arm playfully. "You are a mess. What profound philosophy you have for us."

"Was that what that was?" Cole asked.

She turned and smiled. "It was something like that."

Jesus was laughing too hard to comment. He finally managed, "We like having you along, Liz. You can liven up this party in the snap of your fingers."

"Well, near three days in the saddle and we have not even seen their dust."

"It does get boring at times, this law business. I keep thinking it's worth it to rid this land of the trash."

"Will they ever give this territory statehood?"

"Yes, but no one is impressed with all the empty land we've crossed. They are used to town after town, and farms. Unless the rain patterns change, we won't ever have any dirt farming, except where they have irrigation, and there won't be a lot of that."

"Population?" she asked.

He nodded. "That, and we're the last jumping-off place for all the criminals run out by the law east of here. Texas started back its ranger program in 1870, when they got rid of the federal troops. In time, the rangers will run every scalawag out of the Lone Star State. Where can they come but here?"

She laughed. "They better not, or my husband will find them."

"That's right, and we usually do find them."

The men nodded in agreement.

"Chet?" Cole pushed his horse up with him. "There's a small ranch over by Mayer that belongs to the Green family. I heard they wanted to sell it."

"I don't know them. How big is it?"

"They say a section. It's in that juniper country west of Hampt's outfit."

"You thinking about it?"

"I'd like to."

"Let's talk to my land man and see what he thinks."

"I told Valerie you'd help us."

"If I can, I will."

"Would Valerie live on a ranch?" Liz asked.

"She's got her feet on the ground pretty good. She had a rough life growing up, but she has a big heart. Chet saw that when he loaded her on a stagecoach to come help Jenn in the café up here. She never forgot that, either. We'd like to have a place of our own, and someday run enough stock to be comfortable."

Chet put his two cents in. "She didn't like the business. But she was trapped in Tombstone, waiting tables, and it's a raw place. I knew Jenn would treat her like a daughter and she did."

"I was dumbfounded down there. Here was this lovely woman—in her eyes she looked lost," Cole said. "But a few months later, she had completely changed. When I asked her out, she said she had to go to church. I said I'll go along. She said fine. But she wanted me to know she wasn't the same person we shipped up there."

"So your first date with her was in the church?" Liz asked.

Cole nodded. "Here I was a poor cowboy. Not much schooling, except life's classes, and talking to a young lady who had her feet on the ground. I was awed by my discovery. She never preached to me, but she let me know that she wanted a proper life, and church would be part of it. She also told me that God forgives us, and he had forgiven her."

"Did that transform you?" Liz asked.

"I never raised much hell. My mother would have twisted my ear off. But she sent me to church and Sunday school. Then I started drifting, cowboying, and you know teenage boys can find mischief. Well, I wanted on with this new guy from Texas that bought the big place on the Verde."

"The big man with the aura?"

"You know, ma'am, I never knew what that was about him until you pointed it out. But I met him and shook his hand, and something kinda held me. I wanted to work for him. Of course, it was later that Tom hired me and I got to go with him on that first cattle drive."

"He has that aura," Liz said, and grinned at Chet.

"And, brother, we had enough hell doing that first drive to last a lifetime. Cole shot two Indians," Chet said.

"It was no peaceful cow-herding job," Cole said. "That was for sure."

"But you and Valerie are happy, and that is all that matters. I saw her that first night when she found you on the front porch," Liz said.

"I guess poor Anita thought she was under attack when Valerie rushed past her. She was real glad I was back."

"That was sweet. I saw her dedication to you. You

don't have to tell me. You have as good a marriage as I have with Chet."

Cole nodded and grinned.

"Jesus, you have anything to report while we are catching up on everybody?"

"No, Chet, I like Anita and she is very kind to me. Maybe someday we can find our place together in this outfit."

"I won't speak for Anita, but she seems to me a very proper young woman. I thought maybe I needed a post to lean on in this new land, and that's why I brought her along. I appreciate what she does for me, and she helps Monica a lot. I would not want to say she misses Mexico, but I think some of her heart is down there."

"I agree. I know how much better it is to do what I do here, but I bet there are days when even you think it would be nice to be back in Mexico."

"Only for a few moments, *hombre*. Then I look over and see him and say, 'no Mexico, I have much more here.'"

They all laughed and rode on.

They found out nothing about the threesome, and in two more days were in Gallup. They stabled the horses, and Jesus arranged to have her horse reshod. Chet got them rooms in the Adams Hotel and ordered up bathwater for him and Liz. He told the men they'd meet in the lobby at six for supper.

After their bath, they took a *siesta* in each other's arms and let the past long days in the saddle go by. Sarge had told them about the best restaurants, and they went to Gordon's Mexican Food first.

"Your horse is reshod," Jesus told Liz.

The man who owned the restaurant came by and introduced himself. "So you are the big boss of the cattle drives?"

Chet stood up and shook his hand and introduced everyone.

"I'm glad to meet you. Your men are so nice, and they eat here every month. I know what day it is when they come, but they all have good manners and act very civilized. What brings you to Gallup?"

"I'm also a U.S. Marshal. We're looking for three bank robbers who held up a bank in Arizona, and I thought they might head this way."

"After you eat, give me the information. I know many people in the barrio and places they might frequent, if they were here or are around."

"We'll stay a few days at the Adams Hotel while we're in town. I would sure appreciate any help you can give us on these men."

"Certainly. Eat your food and enjoy yourselves."

A rush of waiters and waitresses came carrying large trays of food. Soon the crew quit talking and began eating, and with a few words bragged on how good the meal tasted.

Before Chet left, he and Gordon went over his list and descriptions of the three bank robbers. They shook hands, then everyone walked back to the hotel. Chet felt satisfied that Gordon might learn something from his contacts about the three.

"Breakfast at seven?" he asked Jesus and Cole in the lobby, and they agreed. "I think in two days, or less, we'll know if they're here, or have been here."

"Think they may slack up, too, if they think the territory line means the law is behind them?" Cole asked.

"That would be our best bet to catch them."

In the room, he hugged his wife around the waist and rocked her back and forth. "I know I tell you this a lot, but you are the spark in my life."

"I am so glad. I have known two men intimately in my whole life. I don't compare you two very much, but you squeeze something out of me that he never did. I don't know why."

"You speak often of this aura you see around me. I see a spark of fire in you that I have never seen in any other woman."

"You had an affair with another man's wife, you said?"

"She didn't have that spark, but she was good and kind. Her husband ignored her and ran around on her. And she was finally going to leave him. Each time I went over, I crossed through that brushy country so careful not to leave a track. I found her in a bed of blood and she had written the killer's name on the sheet in her own blood. She'd written a note to her husband before she was attacked, but I found it on her desk and he never got it. She didn't mention me—but no need to torture another. Her death, despite his misgivings, shocked him. He really wept at her funeral."

"Did they get her killers?"

"They were hung, and some folks blamed me for that." Chet shook his head.

Liz buried her face in his shirt. "A feud going on and then that happened. You did have big problems."

"I think it really was part of the feud, but I couldn't prove it."

"That was not the lady you had to leave when you came here?"

"No, she had parents to care for, and they couldn't make the long journey here."

"I know what Margaret saw in you when you and she rode the stage to Preskitt. Someone tall enough to dance with."

They both laughed.

"And after you left me to go back to Mexico, I thought that cute little chili pepper is gone, gone, and gone."

She squeezed him hard. "No, this little lemon said I wouldn't never get him. But I did."

They went to bed and slept till dawn. Dressing for the day in the cool hotel room, he felt certain they'd get some new information. At least they needed a dim trail to take up. His wife kissed him during the dressing process.

"Well, do you feel better?"

"I always feel better when my wife kisses me."

She shook her head. "I kiss you all the time."

Suppressing his amusement, he hugged her. "I feel good all the time."

"Good. We both do."

Damn right. He wished they could soon be on the outlaws' trail, end this pursuit, and go home again. He hoped that would be the final outcome of their efforts.

Chapter 20

After breakfast in a café down the street, they split up. Jesus and Cole left to check the horse traders and saddle and gun repair shops. He and Liz were going to the county sheriff and the local police department to see what they could learn about the men.

The county sheriff, Lopez, was gone to Santa Fe on business that morning. His deputy, Meredith, had no information on the three, but he acted friendly to the two of them and took down the information from Chet.

"You think they came through here?" he asked Chet.

"There's no reason they wouldn't go to another territory and think they'd escaped the law. But even large sums of money are soon spent, and they must rob again or go to work."

"Most of that kind don't work anyway. I agree that, if they're here, we need to root them out."

"My men are with me and we have help from

some of our friends here. We send the cattle each month to the Navajos, so we have gotten acquainted a little."

"That is where I heard about you."

"Those are my men that make the drives."

"Good to meet you, and I'll spread the word to look for these men. Check back; we may find them. And nice to meet you, too, Missus."

"Thanks."

They left his office and went next to see the town law. City marshal Ernesto Gonzales invited them into his office and was very polite to Liz.

"Mrs. Byrnes, do you go everywhere with this man of yours?"

"Everywhere he will have me." Liz smiled.

"If I had such a pretty wife, I would never leave her at home, either."

They laughed, but Chet figured the thickset lawman was serious as he could be.

"I'm looking for three bank robbers that I think headed this way." Chet went on to explain about the wanted men.

Gonzales leaned back in his chair. "I don't know them, but if they were here, my men would have noticed them. When we get hard cases like that, we watch them like a hawk, señor. But I will have my men double check and see if they are around here."

"I'm at the Adams Hotel for a few days. Send word if you hear anything. There's a reward on them."

"We can do that, and, Mrs. Byrnes, if you ever need a saddle friend, I will ride with you."

They laughed and shook hands.

Back out on the street, he wondered what his men had found out. They checked out a few stores to kill some time, but bought nothing but some hard candy, then found lunch in a diner. He asked the Mexican woman who waited on them if she had seen the three men.

"One is part Indian?"

Chet nodded.

"Those men, or three like them, were hanging around a *fandango* last Saturday night where I was. No one knew them, and someone said they might be *pistoleros* and we should not challenge them."

"Where was this party?" Liz asked.

The woman looked around before she spoke softly. "Don Kataris's. It is on South Catalina. But please don't mention me . . ." She checked around. "My husband does not know I was there."

Liz assured her it would be secret.

Chet gave her a five-dollar tip, then they went to the livery and checked out their horses. The stableman said the Kataris house was yellow and red, and on the right side at the end of the street.

Chet could tell how excited Liz was over their discovery. They trotted their mounts down the caliche-hard street and he soon spotted the dwelling. She stayed on her horse and held his while he went to the door and knocked. No one answered. Then a short man came around the house.

"*Buenos dias, señor.*" Then he saw Liz and removed his *sombrero* and bowed for her.

"That is Elizabeth, my wife. My name is Chet

Byrnes. I'm looking for three men that came to your *fandango* last Saturday."

He nodded. "I am Don Kataris. I know who you mean. We wondered about them. They finally rode away. No one knew them."

"Were they staying here in town?"

He looked around to be sure no one could hear him. "Someone said they were staying at Ramon Egger's ranch."

"Is it close by?" Chet asked in a low voice.

"Take the White Tank Road south to where the Logan brothers have a large set of holding corrals, then turn west a couple of miles. You can't miss their place."

"I'm grateful. Can I pay you?"

"Just don't tell them I told you."

"I won't." He handed him a five-dollar gold piece.

"*Gracias.* Señora, you are a very fine looking lady. Sometime, come to one of my *fandangos.*"

"If I am here, I shall. Thank you, sir."

He held up his index finger. "Trust me. My *fandangos* are the best."

Chet mounted, thanked him, and they rode back to town. Cole stopped them when they approached the stables. "You two find something?"

"Yes. You do any good?"

"No. What did you learn?"

"They were staying at a ranch south of here."

Cole turned to his partner standing on the boardwalk. "Jesus, we need our horses. They have a lead."

Within minutes, the crew was ready and they left for White Tank Road.

"How did you find this out?" Cole asked. "Jesus and I never found a clue."

"A waitress who'd cheated on her husband and gone to a *fandango* last Saturday night said she saw three men there that looked like them. We found the man who had the *fiesta*, and he said those men were staying out at this ranch we're headed for."

Cole shook his head. "You heard all that?"

Jesus shook his head. "Yeah, we never heard a thing all day."

"Then we are valuable to have along," Liz teased.

"Yes, ma'am, very valuable."

With Chet in the lead, they short-loped their horses out through the juniper brush on the dusty road. Unanswered questions crossed his mind. Was this ranch an outlaw hideout? Were there more fugitives there? And how big a fight would those three put up when cornered? All questions, but with no answers by the time they swept around the large set of pens Kataris described. Standing in the stirrups, he wanted to see this place before they rode in blindly. He saw windmill blades whirling and held up his hand for his crew to stop.

The three nodded over the discovery of the mill, and their hard-breathing sweaty horses stomped around some.

Chet pulled out a set of field glasses and gave them to the already dismounted Cole. "Go up high and look for activity. We'll wait here."

Jesus took Liz's reins and she headed for some juniper shelter, no doubt to relieve herself.

After scoping the place out good, maybe Cole

could tell something about what was going on. They might have a shot at capturing the three. After four days on the road looking for them, this was the first and best lead they'd had.

Cole came back, not looking very excited.

"There's a woman and some small kids. She's doing wash. I can't see any saddle horses or men there."

Liz was back and mounted. "You come behind us," Chet told her. "If hell breaks loose, you head for the brush."

He turned to Jesus and Cole. "Get your rifles out. Don't take chances."

Three abreast, they rode up on the small log house. The woman's clothes flapped on the line, and when she discovered their approach, she used her hand to shade her eyes to better see them.

"She knows we're coming."

"She ain't warned anyone," Cole said.

"Not yet. Just be careful. Lots of open ground here to defend yourself on."

"She's gathering kids and coming around front," Jesus said.

"Kick your horse out and go around back, just in case there is someone trying to get away."

Jesus nodded and set out on his fast horse.

"Ain't no one here but me and these kids," she shouted. The three were tight to her skirt, none of them very old. "Whatcha' want?"

"U.S. Marshals. We want Connors, Sattler, and Logan Blue."

She had a hard look on her thin face. She might

have been in her twenties, but a lot of gray streaked her hair. Her eyes were dark and deep set, like she bore some Indian blood in her veins. Her graveled voice definitely had a drawl. "They ain't here."

"When did they leave?"

"I say they been here, mister?"

"We know they were staying here. Giving aid to criminals is a jailable offense."

Jesus came to the front door. "No one in here."

"I tole you that."

"Where did they go?" Chet insisted.

"How am I supposed to know that?"

"Men talk." Chet dismounted. "You heard them say. I don't want to have to press charges on you, but I want an answer."

"They rode for Continental two days ago."

"They have a hideout there?"

"Connors knew a whore there."

"What's her name?"

"Bessie, I guess."

"What do you know about her?"

She shook her head. "She's a black whore."

Ask a question, you should expect an answer. "She live there?"

"They thought she did."

"Where is your man?"

"Prison."

"He knew them?"

"I guess."

"You knew them?"

She shrugged.

"No, you knew them, and they came here because you hide such men."

"I don't."

"Lady, they did not come here for church services."

Her thin shoulders shrugged under the wash-worn dress, and then she silenced a whining child on her skirt. "I don't know why they came here."

"Next time you hide lawbreakers, the sheriff will come out here and take you in irons to jail."

He mounted his horse.

She shook her fist at them. "Fuck you and the horses you all rode in here. You bastards don't scare me none!"

"Better heed my warning. Let's ride." They left the place.

"We were in Continental before?" Liz asked him.

"Three times. We rounded up some criminals there once, and we rode through there going to find the herd and coming home."

"Well, she was tough enough. I'm surprised she told you all she did."

Chet shook his head. "We were a threat to her. She didn't know but that we'd stake her on an ant hill."

"You wouldn't do that to her," said Liz.

"I might have been tempted." He chuckled and she shook her head at him as they trotted for the road.

"We need to get our packhorses and go find them tomorrow."

She pushed in close. "We've ridden a few hundred miles and no sign of them. We had a break and the chase is on. That's how your law enforcement works?"

"We got lucky. That's how it usually happens. You track and track, then use your senses. They show up for a *fandango*. No one else we talked to, from Arizona to here, had seen them, but a waitress who cheated on her husband and attended a party saw them."

"That is a needle in a haystack, isn't it?" she asked.

"Liz, as lawmen, we live on those straws," Cole said, and they laughed. "We were down in Tombstone and they said this guy shot his brother and ran off. Then a man told us he didn't ride his horse, because his horse was still out on the range. Your husband got to kicking around and found a grave, or we thought it was one. But we found the truth when the woman who killed both of them hung herself."

"I had no idea. But I can see how, if you ask enough people, someone may have seen them. I am learning, guys. I am learning."

That evening, they camped off the road at a windmill and tank. The weather was still warm, but Chet expected any day a big cloud bank would come out of the north and winter would kiss them. All the cottonwoods in the high country were golden and they shimmered in the gentle winds. In another day, they'd be at Continental. They'd have to be quiet, for it was a small place and he didn't want anyone to learn who they were before they located the robbers.

"If we ever get somewhere again, I'd be for taking a hot bath and washing my clothes. That water out of that pipe at the windmill is too cold for me to hop in."

"We should have done more of that at Gallup. Sorry."

"No, I can stand any one of us downwind," she teased.

The men all laughed. She smiled and shook her head and went on cooking supper on the campfire.

Continental sat beside the road, with several adobe *jacales* scattered about. Children ran around outside in noisy play, and cur dogs barked at the riders, then slunk away. They went by the saloon and Cole and Jesus went inside. Leading the packhorses, Chet and Liz went down by the dry wash where they had a pump and a water tank for stock. Under the rustling cottonwoods, he used the pump and she watered the horses by twos.

"They haven't gained much population since the last time we were here."

"Oh, maybe a baby or two," he said, working the pitcher pump hard to keep ahead of the thirsty horses.

Chet noticed a woman, wrapped in a blanket, working her way down the hillside. She moved from tree to tree, like she was making sure no one saw her.

"She some old girlfriend?" Liz teased under her breath, not looking at the woman.

Chet only chuckled and let the pump rest.

"Aren't you the lawman came here before?" the woman asked, standing among the horses, so short she would be hard to see.

"I'm a U.S. Marshal. What can I do for you?"

"There are three mean men here. I am sure they are wanted."

"What are their names?"

"One is Paul, they call the other Ken, and a half breed called Blue."

"What did they do here?"

"They raped my younger sister two days ago."

"Oh." Liz gasped and put a hand to her mouth.

"Where do they stay?"

"See that house on the hill with green shutters?"

He glanced that way. "Yes."

"They stay there with her."

"Her?"

"She is a black *puta*. Her name is Bessie, and she is mean, too."

"Where is the law here?"

Looking upset, she shook her head. "Ain't no law here."

"Anyone report the rape?"

"I did with you."

"No, I mean to the sheriff."

"He's not here. He's at the county seat."

"You think they are there today?"

She nodded.

"What is your name?"

"Myna."

"I think my men are coming. I want you and my wife to quietly lead her horse and the packhorses down this creek bottom a hundred yards. Take your time, like you have nothing else to do. I'll go with my men to see if they're at home. Now, real easy, like you are old friends, take the horses down there past the ruined adobe house."

Cole reined up, realizing something was afoot. "You found them?"

"A lady just came and told me. She knew me from before. They raped her sister. She says they are in that house with the green shutters. I wanted those two out of the way. What did you learn?"

"Bessie lives in that house."

"Cole, you ride around back. Unlimber your rifle. They may try to fight their way out." He stepped into the saddle. "Jesus, you and I will take the front. Let's go."

The house was up the hill a hundred yards. He let Cole get around back, then they spurred their horses up the hill. At the front gate, they slid to a stop and he fired his rifle in the air.

"U.S Marshals. Come out with your hands up, or be shot."

There was a lot of cussing inside. Then two shots came from the back of the house. That was Cole's rifle.

"Anyone else wants to die?" he shouted from the rear.

"You alright?" Chet called.

"One's down. Another is packing my lead and went back inside."

"You better get out here. My patience is short," Chet ordered the house.

"Hold you gawdamn guns. I ain't got no gun." A six-foot-tall black woman wearing only a girdle came outside, hands high. "They be coming. Hold you pants."

The next one who came out was a man that answered Connors's description, and he came out with his hands high. The third man, obviously wounded, came dragging himself outside.

Cole came out behind them. "Logan Blue is dead out back. They had their horses saddled and were ready to ride out."

"Bessie, go get dressed. Cole, be sure she don't try anything. People are coming."

"Darlin', they've all done seen my black ass before."

"Cole, get her dressed. Jesus, handcuff the unharmed one and sit his butt on the ground. Be sure they both are unarmed."

Liz slid her horse to a stop. "You all alright?"

"We're fine. One dead breed. One wounded, and the other handcuffed. Cole is getting Bessie dressed."

"Dressed?"

"She was only wearing her uniform."

Her eyebrows crossed. "What was that?"

"A girdle." Unable to hold it, he broke out laughing, and so did his men.

She punched his arm. "You are a devil, Chet Byrnes."

Myna came up to see, along with many wives, children, and men.

"I need someone to haul these men to Gallup. That one needs a doctor."

She shook her head. "No doctor here."

"Cole, see how bad he's bleeding."

"I have a team and wagon. I can haul them where you need to send them," a man offered, obviously needing the work.

"Gallup is the closest town. How much?"

"Forty dollars."

"Thirty," Chet said.

"*Si.*"

"I will pay you five more dollars to feed them."

"*Si, señor,* I can do that."

"My men and I will guard them. They must be clever at getting away."

Cole came back. "He may make it. He may not."

"Whatever. Where is the bank money?" he asked the unscathed one.

"What money?"

He kicked him hard in the leg. "I don't have lots of time. These people would lynch you for raping their young women. You better tell me quick."

"Barn in the loft."

"I'll get it," Cole said, and took off.

"Myna, you can have their horses and saddles. You led us here. They forfeited them, being outlaws. It's a small payment for them raping your sister."

"*Gracias.*"

"Bessie, you have a horse?"

"Of course I have a horse. Why?"

"Get all your things you want to take and you leave this town. If I hear you came back here, I'll have you in prison for hiding these three."

"You can't—"

"Get off your butt and get going—now."

She jumped back and ran in the house, cussing a blue streak.

"Go get those horses that are theirs and bring them around for this lady who helped me."

Some of the men from the crowd that had gathered went to do that.

Cole came back with two heavy saddlebags. "Quite a bit left, boss."

"The Stafford bank will be pleased. Jesus, check their other things for money. Then fix her up." He shook his head warily. "Who buries the poor?"

"I can bury him." A tall man in overalls stepped forward.

"What do you charge?"

"Five *pesos*?"

He nodded his head. "Bury him deep. These people do not want to smell him."

Everyone agreed that was so.

While they waited for the wagon man's return, Liz started to make them some food. One of the women bandaged the wounded man to stop the bleeding. Bessie left with two sheets over her lap that were bulging with things she took from the house, and rode off under a large black hat that flopped to her horse's gait.

Some women pitched in to help Liz and made flour *tortillas* on the stovetop. Soon, lawmen and the rest were eating. Chet wondered where all the food came from. Obviously, they'd brought some, too. No way his wife could have made it all.

"You are like Jesus today, a couple of fish and a

loaf of bread, and fed lots of folks," he said to Liz in passing.

She stopped and whispered, "I paid them for it. They had it ready and thanked me. But I didn't offer to wash their feet."

"That was my job."

"You did a good job at it, too."

They left the next day for Gallup. The way was slow and when they arrived, he put the prisoners in jail and they sent for a doctor to look at the wounded man. He deposited the money, eight thousand dollars, in a bank for Wells Fargo to return to the Thatcher Bank.

"Thank God, lots of it was paper money," Cole said.

Chet nodded.

He telegraphed the bank with his report, and told them the rewards went to his two men Cole Emerson and Jesus Morales, in care of Chet Byrnes, Prescott, Arizona. Then he filed a report with the U.S. Marshal's office in Tucson. They sent telegrams to the families that could get them, then took a bath in a bathhouse. Liz bought them all new clothes, since she didn't figure theirs would stand a washing. Chet looked up the waitress who'd put them on the robbers' trail. She met him out the back door of the café and he discreetly paid her twenty dollars for her useful information.

She kissed him on the cheek. "Just don't tell my husband I was there," she whispered.

He agreed and went to join his bunch to go out and eat at a fancy restaurant.

"What did she say?" Liz asked, taking his arm when he was back out in the street.

"Same thing she did the last time. Don't tell my husband I was there."

They laughed all the way to supper.

That night, the wind came out of the north, and they rode back to the Windmill ranch in four long, cold days in the saddle. The ranch hands took their horses and the pack animals and sent them to the house.

The four of them collapsed in Susie's living room.

"Well, how did it go?" Susie asked.

Cole shook his head. "We rode over there, caught them, and got most of the bank's money back. I still find it hard to believe."

"Would you like a hot bath, sister?" She pulled Liz up from the floor.

"Not quite as bad as I did in Gallup. But, yes, I'd take one."

"Any of the rest of you want a bath?"

They shook their heads.

"Bring us blankets; we want to sleep on the floor," Cole said.

Chet agreed, slumped in the chair. Jesus just nodded his head, seated on his butt and his back against the sofa.

"You win, Liz," Susie shouted triumphantly.

About an hour or so later, the women fed the groggy men. A little rest and they took baths, changed clothes, and answered questions.

"You can stay here another day and rest."

"If you think we'll argue with you, sister, you're crazy," Chet said.

"Good. I'll have company. Now tell us all the story of the bank robbers."

"It all started with a waitress who went to a party and didn't want her husband to know it."

His crew laughed, and so did the collection of ranch hands in the warm living room.

With his arm around his wife's shoulder on the couch, he nodded his head. "I can hardly believe with that bit of information we found them in a few days and it was over."

Well, there was a little more to it than that, and his weary bones told him so. But they were back on his land and everyone was alright. He couldn't believe his wife sat there with him—that was neat, too. What was ahead? No one knew that. He hoped it kept going this smooth. And maybe someday he'd catch up on his sleep. Maybe?

Before they were through visiting, Chet recalled how he had promised to take Liz elk hunting. When the conversation got around to her going elk hunting, Victor spoke up. They were back from their drive and getting ready for the next.

"Hey, I want to be your cook for that hunting trip."

"Sure. We can go next week, can't we?" Chet asked his crew.

"I never shot one. I'll go," Cole said.

Jesus agreed and Liz, seated on the couch, said, "I will be ready by then."

"Sarge, you can spare him for a week?"

"Sure. We've been doing good getting the cattle over there. We have plenty of time. Though we'll leave early the next trip, to insure delivery, since that will be the December one and it might snow early."

"Thanks," Victor said. "Oh, when you get home, tell Rhea I said hi."

"No more message than that?" Liz teased him.

"That will be enough." The whole crew laughed at his expense.

The two of them stayed over a day or so at the Verde Ranch. He showed his wife the Hereford herd at Perkins again, and she was impressed all over again about them. As they came up on the first ones, she exclaimed, "Oh, Chet, they are gorgeous. Is that the right word?"

"Yes, they are that. I worried they were used to better grass in Kansas and might not acclimate this easy. I'm certain the cattle born and raised here will do even better."

"They will calf in the spring?"

"Yes, I'll bring you back. The calves are pretty cute."

"I want to see them."

"You will. I don't deny you much."

"No, you don't. Thanks. We better go see about supper."

He agreed and they short-loped back to the big house. Tom and Millie were coming for supper. Maria had big plans to feed them. Cole and Jesus had rode on to see about their women.

That night, she still was talking about the white-faced cattle. Seated on the bed, he pulled off her boots and she laughed. "I never expected to be in such a whirlwind life marrying you. I have more fun and excitement than I ever imagined. Elk hunting next. Whew."

"You need to rest a few days. Are we wearing you down?"

"No. I am fine. Just thinking how lucky I am to do all these things. I am afraid someday I will have to sit home and be a housewife. I may cry."

"Not until then, Liz. Not until then."

A tear ran down her cheek. "I am sorry, Chet. I wasn't going to cry. I am so happy to be part of your world, I guess I got choked up on it."

He took a clean handkerchief and wiped her tears. "Cry all you want, girl. We do have some life, and I really enjoy it."

"Maybe we should pray?"

"Sure. You want to?"

She scrambled down on her knees beside the bed. "You do it."

"Our dear heavenly Father, we want to thank you for all our blessings you have bestowed upon us . . ."

CHAPTER 21

They prepared to go elk hunting on the rim. The frost had turned the cottonwoods to gold in the valley. Jesus, Cole, and Liz, along with Victor from the Windmill Ranch, who volunteered to be their cook when he heard they were going hunting, were all set. The young Hispanic had become Sarge's right-hand man after working as a cook for that outfit for two years. He'd spent the two years learning the cattle business, and then been upgraded to second-in-command.

Chet noticed how Victor had a lot of interest in his boy's nanny, Rhea, while they were packing the chuckwagon to go hunting. The days were warm, and she, with the boy in her arms, had shown an unusual interest in their preparations.

Up early the morning they planned to leave, he asked Monica about the sparking going on.

"My, yes. I do not know who is the shyest, him or her. Why, Jesus is a Casanova with Anita, compared to Victor and Rhea."

"Oh, we all need someone. They'll figure it out."

"Did you expect your wife to go off chasing those lost cows in Texas with you when you married her?"

"No."

"Well, me, either. She came back from there acting like she wanted to be a painter, telling me all the colors of those bluffs and the waving grass. Who cares? They were so far out no one else will ever see them."

"Liz has a lot of imagination, but she suits me."

"She idolizes you, like Marge did. But I never believed she'd ride off to sleep on the ground with you all summer in a dust bowl."

"She never complained one time."

"No, she never complains about anything that happens here. She clothed all those bare-butted cowboys on that drive, too?"

"She did, and for under a dollar apiece, she told me. I guess one day we'll have more weddings, huh?"

Monica shook her head. "I hope so."

"Are they that serious?"

"Listen, big man, you rub two sticks together long enough, you'll get sparks."

He was eating his breakfast ahead of the others, and amused at her take on the goings-on.

"Don't worry, your son is not being neglected. She watches Adam like a hawk, and he gets her full attention."

"I had no doubt about her or her care of him."

"Are they shutting down the Force?" Monica asked.

"From my last wires with the new man, I think

they are having problems getting funds for it in Washington. You can't operate a successful law enforcement operation any cheaper than we have."

"I know that. Elizabeth told me she expected to find a big marble office building and found wooden benches and tables under a tarp roof."

"We didn't need any fancy buildings. I knew she was shocked at our meager operation when she asked me, 'this is your headquarters?'"

Monica laughed. "You had cowboys for marshals. They can always get by."

"You are so right. And now, I think the rest are coming down," he said, hearing footsteps on the stairs.

Anita came in the kitchen first and apologized for not getting up earlier to help Monica. "What can I do?"

"Make more biscuits."

"I can do that. How are you, Chet?"

"Fine. Ready to go hunting."

"I know. It was fun to have everyone here last night. Victor sure can sing and play the guitar."

"He did that on the honeymoon with my first wife."

"He said he saw the Grand Canyon on that trip with you. Said it was a big, big, slash in the ground."

"He's a good man. You think him and Rhea will get together?"

"I think they will, but she won't give up the boy for him. She is very connected to him. I don't think even his real mother would be that bonded."

"Thanks, Anita. I understand a lot about Rhea, but you've given me something to think about."

"Please don't tell anyone I said that."

"The secret stays with me."

Valerie, who stayed overnight before they left for the hunting trip, came ahead of Cole and greeted everyone. Jesus was behind them. Rhea and his son came next.

"Where is Victor?" Chet asked when Liz showed up.

"I imagine rechecking the chuckwagon. He probably was up before you," Jesus said.

"Go get him to come eat," Chet said.

"I will." Jesus went to find him.

"He may be ready to go," Liz said. They all laughed.

Chet held Adam and teased him until he laughed. It was never hard to get him to laugh and he seldom cried. But that came from all the attention Rhea showed him.

"Will he soon walk, Rhea?" Liz asked.

"Oh, he takes some steps now, but they aren't steady enough. He will be walking by Christmas, I hope."

"That will be nice."

Jesus returned with Victor in tow, and he had been rechecking things. Chet understood his concern that the trip go well. That was how he did things, rechecked them. They said he was even fussier than Sarge about every detail in everything he did. That's what got him the promotion at Windmill.

"Get any sleep?" Chet asked.

"Yes, enough. I wanted to be certain it was all there. And it is."

Victor said something to Rhea in passing her. She smiled and told him thanks. He took a seat beside her and began to fill his plate. "My last morning not to cook. Thanks, Monica."

"You are welcome. Anita has more biscuits in the oven. I will watch them, so she can eat. Anyone need anything else?"

They shook their heads and she refilled coffee cups. "I have my order in for two fat bull elk."

"I bet we get them," Cole said.

Victor drove the team as they set out for the Verde bottoms. Everyone else was on horseback and went ahead in the cooler predawn. Chet noted for the first time that Jesus kissed Anita good-bye. He'd seen Victor with his forehead pressed to Rhea's before they left. Cute lovers.

All of them were anxious to be on top of the rim by evening. They only took a short break at the lower ranch. Tom wished them well and they were on the road again.

It was past sundown when they made a dry camp on the rim in the big pines. Victor had brought plenty of lanterns. They watered the horses from the two water barrels, planning to refill them the next morning at the sawmill. Supper was soon cooking.

Liz's tent was struck, and the horses ate grain out of feedbags hung on their heads. They soon had coffee, and the beef Victor got from Tom sizzled along with fried potatoes and biscuits in the big Dutch oven. Somewhere in the night, a wolf howled and another answered.

Liz scooted closer to him on the bench. "That was not a coyote."

"No, he was a big old timber wolf. They can be calf-eating rascals if they ever get a taste of one. They mostly eat deer, but one bite of beef and they turn bad."

"Did you have them in Texas?" she asked.

"No, we had those smaller red wolves. I think, like the buffalo, they once had them in Texas, but they got shot out early on."

"Oh, we have the red ones in Mexico, too."

"Yes, we heard them when we were down there," Cole said.

"We better help him get cleaned up here," Chet said. "Morning will come early for us to move and set our camp farther up the road."

Everyone lent a hand and things were put away.

"At our next camp, we better swing those provisions in the sky. There ain't no shortage of bears up here."

Victor agreed. "I hope they don't come in our camp."

Later, in their bedroll with his wife, she said, "I never knew Victor before. He is a real smart person."

"Yes, I'm going to talk to Tom about making him the farm manager on the Verde place. I have a young man in the Force who'll need work if they shut it down. Shawn McElroy is a smart, hardworking cowboy who could take Vic's place at the Windmill herding cattle each month to the Navajos."

"I met him down there. He is the quick thinking kind."

"Yes. Roamer can move on to Wells Fargo. I'm certain Dodge wants him to work for them."

She snuggled against him. "What if Victor and Rhea want to get married?"

"They can live in the big house and Adam will be close enough to share with us."

"Think he'd like farming?"

"It would be a challenge. Hampt was a cowboy, but he applied himself and is the best alfalfa raiser I have. Vic could do the same, I bet. Tom is fine, but he has lots to cover. I think Vic could make a better farm operation manager, and we need that."

"We better get some sleep; morning will be early."

"Love you." He really did; she fit right into his life and he really felt dedicated to her. Drifting off to sleep he thought about big elks—with tall racks.

CHAPTER 22

Morning came, with the campfire smoke hanging low and swirling around their legs. Chet knew a storm moving in caused the smoke to hug the ground, and wanted to get set up in their camp that evening before an early snow came in.

With the horses saddled, the team hitched, dishes washed and packed away with the rest of the camp items, they rode north.

"Cold wind this morning," Cole said, riding beside Chet and Liz.

"It will bring in a storm before nightfall."

"If it is coming, in these dang pine trees you can't see very far," Cole complained.

"It won't be long and we'll see it building, I bet," Chet said.

"I'm not going to bet with you. You're too good at figuring weather out."

They all three laughed.

They stopped and talked to Robert and Betty, who wished them good luck hunting, and then the hunting party went on to the springs to make camp. Victor told them to peg down the tents securely, that he was looking for a storm.

Cole laughed. "We're all weathermen."

They busied themselves helping Vic fix supper. The wind came up stronger and clouds began to build afterward. They all turned in, but Chet got up in the night and discovered snow falling in great flakes like leaves.

Back in bed, Liz asked in a sleepy voice, "Is it snowing?"

"Yes, big flakes." Snuggled against her warm back, he went back to sleep.

Come morning, they discovered six inches of snow. Vic's overhead tarp was so weighed down by the heavy snow it had to be shaken off.

"I'm glad Robert promised me hay today for our horses," Victor said.

Chet nodded. "We'll need it."

"Glad I made the deal," Victor said, busy making breakfast. Liz set in to help him. There was coffee for everyone while they appraised the snow.

"You hear that bull?" Chet asked.

"Yeah, he was north of us. Made me feel warm to hear him," Cole said.

"Bet he has a big rack," Jesus added. "He has big lungs."

"Will we get to see him?" Liz asked.

"That's why we came." Chet shook her shoulders and she laughed, then headed to the Dutch oven with the unbaked biscuits.

Mid-day, he dismounted at the edge of a wide-open,

snowy field, and Liz traipsed carefully behind in his tracks in the white stuff to the edge of the meadow. The buck couldn't scent them, but he must have known they were closing in. Chet aimed the .50 caliber Sharps rifle at the elk's shoulders and pulled the trigger. The ear-shattering shot struck the big buck and he half-reared, but the powerful force of the bullet threw him down on his side in the snow.

Chet restrained Liz from going closer, while the big bull kicked away snow in the final stages of his life.

"Oh," she exclaimed. "He is huge."

"Nice bull. Now, if Cole or Jesus have shot one, we've filled Monica's order."

"What next?"

"Cut his throat so he bleeds out, and then go for help."

"Does someone need to stay and watch over him?"

Chet agreed. "I'd hate for a rogue bear or wolves to find him."

"I can ride back and get help."

"Be careful."

She stood on her toes and kissed him. "I will be right back." In minutes, she was mounted and headed for camp.

With her on her way, Chet completed his job of cutting the elk's throat and admired the big six-by-six rack. This was a real trophy elk. He waded off to a downed dead pine and used his small hatchet to chop up branches to make kindling and soon had a fire started in a spot he cleared with the side of his boots. A fire would be nice to warm up by while they dressed the dead animal.

The gray cloud bank above was moving fast over his head and might bring more snow. He started the skinning process on the elk and looked up at the sound of horses returning. It was his wife, leading Cole and Jesus, with two spare horses to pack.

"Wow," Cole said, dismounting. "Boss man, you've shot the big one. Jesus, look at that rack."

"He's sure big," Jesus said, wading through the snow to the carcass. "How are we going to skin him?"

"On the ground," Chet said. "He's too big to pull up."

The men agreed and began sharpening knives.

"Glad you found them," Chet said to Liz.

He turned to Cole. "You didn't get a bull today?"

Cole shook his head. "We saw three nice ones, but we never get close enough for a good shot."

"We saw them. This bull is really a wonderful elk." Jesus shook his head. "You mounting his head?"

Chet was quick to agree. "We better save it."

"Where will you put him?" Liz asked, amused.

"Oh, maybe the Verde house," Chet said, bent over and working with the three of them to strip the hide off his legs and then his body. In an hour, they had the hide off and the elk gutted. Chet used a meat saw they'd brought along to begin quartering the carcass.

Cole used a small hatchet to help him in spots. The meat was soon cut into large portions and wrapped in canvas to haul back to camp. Packed in panniers, they soon had the cape and horns on another. They used Liz's horse for the wrapped-up hide, and she planned to ride double with Chet.

Work weary, the crew finally mounted up, with Liz behind Chet, and headed for camp. With his wife hugging him and her face rested on his back, he felt real comfortable.

"Been a helluva good day," he said over his shoulder. "You glad you came?"

"I am always glad I come along with you. New adventures. Exciting things. You have time for me. I am so fortunate I found this man and he has put up with me."

"But you could be in the warm sunshine on the patio sipping wine in Mexico, instead of smelling like blood and guts."

"But I would not have you. You have spoiled me. You never tire of me. You talk, and listen, to me."

"That is all part of being married."

"No. I do not know a woman in the world lucky as me. Did Margaret ride with you?"

"Some. Did you ride with him?"

"Some. But I bet she didn't go looking for lost herds?"

"No."

"I'm glad I did. I saw so much beautiful country. Historic places that Coronado saw hundreds of years ago and I now ride that land with you."

"Before Christmas, let's go to Mexico and see your *hacienda*."

"Do we have time?"

He knew he had whetted her appetite to go south. "Yes, we need to do it."

"Good, I will notify Manuel to have us a stage-coach at your headquarters."

"We will settle it after we get back home."

"Good, I am excited."

"We'll go."

"I am not worried. You keep your word with me." She hugged him.

He shook his head. Where did he ever find her? Oh, he knew. In a haystack. How damn sweet was that?

Chapter 23

Cole dropped a big elk on the second day. That evening, Victor looked like he was sad the hunt was over. Chet sat down with him after supper and discussed his plan for him to become the farm boss at the Verde.

"Can I think on it?"

"We have all the time."

"Really, I like being Sarge's man. Those cattle drives are exciting and always have something happening."

"Anyone can get cattle to the Indians. Our crops and the Hereford cows could be a good place to learn a lot."

"I will think on it. I appreciate all you have done for me. I didn't ask to be your cook on this trip to find a new job. I always have good times on these trips. I know you miss Marge. I do, too, and your honeymoon was one of the neatest things I ever did. This new lady, Elizabeth, is so nice; you were lucky to have found her."

"Let me ask you something personal?"

Victor smiled. "I wondered when you would ask me about her."

"I'm talking about Rhea."

He nodded. "I don't think she would marry me if she lost her job caring for the baby."

"What if you and her could live on the Verde Ranch with Adam?"

"Oh, I never thought of that."

"I have."

Victor smiled. "I would sure ask her."

"No rush. I better find my wife."

"You always figure out things, don't you?"

"Only because I have such valuable people I need in charge of things."

Victor acted embarrassed. "I still appreciate all you have done for me. How is JD doing down south?"

"Fine, as far as I know. Do you know anything different?"

"No, but he was pretty wild when he came here and nothing suited him," Victor said.

"Maybe he had to grow up. He seems settled down with his wife and the job down there."

"So far, things are fine. He's too busy to do anything else."

"I'm glad. That Reg is a giant. I'm glad he married Lucy. I really got to know her back then, on that honeymoon. She was a real tomboy," Victor said.

"Things have worked well."

"Yes, and your sister is happy at Windmill. We talk a lot," he said.

"I guess I miss Susie as much as anything. We were a team for so long."

"I think she has come to understand that could not last."

"Thanks, Victor. I'm going to go talk Liz into going to bed."

They shook hands and parted.

The group loaded up in the morning and dragged themselves back to the Verde Ranch where they left some elk meat for the household there. Victor and Rhea had a long talk before he left and took an elk hindquarter to the Windmill. Jesus drove the women, Anita and Rhea, baby, and wagon up the hill. The other three rode ahead to the ranch and Monica met them at the door.

Wrapped in a windswept blanket for warmth, Monica came out and asked, "Any elk meat?"

"Plenty." Chet waved. "Jesus has it with him and the women and Adam."

"Glad you all are in one piece. I have hot coffee inside."

The boys took their horses and they went inside and told Monica about the two big elk. Then Cole left for his wife, with word from Chet that he and Liz would stay there until they went to her *hacienda.*

Cole thanked Monica and the others and went for the fresh horse the stable boys had saddled for him. Chet walked him outside.

"Tell her I said thanks for sharing you."

"She'll laugh about that, but I'll tell her. Thanks for the break." Cole swung in the saddle and galloped for Preskitt.

Chet saw no sign of Jesus, but he'd be along with the wagon. The mountain was a tough pull for the animals and would require more time to reach the ranch. He went inside and drank coffee with Liz and Monica.

"Did you get snow here?" he asked Monica.

"It quickly melted. The ground was warm."

"It must have been cold up there, for we mushed in for three days, and there was still snow when we came back."

"Did you enjoy yourself?" Monica asked Liz.

"It was amazing. I was there when he shot the big bull. He was bigger than most horses. Wait till you see the horns."

Monica shook her head. "Weren't you cold?"

Liz shook her head. "I never noticed."

"You have her completely out of her mind, Chet Brynes."

He stood up and hugged her tight. "That's what I got her for—to spoil."

They both laughed.

"Monica, I love what we do. He is even going to take me down to my *hacienda* to see about my things."

"Soon?" Monica asked.

"In a week," Chet said. "I can hear Jesus is here. I better go see about hanging the elk meat in the icehouse."

He put on his canvas coat and told Liz to stay inside. Crossing the yard, he spoke to Anita, Rhea, and Adam before he joined Jesus, and they drove up to the icehouse to unload the meat.

Raphael came in a hurry. No doubt, he had been warned, too.

"You get the big one?" he asked Chet.

"Pretty nice bull. He was six-by-six."

The meat was soon hung, and everyone who assisted admired both sets of elk antlers but gave Chet's kill first place.

Jesus washed up and went to the house with him. Since his friendship had grown with Anita, Chet noticed how he'd become less house shy.

"Well, what did you shoot?" Monica asked.

Jesus laughed at her. "I am only the help. Chet and Cole do the shooting. Someone has to back them."

"Good to have you back in one piece; take a seat. We are all mixed up with all of you coming home, and I did not know my family was returning. We will feed you, no worry, but it won't be right away."

"Thanks, we know," Chet told her. He held his son and bounced him. Adam laughed. He was a good baby, a shame his mother never had a real chance to hold and play with him. But he would grow up loved and be educated. He had many mothers besides his Rhea who loved him so much.

He read the past newspapers while the women made supper. Nothing very exciting in any of the back issues of the *Miner*. Things were quiet in the county, which was good news. Maybe Arizona was settling into being a normal place—but something made him doubt the territory was going to stay that smooth forever.

After supper, he bathed and started to turn in. Liz came upstairs and whispered, "The love birds are holding hands on the couch."

"They won't get in any trouble doing that."

"Sweet. I guess we could have done it that way."

"Maybe."

She tackled him. "I am glad you weren't that bashful."

"So am I."

She agreed.

Chapter 24

They planned the trip for the four of them, Chet, Liz, Cole, and Jesus, plus Anita, to go to Tubac by stage and check with Roamer and Shawn. When they were ready to go to the *hacienda*, her brother-in-law, Manuel Carmel, planned to have the large *hacienda* coach for them, with a guard he insisted on, at the Morales Ranch. In route, they would stop over at a friend's *hacienda* along the way, and then they'd go on to hers.

So they left the ranch, and the five rode the Black Canyon Stage to Hayden's Ferry. The next stage took them to Papago Wells, then to Tucson, and, at last, the Morales Ranch.

Roamer and Shawn were looking for them. Bronco and Consuela, along with Jose and Ricky, had a fun reception for them. Maria had moved to Rancho Diablo, and the other two women said they had been to see her wonderful house.

"Was she happy there?" Chet asked, recalling her hesitation about moving there.

"Why not?" Ricky asked. "She is sleeping with her husband."

They all laughed.

Later, seated in his office, Chet asked Roamer, "What will you do? I asked you to come down here and promised you work after this was over."

"Dodge said I can work for him anytime this job is finished. I want to buy a farm that has good irrigation rights north of Tucson. My wife and kids can handle it when I'm gone. I have enough money from the rewards, thanks to you, and the sale of my place up there to buy a good place. She likes the idea and we'll do that."

They shook hands.

"You said it has been quiet down here."

"Shawn and I have really not had much work the past few months. I think we did what you wanted. Ended the Mexican border bandits. Or damn sure cut them back."

"Good. You ever need anything, let me know. I counted on you and you did good."

"I will if I need to. You saved me from myself. I'd have stayed up there and never had a thing. Thanks; you've been like a father to me, Chet."

"It was good for both of us. We may never be in the history books, or make headlines, but we did close down the outlaw gate down here."

Roamer agreed.

When Roamer left, he sent in Shawn. The youth smiled big and shook Chet's hand. "I hate it that this job is getting over. I've had the experiences of a lifetime. I sure appreciate you letting me come down here and help you and Roamer."

"You did good. I told you I had a job for you. I have another whenever we have to close it down. I'm certain they'll want us to do that soon."

"Good. Doing what?"

"Taking cattle to the Navajos every month, with Sarge and Victor. It won't be as exciting as this, but it will beat just doing ranch work."

"Well, thanks. At least my back muscles won't itch up there riding through some border canyon expecting to be shot."

They both laughed.

"Why not take a few weeks off. Go home and help your father catch up on his ranch, then come meet me at the Preskitt Ranch. We can make plans then. I'll be back from Mexico by then and we can talk some more. I think you're a super person for all you did down here. The ranches are growing. There'll be an opportunity for a person like you to manage things for the operation."

"I was wondering what I would do. Your offer sounds great. Dad can use some help, I figure, and I'll get him taken care of. Tell me how you and the new lady are doing."

"Very good. She rode with us to run down those rustlers, and went to Texas with the three of us and found the lost herd. She sure is different than any other woman in my life—but let me tell you, she never complains."

"You've never seen her ranch, have you?"

Chet shook his head. "That's where we're going."

"Be careful down there. There are some tough guys never appreciated what we did to their robbery business on the border."

"I will, Shawn. It has been a tough job, but you and the team did it."

"I came down here a boy. I hope I'm going home next week a man."

Chet nodded. "You are."

"Thanks; that makes me feel better."

"I'll see you at the Preskitt house if they decide to shut all of this down."

"I'll be there. And thanks, again." When he left, Liz slipped in and kissed Chet.

He explained what had been going on. "I talked to Roamer. He has a wife and four children. I bet she's going to have another."

"Really?"

"They plan to have a dozen."

She about collapsed, and looked hard at him. "Really?"

"My sister thought he was very interesting when they met, and when I told her about Roamer and his wife's plans, she about fell over, too."

"Has it been hard to tell them they may disband your Force?"

"Yes. Tomorrow, I'll talk with the brothers. They have a good start on ranching. I want them to succeed."

"I would never have met you, had you not been down here."

"Liz, I wouldn't have the Rancho Diablo, either."

He wasn't sure why but she was laughing so hard. "Two kinds of hell, huh?"

"Yes, two kinds of hell, for sure." They went off to their bed in the tent chuckling about her remark.

He visited with both Morales couples the next morning. They told him they were proud of all he did for them. They had two hundred mother cows and were becoming ranchers. Someday, they would be large ranchers and it would all be his fault. They'd known the government would eventually close the Force down.

He thanked them and left them a check for his rent and their work. The stagecoach and five outriders arrived from the *hacienda*. Liz introduced the guards and driver to all of them. They had a small celebration that evening, with plans to head south in the morning. Later, in their bedroll, Chet discovered she was crying.

"Are you unhappy with me?"

"No. No. It is not you. It is me. I left that place where they killed him. I don't want to go back."

"That happened years ago. Why does it bother you now?"

"Hold me. Hold me. I will be alright."

He squeezed her trembling body and kissed her. "It won't be bad. That happened long ago. His killers are dead."

"I know. But the memory of his murder has been haunting me ever since I agreed to go back." Still sobbing, she clung to him. "I am not a baby, but it is all I can think about."

"We can do this together."

"Oh, Chet, I didn't want to worry you."

"You aren't worrying me. I'll be there and we can overcome it."

"Thanks."

They left early the next morning, headed for Mexico. At Nogales, the border guards looked under and around the coach, then decided they weren't smuggling anything and let them go on. Cole rode shotgun on top with the driver and that made more room in the coach. Jesus and Anita sat in the back, with Liz and Chet facing them. The strange, flat, tall different cactus began to appear, a variation of the Arizona variety of saguaro that grew in the north. The coach swept along through the dusty rolling desert. They stopped in small towns and watered the two teams and the guards' mounts, giving the passengers a chance to stretch and use the facilities, or brush, whichever was handy.

By Chet's appraisal, Liz had her sadness and regret under control. The first night, they stayed with Don Montrose at his vast *hacienda*, where they had a *fiesta* and party. He and Liz danced under the starlight in the garden to the guitar, fiddle, and trumpet music.

"Are you doing better?" he asked.

"Yes, thanks. I did not do that to worry you. I guess I had to have a cry. I have tried to be brave. I seldom cry. You know me. I am using the strength you gave me. I love you, big *hombre.*" Then she buried her face in his chest and they danced away.

The next day, they reached her *hacienda* and she pointed out the neat vineyards already pruned and tied for the next year. The rows upon rows of grape stalks were on tight wire and stout posts. There were green fields of alfalfa and winter barley, and the headquarters bustled with activity.

He met her brother-in-law, Manuel Carmel, and they shook hands. In his twenties, the handsome man smiled.

"I finally get to see the man who stole her heart. She came home from meeting you throwing things around and clenching her fists in my face and telling me how she had lost her mind. When you helped her down from the stage moments ago, I saw the aura she spoke about. Yes, I see why Elizabeth had to have you. My heavens, man, you have taken her with you to the ends of the earth."

"She and I go many places together."

"She even sent me to go back to read Coronado's adventures and told me where she was."

"We never found the golden cities of Cibola, either." Chet laughed.

"Oh, but you found the lost herd. That was as good. Come to the *casa*, I am such a poor host. My bride-to-be waits to meet all of you."

Chet reached out and hugged Liz before going inside with her.

"I will be fine," she said under her breath.

"I'm still here. Let's meet this young lady."

"Oh, it was not this nice when he brought me here. But Manuel has done well this past year of keeping it in excellent condition."

Chet agreed. The entire place was extra luxurious.

"Elizabeth, where is your son?" Manuel asked.

"Our Adam is just learning to walk. This trip was too long for him."

When Chet came in the tiled vestibule with her, he knew that was where they killed her husband. From there, he could see the spacious staircase across the great hall. Where she had shot the other killer in the chest when the murderer was coming after her.

"What a gorgeous place," he said.

"I forgot. It is that," she said under his arm. "I am glad you've got to see it."

They met Manuel's fiancée, Rickola, a tall, slender, dark-complected young woman who smiled at both of them. Nodding, she looked like he'd expected, a nice young woman from money. Dressed in a very fashionable blue dress, she was a picture of what he envisioned. But friendly.

A band played, so he took Liz's hand and they danced around the tile floor. They circled and swung around the room like they were alone in some canyon with a perfect dance floor. They'd danced a lot before, but never as intense, never this suspended away from the rest of them. She looked up and smiled at him.

"I needed this, big *hombre*. I needed this more than anything in the world. Being away from this place had become a worrisome thing inside of me. You will never know how opposed I was to ever coming back here. Thanks."

"It's a very beautiful place. Like a palace to me, and you fit so well here." He swung her around and around in circles. She had belonged here and he had stolen her away from this lovely setting to sleep in tents and on the ground in bedrolls. But he also knew how empty a house could be without a soul mate. How he had dreaded going upstairs at Preskitt without anyone. Being alone was not the same in every place, but he felt with her in his arms and the music that never quit—how blessed he was about everything in his life.

CHAPTER 25

At breakfast the next morning, Manuel and Chet were the early risers and sat at the end of the great table in the hollow-sounding, empty, great hall. Their voices echoed and he knew her brother-in-law wanted to talk.

"What do you raise on your ranches?"

"Mostly cattle. In the north, I'm crossbreeding Hereford and Longhorns."

"You like them better than the Durhams?"

"I have shorthorn bulls at the Preskitt Valley place."

"That's what I call Durham cattle."

Chet agreed. "They're alright, but I'm unsure which one is better. I have two hundred pure Hereford cows now in the Verde Valley Ranch. We need so many bulls, I thought I'd sell a lot of them, but I need about all they can produce."

Manuel laughed. "She told me you had so many ranches you could not count them."

"I have several, but I know where they are."

"You have a large ranch that goes nearly to the Mexican border."

"That's the largest one, and it costs money now to develop, but, in time, it will be a paying operation. I have a contract to supply beef to the Navajos. That takes six hundred head a month. We have to buy cattle from other ranchers to meet that contract."

"My, that is a large business in itself."

"Yes, but it makes enough money that we've bought several places from our cattle sales. And will buy more that fit our operations. We also have a log-hauling business for a sawmill company up on the rim. We first got into it when the Tombstone mining interest bought his log haulers and lumberjacks away from him. He got more lumberjacks, but pays us to haul his logs. Means we must provide a lot of draft horses, but it, too, pays our other bills."

"And you had a war in Texas?"

"That sent me to Arizona. My brother was shot and killed in a feud up in Kansas, driving cattle to market. But they did me a favor, making us move. Arizona had not seen the rush other places had gone through. There were little markets, no railroads, and we still lack them, but they will come."

"Liz may have told you. Our wine business is the best one we have to make money. So we grow grapes and a lot of them. We have cattle, but the Mexican market is not organized like yours. We even make goat cheese. We buy the milk locally and it is profitable. The same people who buy our wine, buy our cheese. We grow black beans. And I have some avocado groves, orange, lemon, and lime.

These trees my brothers planted are now coming into production.

"We also grow corn. That is a staple in Mexico. And chili and other hot peppers."

"You have lots of people-intensive crops."

"The payroll looks like a country full of workers."

They both laughed.

"But I wanted to tell you while we are alone, my former sister-in-law is very happy being your wife. I read that on her face when she came off the stage yesterday. I knew from her letters that she really was happy going where you went. I could hardly believe that, but I love her. Not like that, I mean she and I were good for each other in building what he started. She made a businessman out of me.

"When he was killed, I was having fun, hunting, and letting my brother do all the details. You might have called me a playboy, huh?"

"I understand."

"The day we buried him, she sat me down and said, 'Manuel, you have to become a man and help me run this place. No more going off to fancy balls in Mexico City and chasing wild women. This *hacienda* needs a leader, not a socialite, at its head. We have to make money at what we do here.'"

"Boy, I bet that was a shock?"

"Oh, a big one. I had to start doing what my brother had done, overseeing every operation. I had to make a profit on everything we did, or this place would collapse. Our first year, we barely slipped by. Money to borrow is expensive. My brother had a good reputation and he had bankers convinced he could make money. They were skeptical of us, and suggested we sell it while we could get top money for it. We sat down and both said no, that we would make this place pay. Each year since then, we have made money, and if we need a loan, bankers will talk to us face to face."

"I am impressed. You both were young to have such responsibilities."

"She said you started running your family ranch at sixteen. I was still chasing young girls."

They both laughed.

"My grandfather told me that my father was losing his mind. The Comanche had kidnapped two of my brothers and a sister. He was so obsessed with finding them, he stayed out too long in his search and some rangers brought him back home delirious. I took over the ranch operation. I wasn't much older than that when I sold my first herd in Kansas. I sewed the money I made in my saddle blankets and came home with it. After that, I used Wells Fargo. But I brought home what I thought was a fortune, and, in Texas, at the time it was, but following that, I made a lot of money and our ranch began to grow."

Manuel nodded. "All at once the quality of our barrels we put our wine in became very important to me. Each year, I knew we had some vinegar instead of wine. Vinegar is very cheap when you sell it. A lot of people have wine go bad, so the vinegar market is not good. Great care is needed in making good barrels. I learned that in twelve months. Last year, I had only one bad barrel."

"You look at barrels like I look at cull cows."

"Yes. Yes, I imagine that is so. I also became the man who got strict with my crop planters not to waste seed. I learned a weedy field robbed the crop. So much to learn, because I had never paid any attention before I was put in charge. I met with my *segundos* every week. I sent men off to other *haciendas* to learn their secrets. When I went to a social event, I asked questions how others handled things. Oh, this has been a real learning process, but when she told me she was going north to live with you and I must step in and become the patron—my heart stopped."

"Really?"

"Oh, yes. I always had her to answer my questions, to find my mistakes, and when she left I would have no one."

"She really told you she was going to live with me?" Chet had never really fathomed that remark.

"Yes. I asked her if you would marry her and she said it made her no mind, she was going to live with you."

"You know her parents came to the wedding?"

"I am surprised. Her father was a big judge, and when my brother kidnapped and married her, the word was out he planned to charge him with crimes he never did and put him in prison for years. And, in Mexico, he could have done that."

"They came and were very polite. I have a young son from my previous marriage. His name is Adam."

"She said you did, and that she held him at your wedding."

"Yes, she did. And her father made Adam their heir."

"Wow, she never wrote me that. She never spoke well of them, either."

"I was aware of her growing-up story."

"No. I knew that. But I am so proud you came down here. I saw yesterday what she told me when she came back from your first meeting. 'Manuel, he has an aura about him.' I saw that when you got down from the coach."

"I had no plans to find another wife. I wasn't hardly over Marge's death. But at first sight, Liz bowled me over."

"Oh, and when you washed her feet, you were made an instant saint."

"She said I became an apostle. Honest to God, I really only wanted to touch her."

They both laughed.

"Well, Manuel. How is the patron role suiting you?"

"I sent her word we made a nice profit. We have no loans out, and don't need any at this time."

"She said she was pleased. When I first asked her who would run this place, she told me she had no concern about leaving it in your hands."

"Barring a disaster, I can handle it. I even enjoy it now. At first on this job, I was not settled down and missed my carefree days. But I realized they were over and I must master this job."

"I did the same thing, taking over our ranch in

Texas as a teen, while other guys got to run off to see the bright lights. I was home saving orphan calves from the coyotes and worrying about oat and corn crops. It took me twelve to fourteen hours a day to oversee it."

"Damn sure a shock." Manuel laughed. "There was a lot to learn and no time to do it in."

"We will come back, in June, is it, when you get married?"

"Yes, we will wed then. I have no idea why we must wait so long. But that is her wishes. I don't mean to pry, but Elizabeth worried so about not having children—"

"Try as we do—no results. I told her not to worry, my last wife was married twice and worried, too, but she had Adam. So who knows? I told her if we do, fine, if we don't, that was fine, too."

"That worried her."

"Yes, but nothing we can do. If it happens, we will be happy. If not, I love her, and that will be enough."

"Tell me about your business as a U.S. Marshal?"

"Have you got all day?"

"No, I think your wife is coming down and so is mine-to-be."

"Old men tales will have to wait."

Manuel agreed. "I still want to hear about them."

"I'll fill you in later."

He agreed.

"Good morning, ladies. How are you?"

"Oh, dreadful." Rickola straightened her back. "I could have slept longer."

"These old men have been talking behind our

backs," Liz said, and broke into laughter. "I bet the two of you have settled the world's affairs this morning."

Holding her chair, Chet said, "At the least, Mexico and the United States."

Taking her seat, Liz said, "Have you told him about your jaguar hunt, Manuel?"

"Oh, Manuel, you shot a jaguar?" Rickola asked, like she'd never heard the yarn, either.

"I went with some *vaqueros* a few years ago on a cat hunt. A livestock killer had eaten many goats and sheep. The people in the village came and begged me to shoot this killer so they could get on with their lives. To make this story short, I brought the *vaqueros* and the dogs to where he made his last kill and the chase was on. We soon treed him and he was a big cat in a live oak tree. I took my 44/40, and took aim and shot him. He fell out of the tree like a shot goose from the sky.

"My horse was gun shy, and jaguar shy, too. So I dismounted and gave the reins to another man. The cat had never moved. I thought he was dead. I got maybe a dozen feet away from him when he woke up and stood on his hind feet, growling mad, claws out, teeth ready to eat me. Then the *vaqueros* shot him so full of holes he was worthless to mount, which I was glad they did, but a few bullets would have been enough."

Chet shook his head, imagining what a shock facing a mad, wounded, large cat would have been. "We had a killer grizzly on the Verde Ranch. Ended up smoking him out of a cave. He was huge and killed several grown cows. I finally shot him escaping the cave, but he stunk so bad it was tough skinning him."

"I have never seen one of those bears. It must have been exciting."

"I simply wanted the cow killer disposed of. Looking in caves for him was no fun."

"We get in some tough situations operating our place. I can see you doing that."

The four talked about his Force. His men and Anita joined them. They nodded to everyone, and the kitchen crew soon brought food to the table.

"Elizabeth, what did you do when they found that lost herd?" asked Rickola.

"I handed out clothes to the men. They didn't have any clothes; they'd worn them out. You can't believe how they were in rags."

"Were you concerned they might hurt you?"

"Ricky, they all treated me like I was a queen. I never doubted that if I raised my voice, I would have had a dozen defenders. Our ranch foreman, Hampt, turned them into soldiers and they turned back a Comanche raid after our horses."

"I am afraid I would have been too nervous to have remained there with all of them."

Liz nodded. "I understand. But I am married to a man that never lets anything even brush me. That country is a grass empire and it goes on forever. I fell in love with Nebraska, but he said they'd soon plow it all under. In Nebraska, every day, trainloads of people and their children got off there, looking for homes and farms."

"You saw so much. Will you write a book about it?"

"No, but someday, I may paint it."

"Can you paint?" She passed the plate of scrambled eggs to Anita.

"No. But when I get time, I plan to learn how."

"I want a painting when you do them."

Liz acted like she'd been caught at something wrong and wanted out. "You may have to wait. I really have no idea what they will look like."

"I still want one."

"I will paint you one."

"Anita, will you be sure she does that?"

"Oh, yes."

"Good." Rickola acted satisfied.

"Sounds like Elizabeth is going to become an artist," Manuel said.

A little amused, Chet agreed. "I bet she figures it out."

She reached over and squeezed his leg beside her. "Thank you, big man."

They all laughed.

After the meal, Manuel took the three men and Liz on a ranch tour. Chet enjoyed his explanation of things, and he found the operation supported by artesian wells to be a very complete operation.

"We grow cotton. We have lots to learn about cultivating it. But there is a gin nearby, so we'd have a market. I have hired a man coming from Texas to show us how."

"Cole used to grow cotton when he was a boy."

Manuel twisted in the saddle, but Cole already had his hands up. "I was just a disinterested boy then." They laughed and rode on.

When he and Liz were a little apart, he spoke to her. "This is a very large operation and I am impressed."

She nodded. "Manuel is handling it very well. That is a relief, but I expected him to do that. His brother trained him well. I am certainly pleased."

"Monica also told me you wanted to paint."

"Oh, it is a whim."

"We will pursue it when we get home."

"Good."

They rode back for lunch and a *siesta*. Operations of the place were typical Hispanic, with no big problems. After lunch, they met his main man, Fredrick Rodrigues, who reminded Chet of his foreman, Raphael, at home. When questioned by his boss, his answers were quick, and Chet would have bet they were accurate.

In their suite, he held Liz in his arms. "You lived like a queen here."

"Are you asking me if I regret leaving here to be your wife?"

"I feel a little short on facilities and atmosphere."

She closed her lashes and shook her head. "This house, this *hacienda*, represents a lack of you, and that to me is more important than all the fuss we have here. I slept by myself for three years. I made all these decisions on what to plant, when and how, and how to sell it. Manuel helped me, but in the end, it was me. I had no one to treat my heart. No one to kiss me. No one to share his thoughts and have his body's warmth in bed.

"I an only a woman. His death made me the

leader, and I am not lazy, but I discovered this was not what I wanted. When we make love, I fly away like an eagle. You made me realize that—in a haystack. I never tired of riding mile after mile, because at the end of the day I would have you.

"Men accumulate ranches and *haciendas.* Women accumulate their kisses and their attention."

He hugged and rocked her. "And I am damn grateful."

Their visit was soon over. They parted with Manuel and his wife-to-be. The coach with guards took them uneventfully back to Nogales, and from there they started the trip by stage to Preskitt. Chet hated that they had not stopped and gone to Rancho Diablo, but he'd do that later. Christmas was only a few weeks away and it was such a large event for everyone in the ranch family. JD and Bonnie would travel north for the holiday and to visit her mother, Jenn.

Liz kept a list of things he wanted for the event. Where would the celebrations be held? What did they need to gather? If they closed the Force, Shawn McElroy would be there looking for his next job. Would Victor accept managing the Verde Ranch farm operation? A lot of questions he didn't have answers for, but it would work out.

They arrived at the ranch after midnight and the place was full of rigs. He turned to her and said, "No sleep yet."

She hugged him and acted pleased.

Cole, riding with the *vaquero,* turned and said, "I

should have known. One of the *vaqueros* said he'd take me to town after he got you two here."

"I would bet Valerie is here," Liz said.

Cole nodded and turned back around.

They were swept into the living room with hugs and kisses. Hampt shook his head. "They didn't skin you up."

"No, we had not one incident. Peaceful place."

"For you, that is a record. Good to have you and everyone back." Hampt hugged Liz next.

When Chet hugged May, she smiled. "He was worried you'd have trouble and him not there."

"We're fine. All is well?"

"Oh, yes. Hampt hired a tutor for Ray. He seems to like it. The young man is really making him work on books. I hope it will get him in a college."

"I'll follow up."

"Good. And good to have you home."

"Anything fall off the wagon while I was gone?"

"No. But we count on you leading us."

He went to see Tom and Millie next. Liz carried his sleepy son over to him. Taking Adam from her, he winked. "He is special."

"Oh, yes. He will steal many women's hearts."

He agreed and handed him back to Rhea, who was smiling. "That wouldn't be some guitar picker over there we know, is it?"

"He brought your sister."

"That was nice."

"Oh, yes. Very nice. I think he wants to talk to you."

"I will talk to him before he goes back."

"Adam is cutting more teeth."

"Better to bite you with, huh?"

"He can bite. But he is a sweet baby. Tomorrow, he will walk some for you."

"You can take him back to bed. I know you're concerned about him getting his sleep." He hugged her. "Good to see you."

"And you."

She was gone and Susie was there. "How was Mexico?"

"Where I was—quiet. She has a large expansive *hacienda* that her brother-in-law, Manuel, runs very smoothly."

"Did you like it?"

He shook his head. "I would not trade this ranch here for it."

"Not your kind of place?"

"No, but it works. I'm in the heart of the land I want to live in the rest of my life. From north to south, I love this state-to-be where we ended up. I want to continue to help it grow, and our holdings as well."

"Big brother, you've done a lot for all of us. Thanks."

He hugged her. "It's worked out well, despite some sad things that have happened to both of us."

"Yes. But you're like me, looking at what lies ahead."

"Right." He noticed small tears in her lashes, but she forced a big smile for him.

Cole came over to join them. "We're going upstairs and go to bed. I've had enough rocking in that coach to want to sleep."

Valerie kissed Chet on the cheek. "Thanks for bringing him back."

"I count on him, too."

"I know," she said. "You all have had a long drive home."

Chet agreed. "But I'm as glad as you are to be here. Good night."

Later, he and Liz went upstairs, too. By then, he was caved in and ready to sleep. Long days, but they were back and the ranches were running on an even course. Good. He'd sleep hard and figure out the rest in the morning. It looked like for the time being, Victor planned to go back and stay with the Windmill.

They had a big Christmas season on the home ranch and at the other ranches. Things settled into a routine, with the added winter duty to feed hay when it snowed. Chet worked hard to note anything undone in the past year. He found lots of chores to tackle, if they had the manpower to get them done. He and Liz attended some social events in town, like the orchestra that came to entertain and several plays. They also attended the dances in Camp Verde. The cattle drives continued smoothly. Barbwire piled up in rolls at the Verde Ranch blacksmith shop, to fulfill the enormous need to build drift fences. And Adam began to walk.

Chapter 26

Spring was moving north rapidly. After Chet, Liz, Cole, and Jesus returned from a visit to Reg's ranch, a wire came one morning about ten to the Preskitt Valley house, from the U.S. Marshal's office in Tucson.

Chet read the wire to himself.

CHET BYRNES US DEPUTY MARSHAL
TWO DAYS AGO THE ARMED ROBBERY
OF A US ARMY PAYROLL HEADED FOR
FORT GRANT LEFT FIVE MEN DEAD.
I AM ASKING FOR ALL AVAILABLE LAW
ENFORCEMENT PERSONNEL IN THE
TERRITORY TO JOIN ME IN TUCSON
AND SCOUR THE COUNTRY FOR THE
CRIMINALS THAT DID THIS BLOODY
CRIME. SO FAR WE HAVE LITTLE
INFORMATION BUT OVER TEN
THOUSAND DOLLARS IN GOLD DOLLAR
COINS WERE TAKEN. SINCE THEY WERE

FRESHLY MINTED THEY SHOULD LEAVE
A PLAIN TRAIL. IF YOU ARE ABLE TO
ASSIST US PLEASE ANSWER AT ONCE.
JOHN THOMAS US MARSHAL

"What is it?" Liz asked.

"There's been a robbery of a payroll shipment to Fort Grant. Men were killed and ten thousand dollars in gold coins is missing."

"That is a lot to carry off, isn't it?"

"They didn't get it in their saddlebags. I have heard and read about train robbers who left thousands of dollars of coins behind 'cause they couldn't carry them."

"What do they want you to do?"

"Help them find the criminals. Let's see, it's . . . John Thomas is the new U. S. Marshal in charge at Tucson."

"Will they, or have they, contacted Roamer?"

"I hope so. I'm going to have to go down there and help. I'm sorry, but there won't be much place for you in this mess. We won't have a camp or a base and it will be hot as hell. If things get straightened out, you might be able to join us later."

"If you will be careful and stay with your men, I can stay home and play with Adam. I understand taking a crazy woman along is like taking too many suitcases."

He hugged her, still in deep thought. They'd switched head marshals so many times, for reasons he wasn't sure about, the job must be hard to handle. He didn't want it. The top man spent all his time setting up courtrooms and finding jurors for grand juries and court cases. People who came to Arizona for the job didn't realize how hot it was there, and how demanding it was to set up trials and that business.

"You need to leave right now?"

"I need to send him my reply, gather up my two men, and wire Roamer and Shawn to meet us, if he isn't already there."

"Alright, busy man. Kiss me and I will help clean up the kitchen dishes and be Monica's helper."

He kissed her and then smiled at her. "Sorry. This should not be too long. You've spoiled me. We haven't been apart hardly at all."

"Both of us are spoiled. But I am very proud of you, and don't worry about me. I knew I married a busy man. I only ask that you be careful, for Adam's sake and mine, and Monica's, too."

"Yes," their cook said. "I don't want to have to break in another cowboy."

They laughed.

Jesus came in the back door and politely knocked. "Did that boy bring trouble?"

"Yes, a large Army payroll was stolen, several men killed, and the new marshal wants our help. I need to write a wire to Roamer and one to this new man and tell him we'll join them."

"I'll take it to the office and get Cole."

"We need Roamer to bring us horses and pack animals from down there, in case we need them. We can take the stage and be there in a day and a half. If we can find them, we need some fresh tracks. Tell

Cole we may be down there for some time. Doesn't sound like he has any fresh suspects right now."

"I will attend to that, boss man. Good morning, ladies."

"That's alright, Jesus," Liz said, holding Adam and teasing him. "We know you two are very busy. Rhea, Anita, and I understand our roles here, and we all will be waiting."

Jesus thanked them.

Chet explained to him the part about the coins. Anita had gone for some paper and pencil to write out his telegrams. Jesus excused himself to go saddle a horse.

Chet wrote out his reply to Marshal Thomas, and then the one to Roamer about bringing horses and when they would be there. He decided to send one to Tubac and another for Roamer to Tucson, in case he was already up there.

"Will you go by and see JD while you are down there?" Liz asked.

"Maybe when it's over. If I do, you can come down and see that ranch."

"I will have my bags packed. You made that offer, if you recall, a long time ago."

"I don't know what this will take, or how long, but it sounds serious."

"Here, you better hold Adam so he doesn't forget you."

The girls at the table laughed.

He took the baby in his arms and talked to him. "Tell those silly women you aren't going to forget me. Are you? Why, no. Soon you can ride a pony and go with me."

Liz looked hopelessly at the ceiling and put her hand to her forehead. "Then I can worry about the two of you."

His son could walk a little but ran most of the time. The women all commented on how he was like his father. Chet shook his head and denied it all. Adam was a nice-looking boy, but he needed two or three more years to have stood the test for what Chet considered survival. Childhood mortality was a large factor in these times, and even carefully handled children took diseases and died. He kept his fingers crossed and prayed a lot for his son's well-being.

In the living room, Chet sat on the floor to play with Adam. The little one went back and forth between him and Liz, who kneeled a short distance away. As time passed, his son became even more precious, and, in bed some nights, Liz cried over her frustration about not becoming pregnant. Despite his reassurances, he had no problem with the situation. He told her the same thing Cole told his wife. If God wanted them to have children, they would, and no amount of crying or pining over the matter would change it. Still, that was the soft spot in their marriage, and he walked cautiously around it.

By mid-afternoon, Cole was there with his war bag and saddle. "I was coming out to see if I could help Raphael today, when I met Jesus on the road. Had to go back and get my things and tell my wife where we were going."

"No problem. I just got the wire this morning. I

thought we could take the stagecoach down there and look for clues as soon as possible. Roamer has horses he can bring up there, easier than us riding down there."

Cole agreed. "They don't have any leads?"

"They don't seem to. But most U.S. Marshals are more administrators and businessmen, rather than range detectives, like you and Jesus."

"Good thing. That means we have a job."

"Yes, how is Valerie?"

"Oh, fine. She and Jenn have been real busy at the café. I appreciate the time I had off to be with her and was ready to get back to work."

"Been a short turnaround, I know, but we don't plan these crime sprees."

"That's for sure. You don't need me, so I'll go find Raphael and some of the *vaqueros* and catch up on what they know."

"Fine. Get some sleep this afternoon and evening, in here or at the bunkhouse. We won't get to sleep much on that rocking stagecoach tonight. Monica will have supper at six."

"I'll be here for that."

When Cole left, Liz caught his arm. "Let us go rest, too."

He grinned at her. "You mean rest?"

She poked him in the muscled gut with her flat hand. "I mean real rest."

They went upstairs with him teasing her privately all the way.

Suppertime, and his men were there to eat. Jesus

sat beside Anita and they helped Rhea with Adam. Cole was telling Liz and Anita about the flowers his wife had planted. They promised to go by and see them and her garden.

"Rhea? Have you seen Victor lately?"

She quickly nodded. "Oh, yes. He took me to a dance last Saturday. He is going to Gallup this week with the cattle herd, so I won't see him again for two weeks at least. The musicians had him play with them a lot, but the cowboys from the Verde Ranch danced with me. They are very polite and asked him if they could."

"Vic is a good guy and a good musician. He is lucky you are understanding," said Liz.

She turned up her hands. "I try."

Liz agreed. "You do try. But being in the shadow of a good man sometimes is not easy."

Everyone laughed. Rhea looked a little embarrassed, but she quickly recovered. Life went on, his ranches and his family were busy, all the time. But they were succeeding, a thing that he worried about making the move from Texas only a few years before. But the threat of the feud had evaporated for him, and he hoped it stayed gone. Those days, now years behind him, were so bloody and hectic, and the thought of his family's losses in those years made him shudder.

Feeling a little guilty about leaving his wife behind, after all their adventures together, the situation niggled him a little. But she'd do fine, and when it was over, they could go to Rancho Diablo and see all the progress his nephew, JD, had made on the sprawling ranch.

Under the stars, Liz sat next to him in the buckboard as a *vaquero* drove them, Cole, and Jesus to the stage office on the east side of town, where the Black Canyon Stage Line would take off around midnight for Hayden's Ferry. It was a cool evening, so his wife wore a shawl and he had on an unlined jumper. He wouldn't need it in a few hours when they dropped off the mile-high elevation into the Valley of the Salt River and the sentinel saguaro cactus. Quite a transition, and he dreaded the heat, but it was only part of what he agreed to do when he accepted that badge.

The coach would then switch from there to the stage that went to Papago Wells, a transfer point to go west to Yuma and California, or south to Tucson. He kissed Liz good-bye. His men loaded their war bags and saddles in the freight holder on the back of the coach. He helped Liz onto the spring seat, and she was ready to go back with the *vaquero* who had driven them down.

"God be with you," Chet told her.

"You too, *hombre.* I will burn candles for your safety, and theirs as well."

He thanked her and she drove off. Climbing in the stage, he spoke briefly to the stage office agent holding the door and felt an empty spot form in his gut.

"Damn you, Chet Byrnes. You can find the purtiest women in this whole world to be your wives. I swear you must be a genius at finding them."

"He damn sure is, Paul," said the driver when he shut the coach door behind Chet.

"Well, I can believe that, too," Paul said, and climbed up on the seat. "Hang on, boys, we're leaving Preskitt right now."

They were off to Tucson. Sleeping was hazardous as always inside the stage. Besides lurching from side to side, it also rocked up and down. In places, the driver ground the two teams up front almost to a halt going off steep hills and grades, then opened them up in the moonlit flats. It was a whirlwind ride, like usual, but Chet did steal some sleep.

He and his men caught breakfast mid-morning at Hayden's Ferry. Then they reloaded for Tucson. The day's temperature hovered over a hundred already. Besides the dust that swept into the coach, the desert heat was like a furnace blast. After several horse changes, they took a break at Papago Wells. The eastbound stage from Yuma was late, and the agent asked Chet to give them a little time because a top man for the U.S. Marshal's office was on that coach. Sheldon Arnold and his wife, Rachael, were the party they waited for.

Obviously, the agent didn't want to listen to the important man's lamenting about any delays. Two hours later, which Chet knew would make their arrival in Tucson be after dark, the stage from Yuma arrived. Cole climbed up with the driver, so Chet and Jesus shared the coach with the Arnolds. He introduced himself as head of the Force.

"Oh, yes, you are the man who shut down most of the border invasion forces that were plaguing the southern territory. I understand you ranch here." Arnold mopped his face with a Turkish towel and then handed it to his wife who looked equally heat stressed. A nice-looking lady, but much younger than her husband. Chet guessed her to be in her early twenties and Arnold in his forties.

"I have several ranches across the state," Chet told him.

"Well, I am pleased to meet you at long last. I was busy inspecting our California operations when I received notice about the payroll robbery."

"You know, Marshal Byrnes, that San Diego is in the seventies night and day?" his wife asked.

"No, I didn't. While it's not that cool at my ranch at Preskitt up in the mountains, it's much cooler than it is down here."

She squinted her green eyes and shook her head. "I hope you two quickly solve this case. I am not anxious to be here very long."

"I think with Marshal Byrnes and his men here, we soon may have this case solved and on our way, my dear."

"Good, Bootsie, because I am really ready to leave now." She looked perturbed and stared out the side window at the boiling dust.

Chet counted his blessings that she wasn't his wife. Taking her along would be torture, compared to Elizabeth and his adventures with her.

"Do you have any idea who these murderers could be?"

"No. But that doesn't mean we can't find them. There are a lot of criminals that filter in here from the more eastern places. Recent restoration of the Texas Rangers has pushed the Texas criminals westward. So I suspect these felons may be unknown to Arizona territory lawmen."

"I know you are familiar with this element better than myself or Marshal Thomas. I do appreciate you coming in to help us."

"No problem. We'll never get accepted as a state until we clean up the crime, and we need statehood for more economic development and growth."

"Spoken like a true American and a businessman. Amen."

"Since they have ended occupation of the South, perhaps we can be better understood in congress as hardworking people needing statehood."

Arnold agreed. Rachael moaned more about how uncomfortable she was from the heat, and her husband, for his part, totally ignored her. Chet tended his own business, and Jesus tried to sleep.

They stopped at Picacho Peak Stage Stop for a horse change. The sun had set and the small peak stood out against the night stars.

"Aren't you lucky you don't have her?" Jesus said privately, standing a short distance from the coach.

"Amen."

"He don't even hear her."

"You're right." They climbed in and took their seats. The Arnolds soon joined them and Rachael continued to fan herself.

Nothing would help the heat except being under a waterfall, Chet mused. They weren't close to where they were going, traveling through the night in a hot wind and churning up acrid dust. Tucson, the walled city, wouldn't be any better, with no place to escape the temperatures as the stage charged through the narrow dark streets. Chet knew he'd be grateful to be at the hotel at last.

Disembarking the stage, he had the agent take care of their saddles and war bags. Then he shook Arnold's hand and spoke cordially to his wife, before they went to their hotel two blocks away. The Arnolds had reservations at the Congress. Chet found it too pricey, and where they stayed at the Brown was adequate.

A street vendor made them *burritos* and they lounged near her spot to eat the meal.

"About time we found some food," Chet said.

"That cook at the Peak hasn't taken a bath since Christmas," Cole said.

"We never eat there," Jesus said.

"Not even starving," Chet teased.

They walked into the Brown lobby and took their room keys. Chet asked to be woke at seven, and when he answered the man's knock, he was thinking he hadn't slept very much.

They took breakfast in the hotel restaurant and went to the federal courthouse to meet with Marshal John Thomas and find out what they could do for him. No sign of Roamer, but Chet decided he must be on his way with the horse stock.

Thomas shook their hands and thanked them for coming. They went in his office and he showed them on the wall map where the robbery occurred. The spot was north of the main stage route, across southern Arizona west of Benson where the road went to Fort Grant.

"Did they have a wagon or did they use the one it was on?" Chet asked.

"We haven't found the Army wagon with our roadblocks east and west on the Butterfield Road."

"They had to have a wagon to haul that many coins, either the Army's or theirs."

Thomas agreed. "We've looked and found nothing. I had some Chiricahua scouts look for it. Nothing."

"When my men get here, we'll look for it."

"If Indians can't find it . . ." Thomas cut him a hard look.

"I have nothing against Indians. But they didn't find it. My men will go up there and look. A large wagon didn't evaporate, unless they burned or buried it. That might tell us more about the robbery than we know now. If they didn't use it to haul those coins out, then they had another conveyance."

"They tell me you and your men are among the best lawmen in the territory, so I'll do anything you wish, but we've not found a shred of evidence we can use to make an arrest or launch a grand jury investigation."

"Give us a week. If we don't turn up anything, I'll go home and run my ranch."

"I thank you, sir, for coming."

"Do you have any witnesses that saw them?"

"They were all masked. They swooped down with what must have been maybe twenty raiders or more, and ran over them, killing anyone they came to and took the rig away. They left the dead and wounded."

"They went south toward the Butterfield Route?"

"We think so, but lost the trail."

"I'm sure we can find the trail to Fort Grant out there," Chet said, convinced.

"What can I do for you?"

"That new coin money should be a flat giveaway if they spend it."

"Everyone has been notified to be on the watch."

"My man will be here with horses for us shortly, and I'll let you know what we find."

They shook hands. Once outside the courthouse, Chet shook his head. "We are late to look at this situation, but we can still follow it. No one steals coins. They're too hard to transport and dispose of. The robbery site must be twenty miles east of here. If I stole it, and if I lived here and had a sound team to drive, I could be home in six or seven hours."

Roamer found them after lunch. He and Shawn had brought the riding horses and pack ones, too. Chet fed the two men lunch from a street vendor, while Cole and Jesus went for their saddles and war bags. By three o'clock they rode east, and about sundown asked a rancher permission to camp at his windmill.

The rancher told them he had been quizzed by the lawmen and had no idea who had done the crime.

"Is there any word about this robbery? I mean, folks talking about it," Chet asked.

"No. I was surprised. I thought maybe Mexican bandits did it, but there isn't much talk about it."

"If twenty men rode up that road, wouldn't folks see them?" Chet asked.

"Sure, unless they went one or so at a time and were local, huh?"

"You have any notion about that?" Chet asked.

The man shook his head like that was all he wanted to say.

Later in camp, Cole said, "Sounded to me like he told you something."

"He has to live here. If that's what happened, that the robbers are people who live here, he would have to keep it to himself. I savvy that's why he isn't saying anything."

"How will we ever prove it, if no one will talk about it?" Jesus asked.

"We need to start thinking about that as possible. I say, 'possible.'"

Both his men nodded their heads.

"Men, it looks like this may be the toughest case we ever tried to solve."

"We heard about it happening down at Tubac, but it has been kind of subdued, like there is something wrong," Roamer said.

"I imagine before we're through, we'll have spent lots of time trying to figure it out. If we can." Chet shook his head. "Why is this robbery so damn strange?"

"Why did they let them get this close to the fort? Looking at that map, they let it get almost there," Cole said.

"They had to have a good road to take a wagon that heavily loaded out of here. The roadblocks east and west on the Butterfield Road turned up nothing. So they either hid it or buried it."

"It may be parked somewhere under a mesquite bush," Shawn said.

"But how many packhorses would it take to haul it away?"

"They might of buried it."

Chet agreed. "Until things cool down. Maybe. Tomorrow, I want both ways from the site of the robbery scouted. Look for anything unusual. If it is an inside deal, we'll learn, sooner or later."

He went to sleep that night in his bedroll, thinking about his wife. They had been together for nearly a year and he was spoiled. Poor cowboy, looking for a little sympathy. *She definitely was not there. Go to sleep.*

Chapter 27

Come morning, it felt cold in the early dawn, stirring around with his crew to saddle horses and cook breakfast. Roamer and Shawn would work north asking anyone what they knew and look for evidence. His three would go south and see if anyone saw anything or had any ideas. When the sun rose, the chill wouldn't last very long, and he'd bet Rachael Arnold wouldn't be up this early to enjoy it. Poor woman must be cooking in Tucson. Glad that he was not her husband, he poured coffee into tin cups for everyone.

"How is your farm doing on the river?" he asked Roamer.

"My wife has a Mexican woman helping her, and they take vegetables to the market every day. Lupe is a real salesperson and they're making money. I'm surprised, but they are really doing well."

"Good."

"Yeah, I was surprised when she set in to do all the

planting, but folks are looking for fresh turnips and carrots and lettuce. I may be a farmer someday."

They all laughed. Chet shook his head. If Roamer ever became a farmer, he'd operate from a chair in the shade. He was a great lawman, but not an industrious laborer.

"Saddle up. We can meet back here. Listen close to any witnesses. But don't put words in their mouth. We need witnesses who saw them."

They spent the day on the road interviewing anyone who would talk to them, coming and going, and stopping to talk to residents who lived on or near the road.

Did they see anyone driving a wagon by on that date?

Anyone strange drive it?

What did they look like?

Jesus talked to the Hispanic people softly and nodded his head at their replies. Chet sat patient on his horse while it switched its tail at flies. Cole rode ahead to look for another witness.

Jesus soon returned and mounted up. "The Castros said they saw the mounted guard go by and it never came back. He said the only wagon that came south that evening was a Mormon bishop named Elliot."

"He say what he was hauling?"

"No, he could not see it, but said his big horses were in their collars whenever they hit a little grade."

"Why didn't anyone else see him?"

"Castro is not a Mormon."

"Jesus, many of these white folks we've talked to are probably of that same religion."

"What should we do about it?"

"We need to talk to the main men from the marshal's office. I'm sure they won't want any trouble with a church group over this matter, but Elliot is the only man we can identify as being seen driving down from Fort Grant."

Cole rode up to join them. "You two learn anything?"

"Jesus talked to a Hispanic couple. They didn't know why he was asking, but the only person who came by that day in a wagon was a ward bishop named Elliot."

"Holy cow. That make him a suspect?"

Chet held up his hand. "Not so fast. We need to check on him and learn a lot more, but so far he's the only one anyone has seen go by. I doubt a dried up little Mexican man and his non-English-speaking wife will make a jury convict a high official of any church."

"That bothers you?" Cole asked.

"Sure, it does. If someone like that murdered the payroll guards and stole the money, they aren't any better than the Mexican bandits we've run down."

"I feel like that, too. Now what do we do?"

"We go back and talk to our boss, and his boss, if he's still here."

"Tomorrow?"

"Let's ride in and get there by mid-morning. We may be able to get a search warrant from a judge and search his place, if they want to do that."

"Maybe Roamer found something."

"I hope it was something more than what we did. Let's get back to camp."

Everyone jogged their horses for camp. Chet had a bad feeling about the outcome of this whole robbery business and was still perplexed by what he knew.

When they caught up with Roamer, he was no help, but he did hear about four men who rode in from the north that day. Someone saw them that day, but didn't know them. They were well armed. Careful with his words, Chet told Roamer and Shawn what they had learned.

"What next?" Roamer asked.

"We go to Tucson and talk to the boss tomorrow. If he don't want to do anything, we won't, and I say we all go home if that is the case. If he wants to get us a search warrant, we'll serve it and apologize if we find nothing."

"Think he'd have the money at his place?" Roamer asked.

"He might think because he is church leader, because of his position, he won't be checked."

"Damn, what will we do?"

"Let our new boss decide."

"Good enough for me." Roamer and Chet shook hands.

Chet could hardly choke down the food Jesus served them. It hung in his throat going down and soured in his stomach. At last in his bedroll, he tossed in his sleep. No crime had ever drawn this out of him. Damn. He fought sleep, and finally slept, but wasn't rested at morning.

They reached the federal courthouse and Chet requested an audience with his boss from Earl at the desk, who went into the back office.

Thomas came out and said his boss was there. That he wanted to hear anything they had to say. Chet said he needed his crew in there.

Thomas agreed. The secretary, Earl, went for chairs and Shawn helped him.

"You've met Chet Byrnes," Thomas said to Arnold. "He can introduce his men for you. This is the Force we have used on the border."

"I met Cole and Jesus on the stage."

"This is Roamer and Shawn."

He shook their hands, nodded to each, and said he was glad to meet them.

"What do you have?" Thomas asked Chet.

"The only man that drove a heavy loaded wagon down that road that evening was a Mormon bishop named Elliot. He's a ward leader in charge of a Mormon church."

"How good is the witness?"

"Jesus talked to him. They are an older Hispanic couple, and she speaks no English."

"What do you think?"

"I think a Mormon church leader drove a heavy-laden wagon by their place after the robbery."

Thomas looked at his boss, Arnold. "Do we need to show him what we picked up at the First Arizona Bank today?"

His boss nodded.

Thomas drew a heavy cloth sack out of the drawer in his desk and spilled the shining coins on the desktop.

Chet stepped closer and nodded. "Who deposited that money?"

"A farmer from upstream named Rickard who paid off his mortgage today with these coins."

"Is he a Mormon?" Chet asked.

"I imagine so. I'd bet eight out of ten farmers on the Santa Cruz River are Mormons."

Arnold broke in, "Byrnes, you live in this territory. Is this going to be another mess, like they had over at the Meadow Valley wagon train massacre in Utah over twenty years ago?"

"No, I know a lot of those people. This never has occurred before, or I've never heard of it, anyway. But they're all covering up seeing any of them on the Fort Grant Road. Except for the one couple who saw him, and I wouldn't want to endanger their lives."

Arnold nodded. "What do you recommend?"

"We'd like a search warrant to look over Elliot's property. If we find any evidence, I plan to arrest him and bring him for trial as a participant in the crime."

"How many will come to break him out?" Thomas asked. "I may need reinforcements to hold the jail."

"If we need to help you, we'll do it."

"Fine," Thomas said. "Let's call in the federal prosecutor and get his opinion."

Chet and his crew rested in the office while Thomas left to find the man. He returned with Alex Prior. After the matter was discussed, the prosecutor agreed if they had strong evidence he would prosecute him.

Thomas then went for a search warrant from Judge Monroe, a judge in his courtroom office.

"You realize to arrest a church leader is a dangerous situation?" Thomas asked, returning with the warrant and handing it to Chet. "Read it aloud and if he resists, subdue him and anyone else dangerous as well. When are you going there?"

"Right now."

His men rose and agreed they wanted it over.

"You know where he lives?" Chet asked.

"North of town on the San Cruz River. I can make you a map. I'm not afraid, but one of us needs to hold the jail tomorrow if things heat up."

After a quick meal from some street vendors, they left an hour later. The ride was hot and dusty. At sundown, they reached the farm and rode up the fenced lane.

A bareheaded man in his late thirties came out of the house and looked them over. "What can I do for you?"

"You Carl Elliot?"

"Yes. Why?"

"I have a federal warrant, issued by Judge Monroe, to search your property."

"What do you want to find?"

Chet ignored his question. "Ask all your family to come out and be in the yard. Children, women, and all."

"I may refuse. You're threatening me."

"Then by the authority of the federal court, I will put you in irons. You have two minutes to get them outside. I don't want anyone hurt, but I will not put up with you resisting me from doing my job."

"What is your name?"

"Chet Brynes."

"I think—"

"Put him in irons, Jesus. Roamer, tell the family to come outside." Chet knew Cole and Shawn were already out back, and he heard some shouting.

"Look what we found," Cole said, with a nice-looking teenage girl in tow. He guided her by one arm and held a bucket in his free hand.

Chet took the bucket. It was heavy, and in the closing light he could see it was about half-full of newly minted coins. A baby cried in the arms of a woman in tears who came out of the house. There were six more kids from preschool to near teens rounded up and made to sit on the ground.

His men brought out from the house more money in containers, and Shawn and Roamer found more in the barn. In a quick discussion, they decided it would require a wagon to take it all back. Chet knew Jesus's relatives would give him a wagon to haul it, and their farm wasn't far from there.

"You realize you will be charged with murder and robbery and no doubt hang for this crime?" Chet said to the man seated on the ground in both cuffs and leg irons.

Elliot shook his head like the charges were nothing and it wasn't going to happen. "You can't ever convict me."

"I guess we'll see, won't we?"

"You're wasting your time. No jury in Pima County will ever convict me."

"I'm glad you're so confident. But the way I see it, this money we found here was part of the Fort Grant payroll stolen ten days ago."

"I will repeat that you will not be able to convict me."

The very notion of the smart-ass words gnawed on him. In irons, seated on the ground, and in the face of the strong evidence they had gathered, this man had no fear of prosecution. There was something else going on, and Chet had no idea what it was. Anyone else would be plea-bargaining by this time. Did he think the federal government wouldn't prosecute a Mormon bishop? Had he set himself up as God? All the members of the family were in tears, and Bishop Elliot was telling them there was nothing to worry about, that he would not serve any time. It was just some inconvenient time he had to spend in jail, and then he would be back home.

Chet's thoughts went back to his first days in Arizona, when he chased down the men who killed his first wife's foreman and his second-in-command. They'd also stolen horses, raped an innocent woman, and threatened another family. He'd chased them down himself, and then doubted if he took them in that this raw territory would prosecute them. Instead, he became judge, jury, and executioner. For their foul deeds, he hung them by himself, in a dry wash outside of Rye.

He'd taken lots of flack for doing that. He'd spent a lot of time since then arresting criminals and making certain they were tried by legal means. But as twilight faded on the hot day, he wondered if this Elliot didn't deserve the same treatment he gave those killers. He was so certain he would get off with killing five men and stealing that much federal money, that might just be called for.

"We've run out of light to look for any more," Roamer said, jolting Chet out of his thoughts.

"You and Shawn stay here tonight. I'm sorry. When Jesus returns with the wagon, we'll take Elliot to Tucson and bring back a crew to scour this whole place."

Roamer gave him a head toss. "I heard that bastard talking. What makes him so damn confident he ain't going to hang?"

"I'm not sure myself. I go back to that Rye deal. I figured those two killers would get off with murder and horse rustling and rape—so I hung them. You know all about that?"

Roamer nodded. "I'm with you. That guy needs his neck stretched for what he did. How will he get off? Brigham Young can't give him clemency down here."

"I'm not sure, but he obviously has no fear about it. You make sure they don't hide any more money. They can sleep out here. Every one of his children must have known he stole it. That older girl was going off with part of it when Cole caught her."

"I'll watch it. But I'm sure confused about him saying that we're wasting our time here."

"So am I, Roamer. So am I."

Jesus returned with a wagon. The money and

their prisoner were loaded and they went back to Tucson. They arrived at sunup, and the prisoner was quickly taken inside and placed in a cell. Thomas and Arnold both shook their heads at the sight of all the money they brought back.

"I want some honest men sent to his place to complete the search. We ran out of light up there last night, but I left two men up there to be certain no more was hidden."

"What's the deal on this man?" Arnold asked. "I heard him bragging he'd be out in three days."

"Marshal, I've heard that for hours. My chief deputy asked if Brigham Young could give him clemency. I have no idea, but he's pretty sold on the notion he will get off scot-free."

"Young has no authority over any federally charged prisoner. Get your man over here. We need to talk to him," Arnold said.

"You want the prosecutor, Alex Prior?" Thomas asked.

"Yes."

Thomas brought him back to his office. "Alex said there would be several Mormons on any jury panel we assemble here. They are a large part of the voter rolls of this county, where we get our jury pools from."

"Is that why he's so convinced he'll never serve a day for that crime?" Chet asked. "Arnold, can we have him tried in El Paso?"

"That would be an awful expensive trial. I doubt my superiors would allow it."

"Wire them. I don't want him walking out scot-free from this courthouse."

"I'll see what I can do, but the response won't be here for a few days."

Chet turned to the prosecutor. "Alex, this is murder and a serious robbery. Can you stall the bail?"

"As long as I can."

"Good. That's our best bet. Move the federal trial to Texas. Men, I'll do anything to see that man is prosecuted. No one is above the law."

"If we can't, what then?" Thomas asked.

"What do you say, Alex?" Chet asked.

"He could be set free by a jury, despite our evidence. Those people are clannish enough."

Chet stomped his foot to let the anger and frustration drain away. "We do all this work to bring crime down in this territory, and we face a wall here. I won't ever understand." He shook his head in disgust.

"My men and I need some sleep. Maybe we can find some justice. I'll check back later. When Roamer and Shawn return today, tell them we'll meet them for breakfast in the hotel lobby in the morning. They have rooms at the Brown Hotel."

"Chet," Thomas said. "No matter the outcome, you came and solved this case. I'll see your men get the reward for the return of the money. I know you well enough to know they get it all. And thanks."

Chet nodded he heard him and went to telegraph his wife. To tell her that he must stay there longer looking for a solution to this problem. *Damn . . .*

CHAPTER 28

Breakfast was a sobering reunion for him and his crew.

"What do they think about his talk?" Roamer asked.

"Alex says that Mormons are eighty percent of the pool they get for jury members from Pima County. All you need is one no vote and the trial is over. I asked Arnold to move it to El Paso, but he fears the expenses will not let them move the trial there."

"So that damn killer is going to get released and go free?" Cole asked.

"That's what we're trying to work out."

Chet looked up and saw Marshal Thomas's secretary, Earl, come in the restaurant. He looked around, spotted Chet, and headed for their table.

"The marshal said to tell you three more people paid off their mortgages on Saturday with those gold coins."

"You have a list of their names, Earl?" Chet asked the young man.

"Yes."

"What does he want us to do about them?"

"He said you could arrest them."

"Let's go get some federal arrest warrants and do that."

Roamer agreed. "Even if they won't prosecute them, they still need to be in jail."

"He said to warn you that over a dozen Mormon lawyers are in the courthouse this morning, shouting for the release of the bishop on bail."

"He need any help? We can clean the halls."

"He didn't ask for that."

"Earl, tell him we're coming." Chet tossed down money to pay for their food.

"Thank you, sir. I'm sure he isn't worried they'll kill him, but they are nasty and loud."

The Force members laughed.

When Chet entered the courthouse, the hall to Thomas's office was clogged with shouting men.

"Wait a minute. All of you get over here," Chet called over the din.

They turned with frowns, saying, "Who the hell is he?"

"This is a federal facility, not a bar. All of you come out here and line up. Who was the first one here?"

"I was."

"Who are you?"

"Joe Lewis."

"Who do you represent?"

"The bishop."

"I arrested him last night. He never mentioned a lawyer."

"I am going to be his lawyer."

"He can't pay you in dollar gold coins, because we confiscated them last night. They were part of a stolen Army payroll, and all people using them will be arrested and charged with the crime. Now, each of you will get a number to talk to Marshal Thomas in your turn, but his recommendation at this time is not to allow any bail for the suspects we arrested since murders were committed during the robbery."

"You can't—"

"I can lock you up for forty-eight hours for disturbing the peace. Now sit down and wait. Marshal Thomas will see you, one at a time, as his time permits."

"Who in the hell are you?" asked a red-faced man in a suit with beads of sweat tracing down his face.

"I am the man about to put you in a cell. My name is Chet Byrnes. I am a U.S. Marshal. This is not a place for a riot. Find a place to sit and you'll have a chance to speak to my boss in turn."

"You can't hold a man of God—"

"That is your opinion. Why did a man representing a religion have possession of thousands of dollars stolen from a U.S. Government agency? I found that gold in his house and even his children tried to hide it from us, and we had a valid search warrant from the federal judge."

"You had no business—"

"No business? Where did you get your law degree?"

"I am a licensed attorney to practice in this territory."

"Maybe you should read it. Sit down and wait your turn." He turned back to them. "Any more questions?"

They shook their heads.

Chet went back and stepped into the office to speak to Earl. "My deputies will hold these lawyers down to a simple first-come, first-see him, and do it orderly."

"Thanks, Mr. Byrnes." Earl smiled. "I guess they learned you weren't going to put up with them behaving like wild wolves."

"At home, I shoot wolves."

Earl snickered.

"We are going looking for the ones who have paid their mortgages off with new coins."

"Here is the information I have on where they live. I'll tell the marshal about your plans."

"Thanks. See you later today."

"Thank you, sir."

He left Shawn to sort out the lawyers. Jesus, Roamer, and himself rode off to arrest the people who got out of debt by paying with new gold coins.

They rode up to a farmer's place south of Tucson on the river. A short man came out of the corral.

"You Carroll Holt?"

"Why?" The man blinked at him.

"Are you?"

"Yes."

"Then you are under arrest for being involved in

a robbery of the Fort Grant payroll and multiple murders."

"I never robbed nobody."

"Where did you get the coins to pay off your mortgage?"

"Why, I saved it."

"No, you stole it. Do you wish to tell your wife we are taking you to jail?"

"I never robbed nobody."

"You had enough of the stolen lot to pay off your mortgage. Jesus, put the irons on him."

"No!"

"Do you have a horse to ride? One of your family can recover it from the livery."

"I ain't going to jail."

"Belly down, or in the saddle. You have two minutes to decide."

"Carroll, who are these men?" a woman shouted from the porch.

"U.S. Marshals, Greta."

"What are they doing?"

"Arresting me."

"What for?"

"Robbing the Army payroll, he says."

"You never done that."

"Ma'am," Chet said loud enough she could hear. "He paid off your mortgage at the bank with stolen money. That makes him a co-conspirator." He'd had enough. "Find him a horse, Jesus."

"You can't take him," she cried, and came hustling off the porch with her skirt in her hands.

Chet wheeled his horse over to stop her. "Don't make me hurt you."

She tried to get by, but Chet used his mount to block her. "Stop, or I'll take you with him."

She shaded her eyes with her hand and swore at him. "Get out of my way."

"Load him on that horse, bareback."

Roamer dismounted and threw the man on the horse's back and tossed the lead to Jesus and remounted on the run. The three left her screaming in the dust.

Carroll Holt was the second man who had paid off his mortgage with gold coins to be put in jail on charges. Chet told the jailer to keep Holt and Rickard separate from Elliot. He agreed that it might encourage them to be uneasy and start talking about the robbery.

The next day, Chet and his men rounded up six more men who paid off their mortgages with stolen gold coins.

Chet was putting his horse up at the livery when a familiar voice behind him made him spin around. Dressed in a fashionable brown dress, Liz ran in and tackled him.

"I couldn't stay home a day longer."

He rocked her back and forth in his arms. "I'm so glad you came. Damn, I have missed you."

"Not near as much as I have missed you. How is this going?"

"Not real good."

"Why? I read the newspapers. You're arresting the criminals and recovering the money."

"First you arrest the criminals, charge them, then take them to trial." He gave his reins to Roamer who hugged Liz and whispered, "Good to see you."

"You, too. You are keeping him healthy."

"I'll put your horse up, Chet."

"Thanks." He turned back to Liz to finish his story. "The jurors come from voter lists. In this part of the country, those people are mostly Mormons. These men arrested are all Mormons."

She nodded that she understood. He went on talking as they walked arm in arm out of the barn. "I'm worried that they can't get a jury to say they're guilty, no matter how much evidence we have to prove they did that horrible crime."

"Chet, you can only do so much."

He agreed. "I don't like losing a war."

"You have won lots of them. Are you taking us all to eat?"

"Yes. I am so excited that you are here—" He whirled around.

Jesus came up on one side and Cole on the other, and they had Anita's arms locked in theirs, grinning like Shawn and Roamer, who were right behind them.

"Where we eating at, Father?" Roamer asked.

"The Brown?"

"That sounds good," Roamer said.

At the hotel desk, Chet secured Anita a room as well as one for Roamer and Shawn. Then they went into the dining room to eat. Seated, they ordered from the menu and the waiter said they had some good locally made wine. He brought them a bottle to see and Chet recognized the bottle.

"We'll take a couple of those and celebrate."

"You know the grower?" Roamer asked.

Jesus laughed. "It is Liz's wine, from her *hacienda*."

"Oh, hell. No wonder he bought two bottles."

They enjoyed a leisurely meal, and nothing broke the fine feelings of being with real friends for a relaxed evening. Chet couldn't believe how much his wife's company settled him.

"How many more will you arrest?" Liz asked.

"I have no idea. Anyone who brings new coins in to pay off their mortgage."

"How much did you recover?"

"I think they are still counting it at the bank," Cole said.

"There was that much?" Liz asked.

Chet nodded. "Jesus had to go rent a wagon to haul it into town. No telling what we missed, recovering it from that man's place. Cole stopped his teenage daughter from hiding a bucket that was nearly half full."

"This all came from the robbery?"

"Let's not talk about it. This will go down as the sorriest thing to ever happen in the territory."

She reached over and clasped the top of his hand. "Chet Brynes, your men have worked hard to make Arizona a better place. You can't win every battle. Justice may prevail yet."

"I hope so. When we finish here in a few days, I want you to see Rancho Diablo. Heat and all. We can look at it in the early morning hours and give JD some support so he doesn't think he's the last man in the outfit."

"I am ready when you are. It can't be hotter than west Texas was herding those cattle."

"It may be," he said, and they all laughed.

"That was plenty hot," Jesus said.

Chet tapped his fork on his empty wineglass. "I want to thank each of you, personally. This may be the most trying case we have ever worked on, and despite any future outcome that might reverse our efforts, you did your jobs. Thanks."

"Amen," the men murmured.

That week, they arrested three more men who paid off their loans with gold coins. Chet heard rumors of other men paying off individual debts with gold coins, but the receivers hid the payments for fear the government might seize them.

Thomas and Arnold shook his hand and each one of his Force members on Friday. Both men thanked them and Arnold reluctantly said, "This crime will go down, I fear, in history books as a sad case. The criminal perpetrators may beat us in court, but not because of the efforts of each one of you men. You did your part and thanks for the Force. I've studied the activities of you and your men, Chet. You've certainly helped bring justice to this territory."

"All of us appreciate the opportunity to help and we'll continue to do that." Chet nodded and they left. At the livery, Roamer and Shawn parted to go back to Tubac to hold down that Force operation, which Chet told them would continue until further notice. The other five went southwest to the big ranch on horseback. Chet offered Anita a buckboard ride.

She wrinkled her nose at him and smiled. "I can ride a horse."

Late in the day, they reached Rancho Diablo. Mexican music wafted across the dazzling heat waves that almost obscured the distant sawtooth mountains surrounding the ranch.

"They have already started to celebrate our arrival," Chet said to his outfit. "I sent him word when we'd get here."

Everyone nodded. Obviously, it was time to have a *fandango* on the *ranchero.*

A very pregnant Bonnie joined her husband, JD, in welcoming them.

Chet lightly hugged her at their meeting. "Did you ever expect to have a child of your own?"

"No." Bonnie smiled. "But then I never expected to be here, either. Thanks; I won't ever forget you. It isn't as hot or bad here as those places I was kept when I was kidnapped. I often think to myself how you and your men came to save me in my darkest hour. No, the heat and my very large baby are blessings. A challenging one, but JD helps me a lot. I told him the next time this happens, maybe I could go lounge at your house in the summertime, but I'd rather be with him. So, forget it. I'm sorry, Chet, I'm hoarding you."

He kissed her on the forehead. "After what we've been doing, you're like a blessed blue bonnet spring in Texas."

Liz stole Bonnie away and Chet shook JD's hand. "How's hot ranching?"

"We're progressing fine. Water development is moving on, like we planned. I've culled the dry cows and have about six hundred head of Mexican two-year-old steers, who are gaining weight despite the heat. They finally have some grass to eat, and water. We're planting, and in three years should have some citrus and wine grapes. I'm learning a lot about farming. We're making progress on our *casa* expansion for the workers. It's about complete. And, every day, I look for rain."

"I bet you do. Now tell me, are you really happy here?"

JD wet his lower lip. "I have to be somewhere to raise this baby that's coming. I need work. This place, I think, is the most challenging operation you have. And we've made progress. I want to go back and find more two-year-old Mexican steers. If you could have seen those cattle, the day Ortega brought them home. And, now, of course, you would not believe the difference. I think we need more of that, if you can find us a market for them. You can do that better than any man I know, finding markets for them."

"Six hundred head is only a one-month supply for the trip Sarge and Victor make each month to take to the Navajos."

"Why didn't I consider that?"

Chet clapped him on the shoulder. "What else?"

"You make things so damn easy at times. I have

only heard bits and pieces about the payroll robbery. How did it go?"

"Not great, but we can talk about it later. That has me down more than anything else. But I'm excited about all your ranch improvements and hard work."

"Well, tell me about Liz and you. She rides all over the world with you?"

"Yes, she came down from Preskitt this week to be with me."

"You look so natural—the two of you. I heard at Christmas how you found her, or visa-versa."

"That was it. We found each other. She is the easiest going woman I've ever known. She never complains. You know, she was very wealthy and gave it all up to be my wife. Oh, well, it is too long a story. I'm blessed to have her."

JD nodded, tight-lipped. "I know now that a good woman is invaluable. I offered to send Bonnie to Preskitt and she refused. We've both grown up a lot down here, being together. We seldom argue and we push each other on to better things and ties."

"Ties?"

"Yeah, we both wanted each other when we got married, but we had our own things that separated us. I thought I could think better alone. Wrong. Now we work together on things and that makes us more supportive and closer."

"Elizabeth and I think a lot alike, and she can soothe me down in no time. When I get upset, she can wink or smile and I know it isn't worth it."

They both laughed. The prodigal one had come home to do his part and Chet felt much better.

The evening was filled with a lot of great food, music, and leisure time to heal some of the gaps he'd felt working on the case. Hay cutting must be going on in the north. From Hampt's alfalfa to the prairie grass that Reg would cut, they had a lot of hay to harvest. Sarge was no small hay producer, nor was Tom at the big spread on the Verde. In another year, JD would need hay equipment for the fields of alfalfa he planned to plant that fall and irrigate with his artesian wells. Always more expenses.

Later, Chet danced with his wife under the Chinese lanterns.

"Are you relaxing some down here?" she asked.

"Oh, yes. I think I've accepted that whatever happens will happen, and I can't change it."

"Good. It is early, and I don't want your hopes too high but we may have a baby coming."

"Will that fulfill your life?"

She closed her eyes as he whirled her around. "Oh, yes. It is too soon to really know, but I could not hold it from you."

He squeezed her against him. "Either way, I'll be pleased."

Standing a little taller in his arms as they danced away, she spoke quietly, "If not, we can try again."

"Oh, we shall, my dear."

Amused, she hugged him tight for an instant. "I am counting on that."

The next morning, early, they left the main ranch on horseback. A *vaquero* took them to see several of the cows and calves at a water hole dug out by the crew with slips and horse teams. The cattle looked very content and filled out, but suspicious of all the intruders sitting on horses.

Next, they came to a windmill, and with the early morning wind it was pumping water out into a large rock tank. Obviously, JD had spent some time locating the mills at a distance a range cow could walk to and graze on the way. His nephew had bowed out of the tour since Bonnie was so close, and he didn't want to miss the event.

Ortega was in Mexico buying more steers, and the night before his wife, Maria, hugged Chet and bragged on her new house.

They rode on and by mid-day had seen lots of development before they swung back to the ranch. They arrived, and men took their horses to put up.

Maria and the ranch ladies had a late lunch ready for his bunch. Many of them acted excited to meet Elizabeth, who talked graciously to all of them. She hugged babies and knelt down to speak to little dark-eyed girls.

Cole asked where the big gray horse was, and Chet thought he was over at Tubac. He had a little dread in his heart for the big gelding, unless Shawn had rode him some since he had ridden him over there. Roamer was not a bronc rider, and he didn't mess with them, but rode the well broke ones. Maybe someday he'd manage to get the big gray up north to use for long trips.

JD and Bonnie joined them. No baby.

Chet gave them his impression. "We saw a lot of good things, and I'm impressed. This desert ranch is a good operation, and I saw some of those steers you've bought. They're full and fattening."

"Oh, that is Ortega's business. He finds them and really buys them cheap."

Bonnie spoke up, "And he is gone a lot, too."

"But we are building a ranch here, aren't we?" JD asked Chet.

"I can see the progress. This will be a great ranch someday."

"How is Adam?" Bonnie asked.

"He talks and walks. So much more even than when you saw him last at Christmas," Liz said.

"What are your plans next?" JD asked.

"The new man, Thomas, and his boss, Arnold, who has been up at Tucson, want the Force to remain. Roamer says he's fine with that, and so is Shawn. Things have simmered down a whole lot on the border."

"Bonnie said all of your work and arrests on the latest case may not get any convictions?"

"I fear that is the case. But the prosecutor is going to try. The new marshal, John Thomas, said we've done all we can in the case. His boss says Washington doesn't want to spend all the money needed to move the trial to El Paso."

"What does that mean?"

"I suspect hung juries that will free them, despite the evidence we gathered from this man, Elliot's, house."

"That make you mad?"

"JD, you know we've tried to bring these criminals in, to try them and get prison sentences or hangings.

If they get off, folks will go back to the rope law. I think that had the men killed not been soldiers and Army payroll personnel, and folks had known them—they would have been hung already. But, see, there is no ground-swelling effort for that to happen. Protect your own."

JD shook his head. "Those folks can be clannish."

"I'm going home in a few days and try to forget it."

JD looked hard across the table. "You ever think about Brigham Young's Angels trying to kill you for what you did up there?"

Chet shook his head. "No, I never worry about it."

"Both of you guys better think about it, along with him," Chet said to Cole and Jesus seated across the table. "They say he has a powerful bunch of enforcers that he can unleash on any enemy of the church."

"Who are they?" Liz asked.

"No one knows. There's a rumor that the head of the church in Salt Lake has hired guns that will clear out anyone who threatens their members in any way."

"You come under that?" she asked Chet with a frown.

"I may, but don't worry. They won't try anything on us."

"If they do that sort of thing, how can they be prevented from attacking you?" she asked.

He hugged her. "'Cause I won't let them."

She rolled her dark eyes and looked to heaven for help. "More I have to pray for."

"Elizabeth, do you ever, I mean ever, regret leaving

your large ranch and marrying him and then being drug all over this dusty land?" Bonnie was smiling and waiting for her answer.

"I tell you what happened when I stopped to buy a wonderful golden horse and I met this tall man who stood so politely at my coach step, inside this great aura that surrounded him." She used her hands to make a round shape. "My mind snapped. He was the thing I did not have in my life to be complete. I had played a widow's role for a long time—almost three years. When I saw him, I wished I had on real clothes, not a black dress of mourning. He would think I still cried for my past one. I didn't. But I had no time to become someone to invite him into my life—our time together would be too short. Would I shock him? Maybe I did, but I never looked back from that first second.

"Then I knew I needed him, not another man—him. That was what my life lacked. My place was to be beside him, and others could run the *hacienda.* Others could make appearances. When I was on that trip to find that lost herd, I saw the sea of grass that Coronado saw. I read that diary, and I rode with the love of my life. The lack of amenities was nothing, not when I could be with him. Does that answer your question?"

Bonnie wiped tears from her eyes with the kerchief her husband handed her. "When Chet told me that you said you would kiss him, but not for the horse, I knew you were the woman he needed and I told him so."

"Thank you, Bonnie, you must have been God's

messenger for me. That very night was the time I was going home in a mad hurry when I stopped and realized—no. If he would have me, I would be his wife, and I about cried since we had no bonds but our verbal ones."

"I am sorry, Liz, I don't have your education, but your description of the sea of grass the two of you sailed over is poetry."

"Maybe someday, I can paint it for you."

"I can't wait. Thanks to you, I shall never again feel sorry for you in your role as his wife at his side in some cow camp."

Liz threw her head back and laughed. "This spoiled girl from Sonora is never in any discomfort when I ride with him."

Cole spoke up. "We'd drag our backside into making camp and there she was happy as a bird in springtime helping us get ready and cook. Halfway across New Mexico, going for the lost herd, I thought that she'd get tired of the routine. Way up to Ogallala, Nebraska, she was still the same, Liz making camp, but he shocked her when he took her to the opera in Denver."

"How did you think of that?" Bonnie asked him.

"Luck. Pure D Luck. I saw some posters and thought she enjoyed the plains so much, why not try music on her?"

Liz, all smiles, shook her head. "He asked me one morning, how dressed up did he have to get to take me to the Denver opera that night. I about fainted. I had been wearing pants for several months. I had no clothes with me. I didn't have Anita to help me fix my hair. But we found clothing, and a hair dresser. If I ever was swept away with this great guy, then he did it that night to me."

"I know we've eaten already, but I recall Susie a couple of times asking you to give a blessing, Chet. This new Brynes is coming, and this ranch never has been blessed. Would you do us the honor of blessing the whole thing?" JD asked him.

Chet agreed.

JD rose and held up his arms to quiet the crew as the sun set off in the west. "My uncle has done miracles for all of us. But he has a side to him many of you don't know about—he's the blessing giver, and he is going to pray for all of us and bless this ranch."

"Thank you, JD. My wife and crew, Cole, and Jesus have seen the wonderful work you all have toiled so hard at on this ranch. It will be a super ranch and only because of all of you. Let us pray."

Vaqueros shed their *sombreros* and dropped to their knees. Women and children did the same, hands clasped tight.

"Father, we come to you this evening as we wait for a new child in our family. Help Bonnie and JD through this wonderful process as your son did when he came here. Lord, we are thankful for our health, the food you provide, and the wonderful desert that these hardworking people are turning into a Garden of Eden.

"Lord, let these people's efforts feed and provide for many. Thanks for the precious water being pumped up to serve us. Thanks for the sun and rain, but most of all, bless and keep all these fine children whose voices and playing make this our home.

"On this day, Lord, we ask you to bless this ranch, the livestock, the horses, and the palm trees they've planted, along with the citrus and grapes. May the harvests be bountiful.

"Lord, be with the rest of our family. Please hold and protect them in your hand.

"Thank you, God, the Father, for we may be far from a church, but this is our altar and the place we cherish. May it grow and be a better place to work and live on. Amen."

"Thanks, we all appreciate that blessing," JD said, and the entire bunch nodded.

Liz told him later, "You don't know how heartfelt those people were over that prayer."

"No, but I saw and felt it, too."

"Good. We're going home?"

"Shortly. I'm ready for Preskitt. Cool nights and away from this mess in Tucson. I may have to come back and testify, but Roamer and Shawn can handle the rest, unless they need us. We can start home day after tomorrow."

"Good. I love the mountains. And your son. But there is not one inside me." She fled into his arms, and Chet felt her sobs and tears soak into his shirt. Damn, she'd had high hopes. Nothing to do but go on. He squeezed her tight.

CHAPTER 29

Forty miles or so north of Hayden's Ferry, deep in the canyon under the brow of the towering Bradshaw Mountains, sat Bumble Bee, the horse change station of the Black Canyon Stage Lines. Chet, Liz, Anita, and Jesus sat in the coach, with Cole up top with the driver, Ira Counts, while they rocked their way north in the desert heat. The driver usually took a ten- to fifteen-minute break at Bumble Bee, depending on the time left on his pocket watch to get to Preskitt, and how fast the agent's, Matt James's, Mexican boys required to switch horses.

The stop would give Chet a chance to stretch his legs and use the outdoor facilities in back of the stage stop. He wasn't looking forward, though, to the fearsome bad odor that the warmer weather brought to the outhouses.

Unexpectedly, with a series of "whoas" from Ira, the driver brought the team to a sudden halt in a dust cloud that engulfed them from behind.

"Heads up," Cole shouted from above the noisy confusion.

"Get on the floor," Chet told the women. Jesus bailed out the far door.

Half-obscured in the cloud of dust, three men in suits stood braced on the east side of the coach against a backdrop of greasewood brush and eroded hillside.

"Get your hands off those guns," Cole ordered. Despite the warning, the one on the right went for his weapon and a shotgun blast ripped through him in return.

Six-gun in his hand, Chet threw open the coach door and in the settling cloud of dust made out the other two men going for their guns. The middle man in the light-colored suit grabbed for his pistol and fired his Colt at Chet. The bullet splintered the coach above his head. Chet shot him dead center in the chest. More shots came from the backside of the coach and dropped the man on Chet's left. He'd acted undecided for a second, then started to draw, giving Jesus time to shoot him. It all happened in less than two minutes, Chet decided.

"You ladies alright?" he asked, turning to see about them.

"Yes," Liz said, as if put out about the whole business, and getting back up on the seat. "Who were these crazy men? Everyone alright?"

Chet holstered his own weapon and said, "I can see everyone. We're fine. Anita, you okay?"

"Scared is all."

Cole had bailed off the top and was standing over the bloody bodies. "Who in the hell are you anyway?"

No one answered.

The stage stop manager, Matt, soon joined them from the building. "I asked them their business and they wouldn't say what it was. Sorry, I never thought they were out there to gun you all down."

"They didn't want you to warn us, Matt. Thanks to Cole, who saw them better than I did and took action."

"We ever see these guys before?" Cole asked.

"I recall that fat guy in the middle. I saw him in Utah when we were up there." Jesus knelt down to look closer and then nodded. "He was there when we stopped to talk to the law in that town—"

"You sure?" Cole asked.

Jesus fished a monocle out of the still man's shirt pocket. "He wore this that day."

"You recalled him?" Cole shook his head. "Let's check them for identification."

"I'll be right back and help you. Now I have other duties." He left for the outhouses, catching the two women on the way.

"Did you know them?" Liz asked.

"No, but Jesus said he saw one man in Utah a few years ago when we went up there and rescued Leroy Sipes. I don't recall him at all."

"Do you think they are those Angels?" Liz asked.

"They could have been anyone, but why pick a gunfight with us at such an isolated spot? Maybe they planned to just ride off at the end. This far from any law, it would be hard to track such a cold trail when the law finally did arrive. But we can talk later," he said, approaching the powerful-smelling facilities.

Liz pinched her nose at the odor. "Good idea."

Anita laughed.

Later, the bodies were covered in some old blankets Matt found while diligent buzzards on the wing floated overhead. Chet's men went through the few identifying items they found on the bodies.

They found a letter from a lady in Idaho inside one man's left pocket.

Dear Shirley,

I miss you so much. When will you be back home here? I hope you can hurry, I think the bishop expects me to marry Johnny Moore. Johnny, you know, has three wives now, Lord knows why he would want me. I promised you I would not marry anyone when you left if you were coming back. Please write me or have one of the men riding with you write one for you. I know you are doing the work of the Lord, but be careful and come home soon.

Your dearest Claudia Clements

General Delivery, Rainy Fall, Idaho

"I am sorry, Claudia, but he is not coming home," Chet said, and shook his head.

"Chet, you know where he came from and what he was doing here?" Cole asked.

"I'm afraid so. They must be part of that bunch JD warned us about—the so-called Angels."

"From that letter, I'd say they've declared war on us. Now, isn't that a fine kettle of fish." Cole kicked some dried horse manure away.

"What is the matter?" Liz asked.

"We think these men are those Avenging Angels," Jesus said.

"Oh, Chet, what will we do now?" Liz asked.

"All I know is, he better call off his dogs. He wants to play tough hand, we can, too. We've done no more than enforce the laws of the United States. That's our job. We haven't done anything threatening or bad to innocent people, nor to members of his church, except those involved in criminal actions."

"But they say he has an entire army." Liz looked very upset.

"Part of them won't carry his banner any longer. And if any more try, they'll find the same end awaits them."

"What are your plans?"

"Liz, I know there are several people here. I'll ask them to keep this a secret. The sheriff can do what he thinks is necessary. I would only say these men tried to rob us and the stage, and they were shot in the act. Matt, is that fine with you?"

"Yes. I will keep it a secret."

"Ira, how about you?"

"Stage robbers is my answer, Mr. Byrnes."

"Thank you. Call me Chet. You want to store their bodies in a shed until the law comes for them?" he asked Matt.

"My boys and I can move them."

"Here, pay them for me." He gave Matt some silver coins and Matt thanked him.

"Let's load up, folks. We'll be late getting to Preskitt."

"No problem," Chet said. "We're unharmed and going home. Thanks to my sharp men." At his side, he hugged his wife and kissed her. He had a lot to be thankful for. Adam, we're coming home.

CHAPTER 30

In his Morris chair, Chet read the *Daily Miner*'s report on the stage robbery at Bumble Bee.

U. S. Marshals Stop Stage Robbery in Its Tracks

Three armed men waited at the Black Canyon Stage Stop at Bumble Bee last Wednesday for the arrival of the north-bound afternoon run. They stood around dressed in suits and were mere passing-by strangers to the station agent, Matt James, who had talked to the three before the afternoon stage arrived for a change of horses. Mr. James said he had talked to them earlier and they told him they were on their way to do some business at Hayden's Ferry and some other places south and only wanted to rest their horses a while. Dressed in suits, he decided they must be salesmen or businessmen and disregarded them, though something bothered him about the three.

> Just as the stage arrived, the three strangers drew their guns. Riding in the coach was area rancher and U.S. Marshal, Chet Byrnes, and his deputy, Jesus Morales, plus on top with the stage driver, Ira Counts, rode another deputy, Cole Emerson. Emerson sounded the alarm about the robbers and used the stage line's shotgun to stop one of the would-be thieves. In thirty seconds, the robbery was over and all three outlaws were dead.
>
> Neither Mrs. Elizabeth Byrnes nor her lady, also in the coach, was injured in any way and the crime was stopped. Let this be a good warning to all you bad men out there, don't try to hold up a stage with U.S. Marshals on board. The results are fatal.
>
> Only one of the robbers was identified so far by officials, a Shirley Algood of Medicine Fork, Utah. All three were interred in the pauper's portion of the city cemetery. Anyone having any information to identify them, please contact the county sheriff's office.

"Time for lunch, dear," Liz said. "Are those men coming this afternoon to talk with you?"

"Yes." He scooped Adam up from Rhea and laughed, making a face at his boy, who laughed back at him. "Bishop Fleming and Bishop Wallace."

"You are talking to them—"

"Yes, they're good people. They sounded very concerned and anxious to settle the issue. I think they're at the bottom of things up there. They support none of the robbers or the men we met south of here."

"Is it over then?"

He swung his son in a circle. "I certainly hope so. So does Adam. Don't you, big boy?"

Adam only laughed at him. What a happy baby. Set down on his bare feet, the little guy ran for the kitchen in a stilted gait, like he needed to be there with granny Monica.

His arm over his wife's shoulder, and along with Rhea, they headed for their lunch. In a few hours, he hoped to learn what the Mormon bishops knew about the rumors and the situation he and his men had faced during the incident at Bumble Bee, and if that matter was settled with the higher-ups in Salt Lake. The two men were coming later that day to meet with him.

Both men, and many of their ward members, sold cattle to Tom. They knew how important Chet's cattle-buying operations had become to local people and to their welfare. Chet felt that had probably been a settling point for them in the matter. Anyway, he hoped so.

To my fans and readers of my books,

Thanks a lot for all the mail. I'm on the straight and narrow for a lot more of the Chet Byrnes Series. I do get complaints from time to time and anyone is entitled to them. I try to answer their concerns, but most of my mail is simply sorting out things. No problem.

I love to hear from all of you, and try to answer each e-mail. With life being so busy, my responses might slow down a bit, so please be patient. My e-mail is dustyrichards@cox.net.

My webmaster has many things going at dustyrichards.com, so please check it out.

The success of my books relies on you, the readers, and I appreciate all of you. If you read one of my books and like it, then stick up a good review on Amazon or one of the other book review sites, so others will read it.

May God bless you, your family, and the rest of the world.

Your cowboy friend,
Dusty Richards